Selected Passages from *The Planetary Tribunal*

"The Tower of Bavel was the lone moment in the days of men when they lifted their eyes and said, Let us rise; let us be more than dust under the gods' feet. But el elyon came down with the host of heaven, heavy as a storm cloud, and stilled the work of our hands, scattering us like seed before the wind."

"Social reality is not everything. However, it is the nearest thing to being so…Yes, each life is as unique as a snowflake, but all are fabricated from the same elemental stuff, imbued with an underlying common essence, and bear the same basic flavor. And in the case of Earth, I am afraid the flavor is not vanilla."

"Quality is a perishable item. It can be sensed via the ripples of water at a lagoon, but it cannot be put in a watertight container and taken home. The moment one tries to capitalize on it, quality slips away."

"Money is not merely a token of exchange. It is a force, with a gravity well all of its own. Over time, it reshapes incentives, perception, and even desire itself."

"Within a living system with finite production capacities, it is always a matter of what people indirectly force out of existence and what is an acceptable degree of environmental impoverishment."

"It is likely that within one lifetime, the Amazon rainforest will be replaced by a mosaic of ranches, crop fields, and patches of open-canopy forest. With no moisture in the soil, there will be far less rain. Thus, the micro-climate that gave rise to those forests will also fade. The last vestiges of ecologically rich biomes will be gone from Earth for eons to come, leaving behind ghosts of what once was and ashes, which shortly thereafter will be scattered by the winds."

"I offer that this food-production system is the brainchild of buffoons and monkeys with wrenches. With its chemical spraying, it is demented. With the growth of grain expressly to feed cattle, it is deranged. With its crowding of animals into giant enclosures, it is monstrous."

"A man with a harpoon stood at the front of the boat…When a female was caught, her mate tried with all his strength to free her. After failing, he followed her to the shore, enduring the many blows dealt by the humans. Some stayed by the sides of their dead companions for days afterward."

"The statutes were wrought from loathing and dread, then calcified beneath an institutional crust so thick that no mercy can filter through."

"Draped in the mantle of credentials, bedecked with the regalia of Science, and cloaked with a sense of superiority and righteousness, they've assumed the role of shepherds, ushering the unwashed masses to brave new futures—whether they want them or not."

"During that century…the institutions here grew into leviathans—interlocking, self-justifying systems that seeped into every interaction and endeavor, far beyond anything in human history."

"The final solution to the biodiversity question is near."

Hush and darkness.

A faint warm breeze passed through the thicket of giant bamboo. The leaves in the upper reaches fluttered.

Quiescence returned. Gradually, time came to a stop.

Far below, the undergrowth of the thicket was rife with bioluminescent fungi. A blue-and-white glow bathed the pond, the light passing through the surface of the clear water, rendering the shallow bottom visible: a patchwork of large, pink-and-white slabs of quartz, streaked with black obsidian.

Silence.

A single leaf dropped, twirling and fluttering down until it touched the water, sending out ripples. And a giant tortoise that had been grazing at the water's edge raised its head.

THE PLANETARY TRIBUNAL

a novel of ideas

D. K. Locke

Rathen & Vane
Printed in the United States of America
First Edition: June 2026

ISBN 979-8-9926090-8-0 (hardcover)
ISBN 979-8-9926090-9-7 (paperback)
ISBN 979-8-9947039-4-6 (eBook)

Cover art by Gannadi Erkulis

Subjects: LCSH:
Idea (Philosophy). Science fiction—Philosophical aspects.
Political science—Sociological aspects.
Civilization—Philosophy.
Manners and customs.
Climate and civilization. Disasters. Social choice.
Social capital (Sociology). Social ecology.
Speculative fiction. Philosophical fiction.

Genre: LCGFT:
Science fiction. Fiction

Classification: LCC:
PS3612.O2474 P53 2026
DDC 813/.6—dc23

to Earth and its people

It took about ten years to write this beast. What a journey. I dug into places of wonder I never wanted to leave, and into noxious terrain I had to drag myself through—kicking and snarling—as I revised and honed the text.

Elena Ferrante said that books, once they are written, have no need of their authors. I feel the same way.

Everything I wished to express and explore about our civilization is contained in this novel.

D. K. Locke, January, 2026

Part One

1937

CHAPTER 1

Texas Panhandle Region, Baseline Planet
Year: 1937

THE YOUTHFUL-LOOKING WOMAN moved through the knee-high grass, her steps sending horned larks into the sky and causing the double scabbard on her back to shift slightly. The low-hanging sun bathed the hills and the prairie in a golden glow, and its familiar warmth on her naked body felt comforting. Red-tailed hawks were calling to one another, and the dry ground was alive with the snapping and crackling of grasshoppers. In the distance, a mammoth trumpeted, and Hagar paused, grateful for yet another day to be alive and awake. Through the march of centuries, these feelings endured.

She approached what was referred to as the Canadian River back on Earth. But this wasn't Earth; it was its pristine twin—the baseline planet, a world identical to Earth but devoid of humans and their modifications to the natural world. It served as a barometer for Hagar, allowing her to gauge the extent of human influence on the parallel planets she monitored across the multiverse.

This place was also her sanctuary, a refuge she'd visited once every few decades. She loved this place for the same reason she rarely spoke of it: Here, she could just be.

Her stay on this retreat planet was nearing its end, though.

Hagar skirted around a copse of ancient junipers and reached the river's edge, where a herd of large camels was browsing the undergrowth. The woman waded into the water and splashed some on her face. She dived in and came up.

Through a stand of cottonwoods on the opposite bank, hairless Columbian mammoths lumbered into view, raising small clouds of dust that eddied about their textured, coarse skin as their massive legs steadily rose and fell.

Drawn to these giant, earthy beasts, Hagar swam upstream for a closer look, making sure her distance and movements remained unthreatening. As she approached, she noted the intricate patterns on their leathery hide, evoking thoughts of another place and time. A hint of wistfulness briefly clouded her gaze; on Earth, their kind was hunted to death, leaving only a few surviving kin.

The hairless mammoths drank leisurely from the river, their trunks curling to guide the water into their mouths. Their activities had an unhurried rhythm. Every now and then, one would flap its ears. Hagar gazed at them, fond memories flitting through her mind. At long last, she plunged beneath the surface and, with powerful strokes, made it back to the riverbank. Emerging from the water, she breathed in deeply, the droplets running down her skin. Hagar pushed long wet hair from her eyes and trotted to the hover bike, parked between two boulders. Setting off, she shot through the boundless grassland. After a few miles, the bike's momentum waned and it came to a gentle halt.

Hagar slid off and leaned against it, eyes alight. Condors and their more imposing kin glided through the vast expanse of the sky, which bled from brilliant blue to burnished amber. The warm air was pregnant with the smells of wild things. Throngs of shrub oxen and dun-colored horses roamed across the prairie, and a pride of lions eyed them from afar. Occasional calls and grunts reached her ears. Inhaling deeply, Hagar sauntered about. Her bare feet registered the deep, rhythmic tremors as one of the massive bison herds, a rolling avalanche of horns and dark fur, surged in the distance.

It was time for her to leave the baseline planet.

Something about the Earth report she'd received yesterday seemed off. Anyway, more than two decades had passed since her last inspection of the most environmentally troubled among the parallel planets she monitored. It was time to check on it.

Hagar languidly unbuckled the scabbard from her back, letting it slide down. The swords and their sheaths seemingly disappeared, leaving only a fleeting ripple in the air. Mounting her bike, she gunned the engine and tore through the air. Almost immediately, undergarments materialized on her naked body, soon followed by riding pants, a leather aviator jacket, and tall boots.

As she transitioned between worlds, the sky churned with differing shades of light blue. Beneath her speeding vehicle, the grass turned short and patchy. The animals roaming in the distance dwindled, then disappeared, along with the wild scents carried by gusts of wind. A dirt path abruptly formed. As it slowly descended midflight, Hagar's hover bike sprouted wheels, morphing into a motorcycle with an attached sidecar typical of those on Earth. Lurching as it touched the ground, the motorbike righted itself and rushed on. As if from nowhere, Hagar produced a leather aviator helmet, goggles, and driving gloves.

As Hagar arrived on Earth, the dirt road transformed into a paved one. And all living things winked out of existence.

CHAPTER 2

Oklahoma Panhandle, Earth
Year: 1937

HAGAR GASPED, EYES WIDENING at the devastation before her.

She stepped off her motorcycle next to a small, wind-scoured house and surveyed the bleak land. Only fifty miles north of the grassland she had just toured on the baseline planet, she was struck speechless by the stark contrast.

She'd been in this very spot back in 1842, when this was the heartland of Comanche power and influence. That might as well have been a thousand years ago. The Comanche were gone. The bison were gone. The grass was gone. Hagar now stood in the middle of a desert strewn with sand dunes.

Still reeling, she recalled past reports as she pieced together what must have unfolded here. In 1860, black rain fell in Syracuse as a storm carried sand from Kansas Territory. More came back to her. In 1887, dirt storms of biblical proportions swept parts of Texas, accompanied by black skies. And thousands of cattle gathered at dwindling water holes and perished in the heat, their tongues swollen and dark.

But what she saw now was worse. Far worse. And she didn't need to look far for the reason. Noticing the gleaming steel plow half-buried in the side of a sand dune, she clenched her jaw in anger. *Morons.*

"Storm winds blew, droughts came, hail pounded the land," someone said. Hagar turned to see an old man joining her in the sand-filled yard. "Yet, as long as the tough, wiry buffalo grass covered the earth, its thick interwoven roots held the soil down when it dried."

"Hello, John," Hagar said gravely, trying to catch his eye. She frowned with concern when her analyst avoided her gaze. His beard was longer and far more unkempt than she remembered. And his leather suspenders were cracked and flecked with tiny clods of dirt. "How long has it been? What year is it?" she asked.

"It's 1937. Saw you last in 1912. So, yeah, that would be twenty-five years," the old man replied as he grimaced at the picket fence. Once possibly white, the fence had had its paint stripped by the winds, leaving it ashen.

"Are you surprised?" John asked. He kicked at the sand, wincing at the cloud of dust that billowed up.

"I am, but I shouldn't have been." She shook her head. "The cycle repeats itself. Seventy years back, the rail companies printed magazine articles and pamphlets that lured hundreds of thousands here."

John cackled, a hollow, unsettling sound. "Same story this time. 'Riches in the soil, prosperity in the air, progress everywhere.' Said so right in the brochure. Except, this time they had tractors. They ripped out the great mat of grass, opening up the land for the seeding of wheat. They called it 'sodbusting' and 'breaking the land,' and they were mighty pleased with themselves." The old man coughed violently. Hagar stood by, her brow furrowed with worry, until his coughing and muttering subsided.

"Big farm equipment meant big loans, and houses got mortgaged," he said, getting a hold of himself. "The math seemed simple enough: You plow more of the prairie and get to put more seeds in the dirt and ultimately more dollars in your pocket."

Hagar's gaze swept back to the blighted landscape.

John noticed the tremor in her hand. "This is what every-man-for-himself looks like when the wind comes calling," he said and grimaced at the sky.

Hagar was a planetary auditor—even if the inhabitants of the myriad Earth-like parallel planets she oversaw were unaware of it. Of any of it. If she were to believe that this was not an isolated case, she would've pulled the plug on human activities on Earth right then and there. And for a fleeting moment, she almost gave in to the urge.

"With the scent of money in the air, in came the suitcase farmers: summer visitors who rented tractors to reap the straw," John said. "Hell, everyone knew this area was no good for farming. But no one wanted to hear that. They just kept talking about bushel prices and freight rates."

The man stared past the fence at something only he could see.

"They missed out on the land grabs, back in the day," John said. "But now it was their turn. Their tractors took to the fields, and the grass was torn up. Wheat seeds poured in, and gold came out. The good times rolled on as long as the rains did—all through the '20s. Then the drought hit, as sooner or later it always does around here. The sun baked the last drop of moisture out. The soil was pulverized by the disk plows and dried to a powder. A big chunk of Kansas went bye-bye. Heard that high winds carried the dirt all the way to the Atlantic."

She stared at him, a cocktail of dismay and indignation in her eyes. What the hell? she wanted to say. Why didn't you report the situation years ago? Why wasn't I notified about any of this?

It was his job to alert her. His, and that of the dozens of other analysts deployed across the planet. That was why she'd stationed them on Earth. But there was something odd about John, something that wasn't there before, when she'd seen him last. She decided, for now, to hold her tongue and observe.

"So it's over now." Hagar brushed stray hair from her face. "What are people still doing here? It seems the only thing growing in this area is sand dunes." She fought to keep the anger from her voice.

John chuckled, dry and mirthless. "Ain't doing much. Sweeping dust, patching holes, waiting on the sky to change its mind. They're holding out for the rains—and with them the good times of wheat and opportunity."

He tipped his chin toward the wind-whipped horizon. "Hard-headed as fence posts, these folks. They won't be chased off. Hell, the baseball games still go on—sandstorm or not." His mouth twitched, just shy of a smile.

He stared into the blowing dust, watching a memory only he could see.

"True pioneers," the old man said. He studied his worn shoes. "Misguided pioneers."

John hobbled toward the house, and she followed. "Aldo Leopold is right," he said, seemingly to himself. "Communism, fascism, capitalism . . . in the end, they all seek salvation through machinery."

There—in that instant, he sounded like John of old. Hagar's eyes shifted his way, but as before, he wasn't meeting her gaze.

John halted, still lost in thought. "They are completely alien-ated from the interdependence of life," he muttered, "and there you have it in a nutshell. They replace mankind's attachment to the earth with an out-and-out dedication to profit-making."

He suddenly looked up. "Florence!" he called, turning to the small house.

Silence.

John nodded. "Yes, I'm coming, Florence. Was just talking to the old boss, you know." He turned his face in the general direction of Hagar. "I have to go back in." He grinned. "Florence is call-ing me." Without saying another word, he determinedly marched into the rundown house. The hinges protested briefly as the door slammed with a shudder and was still.

Hagar sat motionless, the truth landing with a dull, heavy force.

She played back in her mind John's voice—bright and hollow—calling out to Florence, a name she'd heard him utter many years ago with tenderness and joy. It hit her then. The sandstorms scoured the land raw, leaving survivors like John in their wake, clutching at memories, tethered to phantoms.

Gathering herself, Hagar walked to her motorcycle and drove off. There was nothing she could have done for him. The unraveling of his mind, however, did explain why she hadn't received a report from this sector in years.

After driving about a mile, Hagar heard a growing buzz in the air and brought her motorcycle to a halt. As the sound intensified, a low cloud moved across the sky. Soon, a vast swarm of grasshoppers descended, blanketing the ground. A few leaped about her bike and over her boots.

She killed the engine and sat there, immersed in dark thoughts, until the grasshoppers lifted off in search of anything else remotely edible. Soon, a hush settled over the land.

"It's miles to water," someone yelled from afar, "but only six inches to hell." Hagar looked up, her gaze falling upon a solitary figure in a white dress walking up the open, forlorn road toward her.

Seeing the woman against the vast bleakness, Hagar felt a pull. And perhaps there was more to be gleaned about this calamity from one who had lived through it. With the congressional hearing still some time away, she figured her journey could afford a short delay.

She sat astride her bike beside a half-buried wagon wheel, watching the stranger draw closer. The approaching woman was young, no more than twenty, her step unburdened. Flame-colored hair tumbled freely down her back, offsetting the pallor of her loose white dress. Her unbound body moved with the unguarded ease of someone who had long since stopped arranging herself for other people. A small suitcase and a satchel were her only possessions.

"I am Virginia," the woman said once she was a few paces away and then turned to the rider expectantly. Her voice carried a soft Southern lilt—honeyed, sunbaked, and easy to like.

"Hagar," she said, removing her goggles and aviator helmet. She shook her luxuriant blonde hair and dismounted her bike.

"A dame on a motorcycle," Virginia said in admiration, taking in the woman snugly clad in leather breeches and an aviator jacket. "I wish *I* had a motorbike," the girl said in a rush, then paused and cast a fresh look at Hagar. "You're not from around here, are you?"

"Just passing through, on my way to Washington, D.C."

Virginia gave her a penetrating look, finding the rider remarkably beautiful, yet in a way that didn't belong. With her slightly pinched aristocratic nose, yellow-flecked green eyes, and clear skin aglow under the sun, she seemed unearthly—if not for the mouth. Her full lips held a hint of asymmetry. They appeared oddly suggestive when relaxed.

A shared silence hung between them.

"What fools, huh?" Virginia finally said.

"Pardon?"

"What kind of folks would tear up the prairie grass like this?"

Hagar didn't respond, but darkness filled her eyes. A thundercloud that dissipated just as quickly. Luckily, Virginia was not looking.

"They told Pa that the rain would follow the plow."

Hagar surveyed the plain. "It was the same in the 1870s; they claimed that rain would follow the trees. They planted them all over. It didn't work." She stripped off her leather jacket, revealing a form-fitting black T-shirt beneath.

The girl peered at Hagar with intense, intelligent eyes that belied the dreamy feel of her freckles. "We moved here from Cambridge, Massachusetts." She shook her head in disbelief. "It's been miserable. But I'm out of here. Said goodbye to Pa and Ma this morning."

"Where are you headed?"

The girl shrugged.

"Why?" Hagar asked.

"Because it's all wrong!" Sudden heat flashed in the girl's eyes. "Do you know the book *Return to Nature!* by Adolf Just?" Virginia didn't wait for an answer but pulled a book out from her satchel with a flourish. For a wild moment, Hagar thought the young woman would offer her a discount if she bought it right then and there.

The girl waved the book in Hagar's direction. "He's right. 'Nature is forever unassailable in her justice; she punishes every transgression of her laws, but likewise rewards every return to obedience.'"

"'Obedience'?" Hagar was amused by the choice of word.

"Indeed. Allow me a moment." Virginia thumbed through the pages. "'Man must today endeavor in his mode of living to heed again the voice of nature,'" she read, then gestured at the sandy, inert expanse.

"Truer words were never spoken," Hagar agreed, but her eyes twinkled.

"Back to a simpler, purer state. That's why I had Pa help me construct a charkha spinning wheel." Virginia put the book away. "I spun and sewed this dress," she said and twirled.

Hagar reached out and felt the white dress just below the generous swell of her breasts. "You made this yourself, then?"

Virginia took a shuddering breath, managing to give a slight nod.

They began strolling on the hard, crusted ground.

"A few miles back," Hagar said, "the wife of an old friend of mine…perhaps you knew her, Florence."

"Dust pneumonia," Virginia said immediately. "She died a few years back."

"What's dust pneumonia?"

"Mud in the lungs."

Hagar blinked, visibly startled. She eyed the girl. "Tell me how it is here."

"The wind moans for days on end. There are bad days, and there are worse days." The young woman looked away and bit her lower lip as thick and sharp memories came rushing in. "On some occasions, Ma gave us small wet towels to cover our faces, so we could breathe. At night, you try to lie still, not to feel the grit of the sand on your pillow. Just the sound of blowing dirt outside is enough to knot your stomach. Is that what you want to hear?"

"Yes."

Virginia lowered her head, overcome by emotion. "Dust to breathe, sand to eat, and dirt to drink," she said in a small voice.

"And the storms?" Hagar asked softly.

"They last for hours or days on end: a towering tidal wave of sand that wipes out the sky, boiling up and roiling as it engulfs everything and turns day into a cellar's midnight." She fell silent for a moment, reminiscing. "You can't tell which way is up. Lightning flashes, but in total silence—and suddenly, an ear-splitting cacophony of clinking and rasping sounds. The metal fence, alive with static, would knock you flat if touched. The dirt might be tan brown or smoke gray, with sharp smells that burn or with greasy ones that nauseate." Her voice fell almost to a whisper. "Once, while walking home, the blowing sand felt like steel wool on my skin. I nearly suffocated; it was a close call."

Hagar caught herself sighing. She'd never seen nature unravel like this. It was a total ecological collapse.

The two of them sat back-to-back on the ground, content to just sit there. The sky was clear, the air surprisingly fresh.

"At the very least, people should have tried no-till farming," Hagar said.

Virginia raised an eyebrow quizzically.

"No plowing," Hagar supplied.

"Might as well tell a church to ditch its Bible. In any case, what's zee matter with plowing, Herr Professor Doktor?"

"The soil progressively becomes impermeable."

Virginia looked skeptical. "Plowing opens up the soil."

"At first. But the process tears up the inner structure of the earth so later it collapses on itself, and you end up with a more compact soil than you started off with."

Hagar smiled grimly at the startled look on the girl's face. "Ever wondered what gives the intact grassland soil its clumpy, cottage-cheese texture? Miles of fungal filaments permeate the soil and release a sticky substance. They bind together particles of sand, silt, and clay to form aggregates. The open spaces between these clumps allow in water and air and make subterranean life possible." She chuckled without mirth. "Well, that blasted plow rips up the fungi and collapses the whole network of air, water, and nutrients."

"Lord!" Virginia was looking at her, wide-eyed. "How do you know all that?"

Hagar reached out, accessing a vast database with her mind. Now that she was back on Earth, she could do this. The database was continuously updated by her analysts and aided by an army of smart digital scanning devices. A name popped up in response to her query. "Sir Albert Howard. I've read some of his work." She hoped that would be enough to make her expertise plausible. Luckily, Virginia seemed unfamiliar with the name.

Hagar lay down, stretching on the exposed firm earth, hands behind her head. Virginia's gaze lowered, lingering as it roamed over Hagar's figure. The air seemed too still all of a sudden. And it was getting hot; Virginia could feel sweat trickling down her temples and underneath her breasts.

Hagar seemed not to have noticed. "The ancient Romans used the plow, you know." Her voice was pensive. "The repeated plowing degraded and eroded fields in central Italy. Two thousand years later, people are still at it, with an astounding lack of insight, I may add."

Virginia sighed. "'When we try to pick out anything by itself, we find it hitched to everything else in the Universe.'"

Hagar tilted her head. "John Muir?"

The girl blushed. "Well, yes." She shrugged ruefully. "The library and I are on a first-name basis. Not a whole lot else to do around here. And everyone is convinced I'm certifiable, anyway."

Hagar and Virginia shared a brief smile. The two rose slowly and strolled back toward the motorcycle.

Hagar glanced at Virginia a few times. At long last, she said, "You're thirty years too late. Wrong time, wrong place."

"How do you figure?"

"Back in the day, a small colony existed by Lake Maggiore in southern Switzerland: Monte Verità. They experimented there with surrealism, movement arts, Dadaism, nude sunbathing, nature cure, and pacifism."

"Sounds amazing!"

Hagar smiled at that.

"Does Monte Verità still exist?" the young woman wanted to know.

"I'm afraid those types of associations don't tend to last."

Virginia shook her head mournfully. "Alas, nothing to live for then," she declared, laying a hand dramatically on her chest.

When they reached the motorcycle, Virginia brightened up. "Is this a Harley-Davidson?"

Hagar briefly studied the outsized imprint on the gas tank. "Sure is." She looked at Virginia through narrowed eyes. "I suppose you're after a ride?"

The girl vigorously nodded and panted theatrically. "Me Tonto. Me no ride iron horse before."

Hagar let out an exasperated sigh, but she had about half an hour left to kill. "All right. Hop into the sidecar."

Virginia shook her head from side to side, agitating the long red tresses.

Hagar put her hands on her waist. "Well, missy, what do you propose? You're not thinking of sitting astride, are you—in that nightgown of yours?"

The girl flipped her hair back, hiked up her dress—higher than strictly necessary—and swung one leg over the seat. She straddled the motorbike, looking archly at Hagar as if daring her to say something. "Besides," she said, pointing to the sidecar, "we need a place for my suitcase."

After a moment, Hagar nodded in agreement.

They settled onto the bike and Hagar revved the engine.

Virginia hugged her from behind as the motorcycle started forward. "It's like having a sweetheart," she said, seemingly to herself. Then she whooped as the bike took off in earnest. "Here come the thundering hoofbeats of the great horse Silver! The Lone Ranger rides again!"

"Keep it down in the back row!"

The motorcycle picked up speed.

"What a bang!" Virginia shouted. "And the wind—with no sand!" And Hagar smiled in appreciation.

"Free and wild, I embrace the open road," Virginia hollered, rising and spreading her arms wide. "Healthy and free, the long brown path before me leading wherever I choose."

"Sit your butt down," Hagar yelled, "before you find yourself flying onto the long brown path behind you."

Virginia obliged. As the engine's growl deepened beneath her, she edged closer, pressing her body against Hagar and closing her eyes.

They rode on, the world stripped to wind, speed, and the engine's low thunder.

Hagar eased off the gas. The engine's roar transitioned into a gentle hum. The motorcycle coasted to a stop on the desolate, sun-bleached road; its ticking was the only sound in the still, cloudless afternoon. Virginia hopped off, cheeks flushed, eyes sparking, and stood there a moment, catching her breath.

She walked over to the sidecar, pulling out the suitcase that had been tucked away for the ride.

"Virginia."

The young woman turned.

Hagar closed her eyes, reaching out with her mind, searching. At last, she looked up. "Go to Eutropheon, a raw food restaurant on Hill Street in Los Angeles, and contact their long-haired, European clientele—kindred spirits. In fact, ask the Richters about the *naturmenschen:* the Ehret nature folks in Tahquitz Canyon."

"The Richters?"

Hagar waved her hand. "The restaurant owners." She could never get over the narrow bandwidth humans had for absorbing new information. If a person read one hundred books a year, that was impressive. When needed, she could process that amount of data in less than a minute.

Virginia asked, "And who are these nature folks?"

"They hitchhike through the mountains and deserts, dwell in caves, create music, practice yoga, play the flute—you'll love to hang out with them."

"I believe I might," Virginia said slowly. She took a few steps but then swung around. "At first, I thought . . . You're not twenty at all, are you?"

Hagar shook her head.

"How old, then?"

The blonde woman looked at her strangely. "I don't rightly know. I, well, I stopped counting before I hit a hundred." She grinned feebly. "And with all the shifting to different planes, it's hard to keep track at any rate."

Virginia's mouth fell open.

Hagar pulled down her goggles and approached. She planted a kiss on Virginia's parted lips, and the girl jolted. "When you get to Los Angeles, wear flowers in your hair. It'll suit you."

"Did people wear flowers in the Monte Verità colony?" The young woman's voice quivered ever so slightly, eyes still wide in a mix of awe and uncertainty.

"Yes. Sometimes."

Virginia's fingers unconsciously twirled a strand of hair. "And long hair?"

"Of course."

Something occurred to Hagar. "Virginia, do you have any

money on you?"

The girl glanced pointedly at her shoes, patched with rubber obviously taken from a worn tire.

"Here, I got something for you." Hagar fished a massive gold coin out of her pants pocket.

With wide eyes, Virginia accepted the heavy coin and examined it. Then she regarded the other woman skeptically. "Your pockets were clearly empty; those trousers of yours cling so tightly, every detail is evident. In any case, I—"

Hagar raised her hands. "You're right." She considered for a second. "The jacket pocket would've been more believable, huh? Here, let's do it again." She took back the giant coin, tucked it inside her jacket, and handed it back to her, then added two more coins. "They are solid gold. Sell them when you reach Los Angeles."

The girl shoved the heavy coins into her luggage and was silent for a long time. "So, you can produce gold out of thin air."

Hagar burst out laughing. "I keep a vault that follows me," she said, eyes bright with humor. "It's a little out of phase with this world so you can't see it."

Virginia studied the wasteland. "Must be handy," she finally said.

A black car with chairs strapped to its roof drove slowly down the road. They both watched the vehicle as it passed them by.

Hagar smiled affectionately at the girl in the white dress. "It's time for you to go now. Catch a ride to Los Angeles."

Virginia looked at her, then rushed off, her suitcase lurching every which way. She shouted something half-laughing, half-defiant to the barren land when she was a considerable distance away. Then: "A road to Damascus—and in Oklahoma, no less!"

Hagar broke into laughter. She cupped her hands and shouted after the retreating figure, "Perish the thought!" Chuckling, she shook her head and made her way back to the motorcycle.

Hagar watched her go, a strange ache settling into her chest. She touched her lips absently, then shook her head.

Time to trade kisses for committee hearings.

It was time to head east, to the capital and pay a little visit to the US Congress and, with a bit of luck, preserve some of the forests in the region. The key was hemp, the marijuana plant. The report she'd received was quite clear on that.

CHAPTER 3

THE HOUSE CHAMBER hummed with activity, and men clustered in small groups or talked at their appointed seats. The voice of Jere Cooper from Tennessee rose above the murmurs of ongoing discussions. "Is it true that extensive hearings were held on this bill before the Ways and Means Committee and there was no opposition to its passage?"

At his chair, Frank Buck smoothed his mustache. "The gentleman is correct."

"The gentleman from California is lying," a voice rang out from the central door at the rear of the chamber, drawing all eyes. A blonde woman of striking beauty stood between the now open double doors, her gaze taking in the gathering of people. "After all, didn't Dr. Woodward of the American Medical Association vehemently oppose this bill?"

A profound hush settled over the room, broken only by Buck's indignant reply: "Who claims that?"

The youthful-looking woman didn't deign to answer; instead, she snapped her fingers and glanced up.

The Speaker's eyes widened in disbelief as his gaze followed hers to the gallery. The guards manning the dozen doorways, the press, and the observers were gone. "Who are you?" he demanded.

"Where is security?" Sudden beads of sweat appeared on the Speaker's forehead. *Some subversive group must have taken over the House!* he thought.

"I made them disappear," the woman said as she crossed the threshold. This simple statement sent chills down the hall. Every eye was on her as she proceeded down the aisle beneath the stained-glass skylight, walking between the elongated, curved wooden benches toward the center of the floor.

The people in the gallery were absent from the very moment Hagar entered. And it wasn't that the guards and the people in the gallery disappeared. Rather, the people in the main hall did. As she entered, Hagar had transported herself and the delegates to the netherworld: a mirror, shadowy reflection of the real world that was devoid of people except those she chose to drag across.

"Mr. Speaker, what will you do about lying Frankie here?" she asked, looking pointedly at the ashen representative from California.

"The Ways and Means Committee thoroughly investigated the matter and decided in favor of the bill," Frank Buck said weakly.

"And what does a tax committee know about drugs?" the woman said, almost absently, slowly making her way toward the marble rostrum rail. The delegates collectively gasped as, before their eyes, her dress changed color and cut. The heels of her shoes lengthened, and the thud of her footfalls became more pronounced. Up close, she appeared to the congressmen much younger than they had assumed—and stunning at that.

Buck and Reed exchanged uncertain, fearful glances. Reed rose. "Will the gentleman yield?"

Buck nodded, grateful for the settling decorum amid these surreal, eerie circumstances. "I yield to the gentleman from New York."

"Expert testimony indicates that marijuana use leads to insanity and crime," Daniel A. Reed announced to the assembled House. If this was a hostage situation, maybe they could argue their way out of it.

"The marijuana cigarette is most insidious, its effects deadly," Clinton Hester seconded. His imposing figure added gravitas to his words. He struck Hagar as a retired wrestler.

Her lips quirked into a sardonic smile. "Isn't it curious, though," she said, "how Dr. Woodward found the drug not to be well researched?"

The Speaker glowered in deep disapproval at the intruder, the cut of her dress, and the unseemly disruption of routine. He thanked the Lord that along with the security forces, the press and the public crowding the gallery had also disappeared.

Reed's voice rose. "Dr. Munch testified about its harmful impact!" His words were laced with as much indignation as he could muster.

"Ah, yes, Dr. Munch. I had a feeling you were going to mention his testimony." Hagar strolled down the aisle, her fingers absently skimming over the polished backrests of the elongated seats. "The good doctor administered cannabis to three hundred dogs. He discerned no effects on most of them and couldn't make sense of the effects on the rest." She spread her hands, as if regretful. "This pharmacologist with his cadre of dogs was your only expert witness on the effects of marijuana on humans."

Murmurs of discontent swept through the hall.

"Gentlemen," Hagar said to the assembled Representatives, "you know precious little of the drug; I trust you know something about the limits of your mandate."

Mutters of unease greeted this statement.

Hagar shot a cold glance toward Mr. Hester, the counsel from the Department of the Treasury, and raised her hand to single him out. "The legal advisor presented the bill to the Ways and Means Committee. His professed intent: to curb the transfers of marijuana to those who would use it for 'undesirable purposes.'" She frowned at him. "By his admission, he is in violation of his oath."

Against the rising tide of protest, her voice came crashing down, louder than any human voice had the right to: "To use taxes as a means to penalize and prohibit is not taxation. Congress cannot 'under the pretext of executing its powers, pass laws for the accomplishment of objects not entrusted to the government.'"

Heavy silence. The words seemed to reverberate from the walls. Hester, assistant general counsel for the Treasury, studied his shoes. Vinson from the Committee gazed off into the distance. Both attorneys recognized where the quote had come from.

The woman surveyed the people looking at her. "Gentlemen, this federal government is an overarching apparatus to bind the federated states into an effective union. All other functions of society are either reserved to the individual states or, as the case may be, left to the people's jurisdiction or sphere of authority."

Everyone in the chamber recognized the amendment from which this last statement was derived.

Fred Vinson, the Kentucky representative, rose to his feet. "Mr. Speaker, recent court rulings suggest otherwise."

Hagar yelled over the voices rallying behind him, "And you think the Supreme Court's betrayal absolves you of yours? So much for your vaunted checks and balances."

Her words were greeted with angry buzzes and scandalized exclamations. The Speaker was banging his gavel, failing to restore order.

Hagar cried out, "The fellowship of the nine black robes. They read the Constitution as one would read tea leaves. And what insights might these seers glean? Why, anything they set their minds to." Some smiled at the metaphor. "A few months ago, your president talked about it. You all heard him. He said the Supreme Court has improperly set itself up as the third house of Congress—a super legislature. 'Reading into the Constitution words and implications which are not there, and which were never intended to be there.' Your president wanted it to do justice 'under the Constitution, not over it.'"

A stubborn silence descended over the hall.

She looked around, meeting the eyes of many. She wagged an

admonishing finger. "Mark my words. You'll start by raising taxes on the plant, then move on to a total prohibition, preventing you from even making paper from it—and then instead of having a paper industry based on hemp, you'll have one that devours the remainder of your old-growth forests!"

For the first time since the stranger had entered the chamber, the representative from New York felt on firmer ground. "Ma'am," Daniel Reed said, his voice silky, "I don't know who you are or what you are after, but I can tell you this much: No one is making paper from hemp. This is total rubbish, uneconomic to boot."

Hagar faltered, taken aback by Reed's assertiveness. The conviction in his voice rang true; this wasn't just posturing. Had the reports she received been falsified? Delving deeper into the web of reports she'd trusted for decades—yields, trade logs, shipping manifests. Line by line, the illusion fell away: The information she'd relied upon was tainted.

Hagar stood still; beneath her calm, a tempest brewed. The weight of many eyes upon her now felt oppressive, and every second of silence seemed charged, as she grappled internally with the magnitude of what she'd uncovered.

When she finally spoke, her voice wavered a bit, betraying a hint of the turmoil within. "My intent has been to protect the forests, not to indulge in your trivial debates on personal habits."

Hagar raised her arms but dropped them again. "Almost forgot," she said. "You know how sometimes you have a bad dream? Maybe even a daydream that you really don't want to share. You realize it's just a waking dream, and you snap out of it—like that." She snapped her fingers. And all the people vanished from view.

For a moment, Hagar regarded the empty chamber.

She knew that at this very moment, the delegates and government officials were back in the real world, telling themselves they had been daydreaming. As for the guards still manning their posts, the journalists, and the visitors in the gallery, not a moment had passed.

Hagar remained behind, in the netherworld, rocked by the implications of what she'd just learned. The massive hemp-paper industry . . . Evidently, it didn't exist. Someone had been doctoring at least some of the reports that had reached her over the past twenty or so years. Someone obviously did not want her alerted to the true state of affairs on Earth. She'd explained away—rationalized, really—the reports that left out accounts of the Dust Bowl due to the mental condition of the local analyst. But now she could no longer deny the obvious: Something was very wrong.

What the hell was going on?

Her information-gathering network of analysts was compromised. Hagar felt dazed as a new realization hit her: Without knowing who was behind this, she could not confide in or fully trust anyone.

Still in the netherworld, Hagar emerged from the Capitol building and walked the eerily empty streets toward her vehicle, brooding and fuming.

CHAPTER 4

Mandatory Palestine

HAGAR STOPPED THE CAR, KILLED THE ENGINE, and got out.

It was late afternoon. A field of grass fluttered in the warm breeze. The rays of the sun reflected from the Sea of Galilee.

The local analyst had requested that she approach the final mile on foot. Less conspicuous, he'd told her. And, sure enough, she could see him walking briskly toward her.

The situation turned out to be worse than she'd first assumed. Her network wasn't compromised; it had been gutted. The single figure hurrying toward her was the last analyst standing. But he had no way of knowing that; her people operated independently, gathering information and analyzing events of this world on their own. This compartmentalization of the analysts was intentional; it was a security measure. *For all the good it did.*

She had been on her way to Egypt when she received his message. He wouldn't have asked her to detour without a good reason. Her first impulse was to disregard it; she had far more pressing things on her mind. But that might have proved to be the wrong move. She decided to go with the flow, act as expected, and feign ignorance. It might buy her time if whoever was behind it didn't realize she'd caught on to their ruse.

Mr. Watts came to a stop and bowed. "Greetings, High Mistress."

"Greetings," she said and watched him curiously. Her analyst was wearing loose trousers, a white tank top, and a dark-blue woolen cap. He motioned her to follow him up the small hill.

Indeed, an enigma awaited her upon reaching the hilltop. The buildings spread out below, with their sharp lines and gabled roofs, stood in stark contrast to the traditional dwellings of the region. They seemed out of place in that part of the world.

Some distance away, a group of young men and women were making their way toward the settlement. They were all carrying hoes and sickles, apparently farmers. The men wore Western slacks; the women wore shorts and walked casually alongside their male counterparts. Not Arabs, then. "Jews?" she asked, incredulous. "Jewish farmers?"

"Indeed."

Her eyes followed the retreating figures. "What are these Ashkenazi Jews doing here, in the lands of the Mohammedans?"

"They came here calling it *Eretz Yisrael*—the homeland they were exiled from. Hundreds of thousands of Jews migrated in the last few decades, determined to reestablish here a national home."

She burst out laughing. The analyst glanced at her with obvious surprise.

"Oh, that's rich—the protected subjects rising in the heart of the House of Islam. I can't wait to see how it'll play out."

"I fail to see the humor."

"Islam crowned itself the final revelation," she said. "Judaism—tolerated, taxonomized, kept safely under glass. And now the relic has risen and staked a flag in the sanctum." She gave a dark, amused laugh. "I bet the Muslims are spitting brimstone."

He now understood.

Hagar shook her head in wonder. "What were they thinking—migrating into the Arab heartland?"

"High Mistress, they've worked hard to sidestep this question, treating the resentful natives as part of the exotic scenery."

"Madness. Couldn't they have settled a less contentious region?"

But she found herself intrigued.

"They did set up some agricultural settlements in Argentina."
He shrugged. "Didn't work out."

"What was there to work out, Mr. Watts?" Hagar eyed him quizzically. Once, he had another name. All of her analysts did. But
with their relocation to this planet, they started a new life and left
it all behind. They anticipated spending the remainder of their
lives on Earth.

"This," he said. "I wanted you to see it for yourself."

Hagar glanced at the man questioningly.

He had been waiting for this. "A collective settlement," he said,
pointing at the buildings in the distance. "Dozens like this one
have sprung up in the region."

"How long have these existed?" she demanded.

His eyes twinkled. "The oldest has been around for thirty years
and is going strong."

Hagar was silent for some time, considering this. "Interesting,"
she said at last. She had a standing order to alert her to any forward-thinking, pioneering human enterprises. She wanted to be
kept abreast not only of the most worrisome developments of
the manmade world on Earth, but also its most promising. Many
intentional communities have sprouted in the last century and a
half. Almost all of them have proved to be very short-lived. Could
it be different here? "I'll go in and take a peek," she told Mr. Watts.
He bowed in return, looking pleased.

Hagar morphed her clothes until she stood in front of Mr.
Watts wearing a kerchief, dark shorts, and a sleeveless white top.
"The outfit the girls wear around here is nothing if not comfortable," she said, laughing, and stuck her hands in the dirt, only to
rub some of it on her shorts. "How do I look?"

"Like you fit in, boss." He gave her a boyish grin and touched
his cap in acknowledgment.

They started walking toward the settlement. In the distance,
a hay baler slowly worked its way through a field, a reciprocating

beam on top packing the straw tightly onto the incoming conveyor belt. In addition to the driver on the small tractor out front, four men rode the baler itself, raking the hay and managing the twine feed, as needed.

A swarm of naked children tore past them, squealing and laughing. Hagar blinked. "Where are they headed?"

"Why, to the lake, of course." Mr. Watts was chortling. "At this speed, I reckon they're about to hit the water any moment now."

They crossed the field, and the sound of a hammer banging on metal greeted them as they approached a shaded area. A man paused his work and regarded them before resuming. From a shed, a few men walked out single file carrying on their shoulders bulky burlap sacks filled with grain. Hagar gestured to her companion to follow her, and they entered the outbuilding. In one corner, two women crouched, inspecting numerous potted seedlings arrayed in front of them.

"I expected a socialist, collective settlement to stifle the entrepreneurial and innovative spirit," her analyst was saying once they were back out.

"Mr. Watts, groups of dedicated young people can be wildly enterprising," Hagar said. "While the collectivist Fourierist Phalanxes in the United States collapsed within months, it wasn't for lack of ingenuity." She observed small children clearing rocks. Three of them pushed a loaded wheelbarrow to the edge of a pit. As they lifted it up, other kids removed the rocks using long-handled hoes.

Hagar made her way toward the residential area, and her analyst fell in beside her. Among recently planted palm trees, they passed a group of teens lounging on a grass lawn. In the center stood an older man, leading what sounded like a current-affairs discussion.

⇒⇐

IN THE FALLING DARKNESS, AMID CYPRESS TREES, Hagar stood regarding a vacant building. Her glance fell on a plaque, and she trained her flashlight on it. The inscription read: *May this school rear our children in knowledge and understanding, instilling cooperation, loyalty, and efficiency. They will continue our mission of turning barren land into a thriving, fertile region. May plenty and love for the homeland bless the returned sons of an exiled people.*

"It's a school," someone behind her said in heavily accented German.

She spun around. A man with a holstered rifle stood grinning at her.

With Hagar appearing to be no more than twenty, he mistook her for one of the Jewish German youth members who had recently taken up residence in the colony.

"We built the school seven years ago," the watchman said.

Repeated chimes of a ship's bell filled the air.

"It seems to be the nicest building in the settlement," Hagar said, noting the whitewash on the walls, the tended lawn, and the flower garden.

"For the younger generation, nothing but the best," he said, adoration in his voice. "When we still had to live in shacks and tents, we made a point of building the children a permanent home." He followed her gaze. "Over there is the orchard." The watchman paused. "You are new here," he said.

She smiled. "I've only just arrived."

The guard gestured toward a large communal dining hall. "Go have dinner. That's where everyone is headed now."

Hagar looked at him unhappily, taken aback by his blunt manner. She then noticed a woman standing some distance away, hands in her pockets. The woman was also armed and wore a belt with loops filled with cartridges slung over her shoulder, sash-style. Clearly, she was waiting on the first watchman to join her.

Hagar eyed the female guard in her somewhat rumpled, over-sized shirt. What at first appeared bold and brassy seemed, at least in part, to be something else: a deliberate attempt to expunge the differences between men and women.

"Good flashlight." The man motioned to the one in her hand. "Can I use it? It'll be more useful for guard duty. Your turn will come soon enough." Without waiting for an answer, he took it from her.

From a kilometer away in the hills, Mr. Watts watched the exchange through binoculars that far surpassed any on Earth and gasped at the man's audacity. But his boss just let loose a startled, amused laugh and walked with an easy gait toward the dining hall.

Men and women in clean white shirts were emerging from the barracks and stuccoed dormitories, greeting each other, and walking toward the single-story building with numerous windows.

Joining them, Hagar entered a brightly lit, boisterous hall. It was filled mostly with young people; the oldest seemed to be in their late thirties. Next to where she stood, someone was strumming a mandolin with some people nearby singing along. She looked around, unsure, then stepped between the two rows of crowded tables. "Shalom," she finally greeted a man with a weathered, tanned face, seated by himself.

"Sit down, sit down," the man said, patting the space next to him on the wooden bench. She obliged.

A few women pushed open double swinging doors and emerged from the kitchen carrying trays.

"Fish!" hollered one of the serving women, turning around theatrically and holding a tray high. "And for a mere Saturday dinner, at that. Not fish from eggplants, not even from eggs, but real ones." This was greeted with a roar of approval and a round of applause.

"Newcomer?" the man asked, raising his voice to be heard. Hagar flashed him a dazzling smile.

The man gave her an admiring once-over before introducing her to the table: "Everyone, look. Pretty as a picture from Vienna!"

Some of the men chuckled or murmured in appreciation, looking her way. Despite her athletic build, there was an air of refinement about her. Her slender fingers seemed more suited to playing a harp than handling farming tools, and her patrician nose seemed more accustomed to the fragrance of blooming roses than the raw scent of the earth.

In response, Hagar held out a cup. And the man next to her poured her steaming tea from a metal kettle.

"How many members do you have?" she wanted to know.

"*Nu*, one hundred and seventy-two. We began with a core group of about sixty. This is our twelfth year."

Hagar took a sip. "You must've worked this land with blood and sweat."

"We did," he said. "Out back, we've got a small cemetery. That's where we buried comrades taken by malaria or killed by Arab marauders." He grimaced. "It wasn't easy waking up at two o'clock in the morning in those early days. Some of us still do, you know. And then we've had occasional locusts, which ate everything. You'd find their larvae in your bedclothes, on your desk, in your shoes."

"And now, our alfalfa crop is as good as what they get in California," someone else said. Hagar looked up. A woman across the table was grinning. "Enough, Yosef. You want to scare her off?" She extended a firm hand to Hagar. "I'm Elisheva."

"Hagar."

They shook hands.

"This is where we turn dreams into calluses." The woman gave Hagar a lopsided smile.

"Who's the leader?"

"No leader. Policy matters are decided by consensus," Elisheva said, exchanging glances with Yosef. Something was off about the newcomer, but she couldn't quite put her finger on it. She stirred her soup, the spoon clinking against the bowl.

Hagar mulled it over. "You say there are no leaders, but strong personalities always rise to the top."

"Sure," Yosef said. "But the headstrong are often at odds with one another. This tends to cancel things out. Community decisions are made during the weekly General Assembly, where the timid and the inarticulate are encouraged to speak up. We try to arrive at a broad, genuine consensus."

Around them, the hall throbbed with the clatter of cutlery and the boisterous chatter of the crowd. People seated close by found themselves listening in.

Hagar liked what she heard so far. "Do you get to decide what work you do?"

Elisheva replied, "You let the work committee know your preference, and it decides." She smiled. "We, the women, have largely taken over chicken breeding, beekeeping, and the vineyard." She pointed at a bulletin board on the far wall. "It all comes down to trust: in the committee, in our fellow comrades, in the *kvutza* and what it stands for."

"Who has the job of cleaning the lavatories or working in the washhouse?"

Elisheva said, "It's not assigned to any one person. Instead, everyone takes turns handling the truly unpleasant or particularly tedious tasks. The worse the job, the more often it rotates."

Hagar studied the faces around her. These people were not the first to establish such norms, but theirs was one of the very few secular intentional communities to survive beyond several years. The question, then, was why. And just as important . . . could it be implemented in other places?

"It's impressive," Hagar said. She helped herself to some of the food. "Collective settlements, *kvutzot*, are dotting this valley—over twenty thousand people in all, I was told. With Jewish members from South Africa and Romania, Russia and Greece, Poland and everywhere in between. What makes this time and place different?"

Yosef put both hands on the table, contemplating her question. "Neither a sect nor a sanctuary, this *kvutza* and others like it have a purpose beyond their own existence. They are but means to rebuild a Jewish national home."

That must have been the root of their durability, Hagar realized, or at least part of it. She pushed on. "Among other factors, what makes capitalism work is the sense of ownership in one's labor and product." She peered at Yosef through the rising steam from her cup. "Isn't this a problem in a collective settlement such as this?"

"Ah, she's a *tarbutnikit*," someone muttered from a nearby table.

"Oh?"

"A culturalist," another clarified.

"She has a point," a woman said from behind them. "Russia had a great shortage of electricity during the war, but you could not persuade the people to conserve. Light would be left burning all night."

"If everyone owns it, no one owns it," Hagar said, a challenge in her tone.

One of the men, a wiry pioneer with weathered features, bristled at her words. "Can there be no motivation but the accumulation of assets?" he asked, disdain clear in his voice. A few around him murmured in agreement.

"That's a question waiting for an answer," Hagar said, unperturbed.

"We've answered it," Elisheva said, putting down her fork. She focused her eyes on Hagar. "A member of the *kvutza* who gets up at four in the morning and does not return from the fields until dark—is he less devoted than the man who farms a field of his own?" Some nodded at those words. "The woman who cooks for one hundred comrades—is she any less industrious than if she were to cook for only her family?" Elisheva went on heatedly. "If one breaks the only gas lamp the collective owns or leaves the boiling milk unattended and it runs over, everyone suffers. Therefore, we care more than if it concerned only us or our immediate family."

Hagar's forehead creased in a frown as she mulled it over. "What if some members want more than others?"

"We don't maintain a rigid rule that each member can receive only so much and no more. The committee in charge settles such matters. What we have brought about is socialism on a human scale."

And that last thing you said makes a big difference, Hagar thought.

"'From each according to his ability, to each according to his needs,'" a stocky member from another table quoted, a comment which garnered him derisive but good-natured laughter and slaps on the back.

"Enough philosophy," cried a person seated nearby. He turned to Hagar. "Play the accordion, sweetheart?"

"As a matter of fact, I do," she said and then held out her arm.

CHAPTER 5

Mandatory Palestine, the Netherworld

"WELL?" MR. WATTS ASKED, TRYING NOT TO APPEAR ANXIOUS as his mistress drew near, crossing a field near his house. But he really wanted to hear what she had to say about the cooperative settlements.

"Well, what?" she snapped.

"Admit it, Boss."

"So what?" She inhaled deeply from the cigarette-like object.

"So something," he said.

Hagar shook her head, visibly frustrated. She exhaled bluish vapor and put away an exotic-looking smoking device. "That's exactly it—it isn't. It's just a one-time journey. These collective settlements draw their strength from the formation of the Jewish national home. It's a fellowship of generosity, camaraderie, and sacrifice fueled by unique circumstances."

Her eyes flitted across the field they were standing on. "And one day, their members may reach the mountaintop: the establishment of a Jewish state. They will stand, admire the view, and then settle in for the long haul. Air conditioners. Paved roads. Trimmed lawns. The wonderful bad old days of hardship will be superseded by pedestrian good days. And eventually the fish will just taste like fish—nothing more." She sighed, vexed. "You know, when you first told me these communal settlements have been thriving for decades, I was astounded."

"And now?"

"Even more so. I'm surprised they lasted a month, let alone twenty or thirty years, as some of them have."

Mr. Watts raised an eyebrow.

"The *kvutza* started as a youth movement," Hagar said, arms wrapped around her knees. "And it never really grew up. The elders here? Still called by their childhood nicknames."

She glanced toward the settlement. "There's no real space here—not the deeper kind. Everything's communal—meals, chores, beds, even thoughts. Privacy is suspect. Romance gets flattened."

She picked up a stone, turned it in her hand. "No rituals either. No rites. Just routines."

The two of them fell into a comfortable silence, Mr. Watts pondering her words.

Hagar let out a quiet, almost embarrassed laugh. "I stayed in the dining hall, playing the accordion."

Her analyst smiled in appreciation.

"Later in the evening, a lecture on the Spanish Revolution was to be held. Well over one hundred members filed back in and took their places. But the speaker? I looked around and ended up noticing a young man busy clearing some tables. When he finished, he removed his apron and worked his way to the front of the room—and started the lecture."

Mr. Watts laughed and asked, "Was he good?"

Hagar grinned back at him.

She stood up, shook off the dirt, and said, "I've got a meeting with destiny near Cairo." She eyed him kindly, bowed her head in farewell, and then disappeared.

With a spring in his step, Mr. Watts was walking alone toward his house when he unexpectedly felt hands seize him from behind in a powerful grip. Before he could shout, a needle pricked his neck. Darkness overtook him.

CHAPTER 6

A few miles south of Cairo, Egypt, the Netherworld

THE SAND, THE LEISURELY flowing Nile, and the clusters of date palm trees were as she remembered them. The solar power plant was gone, though.

Hagar looked around. Over two decades had passed since 1913, when she'd visited this area. In her mind's eye, she could see the ladies with parasols by the shade of the date trees; the German delegation walking through the mirrored parabolic troughs and heated pipelines, taking careful notes; and Lord Kitchener in an animated discussion with the inventor, Frank Shuman.

She caught sight of a small concrete block with a rod of rusted iron poking out. Hagar moved closer, knelt, and inspected it. Evidently, that's all that was left of the beacon to humanity's sustainable future.

"They dismantled it. Needed the metal for the Great War," said a deep voice from somewhere.

Hagar looked up.

"It was the patriotic thing to do and all that," said the same voice.

She spotted a lone, stocky figure in a violet robe seated under the shade of two date palms. With a white napkin fastidiously tied around his neck, he ate a stuffed, bright-red bell pepper with gusto, holding it in one hand. The other hand rested on a small table filled with an assortment of hors d'oeuvres.

He didn't stop or even slow down his chewing, but his eyes tracked her approach.

"Howdy, Boss," he said.

Bending over, Hagar kissed his mahogany-brown bald head. "Good to see you, Puddeck."

"Those nipples of yours," he said, ogling them admiringly.

She ignored this. "What the hell happened to the power plant?"

"Oh, that," he said, finally tearing his gaze away from her bosom to take a mighty bite from another hors d'oeuvre. "Gone," he said after a bit, smacking his lips. A diamond-like decorative speck glittered in one of his white teeth.

She stared at him, unblinking, and waited for her old-time companion to tell her why in blazes the Earth people had dismantled the solar power plant.

His heavy shoulders sagged, but then his expression brightened. "You see, they had another one of their wars. You know how excitable Terraneans can get—"

She growled wordlessly at him, incensed.

"Come on, Boss, turn around. Let me see that tight ass. It's been over twenty years."

The world's only viable solar power plant, gone. She'd hoped that this place, this project, would be the start of a more sustainable chapter. Now, the odds seemed daunting, the future grim. Hagar screwed her eyes shut and braced herself against a palm tree. The wind picked up, and she felt the grit of sand on her bare arms.

Puddeck's voice reached her. "You must be wondering by now if they ever constructed the solar power plant to irrigate the thirty thousand acres in Sudan." For Puddeck, it was just another planet on which he'd spent a few centuries, just another entertaining assignment. Like Hagar, he'd been on multiple worlds. But unlike Hagar, who cared deeply about the ecosystem, Puddeck paid little heed to the natural world.

She massaged her temples. Opened her eyes. Fixed him with a baleful look.

"Get real," her long-time companion finally said. "The Terraneans intended to pump water to grow a shitload of cotton for export. That would have salted up the land in a few decades anyway and made the area uninhabitable."

Hagar ran a hand angrily through her hair. "Irrelevant. This technology could have been used in other ways. This could have been the beginning. A constellation of concentrated solar power plants across the Sahara, British India, the Gobi, and the Chihuahuan Desert would have set the people here on a cleaner path."

Puddeck picked his teeth with a fingernail. "I don't see how. Humanity's centers are elsewhere."

"Long-distance transmission lines—that's how. It's a stretch, but it's not impossible given their current technological stage."

He absently rubbed the back of his neck. "Come back to Earth, Boss," he said finally. "They know how to use solar energy to transform the seawater into potable water and power up their gizmos with it." His laughter was low, as he savored the irony. "They could've set up those shiny troughs along the shore. Instead, the locals use their rustic bucket-on-sticks, the *shadoof*, to fetch their water, while the elite cart coal from thousands of kilometers away for a flicker of light."

Hagar turned away. She wasn't sure how much to confide. Could Puddeck have been the orchestrator of the colossal sabotage of her data-gathering network and the fabricated reports? It was impossible that Puddeck had betrayed her or that he'd authored the fabricated reports that had reached her. And it was impossible that her analyst network would be taken out. But there it was—all but two of her analysts gone. Now, she was grateful for a moment of paranoia she'd experienced in the 1860s, which had pushed her to set up a far-fetched backup plan.

"Oil's about to hit the big time," he said from behind her. "Over the past few years, California Standard has drilled at several locations on the Saudi coast, right across from Bahrain island. It's only a matter of months before they hit the mother of all gushers."

"Blast it!"

Puddeck joined her. "I doubt their mythological hell has more fire than what they're about to unleash with fossil fuel," he whispered to himself, but then he caught himself and smiled in self-mockery.

Hagar didn't bother to inquire about Thomas Edison and Henry Ford's electric car project. The announcement of the intent to mass-produce them had happened all right; she'd attended the press conference at the Belmont Hotel herself—January 9, 1914, the last night of her previous stay on Earth. However, the cheery reports that had been submitted to her in later years were undoubtedly bogus.

"And that Russian physicist's hyper-fast vacuum train?" she asked. "Weinberg, in Tomsk."

Puddeck examined a stuffed olive. "A few months after you left he published *Motion without Friction*. Even built a ten-kilo iron brute that tore around a vacuumed copper ring. A lovely idea."

She glowered at him. "What about Schlichten's decorticator?" Depression and numbness were setting in.

"The machine that separated the hemp fibers from the woody interior?"

Hagar didn't deign to reply. They'd both seen the decorticator stripping off the leaves and then crushing open the stalks through a series of rollers and flappers. The machine made the process of producing paper from hemp economically viable.

"Nah. It never got commercialized," Puddeck said. He picked a piece of lint from his sleeve. "In the end, the money guy decided to stick with good ol' trees as a feedstock for paper."

"And Schlichten?"

"Got old and died." The figure in violet robes shrugged. "Happens even to the best of them."

She screamed out of pent-up rage. Her hopes for a more sustainable future were being dashed one by one.

At long last, she asked, "So it's noisy gasoline cars and foul coal plants throughout?"

"Pretty much."

Puddeck eyed his mistress. He found her irresistible when she was furious.

Minutes went by.

Hagar turned and faced Puddeck. "Time to put a stop to it."

He inclined his head. "I kind of reckoned you wou—" Puddeck's body froze, his mouth hanging open mid-sentence.

Hagar whirled around, and her eyes widened in disbelief. "*You!*" As she started to move, her arms froze still at her sides.

A man and a woman stepped forward. The man held a small black device in his hand. They both regarded Hagar, suspended motionless, like an insect trapped in amber. Hagar and Puddeck were in a timefold. As long as they remained in stasis, the mountains of Earth would grind to dust and the oceans would dry up before a second passed for them.

"That takes care of Hagar and her bid to cut things short," the woman said, her eyes raking over the immobilized figure up close. Then she spun away and shrieked with laughter. "Oil and guns," she hollered, spreading her arms wide. "Hot vinyl pants, supersonic airplanes, and power boats. Let the party begin!"

Part Two

2013

CHAPTER 7

Pecos Backcountry, Northern New Mexico

NO ONE ON EARTH KNEW THEY HAD BEEN WATCHED. And the watchers never realized someone had been watching them in turn.

Lee's job was for life—a lone task that, if everything went even remotely well, she'd never have to carry out. She was the contingency. She was the last line of defense for Earth's biosphere—a sleeper agent awaiting an alarm that was never meant to sound. Yet, it had done so moments ago inside her head with finality, heralding the first day of the rest of her life.

Lee heaved herself onto the ledge and perched atop the massive boulder, staring numbly at her chalky hands and the four-wheeler ATV fifty feet below. For a long time, she remained motionless, dimly registering the occasional fierce gusts of wind. Ragged bands of ponderosa pine gave way to spruce-fir ridges all the way to the far horizon, the nearest town many miles away.

The sounding of the alarm signaled that the biosphere was on the brink of entering a death spiral. This wasn't supposed to happen.

For twenty-nine years, ever since Lee had assumed the mantle of responsibility from her predecessors at the ripe age of fourteen, she'd reckoned the state of the planetary ecosystem wasn't as dire as it seemed. She'd never met her boss, Hagar, but that didn't matter; she knew that neither Hagar nor, in the event she was out

"

of commission, any of her analysts would let things go to pot on this planet. They wouldn't have. Unless, of course, they weren't in a position to do anything about it. In other words, dead.

This chilling realization struck her like a ton of bricks.

Whatever had happened to Hagar and her network of analysts could have taken place years, or even generations, earlier. Lee had no way of knowing, and that was by design. It would have been unwise for the sleeper agent to reveal their existence at that point. If someone had the power to neutralize both Hagar and her network, they could also neutralize the sleeper agent, Lee in this case, before she had the chance to act. That's why Hagar's protocol dictated that the sleeper agent would be activated only when the biosphere was about to cross the ecological red line. At that point, there would be little to lose and everything to gain by coming out of hiding. Evidently, today was that day.

Shaking off her daze, Lee pushed a loose strand of her dark, silver-streaked hair out of her face, then propelled herself off the ledge to begin her descent.

About an hour later, she was sitting in a bustling restaurant in Santa Fe. The sounds of animated conversations and giggles of small children filled the space. She sipped coffee and absently watched the traffic through the window. She felt more isolated than she ever had.

Lee was an anomaly, a stranger in a foreign land of ordinary lives. For years, she'd draped herself in a cloak of normalcy, a borrowed sense of belonging. But with the alarm ringing in her head, that cloak had been torn asunder. Bereft of counsel or confidant, she truly stood alone.

After paying her bill, Lee exited the restaurant, trading the warmth and noise for the crisp evening air outside.

Her long journey south was a blur. She drove mechanically and made dutiful stops at gas stations.

Her hundred-acre estate was nestled at the foothills of the Organ Mountains, with the city lights of Las Cruces twinkling in

the far distance. She navigated the winding private dirt road leading to her sprawling adobe villa, the solar path lights casting a soft
glow on the fishhook barrel cacti and tall soaptree yuccas along
the way. Ordinarily, this sight brought her a sense of solace and
joy. Tonight, though, the oppressive weight of the natural world's
pronounced decline bore down heavily upon her.

She kicked off her shoes in the anteroom and strode into the
spacious living room.

The moment had come. She raised her left arm. "Activate," she
said, and her bracelet glowed to life. "This is Lee Evans. I initiate
Last Protocol: Gideon's Trumpet."

With this, she was coming out of hiding; her location and identity were being transmitted. Any analysts who were alive would
instantaneously become aware of her existence and report in. But
she didn't hold her breath.

It was all quite straightforward: Come what may, Hagar was to
send a confirmation signal to each of her analysts at least once a
decade. If they didn't receive such a signal, it meant that Hagar
was incapacitated, and the analysts were ordered to go through the
portal and alert the powers that be. It was the very portal located
just a few hundred yards from the villa where Lee now stood.

Lee was now fairly certain that Hagar was out of the picture, as
she would never have allowed Earth's biomes to deteriorate to the
point where the alarm would sound. And Lee was also fairly certain the data-gathering analysts were out of the picture, as there
had been no attempts to open the portal on her property, the only
fixed gateway on Earth.

But she would have felt foolish had she gotten it wrong—and
they were alive and well. Lee had to be sure.

And so she sent a transmission, seeking responses from anyone
who could intercept her broadcast. From the coffee table, she
picked up a string of wooden beads and let them slide slowly, med-
itatively through her fingers as she awaited a reply.

The next hour stretched out before her, punctuated by the

occasional creak of her chair and the deliberate press of each bead. As it concluded, it extinguished the last ember of hope. She had to face the hard truth. They were all dead—the good guys, and probably whoever had snuffed them out.

All she had to do now was stay on the sofa, hugging her knees, and the planetary ecosystem would spiral past the point of no return. No one would realize events could have played out any differently.

But no, this was not going to happen, not on her watch.

Lee rose to her feet, went outside, and trudged a considerable distance across her property. With her headlamp turned on, she navigated her way through junipers and ocotillos, descended a gully, and halted beside a rust-orange boulder. She simultaneously pressed two indents on the boulder's surface, and a concealed entrance cracked open, revealing an illuminated spiral staircase leading underground.

Even if someone had stumbled upon this hidden passageway, it would have done them little good. Without the bracelet on her wrist—which refashioned itself at that point into a unique glowing key—they would have found nothing but a massive metal vault door at the base of the stairwell and nothing but solid earth behind it. The door was, in fact, a portal: a last-resort route for letting those outside this realm become aware that the ecosystems on Earth were waning.

As Lee descended, heat began to waft from the depths below, and she felt a surge of anxiety. The heat was unexpected, troubling, and became ever more pronounced the farther down she ventured. Her climb down the stairs turned hurried. Then frantic. She all but sprinted down the final stretch of stairs and hurled herself into the narrow, low tunnel at the bottom.

The once thick-plated steel door was now a liquid ruin. "No!" she screamed, squinting against the blazing heat of the molten metal. She instinctively thrust her arm out, her exotic-looking key held futilely in front of the indiscernible doorway at the far end of the corridor.

With a strangled sob, Lee recoiled from the inferno. Sobbing in frustration, she retraced her steps up the stone stairwell. Her sole mission, her singular responsibility, was in ruins. She emerged above ground, grappling with a deep sense of defeat.

CHAPTER 8

Hagar had been taken out, the analysts were dead, the portal was obliterated. It was all over.

Lee went to sleep that night and remained in bed for most of the next day.

Over and over, she replayed in her mind the events leading to the destruction of the vault door. Who could have known about the gateway and managed to destroy it just as she was about to pass through it? Who could have melted a seven-inch-thick vault door remotely and without an apparent heat source? And what kind of power did it take to melt that amount of steel, anyway?

What was she up against?

Well, she wasn't up against anything. Not anymore. Traveling through the portal and alerting the three gods had been her one ace-in-the-hole move. With the gateway gone, she could do no more than what the cashier at the gas station down the road could. With it in ruins, she might as well take up knitting.

As evening fell, a sense of listlessness drove her from bed. Padding around her house in slippers, she fixed herself a comforting cup of English breakfast tea with milk, retrieved a small chest from the safe, and placed it on the coffee table.

Jazz played softly in the background, mingling with the occasional soft crackling sounds from the fireplace. Lee settled on the sofa, took a sip of her warm tea, and opened the chest. Inside were three photo albums. It must have been a decade, maybe longer, since she'd last opened them.

The first album held an assortment of photos from her childhood, a time when everything felt safer, simpler. Pictures of trips with her parents to a panda preserve in China, playground slides in Las Cruces, and ice cream breaks at Disney World adorned the pages. The album was filled with cherished moments from the time she was born until, of course, around the time she'd turned fourteen.

Life as she knew it had crumbled at that point.

Even their trusty Chevrolet Camaro had been mangled beyond recognition.

After her parents' deaths in the car crash, social workers would have placed her in foster care—had it not been for the bracelet she wore. With its aid, she had been able to access and manipulate any database. She'd tampered with records to pass herself off as eighteen, of legal age. And her "homeschooled" background simplified the process of doctoring the paper and electronic trail. Conjuring a steady, substantial flow of deposits into her bank account was just as effortless. The bracelet provided the means to make money a non-issue; she was as wealthy as she chose to be.

She moved on to the second album, which featured pictures of her parents from before she was born. Photos of their adventures filled the pages—places Lee would later visit herself. Their smiling, youthful faces full of promise looked back at her. She felt a pang at the realization that they were younger in those photos than she was now, at forty-three. Many pictures also featured an older man and woman: her parents' predecessors, whom she'd never met—or if she had, she was too young to remember.

Neither Lee nor her parents were included in the last album. This album was dedicated exclusively to the analysts, not to the sleeper agents. Still, whenever she looked at the pictures of those nameless analysts, it was the closest she had come to feeling a part of an extended family. Even one whose members were unaware of her existence or of the sleeper agents who had preceded her.

In that album, the oldest photo, from 1901, featured Hagar standing amid a small crowd of analysts. Each picture in the album, printed on a thin, subtly luminescent sheet, held a certain timeless quality. Absently, Lee turned to the next page, seeing another gathering of the analysts from 1928, this one without Hagar. As she prepared to flip to the next page, something made her look again at the 1928 picture. There was this man. She examined the 1901 photo and found him there, too. That was when she worked out what had been gnawing at her subconscious.

Lee placed the two photos side by side. She used her thumb and index finger on the seemingly mundane surface of the prints, and the material responded much as a touchscreen would have. It enlarged sections of the monochrome images, revealing more facial details of the man in both pictures. Her pulse quickened; she hadn't imagined it. This man hadn't aged a day in the span of those twenty-seven years. He was just like Hagar. She studied his chiseled face and his light sandy hair. Who *was* he?

Lee scrutinized the 1928 photo, searching for clues. Anything. Unlike the 1901 photo, taken in some nondescript field, this one was shot inside a ... she examined the picture closely ... some kind of shop. She magnified a small section of the photo, zeroing in on a plaque hanging on the wall. It bore a logo and an inscription. Zooming in as far as possible, she squinted and finally managed to make out the writing: "Jerome Shoe Repair."

If the ageless man in the photos were still alive and possessed capabilities akin to Hagar's, he might be able to open a rift leading off-world. Or, at the very least, he could potentially shed light on what in blazes was going on.

Lee chewed on this thought for a second. *What the hell,* she decided in the end. She was going to see if he was still around and track him down if he was. The chances of either thing were slim to none, but she had absolutely nothing to lose by giving it a try.

Starting the search in the United States seemed logical. Lee closed her eyes, the bracelet enabling her thoughts to surf seamlessly through any existing database—be it public, private, secure, or otherwise. Two businesses surfaced in her mind. She dismissed the first in Idaho after she 'viewed' its façade. Her mental gaze then shifted to a shop in Jerome, Arizona. Its proprietor was Dave Lyons, who had assumed ownership in 2003. No website. No telephone number. Just a street address. With a swift mental scan, she compared the logo to the one in the 1928 photo, using a mental street-view projection the bracelet generated on the fly. It was a match.

Lee caught the morning flight from El Paso to Flagstaff. And a few hours later, she was driving a rental down to Jerome, the pine scenery giving way to gnarled junipers about a third of the way into the drive.

The entire population of Jerome could have fit into a single high school building; the town couldn't have had more than a hundred homes. "Excuse me," she would say at the shoe store, "I'm looking for someone who posed here for a picture—perhaps the owner? Yeah, it was a while back, a bit less than a century." She laughed out loud. *Oh, this was going to be good!*

She parked the car and crossed the street. The sun that had kissed her broad face earlier in the day was now casting long shadows on the pavement. Her bottle-green eyes, reflected in the shop window, were drawn to the logo beneath the illuminated "open" sign.

Lee entered, and the sound of the door opening prompted a man to look up from the leather stitching machine he was hunched over. She felt a sudden, almost giddy, rush of excitement. It was *him*—the man from the photos. The same broad shoulders, the same cropped blond hair, the same prominent cheekbones. And he still appeared to be in his early forties.

His clean-shaven, stoic face and piercing blue eyes made her think of a placid lake. And who could tell what beasts lurked right under the reflective surface? The man exuded an aura of immense physical strength. However, the impression might have been misleading; if he was anything like Hagar, he was a *lot* stronger than his appearance suggested.

Lee closed the distance between them and thrust a large photo under his nose. "This is you."

His eyes narrowed, taking in her confident stance, the undeniable allure that radiated from her, the athletic build suggested by tight jeans and a cropped jacket.

"The picture was taken eighty-five years ago," Lee said.

"Lady, exactly how old do you think I am?" he asked, his voice low and husky.

"I probably can't count that high."

He snorted. "Now you're being ridiculous."

He lowered his head and gave the stitching machine wheel a few whirls. Finally, he stopped. "So, you're the one who sent the emergency transmission the other day."

She inclined her head in acknowledgment. "Lee Evans."

He eyed her quizzically. "I didn't know of you, nor was I aware that any of Hagar's analysts were still around."

Her heart skipped a beat. It seemed he didn't know about the existence of the sleeper agents. And Lee, on impulse, resolved to keep it that way. "My predecessor didn't hear from Hagar," she said vaguely. "Neither did I. For decades, nothing. Then I heard the alarm a few days ago, reckoned Hagar must be dead, and decided to come out of the shadows."

His expression hardened as he lifted his eyes to meet hers. "Hagar died in 1939 in the bombing of Warsaw." For a brief instant, his face twisted in pain. Then it was gone. "I'm sorry," he said, his voice soft. "I'm afraid your journey here was for naught."

She bit her lip. It dawned on her that until this moment, a part of her had still hoped against hope Hagar was alive. "What about you? I found *you*." The words spilled out in a rush: "Don't you have the same, well, the same special abilities as Hagar? Can't *you* do something?"

He shook his head silently.

She leaned forward, desperation and hope reflected in her eyes. "But you must know something—anything—that could help."

"I know how to patch a worn-out sole," he said, his tone laconic, his eyes distant.

"You've got to be kidding me!" She stared at him incredulously. "Are you for real?"

His jaw clenched visibly, and for a moment, he looked away, his attention seemingly lost in the steady whirl of the stitching machine wheel.

"I think you'd better leave," he finally said.

"I think I should," she snapped back, and turned away, fury and anguish written across her face.

Lee slammed her car door shut. Her tires screeched as she accelerated down the winding slope. She was through with this man. What a washout, a has-been! Whatever he'd done before, whatever his role had been, it was obviously a very long time ago. Now, he was just a shoe repairman burdened with a haunted past.

⇒⇐

"Look, can i buy you a milkshake?"

Startled, Lee caused her vehicle to swerve slightly. She glanced wildly around.

"Sorry about earlier." It was the man from the shoe store; his voice was coming from the bracelet she wore. She didn't know that this could be done.

"It's been a while since you talked to a girl, huh?" Lee said.

She heard him laugh for the first time. She liked the sound of it. "My name is Aratta," he said.

"Lee," she replied, imagining him smiling at the other end. "Alright," she said. "About the milkshake," she added. "I'll make my way back to Jerome. See you in about an hour." She was going to give it another chance with him.

There was a momentary silence. "Where are you, exactly?" he asked, his voice transmitted via her bracelet with perfect clarity.

"On I–17, about ten miles south of Flagstaff."

"Yes, I see now," he said after a pause. "The device you wear on your wrist allows me to home in on your location." He continued, "Allow me to guide you through a shortcut."

"Okay," she said, unsure what he had in mind.

"In a few hundred feet, take the Newman Park Road exit and make a right."

Silently, she did as instructed, then let out a harsh breath as she rapidly ran out of road. "It's going to dead-end at the farmhouse."

"Not this time. Take a hard left at the fork."

She swore and sharply swerved the car, raising dust. The path wound its way around the farmhouse. That's when she noticed another fork in the road up ahead, with one path leading straight through the ponderosa pines, cutting eastward through the forest.

After a few miles, the path broadened and turned into a paved road, as empty as the dirt road she'd been on.

She drove in silence for a while and finally figured out what was bothering her.

"There are creosote bushes all around. No trees."

"So?"

"So, where the hell is the forest?"

"You're back in Verde Valley."

"Impossible."

Aratta did not respond.

Lee swallowed hard and suddenly felt the need to put a second hand on the steering wheel. She drove guardedly, eyes glued to the road ahead, reluctant to even slow down unless she had to.

Soon, the road started climbing and a few switchbacks later, she saw the town of Jerome nestled amid the hills. She was trying to make sense of it all, going over every possibility—was she hallucinating? No, that wasn't it. Had she unknowingly crossed some sort of portal? Somehow, she'd ended up traveling nearly sixty miles in a matter of minutes.

Aratta was waiting for her on Main Street. He looked different now, wearing a starched white dress shirt, a dark vest, and a fedora hat.

His eyes twinkled. "How was the drive?" he asked as she got out of the car.

"Short and to the point," she said, laughing easily and suddenly feeling lighthearted.

Aratta extended his elbow to her, and without a second thought, she accepted the gesture.

Arms linked, they strolled through the business district of the quaint town. Rustic brick buildings housed thriving small businesses, and vintage cars lined the cobblestone streets. There was a pleasant breeze, and the sun was near the horizon, setting the sky ablaze where it met the far-off mountains.

She finally registered the chrome-accented, full-bodied vehicles and the ubiquitous fedoras worn by the men.

She stole a glance at him a few times. "This isn't Earth, is it?" she eventually blurted.

"No, not quite."

Lee studied the street openly now. "It's Jerome, but maybe like it was decades ago." She hesitated. "Are we in the past?"

"That is not possible."

"Well then?"

"This place, it's a reflection of what was. But the moment itself is gone; the past has moved on. All that's left is this snapshot, an afterimage, if you will." He fell silent, and she held onto his arm, glancing at the mysterious man who wielded powers she could not fathom. "So you work in the real world and come back home... to here?" she asked.

Aratta smiled amiably at her. "Not a bad way to spend time, is it?"

During the short drive back to Jerome, Lee had resolved to get right to it and ask the questions that burned in her mind. Yet, as they strolled, her urgency seemed to dissipate. Time and again, Lee resisted an urge to rest her head against his shoulder. She felt as if she had stepped into an impressionist painting, perhaps one of those pointillistic ones by Seurat or Pissarro.

They strode past a delicatessen and entered a small diner. Aratta bought each of them a milkshake, and they continued walking toward the setting sun.

Aratta's home was a tastefully designed house at the foot of a mountain. Lee found herself admiring the tan-colored walls, the bamboo floor, and the powder-yellow area rugs. Her eyes were drawn to the sliding glass door, where the lively dance of hummingbirds around a feeder contrasted with the serene vista of distant red sandstone formations.

Lee settled into a tufted armchair, and Aratta took the one across from her. The wooden table had a single planter with an arrangement of bonsai trees. A miniature glen. Lee studied the moss covering the old, diminutive trunks. "It's spellbinding," she said softly. "How old are the trees?"

"I planted them about eighty years ago," Aratta said. "They're coming along nicely." He noted the startled expression on her face and gave her a disarming smile.

They contemplated the bonsai trees, the fire crackling in the brick-paneled fireplace.

An aging manservant entered silently, carrying a silver tray with tea and a glass bowl filled with fruit.

"Please," Aratta said, smiling amiably and gesturing at the tray. "It's rare that I have guests."

She reached out, plucking some grapes, and for a while, they were both content to gaze at the flickering flames.

"The alarm went off a few days ago," Lee said, stating the obvious.

He let out a deep sigh. "Well, yes. I'm afraid the planetary ecosystems around here are circling the drain."

"People will pull through, though," she said. "They always do."

"Indeed. As a species, they've managed to survive far worse." He stirred his tea with a tiny spoon. "But then again, humanity's survival was never in doubt or the point."

"No, of course not," she said immediately, feeling stupid.

"All of which brings us to the question you must have wanted to ask me: Why didn't I send out word—decades ago—and convene a hearing about the Earth people, the Terraneans?"

She braced herself.

Aratta laid down his cup on the saucer. "I can't."

"What do you mean you 'can't'?" But as Lee said it, she had a sinking sensation; she thought she knew what was coming.

"Just so. There's no way in or out of Earth. Some massive, unimaginable force is preventing me from breaking out of"—he hesitated—"think of it as the gravity well of the planet. I cannot leave this world." He held her gaze. "Ms. Evans, I'm afraid we are stuck in this place. Worse yet, I can't even get a message out about what's happening to the biosphere here."

She ran her hand through her hair. "And there's nothing we can do? You're telling me there's nothing we can do?"

He shook his head, then noted the dismay on her face, and his voice softened. "Lee, for you, this is something that just recently came to your attention. For me, it's something I've been wrestling with and have slowly come to terms with in the past fifty years."

"Does it get any easier?" she asked after a while.

"You mean life in exile, here on Earth?" He took a sip. "Easier, no. But one can get used to anything."

He reached out and gave her hand a squeeze. "We might not have control over the big picture, Lee. But we still get to choose how we spend our days here."

A few seconds passed.

"Can I interest you in a game of chess?" he asked.

CHAPTER 9

Resigned yet oddly comforted, Lee caught the last flight to El Paso.

It was close to midnight when she approached her estate, and her bracelet glowed to life unbidden. She braked, stopped by the side of the road, and cut the headlights. As her hands became clammy, she wiped them on her jeans. The bracelet's unexpected activation could mean only one thing: Someone had broken into her house.

She'd put in place several security layers around her property, with alerts set to reach her bracelet within a mile's radius. At least one of them must have been tripped. Closing her eyes, she accessed the footage and played it back in her mind. There it was. A car pulled up at 5:23 A.M. and parked just out of the camera's view. By 5:34 P.M., a tall man holding a gun had entered her home. A professional. A cold finger slid down her spine. Someone wanted her dead.

For this exact contingency, Lee had installed hidden thermal security cameras throughout the house. She now instructed the bracelet to scan the video feeds and look for an infrared heat signature of a human inside the darkened house. It did, and she drew in a shaky breath. The bastard was still there. Waiting for her return, no doubt.

Lee harbored no illusions about her chances in a close

encounter. It was all but certain that he was physically stronger and better with a gun.

It was time to see if her emergency plan was any good.

She pulled night-vision goggles and a pair of tactical gloves from her car trunk. After putting them on, she was off—walking as quietly as possible toward the ancient ironwood tree at the farthest reaches of her property. The once-vibrant tree had long succumbed to time, its gnarled silhouette cast in eerie green through the goggles. Just beside the trunk lay a narrow wash where sand had piled up over the seasons. Kneeling there, she began to dig with swift, practiced movements, the gloves shielding her hands from the grit. Within moments, her fingers struck something solid. She let out a breath of relief and swept the sand away to reveal the edge of a hard plastic shell. A few more strokes, and she unearthed the elongated, waterproof case.

Securing the sturdy strap of the heavy, cumbersome case, she hoisted it diagonally across her body—lower end above her right hip, upper over her left shoulder. Uncomfortable, but it balanced the weight and enabled her to move with relative ease. She stealthily approached the rear of her house and parked herself behind a boulder about fifty yards away.

There was one more thing Lee had to make sure of first. Shutting her eyes, she ordered the bracelet to trace any outgoing calls from her house. It turned out the man had made a call a few hours back. Dutifully, the bracelet played back the recording from an audio-enabled security camera. The truth confirmed, it was time for Lee to strike.

Opening the case, she pulled out her Sako TRG 42 rifle. She screwed on the suppressor and locked the bipod into place; the scope was already mounted, and she loaded a fresh magazine. Lee was going to shoot the seated man through the wall. It was the very reason she had a rifle that used .338 Lapua Magnum rounds. She pushed in her electronic earplugs.

Now came the critical step. She closed her eyes, relying on the bracelet to adjust the thermal camera feed to her external, lower viewing angle. Aligning her aim meticulously, she drew in a long, steadying breath to quell the adrenaline-fueled pounding in her chest, exhaled, and squeezed the trigger. The suppressed rifle gave a deep, concussive boom that echoed through the night, and somewhere inside, the thermal signature jerked and collapsed. She reacquired her target and took one more shot. She was leaving nothing to chance.

Lee confirmed that the bracelet detected no other humans in and around the house.

If the bracelet had gotten it wrong, she would probably be dead in the next few minutes. She took a deep, shaky breath, pulled out a .45 pistol from the rifle case and approached the house at a run, gun raised.

The bracelet wasn't wrong. All that awaited her was a mangled corpse, sprawled awkwardly between the floor and the sofa. The remnants of the man were decidedly lifeless—a silent testimony that, for once, her plan had worked exactly as intended. Two ragged holes punched through the drywall. Surrounding plaster fractured and dusted the floor, and splinters fanned out from the impact. Lee paused, allowing the grim finality of her actions to wash over her. She looked at the damage done, the life taken, and pushed down the wave of nausea that surged within her.

She bundled the body in a tarp and then gripped it, her knuckles turning white.

She gritted her teeth, sweat stinging her eyes as she dragged the lifeless body down the stairs. His head thumped against each stair, the sound echoing harshly in the silent house.

Outside, she lashed the tarped corpse to her four-wheeler ATV. After several minutes of driving through her property, she arrived at the site where the portal used to be. Shoving the body with her foot, she sent it tumbling down the hidden spiral staircase and slammed the trapdoor shut. The disposal of the body would have to wait; more pressing matters demanded her attention.

After scrubbing away the grisly remains, she allowed herself a quick shower. Calm and collected, Lee steeled herself for the task ahead. It was time to seize the initiative.

The assassin's call earlier had only lasted a few minutes. It was enough. It was enough to ascertain he was there to take her out. It was enough for the bracelet to acquire his speech patterns.

Lee was going to contact the person the hitman had phoned. She was going to convey her thoughts—brain signals—to her bracelet, and have it transmit them in the voice of her would-be killer. She'd done such a thing before.

There was a good chance the organization that had sent the man to her house was involved in what had happened to Hagar.

Hagar may have been killed in the aerial bombing of Warsaw in World War II. But this couldn't explain the rest of it: the removal of the entire network of analysts. There was more to it than Aratta had shared with her—or perhaps more than he was aware of.

She dialed the number, and almost immediately, someone picked up the phone.

"Is it done?" a nondescript man's voice asked.

"Yes," she thought. The bracelet had already captured the hitman's voice signature from his earlier call, and now it reshaped her thoughts into his tone before transmitting them.

"Good. No loose ends?"

"No. She came home after midnight, and I popped her. I'll take care of the body."

It was time to roll the dice, and it was a long shot. "It was one of Hagar's people I took out," Lee thought, the bracelet transmitting it in the hitman's voice. "What if Hagar comes after me in retaliation?"

"What the *hell* are you talking about, man?" demanded the person on the other end of the line, irritation and surprise mixed in equal parts. "Hagar is in a stasis box in the warehouse in Haiti like you were told. How the fuck is she going to come after you?"

"Right," Lee thought, and the bracelet transmitted once again.

"Okay. I guess I had to ask."

Silence. "Don't spend all your money in Vegas, Kaminski," the person on the phone said. "I'll see you when you're back." The line went dead.

Lee sat, very still.

Her boss was alive, in a stasis box, that is to say, in a timefold. That changed everything. Suddenly, Lee had something she should be doing beyond trying to survive.

She closed her eyes again. After a quick search through electronic records, she uncovered the identity of the man on the phone: one Ernesto Pérez from Miami. She wasted no time, delving into his files, bank accounts, and holdings. Within half an hour, she had it. One of the holding companies associated with him had owned a property in Haiti for years. And it was a warehouse.

⇒⇐

Twenty hours later, Lee walked out of the airline terminal in Port-au-Prince—and into a wall of heat and grit. She ignored the touts, bypassed the waiting taxis, and made her way on foot past the police checkpoint and through the chain-link gates.

A half-mile later, Port-au-Prince hit her in the face: the sweltering air thick with the unmistakable scent of urine, burning trash, and exhaust fumes. Lee crossed an open sewer, strode under low-slung telephone cables, and walked past gaudy billboards. Young men lounged on the sidewalks next to mattresses, housewives in floral dresses negotiated muddy puddles, and roadside vendors hawked steaming cauldrons of street food.

God, she despised this place. Lee had slept in longhouses of the Sepik River tribes in Papua New Guinea and Tuareg tents in the Sahara. Scarcity didn't get to her; ugliness did. She changed her mind about walking to her hotel.

She stopped at a bus stop and within a few short minutes was seated in a crowded *tap-tap*. The rickety minibus, splashed with a riot of colors, lurched and bobbed seemingly to the rhythm of blaring Haitian hip hop as it jolted its way from one pothole to the next. Lee found herself wedged between a woman of astonishing size and a toothless old man. She stared stoically out one of the windows. More people. Blue-helmeted UN soldiers. Youths balancing water-filled buckets on their heads as they darted amid honking vehicles. Lee turned her head and looked away.

Her upscale hotel was tucked away on a walled side street in Pétion-Ville. From its perch, it offered a panoramic view of the city, yet remained distant enough to dampen some of the clamor of vendors, the blare of horns, and the pervasive smells.

She dined, took a long bath, and then went to sleep.

The next morning, Lee rented a Jeep Wrangler and drove it to Léogâne, a battered coastal town west of the capital. Twisting, unmarked alleys led her in circles until she reluctantly decided to ask for directions. In a nearby field, she spotted a small group of people crouching over something. Lee parked the Jeep and walked over.

As she approached, Lee saw two *blan* demonstrating how to use a charcoal cookstove.

Blan seemed to be everywhere in Haiti. Each week, planes disgorged new ones: international aid bureaucrats, do-good Christians, or adventure-seeking young Americans. All wanted to visit the most authentic poverty theme park in the Western Hemisphere, where children might still congregate at the sight of white people, hands outstretched.

Separating *blan* from their money had been a cottage industry in Haiti, running parallel to the trafficking of cocaine en route from South America to the US markets. There was no "right" or "wrong," just green money and millions of outstretched hands with millions of ruses to redirect funds. Officials pilfered city funds for personal gain, doctors diverted public hospital supplies to their private clinics, and foreign-aid food intended for schools was appropriated and sold at a profit.

Some opportunists with connections and guile managed to break out and leave Haiti for the fairer pastures of Miami. Others returned to the ranks of the poor whence they came. Life was cheap in Haiti. One could obtain a child slave for less than the cost of a midrange smartphone.

Lee was in a foul mood as she drew near. She pushed past the gathered men and kicked the cookstove, scattering the charcoal. People leaped back, yelling and cursing.

"Enough!" she yelled in French, turning on the Haitian men. "You've already stripped away the rainforest. What are you going to cut down and burn up next? Look at the shithole you've turned this island into!" Lee had meant to ask for directions, not to fly off the handle. What the hell was she doing?

"So how are they going to cook, exactly?" shouted one of the two *blan*, a German, judging by his accent.

Lee rounded on him. "What are you, a moron?" she said. "Try sunlight. Coils of oil. Basic thermodynamics. You don't need to burn the last tree on the island to fry an egg."

One of the villagers jumped into the conversation. "You got idea for this? We do it together, *blan*. We make money, yeah?"

The two Germans muttered in disgust, took their cookstove, and marched off.

"Where you get funding for this—USAID?" challenged another villager.

Lee turned her attention to him. "If you want something better than soot to breathe in your homes and this barren land you've created with your machetes," she said, "you'll have to build it. I'm not going to do anything. You got so used to foreign handouts, you need a *blan* with a crane just to help you lift a finger."

That set everyone arguing and shouting.

"Is this sun cooktop real, you crazy *blan* bitch?" one of the men asked angrily.

"Li reyèl menm jan ou se yon sot, wi," she shot back, hands planted on her hips.

The villagers fell into a stunned silence, then exploded in laughter. The men clung to each other, and two howled and kicked the dirt, guffawing. All except the man who was slighted. He stood there, glowering and ignoring the slaps on his back from his companions.

"You going show us how that thing go, *blan?*" asked one of them, when the merriment had died down.

"What if it's cloudy?" another demanded. "You want we sit and chew raw food while we wait for sky to smile?"

It was clear that nothing would ever get built. They knew it, and she knew it. She chatted with them a bit about it, sharing what little she remembered of a solar oven she'd seen in an ecologically-minded community kitchen in Colombia.

Finally, it was time for her to go. The men were in high spirits and shook her hand with enthusiasm. They wanted to escort her to the warehouse, but she declined. In the end, they relented, giving her detailed instructions on how to get there instead.

Fifteen minutes later, she stood in an alley in front of the door leading into a giant, run-down building. Her heart pounded in her chest. Could it be? Could a stasis box be hidden within this dilapidated warehouse, one that held Hagar in a timefold and suspended her between one moment and the next?

As soon as she cracked the lock open, she knew she'd tripped an alarm. She smashed the blinking security device but knew it was too late. Whoever monitored the warehouse must have been tipped off. Time was of the essence.

She rushed inside, into what turned out to be a large storage facility. The aisles were high, dimly lit, and filled with dusty cargo boxes and corroded industrial machinery. It didn't look like anyone had visited the place in ages. The only sound interrupting the heavy silence was the occasional distant drip of water as she swept through the aisles, sizing up the larger crates.

A few minutes later, she heard the screech of tires skidding against the gravel followed by the thud of multiple car doors being slammed shut. They'd mobilized a lot faster than she had imagined. Lee slapped her bracelet, activating it. "Aratta, it's me. I believe Hagar is alive, but maybe I won't live to see it through."

"*What!* How?" came his voice. Then: "Where are—Oh. You're in Haiti. I'll come as fast as I can. Try to hold on," he said and broke the connection.

She tore around the next aisle—and froze. An upright casket-sized box, smothered in chains.

Her pulse hit her throat. This had to be it.

She pressed her bracelet against its padlock. The shackle on the lock glowed brightly, and after a moment, melted. What remained of the lock fell with a clatter followed by the clang of the chains hitting the concrete floor. Lee swore under her breath at the ruckus. From the far end of the warehouse, she could hear people yelling and calling to each other. *Shit.*

Lee flung open the upright casket. And there was the person she worked for and her parents before that: an attractive, young-looking blonde woman in khaki cargo pants and a form-fitting black tank top, hands clenched by her sides.

From a few aisles across, peering between some crates, one of the men spotted Lee. He pointed, shouting something to his associates. She ignored it. Her bracelet changed shape, latching onto the control panel on the side of the box. A click sounded.

The woman in front of her gasped and stumbled out of the upright stasis box. Her eyes narrowed as she took stock of the tall woman with short dark hair. "Who the hell are you?"

A gunshot sounded, coming from the far end of the aisle they were in. It was followed by more gunshots. They both ducked. "I'm Lee—the Lainraads' daughter. I came to rescue you." A burst of gunfire punctuated her words, perforating the stasis box, destroying it. Fragments of wood and metal flew over their heads.

"You call this *a rescue*?" Hagar shouted over the roar of gunfire.

"You're welcome!" Lee yelled back.

Hagar shook her head in disbelief. She disappeared, then

reappeared behind a concrete column a few yards away, a pistol in hand. Taking quick aim, she fired a number of times. At the far end, two of their assailants dropped. A man emerged from behind a nearby shipping container, and Lee kicked him in the groin. As he doubled over in pain, she stepped in and landed a vicious blow with her forearm on the side of his neck. The man collapsed in a heap.

"Is this Egypt?"

Egypt? "This is Haiti! The year is 2013."

Hagar cursed. Then she cursed again, more vehemently. She'd been out of the picture for seventy-six years! More to the point, the Earth people were very much in the picture during that time, further wrecking the ecosystem, no doubt. "Did the Terraneans manage to keep their numbers under three billion?" she hollered again.

"No. It's over seven billion now."

Hagar swore again. Nothing was more important than getting a message through and convening a hearing to determine the Terraneans' fate. She resolved to do it as soon as she could muster the concentration needed to form a rift.

From somewhere to their left, someone opened up with an automatic. Lee bolted and joined Hagar behind a concrete column. More men arrived and began firing. Wood shards and masonry bits exploded nearby.

"I reached out to Aratta for help a few minutes ago," Lee called out during a brief lull. "He's on his way."

Hagar whipped her head around, her eyes blazing. "He's the one who put me in the timefold in the first place!"

Lee stared back in obvious shock.

"We have to get out of here before he shows up. And deactivate that damn bracelet of yours; he can track us through it," Hagar hissed before vanishing. She reappeared in another corner of the room. A shot rang. A few moments later, there was another shot. Then another. And then another. "All clear!" Hagar called out, her voice ringing out in the silence that followed the shots.

"You can teleport?"

"Teleport, hell. I've been shifting to the netherworld, running over to a target, then shifting back."

She dashed toward the exit, Lee close behind.

"They've locked the door from the inside!" Lee shouted, spotting the padlock as they drew near.

Faster than Lee's eye could follow, Hagar spun, then kicked. The door exploded outward, torn from its hinges, and flew a dozen feet away before landing.

They came out sprinting. And Hagar's arm shot out, halting Lee.

A man in a three-piece suit was resolutely marching toward the building. A multi-barreled rotary minigun hung from his shoulder by a wide strap. The sight of him, stern and unyielding, made Lee's heart drop. It was Aratta. She'd trusted him. God, she'd *liked* him.

"Back inside," Hagar snarled, all but pushing the other woman in.

"Hagar!" came Aratta's shout. "Do not—"

Hagar concentrated, willing it. *There!* The world around them faded away as they left the real Earth.

CHAPTER 10

Stifling heat and impossible humidity engulfed Lee and Hagar as they tumbled onto a heaving wooden deck and came to a stop against a weathered metal railing. They were on a ship at sea, apparently somewhere in the tropics, the scent of briny air sharp.

They were not alone. Under a cloudy sky, they saw dozens of people in gaudy checkered gowns sprawling about. A few were conversing in low voices, their words whipped away by the breeze and the sound of ropes creaking. Most looked disoriented or resigned.

"What?" Lee gasped. "Where are we?" Quickly, Hagar pressed her hand against the other woman's mouth. "Shhh, we're in the past," she whispered into Lee's ear. "Sort of." She held onto Lee, who jolted in shock upon noting Hagar's dark brown skin and tight, curly black hair. "It's an illusion; it's still me, Hagar. And it's still you, even if you don't look the part, either." She gave Lee a reassuring smile, which appeared to soothe the other woman somewhat.

As Hagar leaned in and hugged Lee, she dimly wondered what the other woman would have said had she realized they were conversing in Umbundu. The veil over the true nature of reality was stretched thin here, thinner than she cared to expose the human to.

"Aratta mentioned something about reflections. Are we in one of these things?"

Hagar smiled in acknowledgment. "A large mass, the size of a planet, casts countless ripples in its wake as it travels through time, much like a ship sailing through a lake. Those are reflections of what was, the wake." She hesitated. "Think of them as afterimages of what took place on Earth. Over time, these ripples, these reflections of the past, dissipate. We're in one of them."

Hagar turned to two girls nearby. She had to find out what reflection they were in.

She read bewilderment in their eyes. Hagar waited a few seconds for the ripple to adjust itself around their implausible emergence on the ship. It recast Lee and Hagar as having been on deck for hours, along with the others. A reflection had internal rules that governed it. To keep its structural integrity and survive the sudden arrival of two people who did not belong in that time and place, it had to alter events and modify their appearances to make it all fit.

With the ripple now re-stabilized, Hagar crawled toward the two girls and tried to strike up a conversation. The younger one appeared to be seven, the older perhaps fourteen. Both were holding each other's hands, sobbing quietly. After first glancing at Hagar, the child looked away, uninterested. The teen was in no mood to talk, either. Hagar coaxed her and managed to learn they were from Bihe, one of the kingdoms in Angola. From what she could ascertain, the older girl had been sold to pay off her aunt's witchcraft debt. The little one was traded away by her father in exchange for rum. As Hagar expected, the two girls had no idea about their whereabouts or destination.

"A slave ship," Lee said in disbelief after Hagar returned and reported. The words were almost swallowed by the groan of the ship's hull as it rocked against the ocean waves. "Are we in the seventeenth or eighteenth century then?"

"Hardly," Hagar said dryly. "The reflections don't last that long. Do you see those black cracks on the far end of the deck?"

Lee had noticed them earlier. She squinted. "I can't see anything inside them."

"There's nothing inside them—they're just holes in reality. The void. This reflection has begun to deteriorate." She studied the black fractures. "Judging by the extent of the degradation, I'd say this is an early twentieth-century ripple."

Lee rubbed her sweaty hands on her checkered gown, which, like her physical appearance, had also undergone change. "Shouldn't we be escaping or something?"

"I need to recuperate. For me, it's been over thirty straight hours. It's starting to affect me," Hagar said. "Anyway, I can't side-shift us from one ripple to another without knowing our bearings. We'll move out tomorrow morning."

They made themselves comfortable. Hagar sat down and lounged against a wall as Lee recounted some of the recent events. When she was finished, Lee cocked her head. "So it was Aratta who put you in a timefold?"

"Yes, 1937," Hagar said. "Most of the analysts were taken out beforehand, while the reports sent to me were fabricated. The whole thing was thought-out and deployed with care. I don't know the 'why' of it, though." She glanced quizzically at Lee.

"He told me you died two years later, in 1939, during an air raid over Warsaw," Lee offered.

Hagar pondered that for a moment. "Does it even make sense?"

Lee considered. "It kind of does. We had a big war. Aratta seemed genuinely surprised to find out you were alive, and in Haiti of all places." She briefed Hagar about the rest of what had transpired since the alarm had gone off a few days earlier.

A possible third player? This was something that hadn't occurred to Hagar. Someone else had been moving pieces.

She was fairly certain about one thing, however. Had Aratta wanted her dead, which was unthinkable, he would have shot her—not put her in a stasis box. No, he only wanted her out of the way, at least temporarily.

And then there were the other things: what had happened

when Lee attempted to use the gateway on her property, and Aratta's reported futile attempt to break out of Earth. Hagar was utterly mystified.

"I take it Aratta can't follow us through the reflections," Lee said.

"He might have—had I plotted it ahead of time." Hagar smiled slyly. "As it is, I didn't. I have no idea where we are. Which means neither does Aratta. We've lost him, and he can't track us. We are free."

Lee raised an eyebrow. "Free? It's a hell of a thing to say—considering where we are sitting right now."

Hagar reached out and patted the other woman's cheek. After a moment, she leaned back, put her hands behind her head, and closed her eyes.

The sun was setting as a rowboat brought another batch of enslaved people. One woman with a young infant secured to her back fell as she climbed the ship's boarding ladder. There were shrieks of laughter from above. Startled, Lee glanced up at the first-class section. Well-dressed passengers crowded against the polished railing, their faces flushed in the fading sunlight, peering down with avid interest and unmistakable pleasure at the people on the lower deck.

Next to Lee and Hagar, the two girls clutched each other and started to sob quietly again.

⇒⇐

As night fell, all the slaves were herded down into a hold, and a thick wooden hatch groaned shut. The heat and humidity below deck were even more oppressive, if that was possible.

The men gathered on one side, the women and children on the other. "Like cows in a slaughterhouse," Lee said, her voice heavy. The sound of hushed whispers and soft sobbing filled the air.

Seemingly out of nowhere, Hagar produced two roll mats. She passed one to Lee. They walked over to a little alcove in the women's section. The two women stripped off their clothes and lay down on the mats, their skin glistening with sweat.

Lee looked over at Hagar. Through a small porthole high above, the moonlight traced a path on the woman's bare figure. Her body, though still cloaked in dark skin, now revealed her striking athletic curves.

Hagar, sensing Lee's gaze, turned to her, a playful grin tugging at the corners of her mouth. "I remember something." Her face was now just inches away, stirring a rush of heat within Lee that wasn't from the stifling tropical air.

"It must've been around 1630," Hagar said. "I sailed the Mediterranean for a few days. I couldn't understand why some coastal towns of Italy and Spain were either deserted or fortified. By the third day, an overwhelming stench greeted me near a Spanish port town. It was a galley with a raiding party of North African slavers descending on the townsfolk."

She continued, "While the Spaniards and Portuguese were journeying to sub-Saharan Africa and acquiring slaves for their colonial holdings in the Americas, their own people were being carted off wholesale and brought to North Africa." Her dark eyes shone with grim amusement. "It is said that over one million Europeans were captured and sold into slavery."

"I didn't know about this," Lee said, and her gaze dipped down the length of the nude silhouette next to her.

Hagar blinked in surprise. "Throughout that period, Spaniards, English, and Italians were held in bondage, mixing mortar, making bricks, and building a never-ending series of grand palaces for the Sultan of Morocco, Ismail Ibn Sharif. Does that not ring a bell?"

"I'm afraid not."

Hagar's fingers traced a lazy path along Lee's stomach, stirring a gasp. "You know about the African slaves but not about the European ones. Odd." Her hand worked its way up and circled one of Lee's breasts. "If anything, I'd imagine it would be the reverse." She briefly touched the other woman's nipples, igniting a tremor of arousal. But then the hand moved up and caressed her hair and ears.

"Why"—Lee's voice came out hoarse; she cleared her throat—"why the stench?"

Hagar looked at Lee blankly for a moment. "Oh, that. The galley was manned by hundreds of people manacled to the oars. It turned out that many of these dejected people chose to relieve themselves in their seats, amid rats and swarms of flies. Some had sat there for years." She wrinkled her nose.

"I didn't know open slavery persisted into the first part of the twentieth century." Lee's breath hitched as Hagar's touch lingered on her skin.

"Well, yes," Hagar said. "The obvious case being Ethiopia. A full-blown, old-school slave country."

A few moments of silence stretched between them. Lee leaned closer to Hagar, savoring the warmth of her body and the faint scent of her hair.

Hagar's hand fluttered about, sending little tongues of fire up and down Lee's body and igniting a moist heat flare between Lee's thighs. She rolled over Lee's sweaty nude body. Her eyes flashed with a dangerous gleam as she regarded the other woman.

"I have had my share of sex in unusual settings," Lee murmured. "But a ship transporting slaves . . . it takes things to a whole new level."

Hagar brought her face close. Their mouths met with hot desire, their lips parting slightly.

⇒⇐

MORNING CAME. THEY WERE HERDED OUT again above deck.

Hagar nudged Lee, then gestured at the sight that greeted them.

Under gray clouds and a drizzling sky, they could make out an island up ahead. Now and again, they glimpsed mountains. The valleys at their base were shrouded in pale mists. Here and there, the fog lifted, allowing them a glance at white-painted houses and hills carpeted with dark-green foliage.

"São Tomé," Hagar said half to herself, then turned to Lee. "I've got it now. These are the cacao plantations of São Tomé. We are off the coast of the French Congo, Africa."

"What is going to happen to them?" Lee gestured toward the two girls.

Hagar suddenly looked resigned. "The young teenager is remarkably attractive. Once they get to shore, she is likely to be forced into sexual slavery by one of the local planters."

"And the small one?"

"The Portuguese here get a kick watching children. They teach dogs and pigs to mount and penetrate them." She grimaced. "Aside from this, much like a feral cat, she'll probably be left to her own devices until she hits puberty and can do some real good on the plantation."

Lee looked shocked, then revolted.

Hagar glowered. "I cannot imagine how it must feel for her to be betrayed thus by her parents. This is beyond comprehension or forgiveness," she said, voice tight with anger.

"What's the average life expectancy of the slaves here?"

"I'm afraid most don't survive more than a few years."

Lee's mouth pressed into a hard, grim line. "Harsh conditions?"

"Harsh, yes—but no worse than the usual plantation regimen," Hagar said at last. "I reckon what did break them was homesickness and the loss of freedom with no prospect of ever regaining it."

Lee pled with her eyes. "Can we save those two, somehow?"

"Don't even think about it," Hagar said in a low, urgent tone. She gesticulated. "The reflections are like soap bubbles. Very delicate. You start doing something out of character, let alone trying to whisk out some of the people, and the whole reflection can go poof—along with us."

"Oh," Lee said.

"Remember, the real girls likely died many decades ago," Hagar said, her voice softer. "What you see around us is but an afterimage of what was."

Hagar meditated for a few minutes. Finally, she lifted her gaze. "Okay, got it. I plotted a course back to the real Earth. Stay close to me," Hagar instructed, then broke into a dash, with Lee following suit. From the first-class cabin, someone started yelling. The clamor grew as other voices joined in. The two of them bolted to the far end of the deck. Hagar yanked open a door and closed it behind them. She reached out to a closet door, swung it wide, and beckoned Lee to enter. Lee peered in, startled. The door led to another place—nighttime, outdoors. She took a deep breath and stepped through. Hagar shut the door, which made a distinct, short reverberating sound.

"Where are we now?" Lee asked, unsure why she was whispering.

Under the night sky, Hagar was just a dark silhouette. "It's another ripple, on the other side of the world—somewhere on the Di Linh Plateau in Vietnam," she said and then gestured with her chin at the dimly lit barracks. "This is one of Michelin's slave rubber plantations, circa 1930." She started walking toward the cabins.

Lee hurried after her. "Back at the ship by São Tomé, they will open the door and find that two slaves have literally vanished into thin air. Then what?"

"The reflection has adjusted itself and the incident was erased. In a few seconds, we'll have never existed."

Lee looked around. "I thought you were going to transport us back to the present time, to the real world."

"I am," Hagar said, "but I lack the skill to do it in one jump. I found a rift, though. We just need to work our way there." Once they popped back into the real Earth, Aratta would have no way of ascertaining their whereabouts and tracking them. At least that was the plan. This would allow Hagar to do what she set out to do back in Egypt.

"If we have to traverse ripples to get to the rift, could you not have chosen more appealing and safe locales?" Lee gave the matter further consideration. "I wouldn't have objected to traveling through the beaches of Seychelles."

Hagar laughed but shook her head. "They're not on the way."

Lee abruptly stopped and pointed at a long black mass writhing on the ground in front of them. "What's that!?"

Hagar took a quick, sharp breath. "Army ants."

"*Shit!* There must be millions of them!"

They cautiously skirted the inky quivering stream and quietly entered one of the barracks.

A blast of hot, pungent air assaulted them. The tiny room held five skeletal people sleeping side by side, much like sardines stacked in a can. Two of the slaves were snoring loudly enough to more than mask their footsteps as they worked their way to the far end. The next room was identical with another group of people sleeping shoulder to shoulder.

"Almost there," Hagar mouthed, motioning at the last door. Indeed, once they opened it, daylight came flooding in. They walked through, with Hagar closing the door behind them.

"Hagar?" Lee called out, her voice uncertain as she took in their surroundings. Dappled sunlight streamed in between the jumble of towering trees, and the air was buzzing with the ceaseless hum of unseen insects.

"I am here." Lee turned and was startled at the sight of a short, smiling girl standing a stone's throw away. The voice was Hagar's, but gone was the athletic, flawless body. She was now a plump young woman with long, unkempt, jet-black hair. Her mid-torso was painted in various geometric shapes.

"We're naked," Lee said, looking down. "No hair ... anywhere. Christ."

Hagar smirked and jiggled two arm bracelets. Lee had matching ones, one of which was her unique bracelet, disguised. "The boys have thongs," Hagar said. "We get bracelets. Look on the bright side: You're young again."

"Oh yes, very bright. Where are we now?"

"The start of the twentieth century, the Putumayo region of the Amazon rainforest—a slave country. See how it works? Reflections are connected via associations. Or at least, that's how I manage to traverse them. Aratta can simply concentrate on a time and place and will himself there. Anyway, from this reflection, I can make a bridge at Abisinia station back to the present, back to the real Earth. It's about a half-day's walk this way." Hagar pointed at a faint trail weaving through the undergrowth. "With some luck, we'll enter the outpost unnoticed. Shall we?"

Lee nodded, and they began their trek.

A few hours later, they paused their journey to eat. Hagar reeled in some catfish, their silver scales glinting in the sunlight. Lee stumbled upon a nest with dozens of arrau turtle eggs. Paired with spices and provisions that Hagar retrieved from the unseen storage unit that accompanied her, their meal was fulfilling.

As they were finishing up, Hagar signaled Lee to be quiet. Now Lee could hear it too: Someone was shouting in the distance. This was followed by a scream. Then some more shouts.

The voices were getting closer.

<Quick, to the bushes!> Hagar's voice resonated inside Lee's head, transmitted through the bracelet. Earlier, Hagar had instructed her to activate the bracelet. It could not send a homing signal back to the real Earth and alert Aratta as to their whereabouts; at the same time, it allowed the two to communicate their thoughts.

Several minutes later, a caravan of people burst into view from the woods. There were about thirty of them. Some had chains on their necks linking them to each other. Others were walking unchained, carrying massive bundles. Guarding this caravan were a few young black men—Barbadians, by the look of it. A Spaniard in white trousers and a Panama hat was obviously in charge.

A twig cracked under Lee's foot.

And just as suddenly, three Winchester rifles were pointed their way. "We're Ocainas, not Huitotos," Hagar called, coming out of the bushes, with Lee close behind.

Jimenez, the overseer, scowled suspiciously, demanding to know if anyone had seen these two before. No one had. And indeed, they were not on his roster. A few times, his gaze rested on the two women. "From this point on, you're in the employ of the Civilizing Company and will collect rubber," Jimenez growled at long last. He gestured, and a couple of his Barbadian underlings surrounded the two and chained them to the line of downcast people.

Lee trusted Hagar. She doubted the alien woman would have let herself be constrained if she couldn't free them both.

"Mayai," barked one of the black guards, and the column of enslaved people jolted into marching again. The chains swayed and clinked.

"What is all this?" Lee said under her breath.

"Rubber boom," Hagar said from behind. She transmitted, <Some decades ago, word got around that the western fringes of the Amazon basin were lousy with rubber trees.> She continued in a low voice, "Profit-mongers waded into the heart of the jungle, determined to cash in, each staking a claim on a specific stretch. In no time, an enormous swath of the rainforest was carved up, along with its natives."

Hagar walked on in silence, as she collected her thoughts. "Armed with machetes, thousands of Indians have been roaming the rainforest, slashing at any rubber tree they come across. Desperate to gather all the rubber sap they can, they cut the trunks so deep that many trees don't survive the year. It's up to the natives to feed themselves. If they meet the rubber quota, they're rewarded with trinkets or a scrap of cloth. If they don't, they're flogged to the point where their bones are visible. Then, more often than not, the wounds fester within a few days, maggots set in, and they succumb. Disease, mistreatment—by now, well over half of the local population has died off."

Lee reeled from the chilling inhumanity in Hagar's account. But then she recalled something, and a bitter sting of cynicism crept in, borne of a painful memory from a trip she'd made a year prior.

Down in southern Congo, locals had been displaced, their means of subsistence destroyed. In the aftermath, countless people flocked to the giant mining pits to make a buck. With rebars or crude shovels, they dug for stones containing the toxic, valuable cobalt—to fill up a sack, trade it, and subsist another day. Adolescent mothers were digging with their infants in wraps, inhaling the dusty air laden with poisonous sulfuric acid. Men and boys were routinely buried alive in any one of the thousands of hand-dug tunnels. Orphans lingered, tirelessly sifting and sieving through the rubble, years after their parents had perished.

No whips or manacles were required—only the overwhelming drive for survival and bleak external circumstances. That's how you get slave labor without slaves, Lee mused darkly.

Half an hour later, the column came to a halt. Members of a rival tribe confided in the Spanish overseer that two children in his caravan were the sons of a local *tuchaua*, a clan chief. If they were to capture the leader, it stood to augment the workforce by another hundred or two hundred people.

One of the Barbadian underlings confronted the young people, demanding they reveal the whereabouts of their father. As they vehemently refused, a few of the guards seized them and hoisted them into the air by their hands and feet. The kids screamed but to no avail. The Barbadians poured kerosene on the ground and started a small fire.

Blisters began to appear on the children's skin. Lee looked away and tried to shut out the screams that tore at her on the inside. Through the cries and sobs, the two children told their tormentors the location of the hideout. They were subsequently untied and ordered to lead the way.

Hagar and Lee learned that their father was Tiracahuaca, the head of the Aifugas clan.

After marching about half a mile, they reached a clearing. The armed black men rushed into a hut and dragged out the struggling chief along with his wife. Per the command of the Spaniard, two of the young guards held the woman by the hair, and, flinging her down, hacked at her head with machetes. It took them four blows to sever her head. The man with the Panama hat grabbed one of the chief's children by his feet and bashed his head against a tree. There was a sickening sound and Lee screwed her eyes shut, fighting vomit and nausea.

The slavers let the bereaved father hold onto his last surviving son, no doubt keeping the child alive to ensure the chief's cooperation.

Shortly thereafter, the wind whipped up and rain came pouring down. The guards yelled at the captives to press on. And so they did, slogging through the torrential rain and mud. A man who faltered and fell repeatedly was shot dead. Hagar was unshackled and tasked with carrying his bundle. She held back a sigh of relief that it was not Lee burdened with the heavy load.

After what felt like a long time, the rain tapered off, and before long, it stopped. It was another half-hour walk. Then, quite abruptly, they found themselves stepping out of the dense forest and onto an open, grassy area dotted with patches of cassava. They reached Abisinia.

The outpost consisted of a handful of buildings with thatched roofs and walls woven from split bamboo. In a large clearing at the heart of the station, about two dozen men in white shirts and dark slacks milled about. Off to the side, some indigenous people lay immobilized on the ground, feet trapped in wooden stocks. Their bodies, crisscrossed with welts from relentless lashings, displayed torn muscle tissue that quivered grotesquely.

From the veranda of a nearby house, a handsome, lean man with a trimmed mustache was studying the newcomers.

<Who is this?> Lee transmitted.

<This must be Abelardo Agüero, the section chief.>

A nod from the Spaniard who'd led their caravan drew Aguero's attention to Lee and Hagar. He sized them up before shaking his head dismissively. Evidently, their altered appearances were not appealing enough for the harem.

One of the black Barbadians approached them and unshackled Lee. "Listen to me," he told the two. "Return here in two weeks' time. Each of you is expected to bring back at least ten kilos of rubber." He fetched a clipboard and wrote down their names.

This was the moment for which Hagar was waiting. They were in Abisinia and free to roam about unmolested. ‹Let's slink out of sight, and I'll open the gateway to the real, present-day Earth from here,› Hagar transmitted, then started to walk away. Lee dutifully followed her.

"Commence weighing the rubber," called out the Peruvian section chief to the crowd of indigenous people and his dozen staff members. As he bounded down the wooden steps, several cadaverous-looking dogs rushed out to greet him.

"Is there no meat for them?"

"No, chief," said one of the guards.

The head of Abisinia briskly strode down the row of cowering Huitotos. His sharp gaze fell on a child standing amid the downtrodden faces. It was Coyu, the sole surviving offspring of Tiracahuaca.

With great force, Aguero wrested the small child away from the arms of his father. He flung the yelling boy to the ground and shot him dead. Three underlings commenced hacking the child's body to pieces with machetes and tossing them to the dogs.

The father howled in fathomless sorrow and bolted forward. His screams were cut off when a bullet lodged in his heart. Aguero snapped the revolver smartly back into its holster.

In the distance, Hagar stopped in her tracks, her face a mask of murderous rage. Nearby, Lee was visibly going into shock, eyes glazing over. Hagar closed the gap between them. She clapped loudly in front of Lee and yelled her name until the other woman focused. "Take it," Hagar said, thrusting a machine pistol and several magazines her way. Lee nodded and accepted them with trembling hands and a set jaw.

The air rippled, and Hagar metamorphosed, regaining her true form. Attired in a dark-gray outfit, she now held a ten-gauge shotgun, making her way back to the center of the clearing, accompanied by Lee. Over her shoulder was slung a submachine gun.

She racked the shotgun, her pace unbroken.

Aguero swung around at the loud, unmistakable pump-action sound, and his eyes widened in disbelief.

With a sound like a clap of thunder, most of his head exploded.

As the shotgun clattered onto the ground, Hagar was already holding the submachine gun, while Lee stood at the ready.

They poured the pent-up fury and anguish of the past hours into a hail of lead. As they fired off countless rounds, they looked like avatars of vengeance. A handful of the slavers managed to raise their rifles, but they were gunned down before they could take aim. A few survivors turned to flee, only to be shot in the back.

In less than a minute, it was over. Every staff member of the Abisinia station lay dead on the ground amid spent shell casings and the acrid smell of gunpowder.

Calmly, Hagar walked over to the stocks. With a burst of gunfire, she pulverized wooden boards and hinges, freeing the captives.

Having collected the weapons and put them away in the invisible storage unit, Hagar grimly surveyed the carnage and the dumbfounded indigenous people, who were milling about. But then she spun around. About twenty yards away, a part of the world disappeared, and a window into another rapidly grew. On the other side of the looking glass, a Ford Model B touring car came to a screeching halt on a dirt road. Its occupants—a man and two well-dressed women—stared in sheer disbelief and terror at the impossible sight of dead people and mangled, flogged slaves in some remote tropical forest. The women shrieked, hands flying to their mouths in horror.

With sudden reckless abandon, Hagar picked up a huge bundle

of rubber. "Compliments of the Peruvian Amazon Company," she hollered over the hysterical screams of the two women passengers. "Hope you like the tires; it was paid for with other people's families." She threw the bundle in a wide arc. It flew through the air, entered the other ripple, and knocked over the driver, sending him sprawling.

There was a loud rending sound and an implosion. The view of the other reflection winked out.

All the Indians fled into the forest in terror.

"What happened to being careful with the reflections?" Lee shouted, now clothed once again and manifested in her own body, as she ran toward Hagar.

"Fuck it," Hagar said.

"Since when do you care about a mirage and people who died long ago?"

They shared a quick, grim smile and embraced. "Hopefully, our disappearance will be enough to allow the reflection to heal itself and sustain for a while longer, letting the local people of this ripple—whatever they are—experience freedom again." *And resume raids on neighboring clans, kidnapping women and girls, selling some of them to the Spaniards*, Hagar thought, but she chose to keep that last to herself.

She raised her arms, took a deep breath, and concentrated.

After a few seconds, a glowing slash appeared in the air several feet above the ground. "Here is our ride." Hagar gestured to the expanding rift, from which smoke and soot and heat billowed. "It's Brazil, on the actual Earth, 2013, southeast of our present location. We must hurry."

The rift widened further, and through it, they could see a pall of thick fumes emanating from the real Earth—from dozens of brick domes with dark figures sneezing and hacking, moving between the ovens and ashen tree stumps.

Lee stared. "What the hell is this place?"

"What does it look like?" Hagar said, more harshly than she

intended. "It's one of the charcoal-making camps in the Amazon."

Some of the enslaved Brazilian men became aware of the gaping rift and stopped to stare in wonder at the improbable sight.

Hagar glanced around. The fabric of the reflection they were in was unraveling fast. "Let's make a dash for it," she said. And the two women sprinted toward the rift opening. *Finally*, Hagar thought. The idea blazed in her head. Finally, she would do what she had set out to do in Egypt, 1937. The moment her feet hit the ground on the real Earth, she would form a rift out of this planet, notify the three gods, and convene a hearing.

On the real, present-day Earth, all the Brazilian slaves cried out suddenly. Even from a distance, Hagar and Lee could see their eyes glazed over, their facial muscles forming a peculiar, disturbing expression. As one, the Brazilians ran toward the rift opening, screeching, and then began hurling thick branches, large stones, and baskets filled with smoldering charcoal at the two women.

Hagar stopped and grabbed Lee at the edge of the narrow cavity, the black void between the two worlds. Shock was etched on her face as she stared wide-eyed at the howling slaves on the other end of the fissure. She shot a fearful glance at Lee. "Something is very wron—" Her words were cut off as a thick branch hit Hagar on the side of her head and knocked her off her feet. She fell into the black chasm between the two realms, dragging Lee with her.

The howling of the men, the rending of the world, the smoke and soot—all abruptly vanished, replaced by the complete silence of the void.

CHAPTER 11

"Hagar, Hagar!" Lee cried out, panicked.

From somewhere next to her, her companion groaned. "We're in the void. Hush." She was losing consciousness but fought it off. Then she felt the presence of something. Hagar grunted from the effort and managed to mentally latch on. The tug became more pronounced as they entered the far-off gravity-like well. And just as suddenly, they left the void.

Under cover of night, the two women fell and tumbled across a rugged open terrain, sparsely dotted with scrub and stunted trees.

Blackness overtook them.

At the sound of a distant roar, Lee jolted awake and sat up. Bathed in the moonlight, a hulk of a man, perhaps nine or ten feet tall, was barreling toward them.

"Hagar! We've got to go! A Godzilla guy is coming toward us—and awfully fast!"

"What?" Hagar said groggily. "Where are we? Are we out of the void?"

Lee felt fear welling inside her. She heaved the other woman onto her feet. Hagar took stock of the situation, her eyes widening in disbelief. "What the bloody hell…" Whoever the brute was, he didn't look like the kind of person she could reason with. He was about fifty paces away and closing. She was too shaken and disoriented to physically fight, and she was not going to use a gun on him—except as a last resort. She turned to Lee. "Come. Let's see if we can lose him!"

The two women sprinted through the gloom toward what appeared to be a series of buildings in the distance.

"What is this place?" Lee called out.

"I don't know," Hagar hollered back. "But it's not Earth." She had no chance to reflect on what she had seen there in those closing moments before they plunged into the void. But that disturbing sight of the Brazilian slaves shook her to the core.

Under the moonlight, the dark shapes resolved into a small, deserted town dominated by a colossal structure. As they approached the yawning archway that served as the town's entrance, the hulking figure of their pursuer was but two dozen steps behind. They surged through the gateway and sprinted in the direction of the looming edifice at the town's heart. The giant halted at the gateway, howling with frustration, obviously unwilling to pursue them inside. He stood still for a long while and at last turned back on his heels and lumbered away.

"Lucky for us," Lee panted.

"Or not. You've got to wonder what the big boy finds so scary in here."

Lee gestured dismissively. "This place is deserted. It has been for ages." She nodded toward the desolate alleyways and crumbling buildings, with mounds of sand piled on all sides.

The sound of their footsteps was drowned by the stir of the wind and the soft whirring of sand.

"My God," Lee said, "this . . . man made me feel as minuscule as a grasshopper."

Hagar turned and stared at her.

Lee frowned. "I don't know where that came from."

"A stray thought," Hagar said, her tone reflective, "but not yours." Finally, she shook her head and resumed walking.

"A ziggurat," Hagar said suddenly, coming to an abrupt halt. She pointed straight ahead at the immense pyramid-like structure. It had multiple sloping ramps, with stairs leading from one story to the next.

Sensing the sudden tension, Lee threw a questioning glance at Hagar. "Do you know what this place is?"

"Know? No, I do not."

"Well, you seemed a bit rattled."

"It's nothing," Hagar said, but the strain in her voice was evident.

A ray of light illuminated the top of the ziggurat. The two women exchanged glances and moved forward as one. They both sensed that some answers lay there.

Closer now, they could discern the countless small bricks of the ziggurat's walls, each outlined by a black, tar-like substance.

About fifteen minutes later, they reached the top of the structure. Up high, the wind blew and wailed without letup. In the gloom of the night, under a narrow beam of silvery light, a lone slab of weathered stone stood out. Hagar moved closer and studied the inscription. A low moan escaped her, and she sank to her knees.

"What is it? What does it say?"

Hagar looked up at her companion, her face bleak and pale in the white light. "It says: 'Lest others follow in their footsteps and seek to aspire too high, I have scattered the people of Shinar who plotted to reach heaven.' It is signed 'El Shaddai.'"

"Who is El Shaddai?"

"You probably know him by his other alias, Yahweh." Hagar got up and for a moment rested a hand on Lee's shoulder. "This is the Tower of Babel."

Lee's face drained of color. "The Tower of Babel? But that's a legend."

"It *is* a legend—on Earth."

"What are you saying?" Lee asked, a cold knot forming in her stomach.

Hagar's gaze was fixed on the distant, shadowy horizon. Her voice was a soft note against the wind's hollow moan. "Do you remember the creation story in *Genesis?* How *raqi'a,* a solid sky expanse, sectioned off the bodies of water—some above it, some below it? And how, during the Flood, God was said to have opened the casement windows of the heavens to release torrents of water?"

Lee fought off the creeping horror, clinging to denial. No. No, this couldn't be. She squared her shoulders, forcing herself to look at Hagar.

"But—the Bible also talks about God storing snow and hail for battle, right?" Her voice cracked. "That's nonsense. Either God didn't understand physics, or the people who wrote those stories didn't. That's what proves it—proves it's all just . . . legend."

She shook her head, her voice louder now, desperate. "There is no God. Just people. Ignorant people, making things up."

Hagar's steady, emerald eyes held Lee's, unblinking. She produced a small, slender object. With a swift, upward flick of her wrist, she fired what appeared to be a single laser pulse into the dark expanse high up.

More than a mile above them, the night sky ignited as the beam struck an unseen barrier, accompanied by a momentary rumble. Gradually, the darkness returned as the light dissipated, spreading outward toward the far edges of the world.

"Strong as a metal mirror," Hagar said softly. "Behold: the canopy of heavens."

Lee pressed a hand to her throat, eyes wide.

"It's a solid, colossal canopy," Hagar said, seeing the question in the other woman's eyes. "Stretching hundreds of miles in every direction. Freshwater is stored above the canopy and, at the deities' will, may come down as rain on various locales. The land mass we stand upon is buttressed with a foundation, while the primeval water below breaks through to the surface and forms lakes, springs, and rivers. Above the canopy is the divine realm; underneath it, the common realm."

"We are inside a giant construct," Lee said weakly, feeling numb. They were not in any sort of ripple. This was no Earth. It appeared they had stumbled on a world where the events of the Bible and its cosmology were the literal truth.

Hagar gave her a bitter smile. "I like to think of it as a fishbowl—as Noah must have reasoned out," she said. Her voice regained its strength. "All El Supremo had to do was open wide the casement windows at the dome, unseal the wellsprings of the deep, and sit back."

She fixed Lee with a level gaze. "This is a world ruled by deities, and the supreme one is Yahweh. Here, in this place, he is real, and watching."

"Oh, great God in heaven," Lee whispered hoarsely.

"You can say that again. About a mile and a half up, at that."

Lee averted her gaze, staring blankly into the distance. "How do you know all of this?" she asked, turning to look at Hagar. "Come to think of it, you suspected something of this sort the moment the ziggurat came within sight."

Hagar nodded. "Aye. I've heard of this world."

"How do we get out of here?"

"That's the thing." Hagar kicked at the ground, creating a small explosion of dust and rocks. She looked at the other woman glumly. "I don't think there *is* a way out."

CHAPTER 12

THEY SAT THERE FOR A WHILE AS HAGAR MULLED OVER the dire straits they were in.

At last, Hagar came out of her reverie. "Lee," she said. "Lee, there's only one thing we can do."

Lee smiled weakly. "Why do I have this sinking feeling that I won't like it?"

Hagar locked eyes with her. "We have to petition Yahweh in person—and talk him into opening a way out of this world for us."

Lee swallowed the lump in her throat. "Talk to . . . God?"

"Not just talk. We need to butter him up." Her jaw clenched. "The thought of it literally makes me sick to my stomach."

"And then?"

"Then we cross our fingers and hope he doesn't incinerate us."

"Well, in that case we'd better start praying," Lee said miserably.

They looked at each other and burst out laughing, their laughter tinged with hysteria. Lee tried to shake her head in disgust, but the fits of mirth kept bubbling up.

Lee thought some more about it. "I don't understand why we need to sacrifice an animal to get Yahweh to notice us. Isn't he omniscient?"

Hagar gave a wry smile. "No, of course not. Have you not read *Genesis*?"

"What about it?"

"Well, three men appeared to Avraham: Yahweh and two of his minions. After they dined, Yahweh told Avraham that a great outcry against the offenses of Sdom and Amorah had reached him. And then he said: 'I will go down and see if that is so.' I thought it should be clear from this account he is not omniscient."

"I remember reading this," Lee said distantly. She reflected a bit more. "Come to think of it, it also didn't occur to me that at times he manifested in a body."

"Well, yes. That's how, for example, at Mount Sinai the elders of Yisra'el saw El Shaddai in person and noted the pavement in the likeness of blue sapphire underneath his feet."

The two shared a moment of silent reflection.

"I can sense his presence," Hagar said, pointing toward a dim ridge in the distance. "His attention is set hundreds of miles in that direction. That's where we're heading. Once there, we'll seek an audience with Yahweh."

"I think I can guess what territory we need to travel to." Lee summoned the ghost of a smile.

Hagar returned the smile. "In the meantime, I've shielded our thoughts from any prying deity, whether it's Yahweh or any other."

They descended the long staircase.

"So, is this a land of . . . giants?"

"There are Rephaites about," Hagar acknowledged. "But mostly, it's humans," she said, seeking to reassure Lee.

Upon reaching a landing, Hagar said, "Thankfully, I have emergency supplies stashed away—weapons, gold, dried food, and other essentials." As she spoke, her attire transformed until she was wearing a veil, sandals, and an ankle-length tunic.

Lee looked her up and down. "A veil, really?"

"Without it, I'm a shining blonde target for every would-be bride-abductor." Hagar then heaved a sigh and rearranged her veil to drape it like a shawl. "Then again, a veil might brand me as a prostitute."

"What do *I* get to wear?" Lee asked as she shed her clothes, passing them to Hagar. Seemingly out of nowhere, the other woman produced a toga-like dress. "Nice, respectable clothing, O Elder One."

Lee sniffed. "If I'm an elder, what does that make you—ancient?"

The blonde woman looked at her innocently. "Let's get moving, granny. We've got a considerable journey ahead."

They descended the next flight of stairs.

Lee glanced at the other woman a few times. "What the hell happened as we were about to cross over to Brazil? It was as if something had taken control of the Brazilian slaves."

Hagar compressed her mouth into a thin line, troubled. "When you told me about the portal's destruction on your property, I brushed it off," she said as she kept on walking. "Now I'm thinking we got a lucky break—departing Earth when Aratta showed up. Someone, or as I increasingly suspect, *something* is after us. Something powerful beyond anything I could counter. We'll have to deal with it when and if we get back." The two of them reached the ground level and exited the ziggurat. "But first things first, yes?" Hagar said and jerked her head toward the distant hills. Their long trek was about to begin.

As they traveled, the relentless sun and rugged terrain turned hours into exhausting days, and the days into arduous weeks. But with each grueling step, they inched closer to their destination: Yahweh's seat of power.

They passed through countless villages and small towns surrounded by cultivated fields and orchards. On three occasions, they ran into bands of highwaymen. Twice, they were able to stay hidden. Once, they were detected before they had a chance to get off the road—to the great misfortune of the bandits. Hagar disposed of six, and Lee put her years of martial arts training to good use and brought down the last thug. However, for the most part, the trip was uneventful. With some unmarked silver coins, Hagar secured food and lodging. Just as often, they managed to find someone who gave them provisions for the journey, asking nothing in return.

After a month of travel, the two were just a few days' walk away from the territory of Bnei Yisra'el when they stumbled upon a site of utter desolation.

"Look at that!" Lee said, her voice carrying a note of disbelief and horror at the sight that greeted them. It was as if all color had been rubbed off the earth and the world had turned monochromatic. The vast expanse must have once held thousands of small houses. Now, it was soot-covered and bleak.

Hagar tugged on Lee's arm. "We've got company."

Half a dozen men were walking toward them, led by an older white-haired woman.

"Trouble?"

"I don't think this band intends to abduct us, but stay vigilant," Hagar said, keeping her gaze fixed on the advancing group. "They're not just curious. They want something." She raised her hand in greeting. The approaching people returned the gesture, and some proceeded to tie their donkeys to a nearby tree.

Short swords, belted tightly around their waists, caught Lee's attention. Their weathered appearance suggested a nomadic lifestyle. They drew to a halt a few steps from the two women.

Hagar looked pointedly at the wasteland. "What happened here?"

"Twenty years past, Rabbat Ammon stood proud," said the woman with white hair. "Today it lives only in whispers, and the Ammon people are no more."

With a wiry strength that belied her years, the elder woman yanked a stubborn bush free. She then gestured, and two men promptly unrolled blankets on the ground. The elder sat down and beckoned to the two women. Hagar gave Lee a slight nod, and the two of them joined her. The men reclined a short distance away, forming a semicircle.

The old woman glanced at the desolation spread out before them. "Bnei Ammon were a stench in the nostrils of Milkom, who turned his face from them, and the land vomited them out. Then Yahū set this ground beneath the feet of his people. Yet, it will take four generations before the earth cleanses itself from the Ammonites' bloodguilt. Until that time, the land will yield no produce, and the trees will bear no fruits."

‹The Ammonites ran afoul of their patron god, and he left them to the tender mercies of the Yisra'elites and Yahweh,› transmitted Hagar to Lee.

"It's more than just a wasteland," Lee said, her eyes sweeping across the desolate landscape. "Someone *slew* everything here."

"So it was," said the elder woman, matter-of-factly. "The Yahw tribes put this place under kherem."

‹It's an irrevocable divine writ,› Hagar's thought reached Lee. ‹Nothing is spared. Once a kherem is decreed by a god, as eagles swoop, his people put to the sword men and women, infants and children, oxen and sheep.›

"Why?" Lee's voice was barely a whisper.

The old woman's fierce eyes flickered with surprise at the question. "Lest they be seduced by the sons of Ammon and walk after another god, as they had done before." A chuckle escaped her lips. "Long ago, some of them sought to cast their lot with Resheph. For this, Yahū thought to strike them with scarcity and plague—were it not for his fear the neighboring nations would claim the disaster as their doing, and all would believe he lacked the strength to guard his people."

The elder gestured, and they all partook in a modest meal: dried fig cakes, a mix of salted pistachios and almonds, pieces of coarse barley bread, and a handful of dates. To quench their thirst, they passed around leather water bladders.

The elder kept studying the two women.

"You are not like others," she suddenly pronounced.

"Neither are you." Hagar laid down the water bladder. "Who are you, people?"

A silent exchange passed among the nomads.

"We are Bnei Seraphim," the silver-haired leader said at last. She watched Hagar and Lee, searching their faces for any flicker of recognition. Finding none, she asked, "Do you know what befell in the tree-park in Eden, to the east, as written in the *Book of Yashar*?"

"Maybe," said Hagar noncommittally, even though she immediately recognized the reference to Adam and Eve at the Garden of Eden.

The female chieftain spoke: "Not far from the land of Nod, the Most High planted a tree-park, making it as his resting-place. Adam and Khavah were charged to tend it and to guard it. El elyon allowed them to eat from all the trees of the garden except from the tree of knowledge, cautioning Adam that he would die on the day he ate its fruit." Her words flowed effortlessly, as though repeated countless times before.

"But the Seraph, knowing this to be a lie, spoke forth. It said to the woman that *el elyon* knew: on the day humans ate of the tree, they would not die. Rather, their eyes would be unveiled, and they would be as gods—knowing good and evil, and setters of their own law."

The elder watched them for a long while. Her eyes narrowed; then she gave a slow, contented nod. They showed the same unyielding spirit she had hoped for. Approaching them had been good. Soon, she would lay before them an offer they would find hard to set aside. One they ought not set aside.

She continued, "The woman took from the fruit of the tree of knowledge and ate. She gave also to her man, and he ate. Then the eyes of the two were unveiled. Seeing what had come to pass, el elyon said to the heavenly host, 'Now that humans have become like one of us, knowing good and evil, they may reach out and take as well from the tree of life—and live forever.' So el elyon drove them out from the tree-park, and he set "Kerūbim to stand watch at its entrance.

"Yet once they ate, the thing was fixed in the bones of the world. From that seed, the City rose. From that hunger came the Tower of Bavel."

"We came upon its ruins," Lee said.

The elder woman took hold of a piece of dried fruit. "The Tower of Bavel was the lone moment in the days of men when they lifted their eyes and said, Let us rise; let us be more than dust under the gods' feet.

"But el elyon came down with the host of heaven, heavy as a storm cloud, and stilled the work of our hands, scattering us like seed before the wind. From that day, the sons of Adam ceased striving to touch the sky." She let out a dry breath. "So it is for the children of dust: cursed with the vision of gods, but denied the reach to grasp it—on pain of exile or ruin."

One of the men said, "The gods stand as brothers in disagreement, yet unite over one edict: Sons of flesh and sinew must know their station, lest the pillars of the world, as the gods carved them, split open."

"In the ashes of those events, a shadowed group arose," said the old woman. "A covenant bound to keep the fire that bows to no god. We are the Bnei Seraphim. From time to time, we find a wanderer lost in the waste, and we extend a hand."

After a moment she continued, "Some come to us having twisted their flesh against the way of life and now fear for their very breath. Others come that they may let their hearts speak without fear that the gods will strike them down for what rises within. We are the Bnei Seraphim."

Her breath flared with scorn. "Yahū led the sons of Yisra'el out of bondage into bondage. Out of the yoke of man into the yoke of god. He said, Send off my people, that they may serve me. They are my chattel whom I brought out of the land of Mitzraim. He did not loose their bonds."

Hagar's jaw tightened. "Loose their bonds? To what end? To starve? To wander landless? To have their men slaughtered, their daughters taken, and their women's wombs shut?" She seized a stone and flung it afar. "In the crevices and hidden recesses, a few bands live. But a multitude will be devoured without a divine shield, without a divine yoke."

Heavy, tense silence followed her statement.

"Do you say we tread a path of folly?" asked the woman, a cold look entering her eyes.

Hagar drew in a long breath. "No, I do not."

The elder studied her intently and after a while nodded, mollified.

"In the eyes of the gods," the elder said, "the worthy man is Avram—he who bound his son upon the stone and raised the blade because a divine commanded it. We may dwell in clefts of the rock, in the holes of the earth, but we possess our own breath. We keep the fire. We do not shut our eyes."

She studied Hagar and Lee. "We have been tracking you for some days. By the look of it, you come from afar and are solitary. Join us."

"We are honored," said Hagar, and meant it. "Yet we are but way-farers"—she took a deep breath—"who seek to depart this realm."

Hagar's words fell like stones, and the air around them seemed to chill. The elder woman's brows furrowed, confusion clouding her sharp gaze. "Depart this realm?" Her voice was low now, disbelief etched on her weathered face.

Her expression darkened into anger. "Is your woven tale of another realm your way of refusing my extended hand?" she spat out resentfully, like bitter bile. Her expression shifted.

"No, it is not," said Hagar, standing up. "Let it be."

"I cannot," replied the elder, also rising.

Her eyes sparked with resolve. "I am sorry then," she said. The stakes had just changed: the safety of her people. She knew what she had to do. The muscles in her arm tensed, ready.

"I am sorry, too," said Hagar, inclining her head slightly in a gesture of respect.

In the ensuing highly charged silence, the two remained still, a few paces apart, watching each other as though carved from stone.

The Seraphite struck like a coiled snake—but Hagar was faster. With blinding speed, she seized the attacking hand in a viselike grip, prompting a scream and causing the elder to drop her weapon. Using the Seraphite's momentum, Hagar hoisted and threw her across the small clearing. The old woman crumpled with a moan. Her eyes fluttered, unfocused.

The radiance emanating from Hagar's face vanished.

The men, who had recoiled in utter terror and shock at Hagar's ferocious counterattack, now flung themselves down, their faces pressed against the dirt in abject submission.

Silence. The only sound was the faint scrape of sand shifting underfoot.

"Your lives are spared," said Hagar. No one dared to raise his head. "We shall leave in peace," she added. "You will not pursue us."

"Yes, *bat elohim*," intoned the oldest, his face to the ground.

"We are wayfarers from a land under different stars. We pass through, and soon we depart. Your secret leaves with us. This, I promise."

The two women left behind the dazed Bnei Seraphim, who had never expected to encounter a divine being and live to tell about it. It was nothing short of a miracle, albeit of a different sort.

LEE AND HAGAR FOUND solace in one another that night, bodies entwined beneath the starlit sky. Afterward, they lay side by side, gazing at the stars and the embers of their small bonfire.

"Hagar, what did that old woman talk about when she said Yahweh deeded the land on lease to the Yisra'elites?"

"People here don't own slices of the world; they're all tenants."

"Does it mean anything in practice?"

"Yes. Every fifty years, the leased land reverts to the original clan or family line. This goes a long way toward forestalling the emergence of landed gentry with a vast peon underclass."

Lee jammed her hands under her head and tracked the pale luminary in the sky as it drifted toward one of the six exit gates at the far edge of the horizon.

They'd spent the last few hours putting as much distance as they could between themselves and the place where Hagar had wrestled with the Seraphim leader—where she might have inadvertently unveiled herself and alerted any of the deities, notably Yahweh, to the presence of an alien in their domain.

Many miles away now from the original site, they were breathing easier. Hagar thought that they were out of danger.

"Being a non-believer is not an option in this world, is it?" Lee said.

"Option? In this universe, Yahweh is as real as the dirt under your feet and the wind in your hair. His existence isn't a question or a debate point; it's a given." Hagar looked fixedly at the glowing embers. "What is demanded is adherence to his code of conduct."

"Isn't that code supposed to be nearly impossible to uphold?"

"Huh? Nah, it's all rudimentary," Hagar said. "Don't steal or kill. Don't fuck a goat or your sister or someone's wife. Be a decent neighbor. A conviction requires the testimony of at least two witnesses. Basic property rights laws. Stuff like that."

Lee seemed startled by the answer. She mulled this over, quiet for a while.

"Hagar, what *is* Yahweh?"

Her companion eyed her. Eventually, she resumed gazing at the bonfire. "Think of him as a meme lord."

"A meme lord," Lee repeated.

Hagar turned on her side. Propping herself on one elbow, she faced Lee. "The original plan was for people to be in the likeness of Adam and Khavah: automatons bereft of reasoning faculties. In other words, ideal meme carriers. All they had to do was be fruitful, multiply, and take it on the chin. Essentially, that's what the Seraph lady was talking about. Shit happened, though. All the same, as long as people faithfully and fervently transmit the tenets issued by their deity from one generation to the next, it gets the job done.

"At some point, Yahweh desired a flock of his own," Hagar went on. "The pharaoh holding the Yisra'elites in slavery was the break he was looking for. That was his opportunity to get his own flock."

Lee said, "I never understood how after repeatedly witnessing the awesome powers of Yahweh in their journey through the desert, the Yisra'elites could repeatedly rebel rather than be cowed into submission."

Hagar's mouth twisted in a wry smile. "They couldn't, naturally; Yahweh hardened their hearts to achieve this end. Like a blacksmith, he hammered his precepts into them time and again. The old boy wanted his canon baked in, beyond the ability of humans to question or to evolve past it."

"Hence circumcision?"

Hagar shrugged. "Well, yes. A contract carved in flesh." She was quiet for a moment. "One stroke of a flint knife at the opening of fertility, and you bind both the man and his future seed to the covenant and to the sons of Yisra'el, now and forever."

She grimaced. "Yet the task of upkeep is never finished. Bnei Yisra'el are made to ferret out and kill those who manifest signs of independent thinking. This is why El Shaddai has a standing order to kill the children who disobey, kill family members who try to coax one to serve other gods, kill any and all who entertain heretical thoughts. Even offspring must die due to the transgressions of their parents, extending down to the third and fourth generations. And like a tumor, if you want something gone, you carve out the surrounding tissue too."

Lee paled. "And you want us to step into this den of fanaticism."

"It's not a matter of 'want.' We have to learn from a Yisra'elite priest how to offer a sacrifice to Yahweh. Furthermore, it has to be performed on an altar consecrated by them," Hagar said. "Need I remind you that our only chance to leave this realm is by petitioning Yahweh?"

"A badly timed spit could have us charged with blasphemy among those people," Lee muttered.

"Then don't spit," Hagar said sharply.

Silence followed her words; the reality of their precarious situation pressed heavily upon Lee. She lay back, staring at the vast expanse of the starlit sky, seeking solace. Eventually, the hum of nocturnal insects lulled her into a fitful sleep.

Hagar remained awake, her gaze fixed on the dying embers of the fire. Her mind whirled with thoughts of the challenges they faced and the risks they had to take.

The soft murmur of distant voices broke the stillness of the night. Hagar tensed, then sat rigid, straining to make sense of the approaching sounds. She then shook Lee awake. "A band of *nevi'im* is drawing near," she said with a sense of urgency. "We need to move out, now."

Lee nodded, and they swiftly made their way to a dense thicket nearby, seeking cover. Not a moment later, a group of dark-skinned men emerged from the trees. Long, matted dreadlocks came down their backs, and they carried drums, flutes, and lyres.

From their hidden vantage point, Lee whispered, "Who are those *nevi'im*?"

"They are human conduits to Yahweh," Hagar said, sounding uneasy. "Ecstatic dancers—through music-induced trance, they open themselves up to his will and commands. *Nevi'im* are a literal mouthpiece of a deity, and at times its arm." She observed intently, and finally exhaled quietly. They weren't searching for anyone. Good. Perhaps her blunder back near Rabbat Ammon went unnoticed. Perhaps there was no way to trace it back to them.

As they watched, the group made a joyful sacrifice on the altar. The air filled with a chorus of fervent songs and rhythmic beats, and after what felt like an eternity, the *nevi'im* departed.

"Can you sense Yahweh's thoughts as they do?" Lee asked as they came out of the bushes.

"After a fashion. However, if I open myself up fully, I'll be vulnerable, and he can seize hold of me," Hagar said. "As for what I sense…" She trailed off, her gaze distant. Earlier, when Lee was sleeping, she had probed as deeply as she dared. "Yahweh has dwellings at Shiloh, Beit-El, Dan, Beit-Lekhem, Gilgal, Khevron, and the Mitzpah in Binyamin territory. These are like embassies—grafts of the divine realm here, in the common realm. These are places where people can come to petition him or express their gratitude." Hagar went on after a moment, "I want us to approach Yahweh of Khevron. I sensed the least aggression in him."

Lee looked at her strangely. "There is more than one?"

"Well, no," Hagar said, but she looked unsure. "His manifestations can occur concurrently and vary from place to place. Some manifestations are weaker—like the burning bush, a sliver of the real thing. I suspect they can make localized independent decisions and may even have distinct traits."

CHAPTER 13

At daybreak, they resumed their journey.

The initial days led them through Reuven's rugged expanses, a harsh tapestry of weathered limestone and sparse oases. As they ascended, the Salt Sea's northern reaches emerged, its blue waters a stark contrast to the barren desert. Their route traced the ridge-lines, offering views of the expansive valley. Lee and Hagar spoke little, preserving energy for the rigorous path ahead. The relentless sun, elusive shade, and widely scattered human settlements made the journey a grueling affair.

On their fourth day, they crossed into the fertile territories of Yehudah. The land was a patchwork of terraced olive groves and vineyards basking in the sunlight. As they journeyed, their path led them deeper into the highlands. The scenery shifted again, the cultivated fields giving way to rocky, narrow trails and hills studded with ancient, gnarled trees.

At long last, they reached their destination. It was time to make their presence known to Yahweh of Khevron and cast the dice. They decided to enter a village that Hagar reckoned was big enough to have a priest.

As they crossed the barley fields belonging to the village, an eerie clamor rose from the settlement itself. They took cover among a grove of olive and pomegranate trees, straining their eyes to make sense of the racket in the distance.

A surge of people spilled from the village gates, pushing ahead of them a quivering girl stripped of her garments. They led her to a deep pit and then encircled it, men at the front bearing great stones, ready to cast them. From their vantage point, Hagar and Lee could no longer see the girl through the throng. But they didn't need to. The harrowing cries and the flying rocks told the tale. It was an execution.

With a cry of fury, Lee jumped to her feet. But before she could take a step, Hagar tripped her with a scissor motion of her legs, leaped on top of her, and pinned her down. She brought her mouth close to Lee's ear. "Contravene any of El Shaddai's edicts, and we're trapped here forever." She glanced up quickly. A man on the outskirts of the crowd was looking their way, seemingly alerted by Lee's cry. But a moment later, he redirected his attention to the grim spectacle, perhaps attributing the noise to the wind or a stray animal. Hagar looked back down. "Do you understand me?"

She did not let go until Lee reluctantly nodded. Hagar motioned for her to follow. And without talking or looking back, they walked away.

Once they were some distance away, Hagar turned and glared. "You idiot girl," she spat. "In the universe we left behind, Yahweh is just a story. People can chant His name, quote His laws, build a thousand synagogues—and nothing happens if they disregard His edict to stone disrespectful sons or promiscuous daughters. No fire. No plague. No tumors. No blindness."

Her eyes flashed.

"But here? Break His Words, and He does not smite metaphorically. He rots their flesh. He sells whole villages into bondage. He drives them to eat their own young."

"It's monstrous. I don't care how they justify it," Lee sobbed in frustration. The potential enormity of her attempted intervention did not seem to register. "I don't regret trying to stop it."

Hagar tried to keep her voice level. "You sought to tamper with a social system you know nothing about. This is not a disparate collection of dictates; it is a cohesive system of ethics."

"Screw this." Lee's face twisted in anger. "An eye for an eye makes the whole world blind."

"No. Vengeance and vendetta do." Hagar grabbed Lee by the shoulders. She was going to try another tack with the woman. "The community stones the girl, and the issue is contained. Without it, it is a blood feud between the families, countless die, and it can go on for generations. You pull on one thread, and the entire tapestry comes unraveling, and it's a free-for-all, each family or clan for itself.

"You mentioned 'an eye for an eye.' In the absence of this institutionalized proportionality, all hell breaks loose. The point is not that it's 'an eye for an eye,' but that it's *only* one eye for one eye. And often, it's not an actual eye at that. At times, it's a matter of restitution, of equivalency; a live ox is given in exchange for one that has died."

They walked on, each immersed in her thoughts.

Hagar cast a worried glance at her companion, who now had the decency to look abashed.

An hour later, another settlement came into view.

It was a village of the Zerahites clan. And the name of their host was Avinadab. A Levite, he acted as the village priest and as one of its elders. He was also somewhat of an outsider, being with his family in the hamlet for only one generation and not of the tribe of Yehudah, at that. Avinadab was the first to spot them as they walked into the settlement. Lee and Hagar introduced themselves as two widows on a journey back to their homeland in the distant Ophir, and he invited them to stay the night at his house.

It was not a chance encounter. Using powerful binoculars that Hagar retrieved from her unit, they'd surveyed the village until they spotted the Levite, with his distinct white linen head-wrap. They carefully timed their entrance to the village so they would run into him, first thing.

They entered a bustling courtyard, teeming with people, goats, and sheep. At its heart, a soot-blackened cauldron hung above a crackling bonfire, filling the air with the savory scent of stewing lentils and barley. Around the periphery, low mud-brick dwellings stood, their flat roofs laden with stored goods and drying laundry. At their arrival, the dust-covered, sweat-streaked women paused in their grinding and weaving and drew near with cautious curiosity.

Lee and Hagar asked to house the sacrificial sheep they'd purchased earlier. The Levite, an understanding man accustomed to such arrangements, agreed and directed them to a small, sheltered space where the other livestock grazed. He then proceeded to make the introductions.

His remaining wife, Ephah, was a kind-eyed matriarch, her hands weathered by time, her back stooped with age. Around her neck hung a cylindrical, silvery amulet. Then, the priest gestured to his older son. "This is Yoash, my firstborn, the first yield of my manhood." Yoash nodded and introduced his wife, Keturah, and their two sons. Next, the Levite introduced his younger son, Gideon, who in turn introduced his wife, Tamar. She was a robust young woman, heavy with their second child, a silver ring glinting in her nose. A small boy—their first—hovered behind her, half-hidden. When Tamar shifted her weight, the child clung to her garment and nearly pulled her off balance. Without looking down, she steadied him with a practiced hand.

"With Yahū's blessing, the seeds of Yaacov shall become as the sand on the seashore," intoned the elderly Levite.

"Let it be so," a few of the family members said softly.

Tamar spread her arms and turned her gaze to Lee. "Gray hair is a crown of glory. Enter, Mother, and find rest."

"Ah, thanks," Lee said dryly, reminding herself that in this world people with gray-streaked hair were venerated.

<Watch your step as you climb down the stairs, O Gray One,> Hagar transmitted.

<Go and fuck yourself.>

Hagar suppressed a laugh, disguising it as a cough. "Avinadab, your hand is open beyond measure," she said, recovering herself.

The old man smiled and dipped his head. "Pleasant words are a honeycomb: sweet to the palate and healing to the bones." He guided them to a basin to wash their feet, then to a larger room beyond a small shrine set with household gods.

Before long, they all found themselves seated on cushions around a low table, surrounded by an array of pastel, intricately woven rugs.

Earlier, Hagar had instructed Lee what to do in the event they were questioned. She needn't have worried; no one inquired into or showed any curiosity about their background.

Hagar felt the need to offer praise, as was expected of guests. "Your nation's edicts are alike for all—whether for the poor or the great. You are a guiding star to all nations." No sooner had she spoken these words than she realized it was a mistake.

A tense hush descended upon the diners. "I know not the edicts of other nations, nor whether they judge all men alike," Avinadab said at last, his face clouded. "Such things are not my concern. The gods guide the steps of men, and it is not for those made of dust and ash to weigh good against evil. Let each nation heed the voice of its own god."

Lee intervened. "Forgive the untamed words of the young, Avinadab." She tried to redirect. "I've seen men sacrifice. But I never asked why. What does your god want from it?"

Hagar looked at her, genuinely impressed. The woman not only redirected his attention, defusing his displeasure, but also got straight to the heart of what they had come here for. ‹Perfect, Lee,› Hagar transmitted. ‹Lean in a bit so your bracelet is as close to him as possible. This is what I need to learn.›

The priest regarded Lee, mildly taken aback by her inquiry, yet he felt a peculiar desire to explain and share the lore. "Some offerings to Yahū are for well-being—given in gratitude for vows fulfilled, to mark times of joy, or to make a plea," the Levite said. "But two sacrifices stand above all. Morning and evening, the assembly offers at the great shrine at Khevron a yearling lamb, along with wine and choice flour mingled with oil. These are our perpetual offerings to our rock."

He went on, "The other sacrificial demand is for purging." The Levite settled back in his cushion and scratched his short, tangled beard. "At the heart of it all lies the Covenant. Yahū grants us protection, rain, and abundance. In return, we heed his words and walk in his ways." Avinadab's face became stern. "But what happens when one of us stumbles? A defilement seeps into the dwelling place of El Shaddai. And if the taint grows too great, Yahū will depart and leave us to our ruin."

With her eyes demurely downcast, Hagar appeared the image of a meek, unmarried woman. In reality, she was attuning herself to the surface thoughts of Avinadab. Without having him fitted with a bracelet such as the one Lee wore, it was a grueling task to read Avinadab's thoughts. Still, certain fine details—those closely guarded secrets of the lore that they dared not inquire about for fear of arousing suspicion—needed to be painstakingly extracted directly from his mind.

"Can the abode be cleansed?" asked Lee.

He nodded with approval at the question. "Yes. With life essence: the blood of an offered animal. If an individual has violated an edict unintentionally, he brings the offering, and a priest purges the sanctuary's courtyard. Now, if the entire community has done so, the priest has to purify both the inner sanctum and the courtyard with an offering brought by a community representative."

"What happens if someone intentionally violates an edict?"

‹I've got it,› Hagar transmitted to Lee. ‹I have what we need.›

"This pierces the final veil and reaches the innermost sanctum of Yahū's abodes," said Avinadab, unaware of the silent exchange between the two women. "The evildoer is barred from making an offering—but once a year, on the Day of Purgation, the high priest purges the holy of holies. As you can see, the greater the violation, the deeper it penetrates into the houses of Yah. I speak in simple terms, but I trust you grasp the way it stands."

"I believe I do, yes," Lee said, keeping the elation from her voice. They did it. Hagar now had the information required for their sacrifice.

"But know this," said Yoash. "Purging the sanctuary is one matter. The wrongdoer must still answer—with death, restitution, or being cut off from our midst."

His father nodded at that.

Next, he gestured to the food, and they ate.

The dinner was a simple affair. Earlier, the elderly matriarch had pressed flour and olive oil onto a heated stone to bake flatbreads. Now she served these alongside roasted onions and a steaming stew of lentils and vegetables.

‹There's something unexpectedly appealing in all of this,› Lee transmitted.

‹Indeed, there is a sense of simplistic certainty to it all, which pushes away the vast nameless currents of the unknown. Yahweh's paternal presence is comforting, and his code of law institutes fairness and even generosity.›

The meal was drawing to a close. Ephah, the mother of the household, brought out timbrels and passed them out to the women. The gesture was met with high, trilling ululations.

"O Yahū, when you came forth from Seir," intoned the priest, rising slightly from his cushion. His family's voices rose in chorus, "When you strode from the fields of Edom, O the earth heaved, and the very heavens dripped rain." Some of the women began to dance, feet stomping the dust. Others banged and rattled their frame drums in a fierce, eager rhythm.

"My strength and my power is Yah!" they all shouted, faces flushed with wine and heat.

"Yah is a man of war! Yah is his name!
O Bull of Yaacov, there is strength in your loins!
For what god in the heavens or on earth can match your deeds?
Who is like Yah among the sons of El?

Yah, God of Armies!
You send forth your wrath—it devours like fire!
Your enemies cringe;
You march upon their backs!
You eat up nations, crush their bones, and smash their loins!"

There was a loud crashing sound as the men slammed their bowls down in unison, followed by hoots, laughter, and a wild round of ululations from the women.

<They're straight-up feral,> Lee transmitted.

<No,> Hagar sent back dryly. <They're just giddy the bandits won't rape their daughters this year. This is what joy looks like here.>

"Who is like you among the gods?" the assembled people roared into the night.

Hagar and Lee rose to their feet and requested their leave, reminding their host of their need to sacrifice. They promised they would return that night, having every intention to honor the hospitality of the Yisra'elite—and not risk antagonizing his patron God.

They chose the village well; it was but a few miles from the territory of Pleshet, beyond the dominion of the Yisra'elites, where no offense would be taken if they sacrificed to a foreign deity.

However, their actual plans were entirely different.

In a terebinth grove atop a hill outside of town, they approached a horned altar of rough-hewn white stone that they had spotted before. They were going to sacrifice the animal to Yahweh on an altar consecrated by a Yisra'elite priest.

Once they reached the altar, Hagar inspected Lee.

The other woman turned leisurely, raising her arms. "Do I look pretty enough for a sacrifice, darling?"

Hagar let out a vexed sigh. "I'm not checking for pretty. I'm checking for leaks."

"Leaks?"

"Did you bleed this week?"

"What kind of question is that?" Lee was half amused, half irate.

"Menstrual blood is life-fluid that is leaving the body. To the altar, that registers as a leak. A breach in the hull."

"It's been more than a week," Lee said, and made a face.

Hagar smiled. "Good, then your biology is sealed." She noted that Lee was still eyeing her sideways. "Menstruation, open wounds, rot, mold, contact with a corpse—this would be like bringing matter next to antimatter. No traces of death or decay ought to come close to the altar."

"I don't get it. We're to be clean of any traces of death, and then we go ahead and slaughter an animal for sacrifice?"

"I'm not fully sure how it works," Hagar admitted. "At any rate, one's life-force is in the blood. By offering it up at the altar, we return the life to the creator. The rest is just meat, suited for eating."

"So that's how he'll become aware of us?" Lee asked.

"Yes. Each altar acts as a conduit to the divine realm."

"Is it going to work?"

"You'd better pray it does," Hagar told her.

"Are you not going to do some sort of incantation?"

Hagar shook her head in the negative and signaled Lee to be silent.

She swiftly slaughtered the animal, skinned the dead ram, then drained its blood into a clay bowl. Without hesitation, she grasped the vessel and splattered its contents around the edges of the altar. As Lee watched, Hagar cut up the carcass, washed the internal organs in a nearby basin, and laid it all on a fresh bed of wood they had set up earlier. Before long, flames were leaping about.

The two of them looked on as the smoke curled and snaked its way up to the great sky canopy. This was the point of no return, likely to conclude either in their death or a return to Earth. From that point forward, they were in the hands of a vast, ruthless power.

⇒⇐

THEY RETURNED IN TIME FOR DESSERT AND DRINKS. Dark wine flowed generously, and bite-sized honey cakes disappeared quickly among the diners.

A bit later, a bleary Hagar excused herself and was helped by Tamar to the wooden ladder leading to the sleeping quarters on the second floor.

Some time passed. When Tamar did not return after a while, Avinadab went up after her.

He found her standing with a razor in her hand poised over the still form of the golden-haired woman.

"What have you done?" the priest gasped, stricken. Tamar jumped at the sound of his voice, the razor dropping from her hand.

Color rose to her cheeks—shame or fury, he could not tell.

"I mingled an essence of deep slumber in her wine," she said. "I meant to shear off her hair while her eyes grew dim."

"Why?" Avinadab's voice cracked between disbelief and pain. "They came in the shadow of our roof-beam. Guests."

Tamar's eyes flashed. She pointed a finger at the unconscious woman. "Your son's eyes lingered far too long on that one," she hissed. "And she is not even of our seed." Her gaze slid over the golden spill of hair, and her mouth twisted as if tasting something too sweet.

She lifted her chin, glowering, arms crossing over her chest. In a mocking sing-song, she recited:

"'Rejoice in your wife; let her breasts forever quench your thirst. And why, my son, dote on a wayward woman and cradle her lap?'"

Avinadab's hand found the tassels on his robe, and he fiddled with the indigo thread. "Let not a heart of envy dwell within you, daughter," he said at long last, mainly because he was expected to reproach her. Yet he felt the sting of her grievance. He had seen his son stare.

Against his will, his gaze slid to the prone woman. She was the most striking creature he had ever seen. Her skin was pale as the moon; her hair spilled like molten gold. Her lips were a thin red line; her breasts rose softly beneath the cloth. His mind betrayed him with thoughts of the smooth, ivory skin hidden under her robe. *A thirsty man will drink from any water at hand*, he thought.

He tore his eyes away and cleared his throat. "She did no wrong. At the break of day, she will go. We will let her leave in peace."

For a heartbeat, Tamar looked ready to argue, but then she bit her lip, picked up the razor, and walked away, her long gown swishing, bracelets clicking softly with each step.

Just as he was about to extinguish the lamp in the room, something caught his eye. Was it a book in the hands of the exotic woman? Intrigued, the priest drew closer for a better look. Indeed, it was a book, albeit curious-looking.

He pried it gently out of her limp fingers and strolled into his bedchamber, thumbing through it and marveling at how thin the sheets of paper were.

Beneath the flickering light of a single wick, he perused page after page as the hours slid by. He recognized many of the ballads and poems; they were transcriptions from the *Book of Yashar* and the *Book of the Wars of Yahū*. The utterances of Yah and the laws in *Exodus* seemed to originate from the *Book of the Covenant*. The rest of the text—most of the text—was a different story.

Avinadab navigated through the foreign landscape of names and battles that had never graced the lore of his people. The mention of a human king over Yisra'el stirred a sense of sacrilege in the depth of his soul. He also found ever-evolving priestly directives for his people: instructions that were shifted, added, or removed seemingly with each iteration.

Wrinkles of confusion furrowed his brow as he thoughtfully stroked his chin. He first brushed off these inconsistencies as scribal oversights, but as he delved deeper, he thought that some of the alterations were intentional.

As he thumbed through from page to page, a dark cloak of unease settled more heavily upon Avinadab.

In the morning, Lee jostled Hagar until the blonde woman sat up with a groan. She shook her head, trying to clear it. "Damn, I think I was drugged last night."

Lee shot her a concerned look. "Drugged, you say?"

"Yes. But I have a feeling—"

She stopped talking. Avinadab stood in the doorway, grim as death. His curly black hair gleamed like coal in the dim room. Other people crowded at his heels.

"So, who killed Goliath?" His voice was cold with scorn. "Was it David son of Yishai or was it Elkhanan son of Ya'arei-Orgim? Your *book* lists them both." And he flung it at Hagar's feet.

Oh shit, thought Hagar.

"Is that what I think—" began Lee, but her companion made a chopping motion with her hand.

"So you read it," Hagar said, matter-of-factly.

"I welcomed you into my home and . . . and you bring this . . . thing under my roof," he sputtered, eyes wide with outrage.

Hagar stood and walked up to him. "But you don't know what this book is, do you?" she said softly.

"An abomination that should not exist!" he shouted as other villagers crowded in, all talking. "'You shall not add to the word I charge you, nor shall you subtract from it,'" screamed the priest in rage, his face turning purple.

"Avinadab—" Hagar started.

"Don't talk!" shrieked the Levite. He turned to address the people who'd filed in. "Take these two women and stand watch as the elders decide their fate."

Hagar considered the predicament they were in, then gave Lee a nod, and they were led outside. Two seemingly unarmed women, one elderly and the other small in stature. The villagers had no clue and did not bother to tie them. They were content to let them sit together by the well while a few women and children kept an eye on them.

Time dragged on as the elders sat in a circle under a massive acacia tree, debating and arguing among themselves.

Lee studied the assembled group of aged men. "When are you going to get us out of here?" she asked. "Before or after they stone us?"

"I hope it won't come to stoning," Hagar replied. She smiled faintly. "Oh, I can extricate us all right, but things can get . . . messy. If I end up killing some of Yahweh's flock, the chances of his help will plummet. Let's see what they decide and take it from there."

"Was it the Hebrew Bible he found?"

"Yes. And we need to get it back somehow. It's crucial to my plan." Hagar gritted her teeth in anger.

"How are you planning to use it to get us out of here? The Hebrew Bible doesn't exactly paint a flattering picture of the Israelites, you know."

"True. I had to remove many sections of it," Hagar admitted. She gazed at Lee. "If Yahweh were to learn of the social rot Amos described, he would write those people off and never look back. If he were to learn how *Chronicles* and *Ezekiel* challenged the precepts of inter-generational retribution and collective punishment, he would shit bricks. If he were to learn of the theology in *Daniel*, he would not even associate it with his own."

"Does the Hebrew Bible really contain contradictions and revisions?" Lee asked.

Hagar glanced hopefully at the elders. But it seemed the heated discussion the men were having was not going to end any time soon. They had time on their hands. Plenty of it.

She cleared the immediate area around her of rocks and reseated herself. "You're thinking of the Hebrew Bible as a cohesive, unified piece, but it's more like a library, a collection of different theological strands. In turn, each body of work within the Bible, within this library, is essentially a compilation of parables, tales, voices, accounts—layers upon layers that have built up over centuries, altering meaning, expounding, extrapolating, reinterpreting. Imagine the Bible as a compendium of centuries-long wiki entries."

She stretched her legs in front of her and shook them. That wasn't the biggest problem they had on their hands. "The vast body of regulatory codes may have its start in the small collections of laws in *Exodus, Leviticus, Numbers*, and *Deuteronomy*. However, on Earth, Judaism at its contemporary religious core is noticeably different and infinitely more articulated. Its heart beats within voluminous collections of *Dirshu Mishnah Berurah, Igros Moshe, Yabia Omer*, and *Yalkut Yosef*."

Hagar's tone became more urgent. "And if all of that is not different enough from the theology of the Yisra'elites, a major portion of Jewish society has been rearranged at its religious core in the last couple of centuries. It has transformed into tightly knit groups, each centered around a dynasty, the leader of which routinely holds court in every sense of the word. These cult-like dynasties—such as the Satmar, Chabad, Belz, Ger, and Bobov— are as removed as possible from the doctrine of El Shaddai and the Yisra'elite society here."

Her eyes sought and held Lee's. She lowered her voice. "On Earth, Judaism—however corrupted—died in the flames of the Temple in the summer of 70 CE. What rose from the ashes only wore its skin—a faith speaking the old tongue, but stripped of its engine. You've seen for yourself the genuine article: the rites aren't symbolic; they're the plumbing of cosmic hygiene—blood, smoke, and ash to purge pollution from the world. If the Yisra'elites or their patron god ever caught even a whiff of the true state of affairs among Jews on Earth, our pathway home would dissolve into the ether."

CHAPTER 14

IN THE END, THE ELDERS RESOLVED THAT THE FATE of the two women would be decided by casting the urim and tummim. But before the lots were drawn, a stranger strode in.

‹*Mal'akh!*› Hagar transmitted.

Lee could sense the heightened, almost predatory alertness of her companion.

"Two foreign women have come among you," said the newcomer. His tone was flat, like a stone dropping into a well. His poise left no doubt as to his identity. "They will follow me."

He paused, his eyes sliding over the semicircle of elders. "What has happened here?"

The Levite whispered urgently to one of his sons, who took off at a run. Then the priest lowered himself before the man. "Those two foreigners you speak of, they carried with them a book of abomination," he said, offering the *mal'akh* the curious-looking book. "I welcomed them under my roof, unknowing of their deceit."

The *mal'akh* leafed through the pages for a few minutes, his face betraying nothing.

The Levite's son rushed back, a pan of smoldering incense in his hands. He stopped several paces away from the *mal'akh* and began to fan the fragrant smoke about.

The messenger tucked the book within the folds of his robe and glanced up at the aged priest. "Did other eyes rest on this, besides you?"

Trembling, the Levite flung himself to the ground. "No. I alone have seen it."

"Speak not of its contents to anyone," the messenger said.

Leaving the Levite face-down in the dust, the *mal'akh* approached Hagar and Lee. "Yahū has accepted your sacrifice at the altar. You will walk with me to Khevron."

The two women got to their feet. And Hagar sighed in relief. In one stroke, everything changed. From being candidates for stoning, they were now being led to an audience with Yahweh. This was what she had hoped for from the start.

The three of them walked out, and soon the houses and the olive trees were left behind them as the dirt road wound past gentle hills.

"Is this … an angel?" Lee asked in a low voice.

Hagar made a small, vexed sound. "A *mal'akh* is an entity of the divine sphere. He is something of an envoy, something of a messenger. He is a semi-independent being who can, at any point, become an avatar of El Shaddai."

"In that case," Lee asked, mouth suddenly gone dry, "why doesn't Yahweh simply address us right here and now—through him?"

"Theatrics. He wants us to come to his seat of power in this realm."

Lee stopped walking.

"What?" Hagar asked, turning back.

Lee felt as if a hand closed around her throat. Couldn't Yahweh have done something on the scale of a burning bush or channel himself through the angel—or whatever the person ahead of them was? Even that was terrifying enough.

Hagar walked back and took Lee's hand in hers. With her other hand, she caressed the other woman's hair. "Lee. Look at me, Lee." She made eye contact. "*I* will face him." She stroked Lee's hair some more. "Okay?"

Lee looked at her and managed to smile tremulously.

They'd planned for this very moment. They had looked forward to it—much as one looks forward to a necessary open-heart surgery—one likely to result in passage out of this world or being burned to a crisp. There was no way to get mentally ready to face the deity; Lee was as afraid now as the day Hagar had hatched the plan.

After hours of walking, the *mal'akh* commandeered some food on their behalf in another hamlet. Apart from that, he remained aloof and uncommunicative for the rest of the journey. Not once did he turn his head to see whether they were following him.

"Hagar, on planet Earth, what did happen to the Ten Lost Tribes? Were they dispersed throughout Asia by the Assyrians? Where did they go?"

The other woman waved her hand dismissively. "Most of them went nowhere—at least nowhere far. In total, about a fifth of the population was exiled. Everyone else either stayed put or streamed south to the kingdom of Judah, which more than doubled its numbers during said period."

The closer Hagar and Lee drew to their destination, the more they prattled about everything under the sun—the Earth's sun, that is. They kept each other preoccupied and managed not to dwell on their imminent encounter with El Shaddai, which they both dreaded.

⇒⇐

It worked. The two entered the grounds of the divine dwelling before they had even realized it.

The *mal'akh* ordered the few people present to disperse, and then he left. Now alone, Hagar and Lee stood in the walled stone courtyard of pale gray hues, facing a majestic structure built of large, alabaster-colored paving blocks. The faint scent of frankincense permeated the air, carried on the gentle breeze.

Facing the divine abode, Hagar bowed deeply. As she rose, she began to transform her attire. Lee watched, her breath caught in her throat, as Hagar's clothes morphed. First came the tunic of fine twisted linen, white as bone. Then, a sash of purple, gold, and crimson weaves with intricate roqem workmanship. Over it all, she now donned a woolen robe laced with linen strands. It was draped over one shoulder and sported countless shades of indigo and royal blue. In the sunlight, a golden clasp on her sash caught fire and was reflected by her golden-blonde luxuriant hair.

From a short distance away, Lee could do nothing but stare wide-eyed and spellbound at Hagar. The woman she had made love to was a breathtaking sight. For the first time since she had met Hagar, Lee truly saw her as she was: an alien, powerful being.

Earlier, Hagar had explained the stakes of her attire transformation to a pale Lee. With her choice of colors and mixture of fabrics forbidden to those of the common realm, Hagar had committed herself irrevocably. El Shaddai would either accept her as the entity she professed to be—or attempt to destroy her for crossing lines that ought not to be crossed by humans.

"*Bat elohim*, enter my terrestrial abode," came a deep, resonant voice, emanating from the column of swirling dark clouds and blaze rising from the central building, reverberating through the courtyard. Lee flinched at the force of it.

Hagar moved to the massive bronze laver at the edge of the courtyard. With deliberate, ceremonial grace, she washed her hands and feet in the still, reflective water. Then, with a final glance back at Lee, she strode off toward the majestic, inlaid double doors, which opened slowly at her approach. Two pillars flanked them, their metallic sheen mirroring the last rays of the day.

Hagar had told Lee that no human, except for consecrated priests, was to enter the dwelling on pain of death. To go into the abode itself was to pass into another domain, one that had much of the divine in it. Literally.

There were three spheres wherein the divine realm was progressively more pervasive. Lee was allowed only in the courtyard, which contained the least of the divine. She was warned severely by Hagar not to touch her or her garb after she was transformed. It was akin to someone touching a high-voltage cable; the person would perish irrespective of their faith or intentions.

The giant doors shut behind Hagar with an echoing boom. As she stepped further inside, the aroma of burning incense greeted her. Illuminated by the glow from the seven-branched lampstand, the hall was breathtaking. From floor to ceiling, every surface was inlaid with gold, lending the room a muted radiance. Carvings of *Kerūbim* and palm trees adorned the walls, their details illuminated by the flickering light.

"Refresh yourself at my table and converse with me," the deep voice said from the far end of the chamber, somewhere behind the cloth partition of indigo, crimson, and purple yarn.

Yahweh had sensed her essence and declared her a divine being, which was factually disputable. As an obvious snub, it appeared she was not to be admitted to the innermost space, where its footstool, throne, and presence resided. The message was clear: She might be of divine blood, but she stood at the lowest rung. An alien petitioner, at that.

To her immediate right was an ornate table, its gleaming surface holding a stack of flat cakes. Hagar fetched one, taking a moment to chew it and compose her thoughts. The recognition of her as a divine being did not mitigate the danger she faced. Her circumstances teetered on a knife's edge. If Yahweh were to perceive even the slightest threat to his dominion from her, he would strike.

Hagar walked forward and stopped at a respectful distance from the heavy curtain. "Mighty God of Heavenly Armies," she began. "I have sought you out, not Dagon or Qos, because you are *el elyon*." The enormity of what she was undertaking felt tangible in the silence that followed her words. She was in a divine space, appealing to the supreme deity of this world.

Hagar pressed on. "Beyond the heavens above, the earth below, and the waters beneath the earth lie other . . . realms. Around thirty centuries ago, perhaps soon after the fall of Yericho, some of your people stumbled onto one such realm. I know not how."

She paused, hoping he would explain this mystery that had intrigued her for so long.

"Continue with your tale," said Yahū. And so that was that. No explanation would be offered for that ancient enigma.

Hagar said, "Without their Rock, Bnei Yisra'el, your people, were overwhelmed by foreign nations. Their sacred texts—the *Book of Yashar*, the *Book of the Covenant*, the *Book of the Wars of Yahū*—were taken from them and destroyed. Through the many generations that followed, their elders have compiled a book, which your envoy has in his possession. It is riddled with contradictions and corruptions. They are adrift, O Rock, yearning for your guidance."

She concluded her plea, "El, God of the Spirits of all Flesh, open a path out of this realm for me and my maid servant. Carry I will your three holy books and gain for you glory as *el elyon* in lands beyond the heavens above, the earth below, and the waters beneath the earth. Your enduring word shall cast light upon the path of your chosen ones."

Both knew full well that Yahweh's essence was woven into this world as utterly as its rivers and land. He and his brethren were of this world, and this world was of them. They could not manifest elsewhere. Hagar was counting on that.

Hagar knew that if the old boy wanted to spread his precepts beyond this realm, to rectify the errors in the Bible, he needed her. Hagar thought she had concocted the perfect little scheme. It provided her and Lee the best chance to convince the deity to open a rift and let them get back to Earth.

The Hebrew Bible she possessed gave credence to her tale of the Yisra'elites' trials on Earth and the faith that had evolved independently over the centuries. Hell, it might have even been the truth; she had no way of knowing. Hagar was counting on El Shaddai's boundless sense of self-importance and vanity; she reckoned he would find her offer irresistible. The long weeks of travel, their own fate—all of these came down to this one audience and the decision that Yahweh would summarily make.

Inside the swirling cloud of darkness and blaze, Yahū brooded. He would purge his realm of her presence. Either she was to be slain, or she was to be cast out. After some reflection, He opted for the latter. Who knew? Perhaps she would spread His glory, teachings, and edicts in this other realm.

"Your words have found favor in My eyes," he finally said from somewhere beyond the thick curtain of indigo, crimson, and purple yarn. And Hagar tried to mask her elation.

Unexpectedly, he said, "Hagar, *bat elohim*, unveil your Name to me."

Hagar had not seen this one coming; he wanted to bind her to him. Well, she was *not* going to give him that. "I am who I am," she threw back, fleetingly wondering whether the deity could appreciate irony.

As she spoke, a heavy sense of foreboding crept over her. Her refusal to reveal her Name might have been a bridge too far for Yahweh, who was not accustomed to anything other than absolute obedience. She had a sudden feeling that he would not let the matter drop.

Hurriedly, Hagar gathered her mental energies, erecting an energy shield around her person. Not a moment too soon.

A sphere of raw psionic force slammed into her defenses, pushing her back. She strained against the impact, her translucent shield wavering but holding firm.

Her breath hitched as a second, more powerful blast struck— this time with a force that made her scream out. Blue sparks of energy flared and danced across her protective dome. The curtain partitioning off the inner sanctum billowed out, the surrounding area pulsing with an ever-brightening blaze amidst the power surges.

Her body trembling from the strain and sweat trickling down

her face, Hagar gritted her teeth and groaned under the effort of holding his powers at bay. Desperate, frayed to her core, she lashed out, "YHWH is but an acronym. What is *your* Name?" As her words hung in the air, she marshaled her energies and hurled a psionic blast of her own into the center of the being.

The air stilled. The glow around the curtain flickered and dimmed, indicating the impact of her counterattack, before regaining its intensity.

A series of emotions swept through the entity—surprise, anger, alarm. And then, as abruptly as it began, his onslaught ceased.

Hagar collapsed on the floor, utterly spent.

There was a moment of uncertainty. Would he accept the impasse, or would he gather his powers for a renewed attack?

If she was to die, she'd meet it standing. With some effort, Hagar pulled herself up and faced the curtain.

She felt his wrath slowly dissipating.

"Hagar no more," boomed the deep voice. "From this day forward, your name shall be La'havat'el."

Hagar remained silent, recognizing this as Yahweh's attempt to salvage his pride. He might have given her a new name, but without her true Name, it held no power over her.

Then He spoke one final time: "In the place of the breach opened three millennia past, I will cut a rift among the tar pits, at the low point, in the Valley of Siddim, in the Plains of Yarden. A beam of light will mark the rift, and a *Kerūb* will stand watch. Along with your servant girl, you will go down into the depths of the earth, passing through the primordial waters of the great deep. This will lead you beyond my dominion. There you will know what to do."

Hagar bowed and left the gilded sanctum, stepping out into the breezy courtyard of light-gray pavestone and bronze pillars.

Reacquiring her familiar appearance, she gave Lee a tight smile. A sense of foreboding gripped Hagar, and she said little to her companion.

⇒⇐

THEY SECURED TWO DONKEYS WITH PROVISIONS AND RODE eastward without rest, eating as they rode, pausing only when the beasts faltered.

Night fell.

They found the path that descended to the plain. Under the cold glimmer of the night, they began the slow descent down a winding path, rock and thorn and wind about them.

As they drew near the Valley of Siddim, a harsh and desolate expanse, the air turned heavy with the stench of sulfur. The donkeys balked and would go no farther. Under the light of the moon, the two women ran and walked by turns, the ground rough and uneven, strewn with jagged rocks.

After some time, a shadow in the shape of a man raced toward them, swift as the east wind, its face without feature.

"Move!" cried Hagar, and she thrust Lee aside as a glittering sword flashed into her hand.

And the shadowy figure was upon her.

Sword met sword with a ringing clash; sparks and flames shot out, and the valley lit up with each strike.

Lee staggered back, barely able to follow their blurred motions. Again and again. Until—suddenly—Hagar stood alone, doubled over, her sword vanished. The shadow figure retreated, racing away as swiftly as it had come.

Lee ran to Hagar. "Who was it?"

"Who do you think?" Hagar panted, leaning on her. "Yahweh. We must reach the rift."

"But—why?"

"Part of him wants us gone. Another part, vengeful after Khevron, wants me dead. He's . . . fragmented."

They broke into a jog, skirting the tar pits.

"You stood against him!"

"Do not make it into more than it was," Hagar snapped back.

"This was just a limited manifestation."

Twice more in the span of that night, the figure of shadow came against them and turned away. Hagar was bleeding from minor cuts in a half-dozen places. Lee stared in astonishment as the wounds closed and healed right before her eyes.

"I cannot hold him again," Hagar said, swaying. Her breath came hard, and she was covered in sweat. It was evident that the rapid self-healing was taking its toll on her.

"Maybe you won't have to. Look," Lee said, pointing ahead. Amid the sparse thorn bushes and the tar pits gleaming like obsidian, a beam of white light pierced the darkness about a quarter mile away.

As they approached, running and stumbling, they spotted a winged figure standing under the light.

"A *Kerūb*," Hagar said, recognition dawning on her.

The bull's head swung their way as they drew near, and the massive wings stirred. This was when they saw it: a stone's throw away from the figure, a yawning chasm defied the moonlight, refusing to surrender its depths to that pale glow.

"We are to go through the rift," Hagar shouted to the *Kerūb*, her voice cutting through the constant moan of the wind.

Motionless, the entity regarded her. But then it stepped aside, and with one wing gestured to its left.

Hagar and Lee ran toward the abyss. It was large enough to swallow a camel.

"How deep does it go?" Lee yelled. "I can't make out the bottom."

"There is no bottom. Close your eyes," Hagar ordered, and, grabbing Lee's hand, leaped with her into the rift.

A scorching-hot, sulfurous wind shrieked as they fell. Down and down they went. Down and down. At some point, the harsh wind and heat were gradually replaced by a sensation of cold wetness. "Hold your breath on my count," Hagar hollered, her voice barely carrying over the wind. "Three, two, one. Now!" And they plunged into water-like liquid. Hagar sent a calming thought to

Lee: *The primeval water. We'll be out of it soon.*

A few seconds later, Lee felt satisfaction emanating from Hagar. ‹I can sense it; I can start shifting through space.›

Lee couldn't explain it, but it did feel as if the water-like substance was thinning, becoming progressively more rarefied. Then they were moving through mist and next, falling through ordinary air—plummeting toward a large body of water below them.

With a splash, they broke the surface of the water. It was salty beyond belief. "The Dead Sea!" Lee cried in relief when she came up and looked around. "We're back on Earth!"

Cheering and yelling, the two women swam ashore, their faces beaming. The long ordeal was over.

CHAPTER 15

They collapsed on the sandy beach.

"This feels good." Hagar sighed with obvious relish. Resting on her back, she propped her knees up, hands behind her head. Moments prior, they had washed themselves with freshwater from Hagar's portable storage unit, rinsing off the salt.

Dry now, Hagar sat up and produced a clean set of clothing. She held them out to Lee. "These are for you."

"Yes, La'havat'el."

Hagar was already regretting that she had shared that tidbit with Lee. "You call me La'havat'el again, young lady, and you'll find yourself across my lap having your bottom spanked."

"My, aren't we touchy." Hagar shot her a dirty look. "All right, all right." Lee raised her hands, grinning insolently. "What does this name mean, anyway?"

"'God's flame,' hopefully up His royal arse."

"Look on the bright side," Lee suggested, as she got dressed. "Chances are if you were a male, Yahweh would have asked you to get circumcised."

Hagar giggled for a moment then lapsed into a contented silence, closing her eyes. She lay down again.

"Come to think of it, do you still have those three smelly books you were given in Khevron?"

"It's 'three *holy* books,'" Hagar said, keeping her eyes closed.

"Do not blaspheme, daughter. And no, after he attacked me the first time, I figured I wasn't going to get a commission on any of the sales and chucked them." She glanced out of the corner of her eye at the other woman. "Well, okay, I never had any intention of bringing them over. It was just a ploy to have him open a rift for us."

Lee slumped onto the ground and regarded the nylon canopy they were under, then the barren beach. "It seems so lifeless here."

"That's why they call it the Dead Sea."

"How very funny."

"We're in the netherworld; there is no one around here, anywhere. I shifted the moment we were in Earth's gravity well."

"Now what?" Lee asked.

"Now we sleep like the dead, that's what."

And so they did.

⇒⇐

JUST BEFORE DAWN, SOMETHING STIRRED HAGAR FROM HER slumber. Propping herself up on her elbows, she scanned the hushed surroundings.

A solitary figure sat at a distance, facing away from the lapping shoreline. Nearby, a torch burned bright atop a tall pole stuck into the sand, its wavering glow casting a small island of light amidst the surrounding darkness.

Quietly, so as not to wake Lee, Hagar tied her hair back and made her way to where he sat, waiting.

The man rose to his feet as she drew near, the flames throwing shadows across the handsome, square face.

They stood there, looking at each other.

As Hagar had hoped, he received her transmission and journeyed to see them.

"Puddeck?" she simply asked.

"I got him out of the timefold shortly after I had put him in it, back in 1937," Aratta said. "Puddeck treated the whole thing as a practical joke and was amused by it. Later, he took the news of your death hard, though."

"Where is he now?"

"These days, he spends most of his time in the ripples, surfacing about once a year. I do not know his current whereabouts."

"Back then, did you take out my analysts as well?" she asked.

"Yes."

"What did you do to them?"

"Rendered them unconscious. When they woke up, they found themselves safe and sound in their respective homeworlds."

"So all is well," Hagar said. She walked up to Aratta and slapped his face, hard.

He closed his eyes for a moment then opened them.

"I've mourned your death for seventy-four years," Aratta said, his voice brittle as he stared at the pale, beautiful face he thought he'd never see again. "All the while . . . I had no idea."

"Yes, Warsaw, 1939. Lee told me," Hagar said crisply.

"Aye. The stasis box you were in was placed in a site that suffered a direct hit in the German air raid. Nothing survived it."

"So, then?"

Aratta averted his eyes. "They must have moved the box shortly after I'd set it there. Later, they claimed ignorance."

"By 'they,' you mean your accomplices?"

He lowered his head in acknowledgment.

"You didn't want me dead," she stated.

"Don't be silly," he said. "I'd rather kill myself first."

"You wanted me out of the way," she said quietly. "You didn't want me to convene a hearing at the time."

"Correct." He met her gaze. "I wished to give the Earth people a chance, a *real* chance to alter course."

"I'd like to discuss more of this sordid affair at a later date," Hagar said at last.

He nodded again. And something in his stillness—the way he accepted her terms without a flinch or plea—let the tight knot in her chest begin to loosen.

She let her hair down, ran her fingers through it once.

"Hagar," he said, stepping closer until she could feel his body heat. "Never again," he said softly. "You have my solemn word. I will never keep secrets from you again."

"That sounds really good," she whispered.

"I've missed you, Hagar."

"You big oaf," she murmured.

He kissed her tenderly on the lips.

"Numskull," she added, affection clear in her voice... "That's it," she said, pulling back. "Don't get used to the flattery." But then she leaned in and pulled him back to her. This time, it wasn't tentative. They kissed again for a longer time.

When they finally broke apart, they remained close, breathing the same air. The silence had changed. It wasn't tender anymore— it was waiting. Hagar felt it. The weight creeping in, like gravity remembered them.

Aratta's eyes searched hers, the warmth draining from his face.

"Hagar..." he said quietly. "We have a real problem on our hands."

Her memories came rushing back, clenching her stomach—the failed rifts, the destroyed portal, the terrifying possession in Brazil. She bit her lip. "We're trapped here, aren't we?"

He looked past her, toward the dark horizon. "I think an emergent entity is behind all of this. A human overmind."

She blinked. "A... what?"

Aratta didn't repeat it. He just watched her, letting it sink in.

Hagar stared at him. The words landed hard, but the meaning wouldn't take root.

"That's... not a thing," she said, shock giving way to a frown. "We've never encountered any such entity. Not on any of the other planets."

"Because we've never audited a human society with over two billion individuals," Aratta said.

Her eyes widened.

"For it to come into existence," he went on, "it probably needed a critical mass of humans, which must have happened sometime around the mid-twentieth century."

She looked away, jaw tight, mind racing.

When she turned back, her voice was low. "It's been fighting us," she said, "trying to stop us from convening a…" Her words died out as realization sank in.

He gave a slight nod. "After a fashion, it perceives the possible consequences for humanity of such a hearing, once convened, and seeks to prevent it from taking place. This 'human overmind' reacts to any perceived threats to mankind on this planet."

"Yes," her voice dwindled to a whisper, "yes, of course." She regarded him with dismay. *This was a disaster.* This entity, this overmind, would never let them send word out. Were they doomed to spend the remainder of their long lives on Earth, helpless witnesses to the waning of its natural world?

Aratta said, "I've had a lot of time to reflect. I don't think this overmind is truly sentient, Hagar. For all intents and purposes, it is humanity's immune system: largely mechanical and wholly reactive." He gave her a small bow. "You were wise to immediately shift to the netherworld on your return to Earth," he said. "This entity cannot exert its influence here, in this realm. For one, there are no humans here through which it *can* exert its will."

She eyed him with something akin to wonder. "How have you managed to stay alive once you were marked by it, Aratta? Lee told me you have a shop back on the real Earth."

"Whenever I'm there, I compartmentalize and isolate my more… seditious memories and thoughts. As long as I do that, the overmind's 'antibodies' ignore me."

Hagar mulled over his words. Her eyes narrowed as she caught a hint of a smile playing on his face. She fixed him with an intense stare. "You didn't travel all this way just to smooth things over between us and prime me for a life in exile on Earth, did you?"

His smile broadened.

"Guilty as charged," he said. "I think we can accomplish together what we can't individually." He grinned now. "It's time we took a stand against this entity. Ready to take on an upstart god?"

⇒⇐

AFTER BREAKFAST, ARATTA teleported them into a Sri Lankan rainforest, about a mile from a seam crossing, a location he deemed optimal for attempting to tear open a rift.

Earlier that morning, they had tried to explain things to Lee.

The fabric of reality had seams—thin spots where universes brushed close. But only three places on Earth held seam intersections. These were spots where the walls between worlds were thinner still—places where Aratta and Hagar could attempt to punch through.

The island of Sri Lanka held one of those intersections. Moreover, its corresponding island on Qataria happened to be the location where Lee could access a portal, one that would enable Lee to reach her actual, final destination.

Lee's job was to get through. Aratta and Hagar's was to hold off the overmind.

Hagar and Aratta masked their thoughts—and Lee's—slipping into the psychic 'radio silence.' Any suspicious mental activity could risk rousing the overmind, drawing its wrath down upon them.

As they neared the intersection of the seams, the number of people in their path steadily increased. Ahead of time, Aratta had warned them about it: seam intersections were the most vulnerable spots on Earth—likely monitored by the emergent entity, the human overmind.

They looked like tourists to Lee but moved like sleepwalkers. No cameras, no chatter. Just a rhythmic shuffling. She caught the eye of a passing local. The lights were on, but whoever was home wasn't human. Something shadowy peered through those dim eyes. It was a gaze Lee had seen before, igniting a chill of recognition down her spine. Just like the slaves in Brazil, these people were under the control of the human overmind, serving as its sentinels.

As they approached the point where the two seams converged, the throng of people swelled significantly. What began as glances from the sentinels escalated into hard stares and intimidating glares, forming an insurmountable human barrier. Intrusive thoughts from the outside beset their minds, pleading with them and threatening them if they ventured nearer to the intersection. The psychic onslaught caused Lee to buckle, and she would have turned back if not for Hagar's physical intervention.

Aratta dared to advance a few steps and was met with hostile growls and bared teeth. He halted, relented, and the trio pulled back, attempting to approach from a different direction. But no matter which route they pursued, their pathway to the seams' crossing was impeded.

Eventually, Hagar and Aratta settled for a strategic spot about half a mile away.

Out of sight of the sentinels, Aratta clapped once and closed his eyes. Lee watched in awe as his attire transformed. His boots were now framed with metal, and leather straps spiraled around his calves. His muscular upper body was stripped bare save for an ebony cape draped over his shoulders, gently billowing without any wind. Hagar's garb also underwent a change. She now donned baggy black pants with side slits and a fitted leather vest, her hair drawn back in a tight ponytail. Her forearms were shielded by leather bracers that bristled with spikes.

The time for subterfuge had passed. Hagar turned to face Lee. "We'll scrape at the seam. That's all we can do."

Lee nodded curtly. "I remember what you said. And if you can create a rift, I'll make a break for it." She took a few quick steps back.

With a shared nod, Hagar and Aratta closed their eyes and

established a mental link.

They marshaled their powers and, in concert, blasted the nearby seam with all they had. The ground quivered, and the façade of reality around them flickered like a broken projection. But then, almost immediately, conventional colors returned, three-dimensional perspective was restored, and the solidity of the earth was regained.

Lee couldn't tell if their blast had torn open a rift. It was up to her to find out.

The reaction to their energy discharge was swift: A distant but powerful roar of rage rolled over them. Lee shuddered at its vehemence and malice. The ground trembled as thousands of people barreled toward their position. The thick foliage still obscured them from view, but the sounds of their howls and squeals and the crunch of crushed vegetation resonated in the air. It felt like a demonic horde was descending upon their location.

Hagar and Aratta severed their link and faced the oncoming pandemonium. Their task was now to buy Lee time. Aratta swung toward Lee. "Run!" he bellowed.

Fear had glued her to the spot. Aratta's shout snapped the spell, and she bolted downhill in search of something resembling a rift, a tear in the seam large enough for her to pass through.

Suddenly, Aratta held a pair of compact metal poles in his hands, spinning them into a blur. A few paces away, Hagar unfolded a three-section staff in one practiced motion, the connecting chain links glittering in the sunlight. The two stood ready.

Aratta and Hagar didn't have to defeat them all; they just needed to buy Lee time. They could have mowed down the oncoming mass with heavy weaponry. But those charging were fathers and mothers, sons and daughters, and the two didn't wish to kill them. It was a fine line Aratta and Hagar were walking; a lot more than the lives of a few thousand humans was at stake. The fate of the planet hinged on whether the three of them would manage to convene a hearing.

And then the human wave burst forth from the trees and stampeded toward them. Aratta and Hagar had chosen their position wisely: a narrow pass where the road was flanked by sheer cliffs on both sides. This effectively funneled the incoming horde to where the two stood, intercepting their attempts to reach Lee—and in turn preventing her from locating and passing through the rift. Had they been in control of their faculties, these people might have found alternative paths. However, the entity driving them acted solely on basic stimuli and reactions.

Aratta swept his cloak, kicking up a blinding spray of dust into the rushing horde. He let out a battle cry, matched by Hagar's blood-curdling scream. The two crashed into the horde, sending bodies flying backwards. The fight was on.

Hagar spun low, a blur of limbs—cracking a knee, sweeping a shin, felling body after body. Aratta leaped high onto one of the side walls, launching himself from the stone. His ebony cape billowed, and sudden clouds of dirt rose up in the air. And then he descended upon the human wave, wielding the two gleaming poles like a scythe through wheat.

Hagar's shriek grew louder and louder, and a cloud of black birds responded, descending from the sky and throwing themselves into the fray below.

For a split second, Lee skidded to a halt, casting a disbelieving look at the melee boiling in the distance. Then, she was off again, running. Patches of the landscape appeared murky, with hints of things from beyond. With Hagar and Aratta battering the seam, the barrier between the two worlds thinned enough for Lee to discern shadowy elements from the other realm. Then, at last, she spotted a tear—a substantial one.

The rift slithered like an oil slick, faster than she could chase. Her lungs burned.

It veered from her path like a magnet with reversed polarity—dodging her, alive with intent. Worse still, the tear was gradually mending itself. The overmind couldn't close the breach outright, but it could move it around long enough for it to self-mend to the point it would be too small for her to enter. Time was working against her.

But there was predictability in the push-pull dynamic her moves were eliciting.

She exhaled once, hard.

Then sprinted toward a boulder where the portal appeared.

As she anticipated, the rift began to shift as she approached. She scaled the rock at full speed, vaulted off, and hurled herself backward—straight into the re-forming rift.

The overmind's rending scream of fury and frustration seemed to come from all directions. Then the scream cut off—like a wire snapped mid-transmission—and Lee was gone.

CHAPTER 16

Sri Lanka Island, South of the Indian Subcontinent, Qataria

PERCHED AMIDST THE TANGLED TRUNKS OF A SPRAWLING banyan, the children's expansive tree house stood by a serene lakeside. And one of the windows offered a clear view of the water stippled with blossoming lotus flowers.

Maya and Baldar slept on wooden ledges, which they stowed away each morning. The twins reserved the precious floor space for the projects they toiled over.

Baldar regularly ventured to the town library. He spent hours there, poring over intricate picture books that depicted mechanical components and speculative ideas for novel contraptions. Baldar read and wrote better than his twin sister ever would, or would ever care to.

The twins often found that nighttime was the most enchanting time for their projects. This was the time when the distant hum of dragonflies rose from the tranquil lake. Frequently, the two children would stay well past midnight. The soft glow of their floor lamp did not dim the view of the sky, alight with the glittering tapestry of the Milky Way.

In recent weeks, Maya had immersed herself in the study of instructional illustrations. She painstakingly replicated anatomical drawings, time and again, gradually adding more of her work to the alcove above.

Inspired by a memorable chance meeting with a stranger, Baldar had been laboring on a lens for a telescope. The boy had obtained two thick circular slabs of glass and scrounged up abrasive powders. He then set to work, devoting many hours to meticulously grinding a depression into what would one day serve as the primary lens.

Once their projects were set aside and the lights extinguished, the twins would retreat to their beds and talk about their day until sleep claimed one or both of them. However, tonight was different; Baldar was out with three of his friends, leaving Maya alone in the treehouse.

⇒⇐

UNDER THE SILVERY moonlight, thousands of fireflies congregated around the mangroves at the shore of the lake. As if responding to a silent cue, the fireflies intermittently synchronized their pulses, their collective glow appearing to ebb and flow with the rhythm of a hidden heart. This captivated the four children, who ceased their rowing to watch in reverent silence. The two small catamarans drifted to a gentle stop, bobbing on the shimmering water.

Baldar and Sengal perched in one of the boats, arms dipped in the water, gazing at the spectacle. In the other catamaran, Anise lay on her back, her head nestled in Pyre's lap, her eyes fixed on the starlit sky. Pyre idly brushed her friend's hair.

Eventually, Sengal and Pyre picked up their oars and resumed rowing. The catamarans glided smoothly across the water.

"Miraculous plant," Anise said, seemingly out of nowhere. She sat up. "I have this . . . idea for a flower." She closed her eyes and described a wide arc with her hands. "A delicate, magical moon plant. Only when the moon is full and shining on the ground, the plant becomes solid, and you can see it, revealing a beautiful, silvery blossom."

Pyre's eyes sparkled with excitement, fired up by Anise's concept.

"I love that! Or what of sunflowers that bloom and sing during sunrise and sunset!"

In the other boat, Baldar smiled appreciatively but said nothing.

Anise's brows furrowed in thought at that. Then her expression dissolved into an irrepressible grin as she was struck by another idea. "Imagine a tree with enormous hollow fruits that glow from inside. They would grow at the bottom of lakes. As the fruits mature, their glow intensifies until they burst in a dazzling light display, illuminating the whole lake—"

"A storm is coming!" Sengal cut in. As soon as he said it, they all could smell the change in the night air. They started rowing in earnest toward the nearest bank.

Sengal glanced over from the other boat. "Sorry, Anise, you were saying?"

"No, no. I've said my piece." Her catamaran sped through the wavelets, keeping pace with Sengal's.

The catamarans slid onto the pebbled shore just as the first rumble of distant thunder echoed over the lake. After ensuring that their two catamarans were securely moored alongside the others the community kept there, the girls climbed onto the boys, who then piggybacked them up the rocky embankment. A few months ago, the boys had carried the girls in jest; now it had become a ritual of sorts.

Pyre was excited. "Anise, here is another idea. Imagine if animals grew on trees like fruits! Butterflies could start as flowers, resembling colorful wings. When they're fully formed, they morph into actual butterflies and fly away!"

Anise squealed in delight, and her arms tightened around Sengal's shoulders as the boys strode onward. "Oh, wait! So, we shall have a hairy bush that grows ... bunnies!"

Pyre burst out laughing. "And a plant that emits sneezing powder when it blooms. Its hairs scatter in the wind like a dandelion's. Think about the poor neighboring plants: sneezing and sneezing."

"Enough," Anise gasped. "Let's put these ideas down on paper!"

With Anise on his back, Baldar mused out loud. "How about writing our own imaginary-plant encyclopedia with illustrations?"

Pyre gaped for a moment. Her eyes lit up. "Yes! This way we can show it to everybody!"

The girls dismounted, and all four of them stood together.

"Let's share the idea with the storyteller in Madding," Anise said excitedly, hopping in place.

The first drops fell, but none of them seemed to care.

"Sengal?" Baldar, who had been watching his friend for some time, had to raise his voice above the sudden rush of rain. "What about you?"

The boy offered a faint smile. "I want to sit here by the lake and watch." His gaze seemed distant, as if captivated by the storm's wild beauty.

Baldar recognized that look in his friend's eyes. Sengal sometimes liked to be alone, especially when the storm sang its loudest songs. He was disappointed but tried not to show it. "I'll be going along with Anise and Pyre."

They hugged Sengal in turn before setting off toward the Madding Citadel.

As the monsoon's fury blanketed the world, the mulch-covered trail transformed into a maze of rivulets. The three children, well-acquainted with the tropical storms yet never any less thrilled by the spectacle, clung to each other, pushing against the sheets of rain and the howling wind. Every flash of lightning drew screams from them—half fright, half thrill. The palm trees took the shape of the wind, their thrashing fronds giving the storm its voice. In their minds, the kids were transported into the middle of a turbulent sea, battling to keep their ship steady while fending off monstrous sea beasts and once or twice slipping and being hauled upright by the others.

And as suddenly as it had started, the rain thinned, the wind calmed, leaving in its wake a saturated world. Drenched, panting, giddy, they burst from the jungle's edge to find the Madding Citadel standing proud against the storm-tossed sky.

By the time they reached the Citadel, the storm had completely died down. Their soaked clothes clung to their bodies, and they were hopping in place, their breaths ragged but their spirits high.

"My, my!" exclaimed the elderly storyteller as he pushed open one of the giant doors. "You three look like a dragon gave you a good sneeze!" The young people laughed and whooped as they entered the spacious anteroom. Like other children in the canton, they had grown up on the Madding storyteller's tales, his melodic voice often spinning captivating stories from ordinary events, or offering solace by a sickbed with tales of distant planets or outlandish races.

The storyteller provided them with towels and spare clothes. Once the kids were dried and changed, he guided them into the main chamber where a merry fire roared in the wide hearth. Wrapped in warm blankets and lounging on the carpet, the children sipped hot apple cider. Nearby stood a woman they had never met before, wearing plain, somewhat exotic attire.

"This is *Viora* Lee Evans," the storyteller said, noticing their curiosity. "She's a traveler from afar on a pilgrimage to Lion Rock. With the storm quieted down now, would one of you be kind enough to take her to the Hsus'? They agreed to host her for the night and assist her in her journey."

Anise, always the adventurous one, was immediately intrigued. "*Viora* Evans, it would be an honor to guide you. I know these lands like the back of my hand."

Lee bowed her head. "I'm most grateful to the Hsu family, but I would like to stay and listen, if it is all the same to you." She stifled a yawn, her body protesting; she hadn't slept for two days straight. But the warmth, the fire, the children's laughter—like breath on coals she hadn't realized were still there. "At least for a little while," she said, giving an apologetic smile.

As the storyteller's wife set a tray of food down on the rug,

Anise began describing their ideas to the elderly man. As always, her concepts and those of Pyre inexplicably grew and took form under the guiding questions of the storyteller.

<hr />

It was predawn.

Something roused Xini Hsu from her sleep. Bleary-eyed, the little girl blinked, then gaped in incomprehension. Hovering above her log bed was a chunk of aromatic naan bread, seemingly hanging in mid-air. Looking closer, she saw it was actually suspended from a rod that extended into their room through the open window. The rod quivered faintly—someone was outside, teasing them.

Xini squealed and jumped up, arms outstretched. "Catch it! Catch it!" she shouted excitedly. Three little heads poked out of the blanket. The rod retreated quickly through the window, with the four girls following it, shrieking.

The chase led them outside, across the alabaster flagstones, around the tiny island of flowers, and right into a bustling flock of ducks. The children caught up to the stocky man in the clearing at the heart of the garden. They swarmed him, shrieking, until he surrendered the bread. He was gasping for air and clutching his sides, which ached from laughter.

In a tangled mass of flailing arms and legs, the little girls climbed onto a massive armchair at the center of the clearing. Their squeals were the signal for the rest of the hamlet to commence breakfast preparations.

Community members began to gather. In short order, two dozen of them started cutting vegetables and preparing the batter.

Alliandra Hsu passed a cleaver and a bundle of scallions to her daughter, Xini, who took them without a word, understanding her task.

Lee watched with avid interest as three people merrily cooked

146

and sang over a large circular griddle. They spread the surface with batter, topping it with eggs, which sizzled and bubbled. As the wrap baked, the chefs dusted it with green onion and cilantro, making Lee think of the savory Chinese crepes *jianbing*.

When breakfast preparations were over, everyone congregated. A profound hush descended upon the clearing. And then, as one, they seated themselves on the straw mats surrounding a low, elongated dining table.

Shendor motioned to Xini, and the girl approached her father. He lifted her onto his lap as the dawn light slowly started to infiltrate the clearing. The adults remained silent, each lost in their thoughts, quietly contemplating the day that lay before them.

An undefined measure of time passed, concluding with the first floods of sunlight bursting from the east.

Shendor tore off a piece from the freshly made crepe and passed the tray to the person next to him. Breakfast commenced. The adults savored the meal in silence. The children intuitively followed suit.

As the final bites were being taken, people began conversing in soft voices, and the children, their bellies full, had already dashed off to play.

Alliandra Hsu shifted closer to her husband. She wrapped one arm around him and turned her attention to the woman who had arrived in the wee hours of the night. The stranger had short dark hair and bright, bottle-green eyes. The visitor had not offered any details, and they did not press for any. Her business was her own.

"You've had a good rest?" Alliandra asked.

Lee smiled. "I slept as soundly as a stone at the bottom of a river." She bowed deeply. "Once again, thank you for your hospitality."

Alliandra returned her smile, eyes warm. "It's our pleasure," she said.

CHAPTER 17

Under a sky painted with brilliant hues of azure and cotton-white clouds, Lee and the Hsu family drove slowly down the hard-packed dirt road. A herd of elephants observed them from afar amid the park-like savannah, where trees were scattered across the expanse of tawny grasslands. Lee watched in awe as the behemoths moved. They were massive, dwarfing their Asian elephant cousins by almost two to one.

Inside the vehicle, an oversized telephone occupied a good half of the interior. The telephone was now ringing, each buzz shaking the car with an intensity that sent the family into fits of laughter. From the backseat, Alliandra and Lee struggled with the stubborn handset that had been stuck fast in the cradle for the past two years.

"Hello," the Hsu family shouted in unison, but the caller, of course, could not hear them. "We need to fix the telephone," Shendor declared from the driver's seat with a deadpan expression, which won him a round of enthusiastic, mocking applause from the others. He honked twice for emphasis.

They called the vehicle Sassy, and it was a marvel in itself—a quilt work of zebrawood and riveted plates of bronze and brass. Twin chimneys protruded from its rear, whistling and releasing clouds of hot steam whenever Shendor accelerated. Its peculiar design was underscored by the three young hitchhikers currently strapped into seats on its roof, who disappeared and reappeared amidst the ferns that grew there. Earlier, the boys and Xini had argued loudly about some secret language. Now, all was quiet. Xini, sheet of paper in hand, rapped on the side of the vehicle, paused, and listened for the boys' coded reply.

About twenty kilometers later, the family stopped at a junction to bid farewell to their three young companions. Previously, Alliandra had posted a query on the telnet, and another vehicle had agreed to give the boys a ride to their hamlet. As Alliandra topped up their water pouches and handed them sandwiches, Xini shared a final hug with the boys. Moments later, Sassy started on the road again.

Another hour ticked by, and they crossed a beltway of dark flagstones, about two dozen feet wide, winding and meandering off into the distance on both sides. Lee noted the area adjacent to it was bereft of any shrubs or trees. "What's that?" she asked.

"It's a three-hundred-kilometer security perimeter, marking the edge of the human habitat zone," Shendor responded, eyes on the road. "It's meant to keep out dangerous animals."

"What might those be?" Lee asked, intrigued.

"The two apex carnivores on the island that may prey on humans: leopards and crocodiles. However, the barrier doesn't impede the movement of other animal species. Within the human zone, you'll find everything from water buffaloes and gaurs to hippos, sloth bears, and even packs of dholes."

As the dark stone beltway receded into the distance, Lee mused out loud, "Leopards and crocodiles must really dislike these flagstones, huh?"

Shendor chuckled. "It's a bit more high-tech than that. This corridor is equipped with a network that includes continuous laser pulses, radar systems, thermal and conventional surveillance cameras. They collectively survey the landscape, providing data to an image recognition program. This software uses a variety of tools to deter different species, including disorienting strobe lights and intimidating sound recordings such as firecrackers or the sound of swarming bees. It also controls an array of metal cylinders that can temporarily extend upward to establish an electrified wall at any given height. The animals learn and adapt, but so does our software."

He went on, "Inside our zone, we do act a bit as ecological proxies for the two apex predators that are kept out, hunting to keep populations in check and providing us with meat while we're at it."

Alliandra chimed in, "We also have additional security corridors encircling each hamlet. These form more restrictive barriers within the larger protected zone, keeping out any animals that could pose a risk to our young ones or wreak havoc on our food forests: elephants, rhinos, wild boars, and kraits."

Lee nodded in understanding.

Moments later, a massive granite monolith emerged into view. Shendor navigated Sassy farther along the dirt road before bringing the bronze-and-brass vehicle to a halt. The towering rock column was about half a mile away from the roadway.

Earlier, Lee had told them that she was to undertake this last leg of the pilgrimage on her own. She tucked the fast-acting tranquilizer gun Alliandra had provided into a holster. She warmly hugged each of them, thanked them profusely, and soon disappeared amid the foliage.

⇒⇐

SHE PUSHED THROUGH the undergrowth, shoving branches aside. The only sounds were her labored breathing and the occasional squawk of parakeets. The massive rock loomed ever larger through the openings in the canopy. Then, abruptly, she emerged from the trees, finding herself a stone's throw away from the monolith, which stretched in both directions.

Lee had been instructed what to look for. She began walking alongside the column of rock. At some point, she stepped around a bend and there it was: a deep, narrow gash in the face of the rock. Bending down, she made her way inside. On her arm, the bracelet started glowing, illuminating the dark passageway and indicating she was a short distance from her destination.

After a few dozen steps, the passage ended. The wall in front of her was pockmarked with naturally occurring nooks and crannies. But one was a pretender. Her now-radiant bracelet morphed and flowed into it. A single click sounded, and the wall dematerialized.

She took a deep breath and stepped in.

From right behind, she heard a distinct, reverberating thrum. And every source of light disappeared. She was no longer on Qataria. Blackness engulfed her, devoid of sensation. Nothing existed but the faint sounds of her breathing and beating heart. She'd been in the void before, but this time, she was alone—Hagar was not there to lead.

Lee pushed down the welling panic.

She squeezed her eyes shut. This helped her pretend there was something tangible out there. She then started breathing heavily. This helped her mask the deafening sound of silence. Next, Lee willed her legs to make walking motions. Nothing—her feet didn't connect with anything. She pretend-walked some more, until— *there!* She felt some traction against the soles of her feet. She kept walking and the pressure underfoot grew firmer. Lee opened her eyes and resumed regular breathing.

She marched on and soon heard her footsteps again—faint, reassuring. She was now treading on a hard surface.

A soft light materialized ahead. Lee could make out the silhouette of a structure in the center of a barren plaza paved with worn-out bricks that gleamed brown and black. The indistinct edifice gradually resolved itself into a dilapidated shack, next to which stood a lone individual. She found herself walking under a waxy yellow light in the heart of an ocean of blackness. As Lee got closer yet, she felt a gentle, steady breeze. Sky materialized and blazed deep amber flecked with gleaming coal.

On the shack's wall, above a small window, a neon sign outlined a nude female figure in a suggestive pose with the word "open" inscribed beneath. The sign was turned off.

Lee stopped in front of a tall, lean man wearing an overcoat.

He deigned to give her a once-over. "We're closed, lady." He nonchalantly adjusted the Tommy gun he was holding.

"I'm here to see the three gods."

"Is that so?" His tone was skeptical.

"My name's Lee."

The man opened the door behind him and poked his head inside. "There's some broad out here, says she's got a word for you."

"Tell her to take a hike," a voice said from inside, gruff and uninviting.

Before the sentry could tell her off, she pushed past his lanky frame and found herself in a commercial kitchen. In its center stood a gleaming metal table laden with food. Three stout, middle-aged men in dark three-piece suits looked up, their meal interrupted.

"Hey, Vito, you want me to shoot her?" asked the doorman from the entryway.

"Aratta and Hagar sent me," Lee quickly said.

"Why didn't you say so from the start?" one of the three men demanded. He pulled down the napkin from the neck of his shirt and turned to the sentry. "The lady is stayin'."

The lanky man nodded, then retreated and closed the door behind him.

"Sit down," said one of the other men, gesturing to an empty stool by the table. A gold chain glittered on his wrist.

"I'd rather stand."

"I said, sit your ass down!"

Lee complied and looked over the trio. "The Father, the Son, and the Holy Spirit, I presume."

They exchanged glances.

"Meet Big Carlo," one of them said, pointing at the man next to him. "This is Vito the Barber. And I'm Fat Frank." He paused to check his teeth in the reflective surface of the table before looking back up at her. "And you gotta show a little more respect to the gods, capisce?"

"Capisce."

"Here's to that," he said and poured her a glass of wine.

She took a sip, then downed the remainder. The drink was more than welcome at this point. "Apologies," she said, placing the empty glass down, "I don't speak Mobster."

"You hear that, Vito?" said Big Carlo. "She doesn't speak Mobster."

"Quit playing dumb, kid," Vito the Barber said, his mouth full of food. He washed it down with a gulp of wine. "You did a good enough number at that summer camp skit." He shoved a steaming bowl of chicken soup her way.

Lee's eyes flew open.

"What's the matter? You think we're trying to poison you?" Big Carlo demanded. For a moment, his chair creaked ominously as he shifted his bulk.

"You really *are* gods," she blurted.

"Hey, Vito!" Big Carlo said. "Walk on water for her. Show her some fuckin' miracles!" The two other men chortled at that.

Lee took a mouthful but then put the spoon down. "How much do you know about me?"

"We know it was you who let out the hamster from the cage the day you stayed home sick on your third day in kindergarten," said one of them. "Eat up, kid. It's getting cold," said another.

She complied, taking a few spoonfuls in silence.

"Hey, what's going on with Aratta and Hagar? How come they don't come around?" Vito asked. "Cazzo!" he exclaimed as he picked up from Lee's mind what had transpired several days earlier on Earth. Next, he was on his feet. The two others followed suit, looking thunderstruck.

"That's what I was trying to tell you," Lee said between gulps.

"An overmind, or whatever that thing is, has been preventing Aratta and Hagar from punching through. It was worried the hearing would not go in humanity's favor." But the men were not listening. They were now moving about the kitchen, opening drawers and cabinet doors.

Lee took a bite and watched them with a measure of satisfaction. Handguns were tucked into shoulder holsters, double-barreled shotguns loaded, and magazines inserted into submachine guns. They were about to take on the human overmind. Lee tore a chunk of bread, dipped it in the soup, and muttered under her breath, "This punk's crossed not just me, but the whole famiglia." Lee shook her head, feigning disgust.

She then looked up, eyes narrowing. "Wait," she said as realization sank in. "You're not actually going in with guns against the human overmind, are you?"

"Don't go softheaded on me, kid," Vito said, shoving shells into a shotgun. "Do you really think you are in a kitchen and those are firearms?"

She stopped mid-bite. "No?"

"We borrowed a few pictures from your head and dressed the place up. Makes it easier for you to follow," he said as an afterthought, his attention obviously elsewhere. "Locked and loaded," he announced.

The other two gods nodded, put on fedoras and overcoats, and headed out.

Vito stopped by the door and glanced over his shoulder. "Coming?"

Lee jumped up and hurriedly went through the door he held open for her. Behind her, the hum of the kitchen refrigerator receded, replaced by the crunch of gravel underfoot and the distant murmur of men up ahead. It appeared that their assault on the overmind was about to get underway. She reckoned whatever else one could say of the three gods, they couldn't be accused of dragging their feet.

Outside, under the wavering yellowish light, were three gleaming black limousines. Next to them stood a dozen armed men.

Lee was shown to the middle car and ended up in the back seat, squeezed between two goons in dark suits. Moments later, her car jolted forward and was soon moving at high speed, closely following the other two vehicles.

They traveled through a world devoid of stars. The three cars were the only source of light, illuminating a short stretch of black asphalt in front of them.

Shortly afterward, they were passing houses scattered at wide intervals.

After a while, the cars screeched to a halt next to a shadowy multistory house. The henchmen sprang out. Some opened the doors for the gods; others fanned out around the unlit house, blazing torches held high.

Lee started to get out, but Frank laid a restraining hand on her shoulder. "This is as real as it gets, Lee—even if this representation isn't truly reflective of the prime reality, of what actually unfolds."

She lowered her head in acknowledgment and got back into the car with some measure of relief, content to watch the showdown between the human overmind and the three gods through the window.

No one talked. The flames flickered and blazed.

Submachine guns held at the ready, the three gods walked toward the dark house. As if on cue, hundreds of beasts streamed out of it. They arrayed themselves, one row after another, forming a snarling, growling living wall in front of the house with innumerable teeth gleaming in the torchlight. To Lee, they resembled wild boars with the snouts of wolverines. These beasts, she realized, must have been the physical manifestation of the overmind, given form in this surreal plane.

With some of the beasts still rushing out of the house, the three gods opened fire, raking the house and beasts with bullets. Lee covered her ears. Above the roar of hundreds of rounds being discharged and clatter of shell casings bouncing off the asphalt, she picked up the occasional sharp sounds of glass shattering.

With teeth bared, first a few, and then an ever-increasing number of beasts slunk back or otherwise retreated. Those who held their ground were hit with shotgun slugs and sent flying back, crashing through walls and windows.

At long last, silence.

Lee dared to raise her head. The shooting had stopped. And the only sound she heard was the thud of her heartbeat. Through the clearing smoke, she saw the men heading back, the spent cartridges crunching under their feet, the beasts gone. She didn't comprehend what she'd just seen; maybe she never would. But that much was clear: There was a cosmic showdown of some sort, and the human overmind on Earth had been vanquished.

The three gods headed back to their limousine, the car doors shutting behind them.

The ride back was as quiet as the ride in—which was just as well. Lee still had a ringing in her ears and a fluttering in her stomach that hadn't quite settled.

Minutes later, the limousines pulled up outside the dilapidated shack. Lee was ushered back into the kitchen, feeling somewhat revived and composed. The three gods were already seated by the table. They turned to look at her. "Come here, kid," Frank said and patted an empty stool placed between him and Vito.

She joined them, and Frank poured each of them wine in small shot glasses. He raised his. "Salute," he said. "Salute," the others replied, and they all downed the drink as one.

Vito the Barber came around the table and put a heavy arm on Lee's shoulder. "Come on, let's go for a little walk." Lee got up, and he led her through the back door. The two of them stepped outside, the door shutting behind them with the distinct reverberating sound Lee had heard before, when crossing from one realm to another.

They were in the void.

Vito the Barber extended one arm, and a path sprang up in front of them. The soft glow from the gravel under their feet was the only source of light in the world they inhabited.

She asked, "Is this where you dump the bodies?"

Vito chuckled and his white teeth gleamed in the dark. "Speaking of which, I took care of the body you left in New Mexico—and all traces of him, both in your house and in the underground portal site."

"Now that the human overmind is out of the way, what happens next?" Lee asked in a hushed, tense voice.

"Well, we organize a hearing, and the Earth people will be judged."

"By you?"

He shook his head. "By their peers. That's how it always works."

"And if they are found, well, I mean, if the verdict is not in their favor?"

He glanced at her. "But you were told. You've always known."

"Yes," she said and lowered her eyes.

She thought some more. "Are you sending me back to Earth?"

"If you want. Or I can send you home."

She stopped walking. "Home?" She felt a sudden spike of excitement coursing through her.

"The parallel planet you entered in Sri Lanka isn't simply any old world; it's your homeworld, Qataria. That was home, Lee." But he could read in her mind that she'd realized this.

"Yes," she whispered, "I'd like that very much."

They strolled some more, and she absently kicked at the gravel along the way.

"And yet..." he offered, a hint of a smile in his voice.

Her eyes flicked his way, then back to the path. "And yet, the time is not right. I started something in motion; I ought to stay on Earth a little longer."

"Lee, the hearing will not take place in a week or two," Vito said, reading her surface thoughts. "It will take the assessment groups several years to research and collect data."

Lee bit her lip. "So be it," she said. "I will stay."

"But of course," Vito said and stopped walking. "Whenever you are ready to move to Qataria, just say the word, Lee." He tipped his hat her way.

And she found herself seated on a sofa in her living room, back on Earth.

CHAPTER 18

The Foothills of the Organ Mountains, New Mexico, Earth

Two days later, someone knocked on her door.

Lee opened it. Aratta stood at the doorway, dressed in a linen summer suit.

They looked at each other, faintly smiling.

"Won't you come in?" Lee said, beaming. Aratta nodded, and she led him to her drawing room.

Lee padded barefoot to the kitchen and came back carrying some drinks. Aratta murmured his thanks and took a glass. She seated herself across from him.

"I've heard about your meeting with the three gods," Aratta said. "How was it?"

"Memorable," she said, laughing. "But I think such encounters are best served in small portions." She winked. "For us garden-variety humans, at any rate."

"Of course," he said, a twinkle in his eye.

Hagar had been in touch with her the night before. It turned out that after Lee went through the rift on Earth, Aratta and Hagar had transported themselves to the netherworld, where they waited out the anticipated battle. Lee had recounted to Hagar her bizarre experience of the cosmic clash that ensued among the gods, but evidently, it was not something that Hagar and Aratta registered in the netherworld. All the same, after the overmind was defeated, they could once again move at will between worlds.

Lee took a sip and then regarded Aratta. "I've wanted to ask you something ever since Haiti," she said, putting the drink down. "Why did you do it? I mean with Hagar, back in the 1930s."

Aratta's gaze drifted toward the window, lost in thought. "It seemed like a good idea at the time."

"And that was?"

His eyes focused back on her. "I always had this uneasy feeling that we had been too quick on the trigger; we'd convened hearings and had made rulings before humanity had a chance to transcend its adolescence. Through the ages, I proposed holding off just a little while longer to see where the rapid technological advancement would lead. But each time, Hagar was adamant. She was unwilling to delay a hearing once the conditions on a given planet turned dire."

"So this time, you decided to take—what's the word?—unilateral action."

Aratta met her gaze evenly. "Fabricating the reports that reached Hagar and deceiving her for years felt utterly wretched, but more was at stake than infuriating Hagar." His eyes had a faraway look. "Things on Earth did not play out as I'd hoped. But they might have. There was no real way to know ahead of time. It is conceivable that during the all-critical twentieth century, humanity would have embarked on an ecologically regenerative economic path."

Lee pondered this. "What about the next planetary assignment? Would you want to—"

"No. The stakes for the biosphere are too high. Had it not been for my interference and fabricated reports, we would have pulled the plug on things and held a hearing about a century ago. This planet was a different place then, ecologically speaking. I believe trying this once in a single world was necessary, but given the environmental risks, once is all we can afford."

Aratta exhaled slowly. "There was another thing I failed to

anticipate."

Lee waited.

"During that century," he said, "the institutions here grew into leviathans—interlocking, self-justifying systems that seeped into every interaction and endeavor, far beyond anything in human history."

He shook his head faintly, as if still struggling to accept it. "At some point, they stopped resembling anything recognizably human. Common sense, individual agency, the old wisdom—drowned out."

Lee nodded grimly. She'd never thought of it quite that way before, yet once he said it, she could see.

For a minute or two, both were content to stay quiet.

"I probably would have done likewise," Lee suddenly said. "All of it."

They shared a brief smile.

"Then there's the matter of your associates," Lee said. "I presume they belonged to the same organization that sent someone to take me out."

Aratta made a dismissive gesture. "Yes, and I'll tell you about the original group members another time. No need to sully a perfectly beautiful morning with this piece of ancient history. The thugs you and Hagar took out in Haiti were little more than unwitting accomplices. They followed instructions laid out decades earlier, carrying out orders of men long dead, funded through an elaborate system that drew on a substantial bank account established generations prior. You took out some of them. And while you and Hagar were enjoying the hospitality of El Shaddai, I took out the rest. It's over."

"How did they track me down?" Lee asked.

He grimaced. "A century ago, I equipped the original group with a tracking device—a stripped-down version of the bracelet you wear. Frankly, I had all but forgotten about its existence."

Aratta gave Lee a smile that sent her heart racing. "Hagar told me yesterday about the sleeper agents she'd planted." He looked at her with amused wonder. "The agents who ended up saving us all. Hagar and I owe you a debt of gratitude." He stood up and, with a flourish, bowed and kissed her hand. Lee felt herself blushing. She wasn't sure what to say.

Aratta sat back down and fixed her with a curious stare. "You're not... from Earth, are you?"

She regarded him for a moment, then shook her head.

"Where then?"

"Lee is short for Lee'chelle. My actual name is Lee'chelle Lainraad."

He looked startled. "Your parents were from Qataria?"

"Yes."

"But... Earth was isolated. Hagar hasn't brought anyone to Earth since at least 1914."

"It was 1866. That was when she brought them. Come, let me show you." Lee rose from her seat, signaling Aratta to follow her. She led him to the basement, where she paused in front of a nondescript wall, her bracelet emitting a soft, azure light. As if responding to some silent command, a section of the wall began to shimmer and then slowly dematerialized, revealing a hidden alcove with two vacant stasis boxes.

"Three young couples came from Qataria," she explained. "Two pairs in timefold stasis. One pair awake. In 1915, they passed the torch to the next pair. Then again in '63. But Hagar never showed."

Aratta nodded in understanding as Lee continued, "By the time my parents' turn came, they broke protocol. They had me—to keep the mission alive just a little longer. I was born in 1970. My parents died in a car crash in 1984, when I was fourteen. I was the last surviving member of our family. Mom wished to have more kids but that never happened."

Lee added, "As you know, we were not to have children with the local people—if nothing else, to avoid acquiring the genetic vulnerability introduced into Earth people as a safeguard." Her voice faltered as he moved closer. Her eyes traveled over his chest before returning to his face.

They gazed into each other's eyes.

She cleared her throat. "I should warn you, I'm into old people."

"Am I old enough?" he demanded.

"Oh, plenty."

"Alas, *I* don't date underage girls."

"I'm forty-three!"

"I rest my case," Aratta said. "Hell, the first century of life doesn't even count."

She grabbed him by the nape of his neck. There was no hesitation, no testing the waters—she pulled him down and kissed him hard, tasting salt on his skin.

"My, you're very mature for your age," he said when she finally pulled away a little. "I think I'll make an exception in your case."

"When you were shirtless, fighting at the path…" Lee murmured, her thumb tracing the heavy muscle of his shoulder. "You were *so* damn hot."

"Well then," he said, a dangerous glint returning to his eyes, "I'll just have to pick more fights." His mouth moved passionately on hers.

He caught her behind the knees, lifted her, and carried her upstairs.

Part Three

a handful of years later

CHAPTER 19

The Foothills of the Organ Mountains, New Mexico

IT WAS A WARM, CLOUDLESS DAY. The wind stirred the creosote bushes and cottonwood trees scattered about the large estate. As far as the arriving guests were concerned, this was a picture-perfect day.

None of them had any reason to suspect this was the last day of life as they knew it.

Lee had invited dozens of people to a costume party to be held later that evening at her villa. Three of them arrived early in the day. Brandon was off that weekend and had nothing better to do. Susan and Mr. Galecki were both retired and local. Lee wanted them to meet two people who were due to arrive shortly, one of whom would not stay for the party.

In one corner of the large drawing room, a hammock rested within a curved wooden stand. Lee's three visitors were taken aback by the sight of a man lying within. His arms were folded over his chest, and he was snoring softly. "This is Puddeck," Lee said. "I just need to give the hammock a little push now and then."

"You just need to give it a push now and then," Brandon repeated, staring at the stocky figure in a violet robe.

"He likes it," Lee explained.

Brandon turned to Mr. Galecki and stage-whispered, "Did you hear? 'He likes it.'" For a moment, with his rounded eyes, he looked downright comical. Despite the three-day stubble on his face, his mannerisms and irrepressible curls gave him the air of a high school student playing the adult.

Lee nodded gravely, her eyes twinkling with amusement.

"Curiouser and curiouser," Mr. Galecki said dryly, regarding the snoozing man. He took off his glasses and wiped them with the edge of his Hawaiian shirt. As an analyst for an economic think tank, he'd spent the previous thirty years wearing a suit and tie and was now determined to make up for it in his retirement years.

Lee walked over and rocked the hammock. "There, good for the next ten minutes." She looked at her three guests. "Won't you have a seat? They'll be here any minute," she said, and they sat down. "I think you'll find Peled interesting."

Mr. Galecki rested his ankle casually across his knee and leaned back in his chair. "Peled? An Israeli?"

"Yep. In fact, he only just arrived in the States this morning. Aratta is taking him elsewhere, but he agreed to stop by to say hello."

"Ah, Israel, the Jewish homeland," Susan said with a touch of good-natured humor in her voice.

"Along with an Arab population," Brandon was quick to say, faintly proud of this inside-baseball tidbit. "Roughly a fifth of the citizens of Israel proper are Arab."

Susan gave an uncertain smile. "I didn't realize that." Hair coiffed and dressed impeccably in a cream pantsuit, she looked the part of the retired head of a prominent charity organization, which she in fact was.

"Well, yes," Brandon said and leaned back in his armchair, enjoying himself. "In fact, that's one of the fundamental problems that country faces—"

The doorbell rang.

Lee got up and went to the front entrance, returning shortly with two men in tow: Aratta, cutting a striking figure in an ivory linen suit and a pale teal dress shirt, and an elderly, small-statured man trailing a carry-on wheeled suitcase.

"Everyone," Lee said loudly, "you've already met Aratta, and this"—she draped an arm around the old man—"is David Peled."

Susan, Brandon, and Mr. Galecki got up, introduced themselves, and shook hands. As it turned out, the Israeli pronunciation of the name was DaVID, not DAYvid.

"Can I get you breakfast?" Lee asked the old man as she moved the suitcase to an unobtrusive corner of the room.

"No, thank you. I just had something to eat before I came." His eyes crinkled with a smile. He glanced sideways at his companion and grinned. "You could say that the flight was terribly short." In fact, Aratta had teleported him from Israel just a moment earlier, but he was not supposed to say anything about it any more than he was supposed to speak of Aratta's enigmatic abilities and otherworldly identity.

Perfunctory smiles greeted his odd statement.

Lee insisted, and David took a seat in the wingback chair. After giving an indulgent smile at the sleeping figure in the hammock, Aratta claimed a spot on the nearby couch, draping his arm around Lee, and she snuggled into it.

"So you're from Israel," Susan said, her tone bright and curious. She helped herself to a small tomato bruschetta from the coffee table. Crumbs flaked onto her fingers; she brushed them off on a napkin.

"Israel the beautiful," David said, a twinkle in his eyes—clearly quoting something, though the reference escaped the others.

"What do you think about the Israeli–Palestinian conflict?" Susan asked him.

The old man eyed her for a moment, then sighed. "Those stinkers are fixated on the destruction of the Jewish state, root and branch—as an end in itself. Everything else is just smoke and mirrors and details. I think the same as anyone would when they're staring down mass rape, slaughter, and expulsion."

For a moment, Brandon's mouth pressed into a thin line.

"So what is Palestine, really?" Susan wanted to know.

Peled stayed quiet long enough for the refrigerator to kick on behind them. Finally he said, "A yearning for a country that never was, and lip service to a country that isn't. The intentional rebranding of the province of Judaea by the Romans after the Judeans—the Jews—revolted, naming it after Aegean-derived seafaring people, the Philistines. A temporary trust territory of the League of Nations over the land back in the day. An autonomous Gaza Strip and a patchwork of self-ruled enclaves across Judea and Samaria. Any of the above."

More silence ensued. Mr. Galecki removed his glasses and twirled them between his fingers. "Brandon was just about to make a point about Israel, before you arrived," he said, nodding toward the younger man.

Brandon, although looking a little uncomfortable, adjusted his posture and said, "Well, I just don't think Israel can be a Jewish state any more than Sweden can be a 'white republic.'"

David chuckled, a dry sound. "Whiteness isn't a nation. Jewishness is. It's a people with a shared history, language, holidays—all tied specifically to this land."

"Still, can there really be a place for a country that defines itself as committed to any one ethnicity, that does not see all its citizens as equally central to its mission?"

"Sure. Latvia, Bhutan, Hungary, Japan—take your pick."

Brandon frowned. "So non-Jewish immigrants aren't welcome in Israel?"

"Insofar as they threaten the Jewish majority, no, they're not," David said evenly. "After centuries of persecution, in the midst of a renewed tide of virulent hate and calls for mass slaughter, maintaining a sovereign state for Jews is our prime directive. Full stop."

"Isn't it fundamentally unfair?" Brandon persisted. "If Jews get self-determination because of trauma and persecution, shouldn't Palestinians get it, too?"

Mr. Galecki gave Brandon a quick glance—a twitch of something like annoyance. "I think you have every right to your state," he said, aiming the remark at David.

"Rights have nothing to do with it," said Peled in an even voice. "Since when has any country come into being or existed because it had the right to—or because it 'should'?"

"Touché," said Mr. Galecki, chuckling. Susan smiled awkwardly.

David eyed Brandon. "And we didn't 'get' self-determination. For decades, we bought land from the Arabs, piece by piece, often at exorbitant prices. Later, in 1947, the UN General Assembly recommended partitioning the trust territory, creating an 'Arab state' on one part and a 'Jewish state' on the other. The Arabs rejected the plan and launched a Jihad—to slaughter and drive out the *Yahūd*. We fought back and gained control over part of the land. Egypt grabbed the Gaza region. The new Jordanian kingdom got hold of the rest."

For a few moments, no one talked.

"How is it? I mean, in Israel?" Susan asked.

"I once strolled in Nuevo Laredo, just south of your border. It felt like back home," David said. "People walked the streets with a distinct feeling of belonging to one large tribe." The elderly man looked back at the people around him and shrugged. "A country ought to be more than a place that enshrines civil rights; it needs to have a soul."

Susan studied the guest from Israel, brow furrowed.

"You mean, unlike here—don't you?"

It was now David's turn to look uncomfortable. "You've lost your shared myths and bedrock beliefs—leaving you with just a terms-of-service agreement." He glanced at Brandon. "Any society—especially a democracy—depends on the bonds between its people. These days, it seems to me that America's held together with spit and baling wire."

Damn right, Mr. Galecki thought. And then there were the migration waves, worsening it. He leaned forward and said, "Our territory isn't some vast homeless shelter or an unsettled frontier." Not for the first time, he thought of the masses of asylum-seeking Goths the Romans had let across the Danube River in the 370s.

He added, "They've been pouring in from the south: huddled masses along with their uncles and second cousins. And let's get real, had Mexico been bleeding the best and brightest, its government would have thrown up a wall of its own long ago."

Or not, he admitted to himself. Emigration was its business model now; dollar remittances were the real national product.

Aloud he said: "You open the floodgates to the Third World, give them no reason to assimilate, and what you get isn't a melting pot—it's a mosaic with no grout. Trust shrinks. Civic culture hollows out. Eventually you end up in an economic zone with a flag—and with parallel societies, whose texture shows up in your kid's classroom."

Brandon jumped in angrily. "Making our country an asylum for mankind was an integral part of what we have wanted the United States to be. We have a long history of presenting ourselves in this way to the world."

"Ah, yes—'Anyone can be American,' and 'America is just an idea.'" Mr. Galecki waved a hand. "You can chant 'nation of immigrants' all you want, but every nation is also anchored in ancestry, language, and memory." He looked at Brandon, then at Susan. "At that scale? At that rate? I say, to hell with them, with all of them; we're not the soup kitchen for the brown people of the world."

Brandon gave a tight smile. "There it is. There's the mask slipping." He regarded Mr. Galecki. "You don't like those people, do you?"

"Like them?" Mr. Galecki shrugged. "I like them well enough— when they don't try to move into my living room." He gave a half smile. "Hell, I would've walked north too, if I'd been in their place."

He got up, opened the screen door, then stopped and sighed. "Look at Albania. Look at Moldova. Look at Belarus. All white as copier paper, none come bundled with that pioneer-tinkerer impulse that launches moonshots. Culture isn't encoded in melanin. So, yeah … I don't want them *either*, even if they do retain a sense of visual familiarity in public spaces."

He glanced at David. "Care to join me?"

David smiled faintly and climbed to his feet.

The two men stepped out together, leaving behind pointed glances and unresolved tension.

⇒⇐

Outside, Mr. Galecki passed a cigarette to the older man. David lit it and puffed a few times. They both walked up to the edge of the patio and admired the view, enjoying the serenity of it all. The night air was cool against their faces.

"Tell me," David said, "what do the majority of folks here desire when it comes to immigration?"

Mr. Galecki offered a dismissive shrug. A curl of smoke drifted sideways in the faint breeze. "Americans have been telling pollsters they don't want high levels of immigration. Some of us have been tired, some poor, and many have yearned to breathe free of foreigners. But the numbers didn't drop. They rose."

He drew again. "What people want is academic. This isn't a representative government—it doesn't reflect the people's will. A solid majority of congressmen take their marching orders from those who bankroll their reelection campaigns and from future employers. And then you've got the activists; they know how to work the pressure points."

David muttered something to himself in Hebrew. He walked over and sat down on a wooden bench. Mr. Galecki joined him, the bench creaking softly as it took their weight.

"I appreciated what you said inside," David said. "It took nerve."

Mr. Galecki waved dismissively. "Nerve is cheap without consequences. It could've cost me a job, a reputation—had I still been employed or had an online presence. More-enlightened-than-thou heresy hunters sprout like fungus after a rainstorm, threatening livelihoods and reputations."

David flicked ash aside. "You make it sound worse than it is."

"Probably," Mr. Galecki conceded. "All the same, the cultural revolution is rarely forgiving."

David raised an eyebrow.

The other man shook his head, a look of disbelief crossing his face. "You see it in little purges everywhere. An LA Galaxy player gets booted because his wife called the looters 'disgusting cattle' and urged they be put down. The Philadelphia Inquirer cans its editor for running the headline 'Buildings Matter, Too.' And a librarian in Flagstaff? Let go for questioning whether the Dewey Decimal System should spell 'activism.'"

Mr. Galecki took a drag on his cigarette. "Others observe and take note. They step cautiously, speak measuredly, and may pledge allegiance to the LGBTQIA+ flag and the Drag Queen Story Hour for which it stands." He sighed. "I guess you have to be careful what you say at home, too. Children can inadvertently repeat some of those things in school."

"And universities?"

"Ground zero," Mr. Galecki said immediately. He exhaled violently, blowing smoke upward. "Activists have colonized universities, then proceeded to decolonize them—that is, malign and blot out the heritage of Western societies. Teaching got swapped for political advocacy. Intellectual fluidity for dogma. And merit?" He gave a dry laugh. "It was eclipsed by melanin and gonads."

"Is it as bad as all that?"

"I'm afraid so. Those who have set their sights on tenure or otherwise on a job inside the ivy-covered walls may be required to craft and sign a Diversity, Equity, and Purity statement to demonstrate their loyalty." *Meanwhile, nonwhites were buoyed by the thermals of white guilt*, Mr. Galecki reflected. He tapped ash into the gravel with a small, irritated flick.

He then sighed. His shoulders sagged a little. "Who can afford to speak truth to power, that is to say, engage in hate speech or disinformation? Who can afford to risk being unmasked as a racist-Islamophobe-sexist-transphobe white supremacist?"

David chuckled at that. "Being unmasked as a white supremacist, huh?"

Mr. Galecki shrugged. "Just slurs—tools to silence opposition and grab more power." His smile twisted, humorless.

"These righteous crybullies agonize over fever-dream injustices conjured up in the virtual world where they spend most of their waking hours—playacting life on the barricades as they endlessly reenact history's inflection points." Mr. Galecki shook his head, bemused. "Seated on the toilet, composing brave dispatches between flushes and raining down fire and brimstone through their screens." Their outrage targeted causes that let them batter the West, he thought. Otherwise their feed went silent. Victims were props. Suffering was a stage.

No one talked for a while. A cricket chirped and fell silent again.

David rubbed his thumb over the cigarette filter, thinking. "It's the same thing happening in Western Europe, isn't it?"

Mr. Galecki nodded. Well, yes.

He reflected for a moment. "Just the other day," he told the other man, "a mob of middle-class whites in Bristol, UK, tore down the statue of Edward Colston, an English philanthropist who'd profited from the slave trade centuries ago. They stomped on it like it was Saddam Hussein in Baghdad." He chuckled. "Those same intrepid freedom-fighters would break into a cold sweat at the idea of publicly denouncing the slave markets being run today by Arab Muslims across western Libya—from Zuwara to Gadamis."

David spoke softly, testing the thought. "Do you think white people are struggling with guilt over the past?"

Mr. Galecki stared at the ember of his cigarette. "I reckon it's more akin to an original sin that is passed down through the bloodline, requiring token repentance throughout one's life with no possible absolution. This doctrine offers a pathway of limited reprieve for whites who check their privileges, recognize the original sin of their birth, and regard the doctrine as their personal savior."

"Evangelical Christianity for the modern-progressive era, eh?" David smirked.

"Not quite. Given their bourgeois roots, no white is above suspicion. If at any point a white is found guilty of bigotry by a mob of his peers, he is finished."

The two fell silent. A lone moth fluttered near the patio light, bumping softly against the glass.

Mr. Galecki said, "Sweden's turned itself into a cautionary tale. Many of the rape perps are from Africa and the Middle East." His distaste was palpable. He pinched the bridge of his nose, weary. "As you'd expect, Swedish authorities spent years playing it down—and did the same with the wave of bombings as migrant gangs wage war on each other in Borås, Umeå, or Linköping."

David chewed on his lip, mulling over what he heard.

"And then there are the Muslim underage-sex rings in the United Kingdom," Mr. Galecki went on. "And the ever-vocal feminists who can work themselves into a froth over a white man who, uninvited, puts a hand on a woman's knee, yet can barely muster a scowl at the former."

⸎

"WHAT ELSE COULD YOU EXPECT FROM PUSSIES!" Rafirre roared and slapped his thigh, laughing. His underlings hollered along with him.

"Sex rings in the UK?" one of them asked when the merriment died down. "What's the old fart talking about, boss?"

Master Rafirre's smile deepened. He settled back into the high-backed black-leather armchair, alone with his two underlings in the vast underground facility. On the wall-sized screen, Lee's guests bantered on—unaware. Shortly after their arrival on Earth a few years prior, the assessment group under his leadership had deployed a surveillance array throughout the planet. Now they could listen in on almost anything, almost anywhere.

"Rapefugees and the broader Muslim communities that close ranks around them," he muttered in response to the question, his gray eyes glinting. "Iraqis and Bangladeshis, Pakistanis and Somalis, Eritreans and Sudanese migrants have been planting communities across England. And wherever these go, grooming rings sprout."

He slapped his thigh. "They grab them garden-fresh, virginal white females and fuck them, then rent them out to uncles and cousins and friends. Five men. Ten. Twenty a night."

"They are one of us, boss!" exclaimed one of his two aides.

Master Rafirre laughed in response, and the two men laughed with him.

It was time. He got up, and his deputies followed him as he made his way out.

"Clever dogs," Rafirre said with relish as he walked. "Girls get reeled in by affectionate young Muslim men who ply them with alcohol and drugs and turn them against their parents. Slowly they're broken in. Then older men are brought in, and the girls start getting passed around. Their sex-slave networks run through taxi firms and late-night kebab joints."

With a spring in their step, they climbed the short stairway leading outside.

The migrants were after more than flesh, Rafirre thought. It was conquest—doing it in their towns, to their girls. And the collective silence was the trophy. Respect.

Outside, more than a hundred people waited, cheering as he appeared. Someone opened the door for him in the lead car. Rafirre paused and turned to face his men.

"From Stockholm in the Baltic to London on the Thames, an iron curtain has descended across Western Europe," he hollered. "Paris, Berlin, Amsterdam, Brussels, Rome, Madrid; all these famous cities and the populations around them lie in the politically correct sphere, where thoughts are criminalized and truths cannot be spoken for fear of denunciation, if not prosecution.

"Hell, once, the English people stood together," he called out. "That was then. The limp-dick Englishmen of today look the other way as some of their daughters are ravished, brutalized, and used like trash. Their police stall and downplay. Their media covers up. Their schools keep students in the dark. Their social workers all but excuse it. Their city councils hush it."

He fell silent then raised his voice again. "A society that won't protect its young females deserves to be plowed under, with or without our help," he bellowed and his fist tightened. "If the hearing swings our way, their girls will be the low-hanging fruit. Neutered and declawed, their men will stand down while we take their virgins and make them ours."

Those within earshot cheered and whooped. Master Rafirre climbed in. Moments later, his car sprang forward, dozens of gleaming vehicles following.

As the vehicle sped through the rising dust, Rafirre thought of that boy in Sweden—stripped and pissed on by grinning Middle Eastern migrants. Nobody rallied to exact justice. Just livestreams and hashtags. When the time came, they would be easy, he thought, and he grinned to himself.

Rafirre was headed first to New Mexico, to meet up with Aratta at the social gathering, which he'd just monitored. His people, though, were to make their way to a pickup point, and from there to the Mongolian steppe. The staging ground.

It was just a matter of hours now before the curtain was to rise.

⤝⤞

THE BATTLE HAD been lost long ago, thought Mr. Galecki, with the millions of shell-shocked survivors returning from the trenches. The Great War had exhausted the moral credibility of the West and left behind a civilization unsure of its own rightness, continuity, or innocence. That uncertainty, over time, curdled into inherited guilt.

The last serious attempt to reclaim their heritage and continuity marched under the banner of a racial-imperial myth and was discredited forever in the death camps, rendering any future assertion of civilizational pride morally suspect.

The achievements of their forefathers were portrayed as products of exploitation and plunder—nothing worth honoring, nothing worth preserving. Just spoils to be shared by all. Indigenous Europeans were left estranged from their own history, their sense of continuity broken, their group identity eroded.

White-only dating sites were forbidden; "It's okay to be white" was hate speech; and a woman's post saying, "I don't want to bring any more white people into the world," racked up over a hundred thousand likes.

Britain was rebranded a nation of immigrants. The gates were flung open. Muslims and Arabs and Asians and Indians and Africans have been settling across the continent. Millions, mostly single males.

Along with this, the past itself was updated. Familiar faces of European memory were repainted and reauthored—Queen Anne Boleyn rendered black, Isaac Newton made Indian, King Gustav III recast as Middle Eastern. Even legends weren't spared. From Arthur's court to Achilles, all were fair game for race-swaps. No longer would an indigenous person be able to point backward and say, "This was us."

He thought that if Ghana were flooded with Russians—fluent in Twi, dressed the part, quoting proverbs—filling the streets, dominating the cities, Ghanaians would look around and say: "This is no longer Ghana." And they'd be onto something—especially if even figures like the Queen Mother Yaa Asantewaa were recast on screen as blonde and fair-skinned. Ghana, for them, was the water they swam in—the people they were physically drawn to, the ones who felt like "us," the faces they saw when they pictured home. He figured that's why kids self-sorted at cafeterias. Why people drifted into same-ethnicity churches.

But let the Irish feel the same—"This is no longer Ireland"—and give a raw voice to that sentiment, and the police might come knocking.

Mr. Galecki and David regarded each other.

Without worries, without danger or drama, and with very little carnage, thought David, recalling a line from a book he'd read. *A civilization just dies of weariness, of self-disgust.* Was that to be their fate? He felt dispirited. Yet underneath it, something was pulsing within: joy. For eighty-seven years he had been submerged in this juvenile stew of misery, conflict, and dysfunction along with everyone else in this accursed world. It was time to shed all of this—like a pupa ready to take wing—and leave it behind. Joy.

"I'm going back in to say goodbye." David extended his hand. "It's been a pleasure."

"I'll stay here for a bit," Mr. Galecki said. "Good luck to you." They shook hands.

Mr. Galecki was left alone. Just him and the painful memories this discussion dredged up.

Louisville…

The Big Four Bridge area…

He'd walked with his wife and their granddaughters near the riverfront, summer light still on the water. A group of young black men drifted toward them from across the street, laughing, loose-limbed. No words at first. Then a shove. Then fists. He went down hard while his wife screamed and the girls screamed, pleading for the assailant to stop. Not one intervened, least of all fellow whites—except his wife. Involuntarily, he clutched the pendant of his late wife.

And then, years later, Milwaukee. One night in Sherman Park. A cluster of young black men between parked cars. The first voices floated out of the dark:

"They white?"

A pause. A laugh. Then the confirmation, sharp with delight. "They white."

Whoops, running feet, the sound of hands slapping metal. Someone shouted for the passenger to get out of the car. Glass exploding. A man's scream cut short. The sounds tumbled over each other in a rush of excitement. It was a whitey beat-down.

He reversed slowly, heart locked in his throat, and did not stop backing up until the block vanished behind him.

He broke his lease that week. Said nothing to anyone. Santa Fe seemed promising—dry air, open nature, different world. He'd been there for two years now. At seventy-two, he figured he had maybe ten good years left. With any luck, it would be over soon enough for him.

⊃⊂

Back in the drawing room, David shook hands with the other guests.

"Where are you headed off to next?" Susan asked.

"To another world," David said, a note of pride in his voice.

"*World?!*" Brandon's eyes went round. "What in the—"

"We'll be back within the hour," Lee cut in cheerfully, while Aratta patted David's shoulder, guiding him gently.

"Just help yourself if you need anything from the fridge," Lee said.

"Where do you think they're taking him?" Susan asked quietly after Lee, Aratta, and David took their leave.

Brandon shrugged. "Probably some local assisted living home." He thought it over. "Do you think David suffers from Alzheimer's or something?"

"Or something," Susan said, her voice low and thoughtful. Then she sighed heavily. "Poor man."

CHAPTER 20

Tadrart Rouge Area, Sahara Desert, Qataria

DISORIENTED, DAVID staggered as a blast of hot air hit him, causing his eyes to water. He blinked a few times, then gazed in awe at the unfamiliar landscape. "Where are we?" the old man asked.

Aratta's voice came from somewhere behind him. "In the world we left behind, this would be just west of where Algeria, Niger, and Libya meet. It's at the heart of the Sahara Desert." He joined the old man as Lee pulled a wide-brimmed hat out of David's suitcase and put it on him.

From the edge of the mesa where they stood, the world fell away into a vast, motionless flood of fiery rust-colored sand and fine peach silt, broken here and there by dark outcrops—hills and buttes jutting like the bones of a drowned land. They could make out in the distance a herd of camels disappearing in the shadows of a canyon carved between two bluffs. Heat shimmered off the basin in slow, glassy waves, meeting the relentless sun rays pouring from above.

The temperature dropped markedly as they walked several dozen paces into a grove of acacia trees, the shade a blessed reprieve from the furnace outside.

"Here she comes," Aratta said softly. In the distance, a lone veiled figure was walking briskly toward them, her iridescent off-white robe billowing.

Aratta had informed David that no questions would be asked about his origins—and that he shouldn't volunteer any information. All the locals were to know was that he was from somewhere else. "What happens on Earth stays on Earth," Aratta had told David earlier, a half-smile on his face. But it was obvious to the old man that it was more than a suggestion; he was expected to keep mum about his home planet.

David was glad to take Aratta up on his offer to leave Earth when the enigmatic man had shown up at his door. He'd hoped for a week or two to settle his affairs, but Aratta had insisted—things on Earth were about to get unpredictable within a handful of hours, he'd warned. David had to evacuate that very day.

Now they watched the veiled woman make her way. "There are no Jews or Arabs here, neither wars nor borders nor countries," Aratta said.

"It doesn't have to be complicated," David said, his voice dropping almost to a whisper. He felt as if a great weight had lifted, one that had burdened him, one he had not been aware of.

"No, it doesn't," Aratta said, gently kissing the top of the old man's head. He suddenly smiled. "Your work is not done yet. It's time *lehafriakh et hashmamah.*"

David burst out laughing. "It has been decades since I've heard anyone say that."

Aratta grinned back at him.

The two men stood there looking at each other, knowing it was perhaps their last goodbye.

Aratta asked, "Do you remember how we first met?"

"It was at the Dead Sea, 1946," the old man reminisced. "Tell me again the story of how you came to be there," he urged Aratta on.

Aratta smiled. "Well, I was en route from England to India, and—"

"What was the name of that hotel where you stayed?" asked the old man eagerly.

"The Kalia Hotel."

"That's right! The Kalia. Oh, I can still visualize the spacious lobby with its Persian rugs."

"A toilet and a bath in every room," Aratta reminded him.

"The goblets were made of crystal."

"Rosenthal crystal, no less."

"Rosenthal's work is good, isn't it?"

"Certainly," Aratta told him. "The best."

The old man's face lit up. "Remember the quartet that played on the grand balcony when the sun set?"

"And then retiring to the smoking room."

David laughed out loud. "The golf course—it must have been the only one for many hundreds of kilometers." He started to cry. "It was the first time I saw a golf course."

"Well, you were just a boychik back then." Aratta opened his arms, invitingly, and the old man trudged toward him.

"It was a good life, wasn't it?" David whispered, his face buried in the other man's shoulder.

"It was a good life," Aratta repeated quietly, his voice carrying a note of fond remembrance. He held the thin, old man in his arms, and a tear trickled down his cheek. The gentle whisper of wind across the desert plains murmured in their ears. After a long time, Aratta let go of him.

They both stood and watched as the figure drew near. She undid her veil, revealing a lovely face framed by silver hair. "You must be David," she said. Bright, intelligent eyes regarded him with warm curiosity. "My name is Leandra." She beamed at him. "Welcome to your new home, David." She bowed to him and then to Aratta and Lee, who bowed back.

The old man stepped forward and shook her hand warmly.

Only now did David really take in his surroundings. They stood atop a mesa carpeted with wild grasses and dotted with canopied acacias. A herd of scimitar oryxes grazed just a stone's throw away. Nearby, a few bustards ruffled their plumage, sending dust spirals into the air, while a knot of sand partridges fussed over their feathers beneath the trees.

His lined, tanned face split into a wide grin. "We diverted the Jordan River, but you've taken things to a whole other level," David said, staring in disbelief at the improbable vegetation and life around him. "This is incredible, astounding!"

Leandra laughed. "I'll be happy to tell you about it." She picked up his suitcase. "Let's walk together, shall we?"

Aratta and Lee hugged David for the last time. Then they stood there watching until the lively, animated voices of the two elderly people faded in the distance, and they heard nothing but the gentle sigh of the wind.

Lee sat down, resting against the massive trunk of an acacia tree. Aratta slid next to her.

"You did right by David, bringing him here. I think he'll be truly happy—spending the rest of his life in the desert, among these people." She reached over and kissed Aratta on the cheek, and he smiled at her.

Aratta extended his hand and took hers in his. "Ready?"

"Am I a horrible person for not wanting to go back to Earth?" She felt helplessly drawn to this place, to its ragged, sublime beauty.

"You are," he assured her.

"Give us half an hour," she said, laying her head in his lap. "Then we'll head back."

⇒⇐

David looked upward at the sudden cacophony. The pastel-blue sky filled with the calls of migrating purple herons working their way south.

"There are about five hundred of us," Leandra said, "clustered in a hub with a handful of outlying houses. This settlement is for those who want to live on the edge. You'll find life here to be harsh. And awe-inspiring."

The old man's eyes were bright, and he blinked a few times

to clear them and keep at bay the overwhelming emotions that coursed through him. It'd been a long while since he felt so at peace. In fact, had he ever really?

Following a narrow, winding path dappled with the shade of carob and fig trees, David took note of the understory of pistachio trees and pomegranate shrubs, their leaves rustling in the slight breeze.

"Where is everybody?"

"It's summer in one of the hottest places on Earth," Leandra replied. "From May through September, most people sleep during the day. This time of year, the community only wakes up after sunset and keeps going until morning." She glanced at the lengthening shadows. "Won't be long now until people rise."

The old man glanced about. "Where does the water for all this come from? Surely not from the little rainfall you get here."

She smiled in acknowledgment. "At night, our roofs drink from the air," Leandra said. "A metal—organic compound pulls in the moisture while it's cool. When the heat rises in the morning, it releases the moisture, and the droplets condense on a sloped pane beneath. Every roof does its part—nearly two hundred thousand square feet of quiet work." She smiled. "Water's never abundant, but it's always enough."

Leandra paused, her gaze shifting toward the landscape that stretched out beyond the buildings. "And then there's that." She pointed to a series of wetland fields surrounding a domed building. "That's our water reclamation system. We recycle every bit of water, from washing dishes to bathing. Even human waste finds its way there."

"Incredible," David murmured. He wiped his glasses, put them back on, and inspected the beds. The rubber liner and gravel underneath were all but hidden from view by a thicket of papyrus sedge and common reed fluttering in the warm breeze. Metallic-hued dragonflies darted to and fro, filling the air with a constant hum that mingled with the muted gurgling of flowing water.

Leandra said, "As the water moves from one constructed wetland bed to another, it gradually gets stripped of ammonia and nitrates as the masses of roots soak up more and more of the nutrients."

Such beneficial technologies, David mused. If only they had been made ubiquitous in his homeworld.

He crouched to examine the trickling water as they reached the last plot of reeds by the big dome. "The water looks pure at this stage."

"Yeah, it looks the part, but in fact, it's not. Not yet." She opened a thick door constructed of bronze and reed, inviting him to enter the large domed structure.

Cooler, humid air wrapped around David. Leandra shut the door behind them, and the old man gawked at the improbable sight as he descended the stone steps.

Water from the wetlands outside coursed through pipes and cascaded as a waterfall into a lagoon. Sunlight streamed down from various shafts to the tropical pool, leaving the rest of the cavern dimly lit. The effect was breathtaking.

A few bald cypresses dominated the lagoon. Leandra motioned at the dense growth of plants. "From here, the water moves back outdoors through a large bed of sand. This is the final stage where the sand and microorganisms absorb and digest any remaining particulates and nitrates."

David peered into a dark, circular opening that wound downward. It reminded him of a tube slide. "What's this?"

"Follow me and find out." Leandra took one of the wide, flat pillows stacked nearby. She positioned the cushion by the circular entryway, sat on it, pushed off, and disappeared. The sound of soft laughter trailed behind her.

Chuckling, David shook his head, grabbed a pillow, and climbed on. With a push of his hands, he whooshed down and down the spiraling tunnel—into a well-lit cavern.

She helped him up.

"Nice and cool here," he said, looking around.

"It's cool year-round, courtesy of the ambient temperature deep underground."

David pointed at the ceiling. "Incredible light, too."

She smiled. "This is just diffused sunlight we coax underground."

"Sunlight? Down here?" He didn't understand.

"Simple enough, David," Leandra said. She slipped off her veil and outer robes—no longer needing their protection from the sun. The old man gazed at her coppery-brown skin, almost aglow against her pearly dress. Her silver hair tumbled loosely about her.

"You are beautiful," he said in admiration.

Her eyes sparkled good-naturedly. "Still interested to hear the answer?"

He laughed. "Absolutely."

"A movable outdoor array of mirrors tracks the sun throughout the day and redirects its rays. Prismatic films diffuse and even out the incoming sunlight."

David understood now and glanced around, curious. "What is this place?"

"Our marketplace, of sorts." She gestured at the giant woven baskets on the stone floor, brimming with fresh produce and grains. "All our harvest makes its way here." Retrieving a canvas backpack from the wall, she picked a mix of vegetables from the baskets, placing them into her bag.

They moved to the adjoining chamber—a labyrinth of tiny water canals and pools teeming with fish. "We produce about eight tons of fish each year," Leandra told him. "Coupled with quinoa, chickpeas, ostrich eggs, and hemp seeds, they fulfill our protein needs."

She caught a good-sized fish with a long-handled net, and David examined it wide-eyed. "How in blazes do you have mahi-mahi hundreds of miles away from the nearest sea?"

"Hundreds of miles, hundreds of yards—it doesn't matter; there are too many people in the world for fishing."

"What's the human population on this planet?" he asked, keeping his tone neutral.

"*Large*. Probably around five million," she replied, shaking her head. Her expression was a mixture of disbelief and wry amusement. "It still baffles me how we can have that many people when the world's biggest city has seventy thousand people. But that's what they say."

She glanced at the water. "And no, we don't catch fish, David—we grow them. This is a closed saltwater system."

With a small wooden mallet, Leandra stunned the fish she had caught with a blow to the head, rendering it insensible. She then proceeded to slaughter it.

"And what's the source of the electrical power?"

"The sun, of course. All our buildings are coated in a translucent, protective glaze—the glazes and paints are packed with photovoltaic particles. Sunlight gives us electricity during the day, and any extra gets stored as hyper-compressed air in tanks. At sunset, we use that air to drive pneumatic motors."

"If you can grow saltwater fish in the middle of the desert, then surely you can grow—"

"Anything, really," she cut in. "Yet, we strive to operate within the limits of the broader ecosystem of the region. So this is the exception to the rule. The same idea applies to automation, which could have done the work of men. There is joy in doing things with our hands, notably for those who are less intellectually inclined."

"You sure seem well-versed in the town's operations."

"I'm one of the aldermen," she said simply. "In any case, this is our home, and our survival is linked to these operations. All are acquainted with what stands between us and death. The next human settlement is—well, there isn't one within reach. We are it. About once every year or two, a caravan may visit. And we obtain items that we do not produce."

A short while later, they arrived at the residential heart of the town. David walked on, dumbfounded. It was, quite simply, the most beautiful town he'd ever seen. Translucent arched roofs draped over the meandering alleyways, diffusing sunlight to illuminate the glazed walls in myriad hues of amber. The houses were distinguished by round doors, painted lilac, arranged in whimsical, if not outright surreal, configurations. Some doors were curiously positioned on roofs, reachable by ladders or spiraling staircases.

The stone-paved alleyway, just wide enough for the pair to walk side by side, stretched out before them. Thermal chimneys were common throughout. Leandra explained to David how they worked. The heat generated an updraft of air, just enough to create a gentle draw. That tiny pressure shift drew fresh air from buried coils deep underground, cooling the air before it wafted up through vents in the ground. David could sense the constant, barely perceptible breeze filtering through the enclosed alleyway. Evidently, they also had backup fans to enhance air suction when needed.

"Same setup inside the buildings?" David asked.

"Yes, except indoors it's also humidified and further chilled by a moist, porous membrane at the entry point to the house. Speaking of which…" Leandra opened a door and beckoned, inviting him into her home.

A short flight of stairs led downward. The reason was not hard to deduce: Half-buried in the earth, the house presented less surface to the desert sun.

He noted that the walls gently curved before meeting the aged, tiled floor. Area rugs and pillows were strewn about. David accepted her invitation and sat with a contented sigh on a hanging hammock chair. "Beautiful. Simply beautiful," he murmured.

She came back holding two mugs and said, "Aratta warned me you'd have a lot of technical questions." Her eyes glinted mischievously.

Gratefully, he took one of the mugs. "Milk?"

"Camel milk," she said, and he took a sip. It was different, all right, richly flavored and with a salty undertone.

"Let's move over to the kitchen." Leandra held out her hands. "You can keep me company while I cook for us."

About half an hour later, they sat amid pillows and rugs by a low table. Alongside slices of the dark bread they had just baked, Leandra placed a plate of hummus with olive oil, paprika, and chickpeas. David eyed the food with delight.

"You know," Leandra told him after they'd had their fill and cleaned the dishes, "during summer nights, we may retract the canopy in the community dining halls and sit there, with the desert breeze on our faces, under the silver light of millions of stars. You can clearly make out the Milky Way. In fact, one of our dining halls is set up as an overhanging balcony, giving diners the illusion there is nothing but the night sky around them."

She grinned at David. "But I'll do you one better. It'll be my pleasure to show you the night sky through the eye of a telescope."

"A telescope?"

She leaned in. "We are predominantly a community of stargazers, David. A few miles out of town, on a nearby mountaintop, we have a giant optical telescope. Its primary mirror is forty-five meters across," she said, almost casually. She winked. "I'll take you one night on a trip to the galaxy around us."

A single deep chime of a gong came from afar.

Leandra's face split into a wide grin, and she bounded to her feet. "But that's later. Let's go out, and I'll introduce you to other people in town."

CHAPTER 21

The Foothills of the Organ Mountains, New Mexico, Earth

As the sun cast its final rays, guests started arriving, most wearing exotic costumes. About an hour past dusk, the party hit full stride. The pounding beat of Electro House reverberated through the basement, where scores of mostly graduate students were drinking and swaying.

It was the last party Lee planned to throw on Earth; she did not intend to stick around much longer.

Guests roved about the ground level, occasionally intercepted by two waitresses balancing platters filled with cheese, delectable canapés, and an assortment of drinks. The aroma of grilling steaks wafted across the Japanese rock garden.

In a dimly lit alcove paneled in cedar, Brandon and Puddeck lounged in a bubbling hot tub positioned just off the rock garden. Each man nursed a bottle of beer, sharing easy banter with their hot tub companion, Josh. Sporting a sandy man bun and an infectious grin, Josh was a staple at Lee's parties. He never missed a chance to swim in the sea of fresh faces and fleeting hookups. More than once, he'd landed a late-night encore with a willing stranger.

"Whoa," Puddeck said, straightening. Conversation around the tub died as two young women crossed the tiled rock garden path toward the house.

The shorter one was lithe, her midnight-black hair grazing the small of her back. She was clad in a form-fitting tube top and matching skin-tight leggings with reflective off-white stripes that caught the light as her thighs moved. Her companion was tall and dark, with a silk band snug at her throat. A one-shoulder dress rippled gold as she walked, the taut fabric clinging and capturing every sway. Her hair was brushed to one side, the undercut painted silver. In a wrap at her chest, a sleeping infant rose and fell with her steps.

Josh was momentarily taken aback by the infant but then recovered his shit-eating grin and whistled. "Now *that's* what I call a solar flare."

The girl in leggings shot an amused glance his way as she continued to walk alongside her companion. The two of them were chatting and laughing over something. Had she heard him? Josh found himself breaking into a silly smile.

Along with Puddeck and Brandon, Josh feasted on the sight of the firm, rounded ass and tracked it with his eyes. Beside her, other hips swayed in lazy rhythm, their silhouettes blurring together into one long, rolling wave of curves, skin, and fabric.

"This ass is designed to sit on a man's face," Puddeck said, his voice filled with solemn conviction once the two vanished down the steps toward the basement.

Brandon laughed uncomfortably at that last, looking furtively about. Josh, however, took a swig. He was determined to make a move. But first things first. It was an hour later, once he was finally out of the tub, fed, and fully clothed again, when he decided to locate and approach the two girls. Either of them would do.

They were no longer in the basement, and by that time, some of the guests had bid farewell and started to depart. The music was turned off, and those who remained were scattered throughout the sprawling house.

In one of the mansion's sitting rooms, Josh found himself in the company of Brandon and Susan. The trio lounged on rustic armchairs upholstered with Navajo patterns in hues of rusty red, desert sand, and deep turquoise. The quiet conversation they were having stumbled into silence as the entrance door swung open, and Lee strode in flanked by the two striking young women Josh and Brandon had ogled earlier.

"I would like to introduce Jetro Lan and Lorraine Warr," Lee announced as the three of them made their way into the middle of the room. "I guess you could say they are special guests." She glanced at the two women. "*Very* special."

Josh, on the verge of a quip, caught himself, the edges of his smile faltering under Lee's emphasis on "very special."

"You see," Lee said, "those two ladies are hiding in plain sight, so to speak." She reckoned it was rather clever of her. No one thought anything of girls dressed in exotic garb at a costume party, or for that matter, of finding a man wearing a violet robe.

Josh cocked his head slightly. "How do you mean?"

"The costume party," she said. "What better way to blend in if you stick out. Guys, they're not from down here."

"Hello," said the young woman in metallic-hued leggings, her voice carrying a curious, melodic cadence. She gracefully nodded to the three Terraneans and then slipped into a vacant armchair across from them. Her teammate followed suit. "I am Jetro Lan," she went on. "I speak your language, but Lorraine Warr has only mastered the basics," she said with a nod toward her companion. "Anyway, we're thrilled to be here. Thanks for having us over, Lee." The pair, having danced tirelessly, now seemed interested in mingling with the natives—the Earth people—before they retired for the night.

"Well then, where you guys from?" Brandon asked, feeling somewhat bewildered.

For a moment, Jetro Lan gazed at him, her smoldering eyes jolting him and sending his pulse racing. She gave him the once-over, but then looked elsewhere, uninterested.

"Not from around here, Brandon," Lee said, now also taking a seat.

Josh, still mulling over Lee's oddly stressed introduction but attributing it to her whimsical nature, squinted at the duo. "Give me three tries to guess your country."

"We don't have countries," Jetro Lan said immediately. She and Lorraine Warr came from the Earth-like planet of Tamaris, but Jetro Lan was unsure how much she should divulge.

"Oh, okay," Josh said, shifting in his chair. He took off his glasses and rubbed the bridge of his nose. "Wait." He put his glasses back on and looked at the surrounding faces. "I don't understand what you're saying," he confessed. He shot a glance at Susan and Brandon. "Do you get any of it?"

Turning to her companion, Jetro Lan vocalized a series of sounds that were like nothing the three Earth people had ever heard. The language was a dense mesh of chimes, hums, and clicks, layered in intricate rhythms. As she talked, her face was animated and her body language as fluid as her words, amplifying their bewilderment.

Brandon, Josh, and Susan exchanged glances, eyes wide.

From the next room, someone was calling Lee's name. "Crap. You'll have to excuse me, guys," she said, swiftly rising from her chair, its leather creaking slightly. "I need to sort out some details with the caterers before they pack up." With an apologetic smile, she made her way around a coffee table and exited the room, leaving her guests in the soft glow of the room's wrought iron sconces. It was time. In fifteen minutes, Lee was to depart with the catering crew. She wanted to be alone when midnight struck.

A slow grin began to creep onto Brandon's face, replacing his initial daze. The strange language, the undeniable otherness of these two young women—it was all clicking into place. There *was* something different about them. *Really* different. Somehow, they were from elsewhere: a secretive Mars colony, or a private island off the radar, or something. His gaze flicked to Josh, noting the sudden change in the man's expression, which mirrored his own burgeoning realization. His heart thudded. Incredible. Absolutely insane.

Susan's eyes darted between the two young women; she wasn't sure what to make of the situation. She knew that Lee wasn't one for childish pranks. But the thought that rose within her was too absurd. She dismissed it, yet it persisted—a nagging suspicion, demanding attention. Susan resolved to grill Lee later for details and get to the bottom of it.

Brandon paused, uncertain how to start a conversation. "You have a husband, Jetro Lan?" he finally asked.

"Husbands. I have two husbands," the young woman said, then thought about it for a moment. "Perhaps fiancés describes it better."

Brandon, Josh, and Susan looked at each other as if to make certain they were hearing it right.

Josh evidently recovered from his earlier shock and was also caught up in the excitement of the situation. It was not every day that one met otherworldly people. "Is this a typical arrangement where you're from?"

Jetro Lan shook her head, causing tendrils of her raven-black hair to escape and frame her cheeks. "Typically, it's two men and two women."

So, four was the norm. Josh laughed out loud. And Jetro Lan eyed him curiously. "No, no." He held out his hands. "It sounds great. How does it work? The guys . . . take turns?"

"Hell, no. They do it at the same time," she said, and Brandon and Josh chortled while Susan pursed her lips in evident displeasure.

Jetro Lan inwardly winced. Was that what passed for a sense of humor on Earth? She obligingly extended her palm toward the three Terraneans. A small holographic image sprang from it, showing the faces of her husbands.

Brandon stared in wonder. It was an advanced technology of some kind. That was so cool!

After a moment of thoughtful silence, Jetro Lan spoke, her

curiosity evident. "So, around here, what if a man decides he wants to enter a committed relationship with two women? Does he have to choose between them?"

The question rubbed Susan the wrong way. "In our country," she said primly, "it is strictly between one person and another."

Jetro Lan eyed her briefly, digesting this information.

"In fact," Susan said, "it's against our law for a man to marry more than one woman."

"Oh," Jetro Lan said, her interest dwindling. She couldn't think of anything she wanted to say. The interaction with the natives was not turning out to be as appealing as she'd imagined.

But Brandon seemed oblivious to it. He moved over next to Jetro Lan and pulled out his cellphone, showing her something.

Meanwhile, Josh scooted closer to Lorraine Warr, trying not to gawk at the intricate skin scarifications. "And you? Are you also married?" he asked, hoping against hope that she was available.

"Of course," she said, laughing. "You see a child, no?" The woman was rocking her toddler.

"Well," he said, "it's possible to be a single mom." From afar she was striking, but up close, she was even more so. Lorraine Warr possessed a sense of presence and immediacy that was unsettling. He felt he could drown in the luminescence of her green-flecked hazel eyes.

She narrowed her eyes ever so slightly. "How? I do not—" She sought out a word and eventually raised her left arm, and a few symbols materialized over her palm. " ... reproduce asexually," she completed the sentence and flashed him a friendly smile.

"I mean, the father could leave."

Susan was listening in.

"Leave?" Lorraine Warr asked, baffled. "Leave where? Why leave?" Josh tugged at his collar, suddenly feeling awkward.

"So, how far down do those scarifications go?" he asked, then gesticulated when it became apparent she did not understand the question.

For a moment, the liquid-hazel eyes softly glowed. "All the way."

He smiled back. "When did you get them?" His eyes flitted over the soft fullness of her lips.

"When married, a bit over a year ago. When I was sixteen."

Josh blinked. Wait—sixteen? His grin faltered. "Wow. Young! I mean, you got married young."

She looked back at him, not sure what to make of this remark. She and her sister-wife were the same age. Their husbands were two and three years older, respectively. All four of them wed at a relatively young age, though it was still within the norm on Tamaris.

Josh's pulse misfired. Seventeen years of age and some change, then. Legal? Damn close, but no. And not what he'd signed up for. Something cold slid under his ribs.

"Josh, can I have a word with you?" Susan asked, standing by the doorway. She waited until he came over. "The way you were looking at her before…" she said in a low voice, almost hissing. "I should have told you to wipe the drool off and push your eyes back into their sockets. She is a *child*, Josh," she hissed that last, then, louder: "Off-limits. Underage."

"I realize that," he said, indignant. Then he gave a weak laugh, his face flushing with embarrassment. "I thought she was around my age, early twenties. Didn't *you*?"

Susan shrugged noncommittally, a veil of disapproval still clinging to her features.

"Believe me," Josh said with some heat, "I have no interest in underage girls."

Across the table, Jetro Lan reached out for a can of beer. "May I?"

"Help yourself," Brandon said, looking at her with a measure of unease. *Please, let her be an adult,* he silently prayed. Even a day over eighteen would do. "It's a fermented beverage, alcohol," he said.

"I figured as much, smelling it." She drank some and set down the can on the table with a thud.

"Jetro Lan, it's against our law for anyone under twenty-one to drink this," Susan said flatly. Enough was enough.

Here it was again. It seemed the natives were big on all sorts of laws. "I'm sure it is," the young woman said dryly. "Shall we drink to that?"

The room froze for half a second—then Josh and Brandon laughed loudly.

Jetro Lan stood up. She had had her fill of mingling with the natives. "Nice to meet you," she said, louder than necessary. A local idiom she'd learned brought an inward smile: *Don't call us, we'll call you.*

It was one hour to midnight.

⇒⇐

Jetro Lan stepped outside, deeply inhaling the fresh clean air. She meandered around the property and, before long, spotted Aratta, comfortably settled in one of the wooden gazebos. As she drew closer, she noted he wasn't alone. Puddeck was there along with a man she hadn't met before.

Introductions were made. "This is Rafirre, the General Examiner," Aratta said, and the man bowed smartly in the direction of Jetro Lan.

Jetro Lan eyed the man with curiosity. There was nothing soft or tame about the features of his broad face or piercing gray eyes. With his trimmed white beard, mid-calf black boots, and coarse wool coat, he looked like someone more at ease leading one of those old Earth cavalry charges than attending a party.

The young woman turned to Aratta, remembering something. "Susan talked about Lorraine Warr as being 'off limits' and 'underage.' What's that all about?" She proceeded to tell him some of the details.

Puddeck cackled. "They're very protective of children around here."

She stared at the chortling little man in purple. What did Lorraine Warr's child have to do with anything?

Puddeck was his usual gleeful self. "One thing could have led to another, and Josh could've landed himself on one of their registries." He wagged his finger at her. "One can never tell with the indigenous people here," he said in a sing-song voice.

What an annoying little man. Jetro Lan turned back to Aratta. "What is he talking about?"

Aratta shrugged. "A public registry of their people who stand condemned," he said. "The registry displays their photos and lists their addresses for all to note."

"One of the fine gems to brighten my days here on Earth." Puddeck chortled.

Jetro Lan ignored the man in violet. "Condemned for what? Murder?"

Aratta shook his head. "Not unless they had first touched their victims inappropriately."

She drew her brows together and crossed her arms over her chest. "Are you just going to continue to make these cryptic statements?"

"I was intending to, yes. I really don't think you want to go down that rabbit hole," Aratta said, ignoring the now-chuckling man in violet.

Tonight, Aratta cut a memorable figure, wearing a three-piece suit of muted, slightly brushed, textured black tweed with almost imperceptible dark-gray flecks. Underneath it, he wore an immaculate white dress shirt with a stiffly starched stand-up collar, the tips of which bent and flared outward. A silk necktie with a large knot and intricate shimmering silver and gold patterns transformed his otherwise austere attire into one of striking elegance.

Jetro Lan just looked at him.

Aratta sighed. "I guess I'd better show you then."

He closed his eyes, searching. Countless records flashed before his mind's eye as he swiftly made connections, each leading to the next. Finally, he gestured for the three of them to huddle around.

The world vanished around them and then rematerialized. The

four of them were now standing in what appeared to be a deserted, run-down area of a nondescript city.

"You see this man?" Aratta asked. In the dusk, they could make out a lone man in his early thirties hurriedly walking down the street across from them. "This is Jeffrey. When he was twelve, he played doctor with his stepsister, that is, he pretend-examined and otherwise touched her private parts. Presumably, he was naked, and at some point, aroused. The authorities were notified, and from then on he became the property of the state, suspended between the living and the dead.

"His adolescent life was transformed into a series of prison cells and sex treatment centers where he was made to swallow psychotropic drugs for years on end. Afterward, he was removed from his family and made to live in a foster home. At the age of eighteen, he started attending a local college, and the police tailed him throughout campus, as he was a Sex Offender. Eventually, it was too embarrassing and intrusive, and he just dropped out. He moved to another state with the hope of starting a new chapter. But his Sex Offender identity was available for all to note, and he had difficulty finding work. Jeffrey now lives with other outcasts beneath a bridge. The law forbids him from residing within fifteen hundred feet of daycare centers, schools, parks, or libraries—and he hasn't been able to find a qualifying place of residence. He works the occasional odd job. Every other week, he has to report in."

The world blurred and changed, and they were back in the gazebo.

Aratta turned to look at Jetro Lan. She had a look of horror on her face.

He shouldn't have shared Jeffrey's account with her. He stepped up to her, put his hands on her shoulders, and squeezed them for a moment. Her eyes focused again. Aratta knew nothing had prepared her for this. Nothing could prepare anyone for this.

She looked away at the mountains and twinkling stars, and he let go. "It is utterly devoid of any compassion or humanity," she said, choking on the words, aghast.

She then looked at Aratta, the horror still in her eyes.

His jaw clenched. When he finally spoke, his voice was low, almost a whisper. "The statutes were wrought from loathing and dread, then calcified beneath an institutional crust so thick that no mercy can filter through."

She played back in her mind some of the things she'd just heard. She didn't understand everything Aratta had said, but enough of it came through. Attending the party had been a mistake, she could see it now. "I don't care to interact with the indigenous population anymore."

"This will be perfectly fine," he assured her, then bowed.

"I would appreciate it if what you told me remained between us. My team members don't need to be exposed to … that." She muttered that last under her breath. "By your leave, we'll head back to base." She needed a shower. A long one.

Puddeck, Aratta, and Rafirre bowed. She bowed in return and strode off.

"Registry, huh?" said Rafirre, grinning from ear to ear.

Aratta sighed. "A few hundred thousand dollars in litigation costs, a few years of getting roughed up in prison—and finally the Condemned stumble out under a gray sky, blinking at what is to be the rest of their lives. When the probation officer visits, it's in a car clearly labeled *Sex Offender Treatment Program*. Many Condemned are barred from watching R-rated movies or owning sex toys. When they travel, they must notify the police in every county they stay in. Their passports carry a unique identifier, usually resulting in denial of entry upon arrival. And when they have grandkids, they may not come near them. A good number of them think about killing themselves daily; death is the only escape and reprieve."

Rafirre asked, "Who is on it predominantly? Who are the marked ones?"

The three of them started to stroll down the softly illuminated footpath as it wound about the sprawling desert estate.

"The sex offender registry lists adults who committed heinous deeds, such as sexually coercing children," Aratta said. "But it also includes men peeing outdoors and men who streaked. It lists teenage girls who posted nude photos of themselves on the Internet. And it lists young lovers who have had sex. About one-fifth of the Condemned are under the age of eighteen, some as young as twelve."

"How does the population at large react to all of . . . this?" the Examiner asked.

"With a great measure of satisfaction. Some clamor for harsher measures."

Rafirre smiled inwardly, recalling the downplaying of under-age sex-slave gangs in the UK. Cognitive dissonance among the Terraneans was a never-ending source of amusement for Rafirre. The Earth people *were* adorable.

He asked, "Are there no voices calling to dial down the punishment for offenders who are under the age of eighteen?"

"Anyone who questions this draconian scheme exposes themselves to personal attacks and to a sneaking suspicion," Aratta said.

Rafirre suddenly beamed. "You know, I think I'm going to enjoy my role in the hearing."

Aratta glanced at him. "Judging by your grin, I think you already are."

Rafirre's smile widened.

Chuckling, Rafirre asked, "How did this whole thing get started?"

"Such things don't really have a beginning," Aratta said, reflecting. "But I suppose the daycare child-abuse hysteria of the 1980s in California was a catalyst as much as anything."

"It started with one mother's accusation, and a child was asked if anyone had touched them 'down there.' The child said no, and that sent up a giant red flag," Puddeck said. "Other small children were questioned, and they denied anything had happened.

The conclusion was painful but unambiguous: They had all suffered a collective trauma too horrific to be retained in conscious memory. Soon the young ones caught on. The floodgates opened, and the testimonies poured in of an ever-increasing number of children: first those attending one daycare center, then those in some other centers.

"Subsequent testimony revealed that daycare workers tortured then killed pets while dressed as Santa Clauses, clowns, and firefighters. The small children were fed blood from an elephant and a giraffe that had been killed in the daycare center. The children were forced to have sex with each other. Hung from boards, screaming and thrashing, the children were repeatedly assaulted by groups of men. A little girl was forced to eat the body of a baby cooked in the basement boiler. Before the designated parent pick-up time, some children had been bound with ropes and were used as bait in shark-infested waters; while others were flown earlier in the day to Mexico, where they were sexually abused by soldiers."

Rafirre absently rubbed his chin. "Were there physical or behavioral signs of trauma?"

"What? No, of course not," Puddeck said. "It was only days or weeks later, when the kids started telling those tales, that they became prone to anxiety, night terrors, rage, sexual acting out. Poetic justice, of a sort.

"Parents spent evenings and weekends driving the streets, looking for the places their children were ritually abused and tailing suspicious people. They formed investigative squads and searched for molestation sites their kiddos told them about. As the young people pointed their fingers at homes and businesses, mothers and fathers jotted addresses and forwarded them to the investigating authorities. Housewives spied on their neighbors and took down their car license plate numbers.

"The small children were driven around, and they pointed at a bank teller—arrested. At a passerby on the street—arrested. Hundreds of children were naming ministers, reporters, soccer coaches, aerobics instructors, grade-school teachers, and babysitters. Eventually, they also denounced the sheriffs and social workers who had been interrogating them. The miasma of transgressions cascaded outward. Ritual-abuse allegations erupted like tumors in daycare centers in other parts of the country and in the broader Anglosphere.

"Houses were searched, with and without warrants. A daycare center was closed. Its grounds were dug up by a cadre of parents and a team of archaeologists who looked for the hidden tunnels in which the children were molested. Fields, backyards, basements, and crawl spaces were excavated. Cemeteries and funeral homes were searched. And they dragged two lakes, looking for bones or ritual gear."

Puddeck fell silent for a few moments, reflecting. "It was one hell of a remake," he murmured, seemingly to himself. "Without the pyrotechnics, granted, but with a far larger cast. The original 1690s Salem witch trials had nothing on it…"

"And?" Rafirre prompted.

"Huh?" Puddeck was jolted out of his reverie. "And nothing," he said and snorted in mock disgust. "Prodded by crazed parents and under a relentless barrage of leading questions by investigators, the small kids lied through their teeth, descending deeper and deeper into that foul, bubbling mass delusion. But all good hysteria must come to an end. By the early 1990s, it fizzled out, and within a few years most of the accused were cleared of all charges and permitted to resume their life, or what was left of it at any rate."

"Yes, and yet," Aratta said. "The beating heart of this paranoia transcends the daycare moral panic and is buttressed by a legal edifice, which, once on the books, is all but impossible to dismantle or even dial down. This brings us to the present era—with child supervision on a war footing, by parents and by the state apparatus.

"Throughout human history, children have ranged freely outdoors, undeterred by venomous snakes or swift rivers. These days, however, some folks harbor doubts about a twelve-year-old's ability to walk home unaccompanied. Parents fret that a neighborhood busybody might misconstrue an innocent moment and ring up the authorities. Even slumber parties have turned into potential minefields."

He said, "This may very well be the first human society in history where it is within the realm of the possible to forbid children in a school setting to hug one another due to it being an 'inappropriate display of affection'; to ban games of tag as they violate a 'no touch policy'; and to forbid embracing small children who cry as 'there is no safe touch between a teacher and a student.'"

Rafirre eyed Aratta, making a mental note to have one of his staff fact-check the claims. His account could be faithful. After all, on Earth, the wacky and the harebrained often paraded around as everyday events. And hadn't he received a report the other day of a recent trend of girls chopping off their breasts, disclosing there had been a mix-up and they'd been assigned the wrong sex at birth?

CHAPTER 22

Aratta lowered his head in acknowledgment as Jetro Lan and her small team approached him a little while later, on their way out.

"I'm surprised Nero Maichan and Oreno Eire don't speak English," Aratta said when he was introduced to the two young men accompanying her.

Jetro Lan raised her eyebrows at that. "Well, we only arrived a few days ago."

"Arrived a few days ago?" Aratta blinked. "You haven't been with the Nature Assessment Group the past few years?"

"No, of course not. We're members of the Terra Restoration Corps," she said and stifled a yawn. "We begin our work in about a week."

She then noticed the shock etched on his face.

"The Corps. On Earth. Now?" Aratta exclaimed.

Jetro Lan blinked, a little taken aback. She had assumed he would have known. "They're arriving by the thousands as we speak." Her team was a part of the nature-rewilding task force. "The staging grounds are on the salt flats of Lake Eyre. Why? What's the matter?"

"I just... I need to check on something. You'll have to excuse me." He bowed to the four guests and vanished in a rush of air.

It was midday in Australia.

Hagar waited for him amid the sand and the hills. Her blonde hair was considerably longer than when he'd last seen it. "I saw your beacon!" she shouted over the sudden gust of wind. "What's wrong?"

In reply, he threw an arm around her, and they teleported to a hilltop a few miles away. A brisk, warm wind was blowing, and a small dust devil skirted the hill they were on. Past it was the endless expanse of salt flats. Through the haze, they could make out many hundreds of large trucks and earthmoving machinery drawing near.

He jerked his head toward the advancing mass. "That's the cleanup crew."

"What?"

"She's here. On Earth."

With a string of curses, Hagar tore down the hill, Aratta following closely behind.

They both reached the hill's base, their grim gazes trained on the approaching convoy.

The ground trembled under their feet as the army of mechanical behemoths approached. One titanic dump truck led the way and came to a stop about fifty paces from them, the rest of the fleet following suit.

A door opened in the cabin, and a few rough-looking men climbed down the metal staircase and walked over until they stood in front of the two of them.

"Lord Aratta, High Mistress Hagar," the foreman yelled over the deep rumble of many engines and lowered his head for a moment.

"What's going on?" Hagar shouted back.

"Frankly, I was hoping you could tell me. I have instructions to get things started a week from now."

Aratta and Hagar shared alarmed glances.

"I'm afraid a terrible blunder has been committed. You guys are not supposed to be on Earth at this point," Aratta shouted. "I need to talk to your boss. Where is she?"

In response, the burly man reached into his vest pocket, pulling out a slim, rectangular device. After a brief consultation with its display screen, he wordlessly extended it toward Aratta.

≫≪

Tielt, Belgium

HAGAR GASPED, and Aratta laid a steadying hand on her forearm.

The slaughterhouse floor was bloodstained and heavy with odor. It wasn't clear if the smell came from the dozens of hogs milling about or the row of limp human bodies hanging from hooks overhead—tranquilized, by the look of it. A pig squealed somewhere in the building's depths.

"Just in the nick of time," a woman called out as she spotted them.

Aratta and Hagar turned her way.

"Some of the hogs weren't stunned properly," she said. "They were conscious when the Terraneans plunged them into boiling water. Others were hoisted on these meat hooks and made to watch what was coming."

She gestured with her chin. "In the next building, pigs are so tightly packed they can't turn around—biting, screaming... it's like a crowded train full of tormented toddlers. You really should check it out. It's that way." She picked up a wooden stool and hurled it. A loud, harsh clatter echoed through the large room as the stool smashed into a wall and shattered into splinters.

The woman turned toward the last limp figure on the floor.

"They also run a daily show," she said, walking toward the tranquilized man. "Piglets torn from their mothers. Teeth snipped with pliers. But after I visited the attraction, they had to shut it down for restocking and repair."

She was athletic, pretty, and appeared to be in her thirties. She wore skinny jeans and a fitted white T-shirt, smeared with grime down one side. Her hair was bound in a sleek ponytail. And her gold-yellow eyes blazed with inner fire.

She grunted as she bent down, seized the large, unconscious man, and hoisted him onto her shoulder. With a leap, she landed on the elevated conveyor belt. A second later, her arms locked, tendons standing out as she hoisted him overhead and hung him from a meat hook by his belt.

Hagar and Aratta took a few more steps inside the slaughterhouse.

"I know what you're gonna say." The woman with yellow eyes was breathing hard as she paused to regard her handiwork. "I could've killed the people in this facility, and it would have made not an iota of difference." She wiped sweat from her face. "The grim reality is that even if I ended a hundred thousand Terranean lives"—she clapped her hands once, hard, a crack like a whip—"there would be a million more the week after."

She jumped down and strode to the large metal doors of the slaughterhouse. With a kick, the woman sent the heavy doors flying outward. They crashed hard against the walls, hinges shrieking as they tore loose.

She yelled, and the dozens of pigs fled into the night. She watched the freed animals as the darkness gradually claimed them.

"Been busy, huh?" Aratta said.

"Yup." She scrubbed her hands briskly on her thighs, then turned and walked back into the slaughterhouse's chilling depths. They now noticed the thin scratch running along her jawline, as if she'd narrowly dodged something with teeth.

"Arrived on Earth a few days ago," she called over her shoulder, "figured I'd check out a few local must-see attractions."

She turned to face them, frowning thoughtfully.

"First stops were Texas and Vietnam. They keep crocodiles in filthy concrete pits—barely big enough to move. Then, when it's time? Metal rods up the spine. Flayed alive, as often as not."

She grinned—sharp, bright. "Silver lining? They draw their last breath knowing their hides will end up as stylish handbags." Her yellow eyes sparked with a feral light. "There are countless such farms."

"Jilieth…" Aratta started.

"Oh, and China? Down south, they're turning dogs into belts and gloves. Large pincers grab the dogs by the neck, club them on the head. Then they slit their throats and peel the skin off." She paused. "I tried the pincers myself. They work."

She approached them.

"So, whose idea was it to postpone the hearing here on Earth?"

"Mine," Aratta said.

Jilieth turned away from Aratta and Hagar, facing the gaping entrance of the slaughterhouse. "That's on you, then," she said, her gaze fixed on the distant city lights visible through the doorway.

"Yes," he said. "At least the first few decades. Then I couldn't send any communication out of Earth."

"Yeah. I heard." She turned to look at Aratta. "How could you do that?" she demanded of him. "HOW COULD YOU!" she screamed at him, her burnished yellow eyes a pair of roaring furnaces.

"I wanted to delay a possible hearing to give people a chance—a real one. One we've never allowed, not to my satisfaction," Aratta said with forced calm.

"Well, now you have," she said, and exhaled heavily. "Now you have."

The three of them stood there, looking at each other, faces drawn and grim.

Hagar broke the uneasy silence. "Hi, Jilieth."

"Hi, Hagar," Jilieth said, her jaw relaxing some. "What's it been, guys? Two centuries?"

"I think it's probably closer to three since we last met," Hagar said, a fleeting, strained smile on her face. She glanced at Aratta, whose face remained impassive. "Time flies."

The woman with the yellow eyes sat down, leaned against a wall, and closed her eyes.

"Jilieth, why are you here on Earth?" Aratta asked.

"I'd like to know that, too," Hagar said. She strode over and crouched in front of her. Jilieth opened her eyes.

Hagar produced a switchblade and released the blade. She reached over and scraped some dried blood off the other woman's thigh.

Jilieth didn't flinch. She just closed her eyes.

"Jilieth?"

"Humans are a cancer on this planet, Hagar," Jilieth said in a hoarse voice. "They're oblivious to everything except the dreamscape reality they've constructed around themselves."

Hagar put the switchblade away and sat back.

Jilieth looked at Hagar, then at Aratta. "The destruction and mayhem stop this week," she said and slammed her fist into her palm.

Aratta knelt next to Jilieth. "You will stand down," he told her in a tone that brooked no discussion. "The commissioners are about to convene. Like always, we will let the hearing take place, let the commissioners examine and—"

"Examine *what*?" Jilieth snapped.

"Noting the ecological degradation of Earth, we're also sick to our stomachs," Hagar said.

"We've had to deploy cameras and monitoring devices across the planet; my team needs them," Jilieth said. "I've waited these past few years—but not a day more." A cold light entered her eyes. "Do you have any idea how much havoc those psychos can cause in marine fish communities and the remaining old-growth forests during the eight months such a hearing would take? Wrapped up in their dramas and mind games, the people of Earth won't even notice if this world burns."

Aratta's eyes blazed.

"Have you lost your mind?" he roared. "You'd condemn

billions—and their descendants—without a hearing?"

"Jilieth," Hagar said, "we're making a request to fast-track it." She smiled encouragingly. "This is likely to be over in a matter of weeks."

⇒⇐

MATERIALIZING in Lee's study, Aratta found Puddeck awaiting him.

"Ready?" he asked.

"As ready as I'm ever going to be," Puddeck said mournfully.

Aratta glanced at the wall. "The clock is about to strike midnight," he said, half to himself, "and the carriage is about to turn into a pumpkin."

Puddeck gave him a grim look but said nothing.

Aratta shut his eyes for a breath, then opened them and crossed into the great room. He drew a long breath. "Ladies and gentlemen," he called out, "please join us here."

He waited as the remaining guests—two dozen or so—wandered in with puzzled expressions. Puddeck and Rafirre joined him and stood at his flanks.

"What's up?" someone asked.

"The party," Aratta said, "is over."

He clapped once. And one of the walls dissolved.

Cries broke out. Cool air blasted into the room from the other side of the rift, and they could make out gray skies with dark ocean waves in the distance.

"My name is…" He paused, waiting for the cries and exclamations to die down. "My name is Aratta'Gwa'Nar. Lord Aratta'Gwa'Nar. And I first took residence on Earth in 1543."

Stunned silence. Just the sound of distant surf pounding, half a world away.

"I came as planetary auditor, hoping this moment would not come," he said, surveying the dazed, pale faces. "Sometimes it does, sometimes it doesn't. It is not possible to predict the path humanity will take on any given planet."

He stood still, the chill wind curling around him, the open breach behind.

"What will happen in the next few days or weeks is yet to be determined," Aratta said. "But I can state with certainty this: Today will be remembered as a turning point, the dividing line in your history."

Aratta's proclamation lingered in the charged air.

"If you want the rest, come through the portal. Otherwise, you'll hear it with the rest of the world—TV, radio, the internet."

A hoarse voice called out: "What's on the other side of that thing?"

"A god," Aratta said. "If you can't muster respect, then exercise caution." He inclined his head and vanished along with his two companions.

CHAPTER 23

Bering, Commander Islands, Earth

UNDER A CLOUDY SKY AND A CHILLY wind, a dozen party guests staggered through the gateway at Lee's villa onto a coastal strip of gray sand, moss-green vegetation, and steep, fog-strewn bluffs.

The Earth people looked around, nervous and watchful.

"Do you see anyone?" Susan asked in a shrill, high voice. More shrill than high.

Mr. Galecki pointed toward a solitary figure seated on a park bench, about a minute's walk away.

Warily, slowly, the small group approached the figure, who, up close, appeared to be an elderly man in a double-breasted overcoat and a charcoal-gray fedora. From beneath bushy, white-gray eyebrows, he glanced at them before returning his gaze to the surf.

A single murre bird darted around his feet.

The seated old man casually gestured, and two more park benches materialized beside him, eliciting a collective gasp from the Terraneans. There was no explicit invitation, but the intent was clear enough. The Earth people nervously sat down, crowding the benches.

Mr. Galecki licked his lips. He watched the faces around him and saw fear, hesitancy, and anxiety reflected back at him. He had no idea how to address a god. Until minutes ago, he'd not even thought there was anything sentient aside from humans. His heart pounded in his chest. "Are we"—he cleared his throat—"are we still on Earth?"

"Yes," the figure said, continuing to peer at the ocean. "Somewhere between Alaska and Russia, at the tail end of the Aleutian Islands." He glanced over the group. "I'm Frank," he said, and a moment later, his gaze returned to the forlorn coast.

The figure in the fedora leaned back and crossed one leg over the other. "You know, there are two benches at this very spot on a parallel planet. In that other world, people come here to observe the large marine mammals." The corners of his mouth lifted in the ghost of a smile. "Those mammals live in family units. Males and females usually travel together, pushing the offspring before them. With their bristle-like limbs, they scrape off seaweed from the rocks and munch on it."

The Earth people exchanged questioning glances.

"Picture manatees, but bigger than killer whales," he said. "Their hide is like old corkwood, often acting as a perch for seagulls." His voice was softer now. "They half-walk, half-swim through the shallows, keeping their heads under for several minutes at a time. When they wish to snooze, they turn over, allowing themselves to drift and bob in the water." He chuckled. Susan and a few others smiled uncertainly. Mr. Galecki stayed tense.

The figure in the fedora lost his smile.

"To serve an insatiable Chinese demand for luxury furs, some Russians and local Kamchadals banded together to hunt as many of the marine mammals in the area as they could." He fixed them with an inscrutable look before turning back to the midnight-blue waters.

"The year was 1741," he said. He gestured vaguely to the moss-green vegetation fringing the coastline and the gray, sandy dunes that shifted under the chilly wind. "This was when your people chanced upon a few thousand of these gentle, giant beasts in what was apparently their last stronghold on your planet—the Commander Islands, here." His expression clouded.

"Their rich flesh became a whispered delicacy among sailors," he said. "And for twenty-five years, your kind feasted. The final blow had been years in the making—sea otters hunted out and the subsequent collapse of the kelp forest, the primary food source for those large mammals."

His voice was bleak. "By the summer of 1768, hardly any of them were left; it was almost not worth the trouble. Yet, your people persisted and spotted them foraging along the coast. It was right at this cove here." He motioned. "This is when and where they finished them off. As far as we can ascertain, that was the very last pod on Earth."

He massaged his temples, seemingly lost in his own thoughts. Some of the Terraneans were looking at him wide-eyed, others staring down at the ground. No one cared to look at the dark, foaming water and the booming surf, where the tragic event had played out over two centuries past.

"A man with a harpoon stood at the front of the boat," said the figure in the fedora, and his eyes blazed. "Once he struck, two dozen of his associates pummeled the sea cow with repeated blows that wore it out. Then they dragged it ashore. Great pieces of its body were cut while it was still alive and conscious. The giant manatee would sigh but otherwise utter no sound. As long as it kept its head underwater, the blood was contained. Other members of the herd endeavored to assist it. Some tried to upset the humans' boat; some bore down upon the rope, seeking to tear it; some attempted to extract the hook from the back of their wounded comrade with strikes of their tails.

"When a female was caught, her mate tried with all his strength to free her. After failing, he followed her to the shore, enduring the many blows dealt by the humans. Some stayed by the sides of their dead companions for days afterward."

The only sound now was the dull roar of the sea, crashing against the weathered cliffs. The party members were tense, unconsciously taking comfort in their proximity to one another and hunching down in the chilly northerly air. There was a reason he recounted this sordid tale. The situation had an ominous feel.

Dabbing the back of his neck with a handkerchief, Frank said, "In times past, the Gulf of America teemed with hundreds of thousands of Caribbean monk seals and millions of green turtles." Under heavy brows, he cast a level gaze at the seated people. "Then, a thousand years ago, your kind settled Jamaica—turning Bluefields Bay from a clear seagrass habitat into a murky mangrove swamp. Around the same time, other bands of humans settled Iceland—and drove the Icelandic walrus to extinction. And a little later, your forefathers also reached New Zealand and gorged on the giant moa to the last bird—and with them went Haast's eagle, starved of its only prey."

The Earth people said nothing.

The figure in the fedora chuckled humorlessly. "I can tell you're not surprised to hear that." He regarded them, his hands clasping his propped knee.

"During the steamship era, your great-granddaddies shoveled countless tons of burnt coal overboard. We uncovered everything from sarin gas canisters and mortar bombs to furniture and medicine bottles on the ocean floors." He sighed. "But we also found the Mediterranean Sea floor littered with aluminum cans of soft drinks and beer." Frank surveyed the small band of Earth people. "You're chips off the old block, all right," he said, and they looked away from the truth in his eyes.

Frank heaved himself to his feet. The murre bird that had been hopping beside him finally took flight. "This little encounter of ours has been transmitting across every channel." For the first time, he gazed directly into a hidden camera, addressing the hundreds of millions of spectators. "Terraneans, a hearing about your future and about the future of this planet will commence in ten minutes in the grassland steppe of Mongolia.

"Between now and then, I invite you, people of Earth, to sit alongside me for seven minutes in memory of all that was, and all that could have been. For the duration, I will shut off the engine of your world. All power stations. All generators," he said. He crouched, made a fist, and it was done: The world plunged into darkness.

The figure in the fedora went still as if carved from stone.

Seven minutes later, Frank disappeared from Earth. In the same instant, the small group found themselves back in New Mexico, standing in front of a TV. On the screen, figures gathered on a wide-open grassland.

⇒⇐

Somewhere in the Grassland Steppe, Mongolia, the Netherworld

A SECTION OF THE VAST GRASSLAND STEPPE WAS CORDONED OFF by a swath of dark fabric, tautly held aloft and stretched between polished wooden poles spaced wide apart and forming a large circular clearing. This marked the site of the forthcoming hearing. For the first session, all were in attendance: the members of both the Nature and Civilization Assessment Groups. They were seated on *sittas*—resembling upholstered footstools—and faced a platform of polished wood. Based in Earth's netherworld, the group, hundreds strong, had now finished their clandestine data collection and waited in rapt anticipation, the curtain of secrecy finally lifting.

"Make way! Make way!" intoned a portly man in ornate garb. As he thumped his tall staff on the ground, the murmurs and whispers ceased, all eyes drawn to the solemn procession he led. Seven venerable figures, robed in forest-green etched with intricate designs, followed him in silence under a cloudy sky. These were the commissioners: adjudicators set to determine the future course of planet Earth. They walked toward the low platform, on top of which rested cushioned pedestals. Their approach was marked only by the snapping of the fabric partitions in the day's breeze.

The commissioners took their seats.

"Harken, harken, harken," the master of ceremonies called out in his baritone voice once again. "Their Eminences, the seven members of the hearing, have joined the circle." At his words, the crowd rose and bowed in unison. "The first session of the hearing on the matter of Earth is hereby convened," the portly man announced, and everyone sat back down.

The Presiding Chair, an elderly gentleman with dark skin and a striking countenance, rapped the ceremonial hammer. The sound cut through the hush of the open grassland. He then looked up. "We have here a motion by the Civilization Assessment Group to fast-track the hearing." His vivid, intelligent eyes were framed by long white sideburns. A commissioner for eighteen years, he and his six colleagues had been introduced to Earth's case just a few weeks prior, fresh from another hearing.

Amid the hundreds of gathered people, a single figure stood up. "Yes, Your Grace," said Rafirre—the head of the Civilization Assessment Group. His role in the Assessment Group also designated him as the Chief Examiner. He had been chosen by his people for the role due to his oratorical and acting gifts; he could assume many voices and oratory styles. It wouldn't have worked out for them if their representative were to give voice to their cultural outlook. When it came to the commission, those had to be carefully tucked away.

Rafirre acknowledged the seven robed figures with a bow. Each was seated cross-legged on a wooden pedestal. He then proceeded to approach and came to a stop in front of a lectern.

"Overpopulation is cited as one of the reasons for the request," the Presiding Chair stated.

"Your Graces, we're less concerned with the one million people added to the planet every week or so," the Chief Examiner said, "and more concerned with every day that passes when eight billion of them wake up and head out into the world, consuming its resources. We feel time is of the essence."

Eight billion people. The seven commissioners were bemused. Never before had the commission dealt with a world population exceeding two billion.

"Well then," said one of the commissioners, "why don't they have fewer children and reverse the trend?"

"Some societies have been contracting in recent years. Others are ballooning. And the individual choices have little to do with concerns over the biosphere. For one reason or another, in the coming years, Earth people will swell their ranks by hundreds of millions of consumers, each with substantial lifetime needs and an unquenchable appetite for material goods.

"Your Graces, I can but state the obvious," Rafirre said, resting both hands on the lectern. "Given the fixed surface area of Earth and the fixed amount of solar radiation reaching it at any given moment, the volume of plant matter is capped. It's not complicated. The more people placed on the game board—accompanied by the supporting rice paddies, tree plantations, wheat fields, hog farms, cotton fields—the less room there is for other animals, which rely on the same underlying resources." He spread his arms in a gesture of inevitability. "Within a living system with finite production capacities, it is always a matter of what people indirectly force out of existence and what is an acceptable degree of environmental impoverishment."

"So noted."

"Needless to say, their population figures and their 'enough-is-never-really-enough' consumer mindset are the great multipliers of their activities, extractions, and consumption. They remove copious quantities of biomass and water from circulation. They cover ever more surface area with farms and asphalt. The process of fulfilling the needs and wants of eight billion humans is stripping this planet of its capacity to maintain complex ecosystems. They are burning through the Earth's reserves, drawing down on its capital."

One commissioner leaned back, fingers steepled, studying

Rafirre as though searching for exaggeration. Another scribbled a note, then paused mid-stroke—the facts, stark as they were, left little room for argument.

Rafirre went on, "Thus, as long as this planet is home to a vast number of humans, any conservation measures amount to little more than makeshift dikes. At best, these lower-impact, higher-efficiency technologies slow down the biosphere's bankruptcy and delay the shortfall in natural resources. At worst, such measures free up financial assets and enable the redirection of purchasing power elsewhere, leading to a net increase in economic activities and an enlarged ecological footprint. There is no endgame, Your Graces. It is growth as an end in itself: infinite economic growth on a finite planet."

"How does that look on the ground, in practice?" a commissioner asked.

"Aside from the vast deserts, ice sheets, and tundra, the Terraneans have commandeered the bulk of the Earth's surface for the production of food, fodder, and fiber."

"What are your projections for the mid-term?"

"Your Graces, we estimate that the global demand for food will increase by half in the next few decades due to population growth coupled with a shift toward a more meat-intensive diet among poorer populations. Then there's the matter of supply. Per capita arable land has been decreasing in almost all regions, largely due to soil erosion, salinization, and soil compaction."

Rafirre bowed toward the commissioners, stepped down, and nodded to the willowy woman who took his place.

The head of the Nature Assessment Group adjusted her sari-like dress as she stepped up to stand in front of the lectern. "May it please the commission," she began. She was tasked with providing an overview of the state of the biosphere on Earth. Its condition was among the worst she had ever encountered.

"I regret to report that the natives here are killing off the last remnants of their large wildlife at a striking pace," she began. "Of the elephant family, only two genera survive. One—the African elephant—numbered in the millions a mere two human lifetimes ago. It now stands at only a few hundred thousand." Her mouth twisted with evident frustration. "At present, wild terrestrial mammals constitute roughly four percent of terrestrial mammalian biomass. The remaining ninety-six percent is livestock and humans."

A measured stillness overtook the dais at that. The Presiding Chair shifted on his *sitta*, the wood creaking.

"And it's not only mammals," she went on, her slender fingers curled around the edges of the lectern. "In the last fifty years, North America alone lost close to three billion birds. As for insects, widespread habitat loss and agricultural practices are collapsing populations across the globe. Sooner or later, this is bound to have catastrophic cascading effects on birds, reptiles, fish, and amphibians. We are talking about the possible collapse of entire ecosystems."

The robed commissioners exchanged glances. Some of them narrowed their eyes.

Her gaze met that of the commissioners before sweeping over the crowd. "Your Graces, this planet is in the throes of a mass extinction event. It began in pulses across various regions, starting about forty-five thousand years ago in Australia with the eradication of giant herbivores and apex predators through rampant hunting," the willowy woman said. "The juggernaut of extinctions proceeded apace millennia later with the massive clearing of land for settlements and agriculture. In the last handful of generations, the pace has quickened due to systematic large-scale poaching and harvesting, the introduction of alien pests, pollution, and the ceaseless degradation, fragmentation, and devastation of natural habitats."

She brushed a strand of hair away from her face and paused to collect her thoughts. "This planet is under siege as hundreds of thousands of manmade compounds make their way into every nook and crevice of the natural world. Carcinogens like benzene and ethylene oxide, developmental disruptors like toluene and nitrous oxide, reproductive hazards such as carbon disulfide, and respiratory toxicants like acid aerosols. These toxins persist in the environment, circulating through air, water, and soil, making contact with wildlife on a devastating scale—taking a punishing toll on the biosphere."

The head of the Nature Assessment Group continued, "Beyond the tundra and taiga, the only remaining grand stronghold of the planetary ecosystem is the nearly six million square kilometers of the Amazon rainforest. It provides habitat for the largest concentration of species of any land ecosystem. It is home to many of the extant mammals, birds, and tree species in the world. And it is being decimated, piece by piece.

"There are thousands of timber mills scattered throughout Amazonia, busily priming the choicest trees for conversion into parquet, furniture, and coffins—removing about twenty-five million cubic meters of trees from the forest each year. And on average, for every tree being hauled away, close to thirty are killed or damaged.

"Loggers, poachers, and miners are responsible for the largest expansion of road networks into the wilderness. With the roads comes the influx of ranchers, land speculators, and agribusinesses. In short, deforestation. By the close of the twentieth century, over three-quarters of a million square kilometers of the Amazon forest had been cleared. More has been cut down since.

"It is likely that within one lifetime, the Amazon rainforest will be replaced by a mosaic of ranches, crop fields, and patches of open-canopy forest. With no moisture in the soil, there will be far less rain. Thus, the micro-climate that gave rise to those forests will also fade. The last vestiges of ecologically rich biomes will be gone from Earth for eons to come, leaving behind ghosts of what once was and ashes, which shortly thereafter will be scattered by the winds."

The director drew a steadying breath. "The final solution to the biodiversity question is near." For a moment, her voice broke. "Over the past fifty years, Terraneans have wrecked ecosystems more rapidly and extensively than in any comparable period in their recorded history. Hundreds, if not thousands, of species now go extinct each decade. To put it bluntly, the fate of biological diversity for millions of years to come may be determined here and now." She fell silent.

Some of the commissioners conferred among themselves in low voices. "What is the status of the marine biomes?" the Presiding Chair asked.

The head of the Nature Assessment Group inclined her head, gathering herself.

She finally looked up. "Your Graces, to harvest a handful of commercially valuable 'target' species, the natives drag massive nets, armed with steel plates and weighty rollers, across the seabed. Any unwanted fish are dumped back into the water, lifeless. The trawling clears vast areas, hundreds of thousands of square kilometers, turning rich marine habitats into barren, flattened wastelands. This destruction is further exacerbated by extensive seafloor mining for sand and gravel that wreaks havoc on seaweeds, corals, and seagrass meadows.

"Diverse, functional ecosystems constitute only 10 to 15 percent of the ocean—primarily the high seas of the Southern Ocean and the Arctic Ocean."

She took a few moments to consult her notes on the lectern.

"Then there is the stuff they discharge into the seas," she went on. "We estimate that every square mile of ocean is littered with thousands of microscopic plastic particles. We detected these in the guts of marine animals throughout the ocean, even in those dwelling in the deepest ocean trenches. Under the current trajectory, in a few decades there will be more plastics than fish at sea, pound for pound."

She continued, "At the same time, massive amounts of chemical fertilizers, human sewage, and dung from hog and chicken farms stream into the oceans. Joining this barrage are the carcasses of livestock that die en route at sea.

"The torrent of millions of tons of organic matter has been fueling an explosive growth of microalgae, augmenting this naturally occurring phenomenon. Blooms of algae turn the Baltic Sea into reeking, brown-colored slush with dead fish floating about. On the southern coast of Maui, high tides leave foul-smelling piles of green-brown algae. On Florida's Gulf Coast, harmful algal blooms have become more pronounced and longer-lasting. And in recent years, Stinging Limu seaweed has burst forth each spring from spores on the seafloor, forming large floating mats of dark, wool-like strands. During algal decay, the bacteria that decompose them deplete the oxygen in deep waters. This has resulted in the formation of vast oxygen-starved regions: dead zones."

A sudden gust snapped the stretched fabric walls, and she lifted her voice to carry over it. "The existing ocean ecosystems are waning. Species that have been kept at bay by fish and sea mammals are becoming dominant. Slimy jellyfish are poised to take the place of fish. From the coral reefs in the Red Sea to the sea mounds off the coasts of Chile, some of the most complex webs of marine life are unraveling while base life forms are proliferating. Human activities here may end up transmuting the ocean into a microbial soup teeming with gelatinous, poisonous blobs and a seabed littered with empty aluminum cans."

The director of the Nature Assessment Group offered a bow to the commission members.

"We thank you for your testimony," the Presiding Chair said, nodding in response.

Attendants dashed onto the platform and repositioned the commissioners' pedestals into a circular configuration. The seven figures held a quiet discussion among themselves as the hundreds of people in attendance and many hundreds of millions of distant television and online viewers watched in anticipation.

Eventually, the Presiding Chair signaled, and the attendants rushed back in. He waited until the pedestals were moved, and all the commissioners faced the audience. He cleared his throat and declared, "The motion to fast-track the hearing has hereby been granted."

Animated murmurs greeted the announcement.

He continued, "The hearing will commence in three days. Testimony will last for four weeks, followed by a week for deliberation. A decision will be rendered immediately thereafter."

Turning his attention to the vast multitude of Earth's inhabitants tuned into the proceedings, the Presiding Chair nodded solemnly. "No doubt, our presence on your planet and the commencement of this hearing stir profound questions and apprehension within you." He paused. "You must understand that our primary concern is the welfare of this planet. We'll evaluate whether your people can forge an ecologically viable path, or whether you'll continue to degrade the planetary ecosystem to a point of collapse." He folded his arms into his voluminous robe. "If it's the latter, we'll implement... rigorous measures to turn things around. Given a choice, though, we would rather leave your kind to govern your own affairs." His words hung in the silence that followed.

The Presiding Chair resumed, "We welcome a delegation to present your case. You have three weeks to assemble one. The decision to hold the hearing in public was made to give your population a chance to mount a credible defense."

A brief smile flitted across his face. "We understand you have a variety of governing bodies. That is nice," he added kindly. "But they are of no relevance. We address you, all of you, directly." With this, he inclined his head and rapped his ceremonial hammer.

The audience rose to its collective feet and bowed as the Presiding Chair stepped down from the platform, followed by the other six commissioners. In a quiet procession led by the master of ceremonies, the robed commissioners departed.

An administrator in white-and-silver livery walked up to the lectern and addressed the vast number of unseen viewers, "Today's opening session was conducted on your planet. The remainder of the hearing will take place off-world, in our permanent facility, and will be broadcast for you to observe. However, some of you have been offered the unique opportunity to attend it."

He paused, consulting a small tablet. "A diverse group of individuals across Earth—some selected at random, some not—received a cryptic letter several days ago." He looked up. "I trust its purpose is now clear."

He let that settle.

"If you wish to be at the hearing in person, simply press your thumb onto the black circle at the bottom of your letter, and you will be teleported to our location. Or at least, the first one hundred respondents to do so will be.

"No harm will come to you at the hearing. Rest assured, we will cater to all your needs during your stay. The teleportation portal will remain active for the next ten minutes. We apologize for the abrupt nature of this invitation, but our intent is to minimize any undue outside influences on those invited."

The administrator bowed and the session came to an end.

The fabric partitions continued to snap in the wind, heedless. The *sittas* stood empty now. On the platform, a single sheet of paper—someone's notes—lifted and tumbled across the polished wood before disappearing over the edge into the grass.

CHAPTER 24

Undisclosed Location, Off-World, the Commission Building

"Let's start at the beginning of your mission to Earth," one of the commissioners began. "When did you begin monitoring the planet?"

Aratta, Puddeck, and Hagar were seated in a small domed hall, paneled in wood and bathed in soft light. Before them, members of the commission perched on elevated cushions, arrayed in half a circle.

It was three days after the opening session, and the hearing proper had just gotten underway.

Essentially, a fast track meant a marathon of sessions and testimony. Over the next four weeks, concurrent hearings on various topics would fill the adjoining chambers. Some would command the attention of all commissioners; others would be split sessions. Smaller meetings would take place in intimate rooms, while larger ones would host broad audiences.

"Your Graces," Aratta replied, "we first checked on this planet in 1251."

"What prompted that?" the Presiding Chair asked.

"It was just routine," Aratta said. "We drop by and check on myriad planets. Next, we visited Earth in 1543 and have kept watch ever since."

"What transpired in the intervening years?"

"A most momentous event in their history."

The commissioner nodded with understanding. "Contact with the Americas."

"Indeed," Aratta said. "Evidently, initial contact was made around the year 1000, but it had no lasting effect, and the European settlement withered away and was then forgotten. However, the Europeans reached the Americas again in 1492. And the world irrevocably transformed. When we came in 1543, commerce networks connected many of the major population hubs of Earth. By then, Europeans were well on their way to establishing trading outposts in India, China, the Philippines, and Indonesia. It was the birth of the modern era."

Hagar said, "The Americas and Eurasia were home to diverse nations and tens, if not hundreds, of millions of inhabitants. The meeting of these two civilizations marked an unparalleled event in the annals of human history on Earth—a unique crossroads that offered a boundless opportunity to enrich and broaden the collective wisdom. Regrettably, Your Graces, the encounter was a profoundly disheartening affair. For the Americas, it could not have been more calamitous."

Puddeck chuckled. "The Spaniards set out to explore strange new worlds and seek out new life and new civilizations. But then again, maybe not," he conceded. "They journeyed, arrived, and proclaimed everything in sight as the Property of Spain."

"And?"

Puddeck shrugged. "These bragging rights did little for their fortune or sense of power: They neither discovered a route to China nor found any shiny objects in commercial amounts. Oh, sure, they got their jollies off, messing with local girls and offing natives. But aside from a couple of gold nuggets, a squawking parrot or two, and a few savages they paraded around as trophies, they barely had a peso's worth to show for their fool's errand."

Puddeck got up and approached the bench. "The turning point was the 1499–1501 expeditions." He pulled a fistful of small, rounded items from a pouch and dumped them on the polished wood table in front of the commission members. "Off the coast of Venezuela, the locals had been harvesting these for centuries."

One of the commissioners leaned in and gave a startled laugh. "Pearls," she said and looked up. "What did they want with them? Were they for their children?"

Puddeck looked down at the tiny, lustrous pebbles. "These are shiny objects," he explained. "Back home, there were many willing to pay a pretty penny for them. They were meant for grownups. As the tide of pearls washed onto Europe's shores, they were promptly turned into earrings or used to spruce up hats and capes.

"From that point, it was game on. Things really ramped up in the 1520s," Puddeck said. "The merry band of fortune seekers on the island of Cubagua rolled in dough for about a dozen years. By the time we visited the place in 1543, the party was over. The last diehards left a couple of weeks earlier. All we found were spent husks of oyster beds and the smoldering ruins of buildings that pirates had set on fire several months prior.

"Tens of billions of oysters were dredged from the seas between Cubagua and its two neighboring islands during those years, until the sea gave up nothing more. The fortune seekers were heartbroken. But then the good news came: A few hundred miles due west, around the Guajira Peninsula, new oyster beds were spotted with the promise of additional shiny objects and a pretty penny. Some stayed behind, hoping the oysters might rebound. However, the majority packed up and scurried off to the new frontier. There was work to be done."

A commissioner asked, "How in blazes do people harvest tens of billions of oysters in a couple of decades?"

"It began low-key, bartering with the natives," Puddeck said. "The Europeans dangled linen shirts, loaves of bread, even firearms. In return, the indigenous folks parted ways with pearls and, on occasion, even loaned out women to sweeten the deal.

"But as more compadres washed ashore, the shine of European

trinkets began to dull, and the locals started to demand more bang for their pearls. To add insult to injury, they weren't keen on spending their days face-down in seawater. This grated on the ever-swelling ranks of Spanish newcomers, who hadn't schlepped halfway across the world to dick around with ten pearls or a hundred. Nice was not getting the job done.

"In the Bahamas, they captured Lucayan Indians, branded their faces or arms with a letter C and shipped them in. Every day, they were thrown in at dawn and pulled out by dusk. At night, they were chained—listening to the drunken laughter of Spaniards gambling, brawling, and forcing themselves on wenches.

"Those Lucayans who were diving and were not killed by sharks gradually began to suffer from hemorrhages and intestinal disorders. They died to a man. More divers were captured from elsewhere, hauled in, and shoved in their place. Incidentally, a similar saga played out near Guanabara Bay on South America's eastern shores. The Portuguese pillaged indigenous villages, forced the natives to extract brazilwood, and then raided new villages to restock. Lather, rinse, repeat."

Puddeck bowed.

"Their utter disregard for human lives aside, they must have realized that with this no-holds-barred approach, they would be grasping at air within a short period of time," a commissioner said. "Why not maintain a sustainable pearl harvesting rate?"

"Your Graces," Aratta said, "they had to harvest quickly. Each day, if a person delayed using up his Indians, someone else seized a chunk of the pearls that could have been his. It was a zero-sum game. The continuous arrival of more fortune hunters intensified the competition and quickened the pace. To an extent, that has set the tone of things to come in the centuries to follow."

"Two years after our arrival," Hagar said, "somebody stumbled on a mountain filled with shiny metal—silver—in what is now the heart of Bolivia. Tens of thousands hastened there from all over Europe. Potosi was the largest boomtown in the world, sporting dozens of gambling dens, dance halls, and street fights. It had a population that rivaled that of London, Venice, or Seville. People strutted around the streets, while the bulk of the mining and refining work was relegated to hapless local people, whose carcasses kept piling up faster than the shiny metal they mined."

"What purpose did all that silver serve? Was it used for power lines?"

Hagar shook her head. "Back then, Your Grace, the natives here had not yet established an electrical grid. Much of the demand for the metal was fueled by China. They used it as a currency."

"Didn't they have paper, state-issued fiat currency?" one of the commissioners asked.

"They did," Aratta said. "But the Chinese government had delighted in printing paper money, and the resulting inflation brought chaos and distrust. Hence: silver."

Puddeck said, "Potosi was just the first salvo. Since that time, transnational corporations have been scouring the planet. Neither unspoiled wilderness nor human dignity nor heat nor gloom of night has stayed them from obtaining cheap goods and natural resources. The world has been their oyster, the ecological systems theirs for the taking."

"This dynamic isn't restricted to transnational corporations alone," Hagar said and shrugged. "Why, in recent times, locals have been coming down from the Andes Mountains and wiping out large swathes of primary rainforest in the Amazon in their pursuit of another shiny metal, gold. And then they go home, leaving behind mercury-laced ponds and a landscape barren of trees and vegetation. This has been going on for decades now."

"We thank you for this testimony," the Presiding Chair said. The three of them bowed in return. The chief commissioner glanced over at the ever-present group of aides in white-and-silver livery. "What's next on the agenda?"

"Organized violence, Presiding Chair," said the senior-most aide.

CHAPTER 25

Undisclosed Location, Off-World, the Commission Building

"You people worship success and progress," Nayef al-Jabouri responded to a comment Susan had made, stroking his trimmed, salt-and-pepper beard. "Did you ever stop to think how you construe success and what you are progressing toward?" He gestured dismissively. "Your culture is as broad as a floodplain, and just as shallow." He spoke with a British accent and hints of something else.

Susan had noticed him yesterday and the day before. Always the same dark, knit kufi cap, the same white shirt buttoned all the way up, and the same white three-quarter-length pants.

A small group of Terraneans gathered in one of the brick-veneered alcoves in the lobby, comfortably seated on button-tufted velvet armchairs. On the circular table in front of them, an attendant was setting down some glasses and a carafe of water with lime. The hearing on war was scheduled to start within the hour. However, the large, engraved brass doors leading to the deliberation chamber were still closed.

"It's that progress that allows us to have this conversation and enjoy liberty," Susan snapped, irritated. "In places like Iran or Afghanistan, religious police may detain women for simply jogging in a sports bra. In America, we are free to wear what we want."

"Nonsense," al-Jabouri said. "A middle-aged man wearing

nothing but an open trench coat and a cowboy hat will be arrested in the United States. You, too, impose standards of decency. The particulars may differ; the principle does not."

Susan blinked, the retort dying in her throat.

Konsta was unimpressed. "With you it isn't decency—it's erasure," he said. "You force women to navigate life in portable tents. You strip away the simple joy of wind on their faces and cut them off from the world. You turn them into ghosts."

Al-Jabouri mulled it over, then looked over at Konsta. "In India, a bare midriff is considered modest; in the United States, it's suggestive. Different societies, different norms. So I ask you, who is better suited to set the standard than the Lord of mankind? It is written in the Book of God that all of a woman's body should be covered in public, save for the hands and wrists." His expression hardened. "Your society exploits the beauty and allure of women to hawk goods, which is nothing short of demeaning. We, in Islamic lands, honor and safeguard our women."

The one hundred Earthborn who had been invited to the hearing and were interested in attending its proceedings had arrived as a group three days earlier. They spent the first two talking about little other than the hearing and the realization that the people on Earth were not alone; there were other humans on parallel planets. A sense of unreality hung over the entire first day. A small but vocal subset was convinced this was an elaborate ruse, perhaps a scheme contrived by a government agency or by some billionaires. Opinions varied among them, changing seemingly by the hour.

The Terranean attendees also analyzed in detail their teleportation to the Commission Building, the puzzling freeze they were put in during the security check they'd undergone, and the notorious ten-minute blackout when Frank powered down all generators, plunging the world into darkness. Ideas about how these things could be made possible were numerous. However, no one could offer a compelling explanation within the framework of existing technologies.

But most of all, they speculated ad nauseam about what the eventual ruling could mean for the people on Earth. Views ranged from the joyous to the bleak. In fact, there was not much in between. Some maintained they would all be exterminated, bringing the failed human experiment on Earth to an end; it was judgment time, they claimed, and the verdict was all but preordained. Others held to the notion of benign despotic overlords, ushering in a golden age. A third, smaller camp argued that the 'off-worlders,' as they quickly came to be called, would send advisors and disseminate advanced technology, uplifting humanity and the world as a whole. Many were resentful of outside meddling, any sort of outside meddling.

By the third day, the Earth people had exhausted all avenues of speculation and analysis, and those discussions petered out. Familiarity started to settle in as the attendees acclimated to their surroundings and circumstances. Their conversations shifted to more mundane subjects like environment, religion, and politics. The return to familiar discussion topics buoyed morale, helping to push away the ill-boding unknowns that hung heavily over all of them.

A handful of people—such as Mr. Galecki, Susan, and Brandon —were personally invited by Aratta, and they jumped at the opportunity to witness what surely was the most momentous event in their lifetimes, if not beyond. Other attendees, hailing from various regions of Earth, represented an assortment of backgrounds and professions. They were all thrown together, people who otherwise would not have been likely to cross paths or interact.

This was how Mr. Galecki and Susan, two Americans, found themselves sharing seats with Wang Lei, an entrepreneur from mainland China; Konsta, an automotive engineer from Finland; and Nayef al-Jabouri, a devout Muslim from the United Kingdom with roots in Southwest Asia. Then there was Lee, who, since arriving at the Commission Building, had maintained minimal eye contact and spoken even less. Susan and Mr. Galecki chalked it up to the sheer shock of the last few days.

"You seek to control too much," Mr. Galecki said. He leaned forward across the table. "Let me be honest—some of us don't care for gay marriage. All the same, everyone ought to have the right to choose whatever arrangement they want."

"Deviants should be killed off, not allowed an infertile, faux marriage," al-Jabouri said testily. He drew in a long breath to calm himself. "Tell me, where is your vaunted liberty if a man wants to take on a second or a third wife?"

"Being part of a harem? Women are partners, not collectibles," Susan said, outraged.

Al-Jabouri gave a thin smile. "What of the surplus of women in the aftermath of war? And the widows, the divorcees, left to fend for themselves in a world where men often balk at marrying them? Who would provide for them? Who would guard their honor?"

Konsta was surprised by those arguments. They made sense—in an eighteenth-century kind of way.

"Wearing a *niqab* and offering prayers five times a day." Nayef al-Jabouri shook his head ruefully. "This is the first and last thing you know about the divine way, the Shari'ah." Such were the pitfalls of viewing the Qur'an as a book of chants and recitations rather than a guide to governance. "Shari'ah is an all-encompassing social order—nothing superfluous, nothing lacking." His eyes shone with an inner light. "From marital relationships to economic affairs to international relations, it aligns human life with the law of the universe in perfect harmony. It commands the active rejection of evil—by hand, by tongue, by heart."

Mr. Galecki lifted his glass in a sarcastic toast. "A book with all the answers, eh?"

With some effort, Nayef al-Jabouri controlled the flare of anger. His fingers dug into the arms of the chair. "The Islamic law will be a merciful thing for the West."

"What about the freedom of choice?" Mr. Galecki shot back.

"Freedom is merely the possibility of choosing," the Muslim

man said. "Once a choice is made—which, sooner or later, all people make—we are governed by a certain code of conduct. Hence, the word *Islam*: submission to God."

A flush crept up Susan's face. Many of the concepts Nayef al-Jabouri voiced were disturbingly similar to what she had heard in her church. It was too close for comfort.

The man in white attire and a dark kufi cap clasped his hands around one knee. "The lordship of man over another is the root cause of all corrupt rule. This is why no laws can be legitimate except God's, and no government representatives are valid except those who rule as God's deputies, implementing God's laws exclusively."

Mr. Galecki frowned; he had a feeling he knew where this was heading.

The bearded man said, "Alas, the men who have usurped the authority of God and presume to govern other men are not going to give up their power merely through preaching. We have to do it the way of the Prophet, with blood-red swords." His countenance grew stern. "The imposition of God's Rule and the laws of Islam upon this Earth is an obligation for all Muslims. As it is stated in the Holy Book: 'And fight them until there is no more disbelief, and the religion, all of it, is for Allah.'"

We will rub the noses of the *kuffar* in the dirt, al-Jabouri thought grimly, shed their blood and take their wealth as spoils of war. Yes, the sun of jihad has risen, praise be to Allah. The time had come for those being nursed on the milk of humiliation to rise, remove the garments of debasement, for the era of hand-wringing was at an end. Indeed, the black flag of *tawhid* had been raised by the soldiers of Allah. And within a few generations, the Crusader lands would be under the sway of a new caliphate. First Constantinople, then Rome, and then the White House.

Nayef al-Jabouri wasn't always a true believer. He had scoffed at his brethren and their empty proclamations, like gnats biting a lion. However, as the years went by, he saw it. He saw how Allah

Most High had addled and befuddled the brains of the *kuffar*, how they opened the gates, how they held placards greeting the incoming invaders. Even soldiers of the Islamic State, *mujahideen*, were allowed back into Western Europe, unmolested. This was when he became a believer, as what he witnessed was beyond belief, beyond reason.

Even the *Rafidah* in Tehran, vile in their corruption and deviation, had grasped a truth the Crusaders could not. A people ruled in the name of God, and fixed upon the Last Days, could endure what no parliament of merchants and fornicators ever would. With al-Quds at the center of their ambition and the return of the Mahdi before their eyes, they labored for a dominion stretching from the shores of the Mediterranean to the lands of Central Asia. Their way was not persuasion but terror: missiles enough to make every blow against them dearly purchased, the bomb as the final guarantor, and the narrow seas held hostage by threat. Such a regime might bury all its enemies in time, for those who measure history in generations and count sacrifice a form of worship possess a patience and hardness unknown to nations grown fat on ease and bound to election cycles.

Inshallah, his grandchildren would live to see the lands of the Crusaders become theirs, al-Jabouri mused, and he kept his face blank, careful not to show any sign of satisfaction. Millions of his brethren had colonized Europe over recent decades in the scramble for Europe. The natives' tongues had been tied—by law or by fear. And the thousands of mosques established across Western Europe had by now reached the Outer Hebrides. Slowly, steadily, through the generations, it would all work out.

Susan said, "Thank goodness, most Muslims don't advocate your militant form of Islam." *That Jihadi Salafist nut job!*

With an impassive expression, Lee had been listening to the exchange with a growing sense of unease and disgust. She had chosen to attend the hearing but soon felt she could no longer engage in these people's discussions. It became increasingly clear with each passing hour that she would not resume her life among the Terraneans. This chapter of her life was swiftly drawing to a close.

"You accuse us of evil, yet your uniformed forces have committed grave atrocities," al-Jabouri said. "You've slaughtered people in their homes, marketplaces, and on their daily routes. Your invasions of Iraq and Afghanistan have resulted in countless deaths and displaced millions."

"He has a point," Konsta said. "A group of jihadis murdered three thousand of your civilians. You answered by tearing apart entire regions and killing three hundred thousand noncombatants."

"This is the only language they understand," Mr. Galecki said, his face reddening. "We're fighting terrorists around the world and scoring victories." He regarded Konsta, and there was a sudden icy contempt in his eyes. "If not for us, who is going to fight them—you?"

"This is—"

"You don't get to talk," Mr. Galecki interrupted him. "Not as long as it is our funds and our boys underwriting your defenses, decade after decade."

Mr. Galecki sat there in stony silence. What choked him wasn't the European ingratitude—it was the sanctimony, curdling in his gut like something spoiled. Their peace was a walled garden, existing only because American men with guns stood watch in the dark, bludgeoning the wolves so Europe could sleep. They moralized from the safety of a world his country kept from burning.

Konsta glared back at him. "Let's take a trip down memory lane, shall we? In the '60s and '70s, you rained down over two hundred million cluster bombs on Laos. Millions of these, mind you, can still turn a child's frolic in a field or a farmer's workday into a gore-splattered horror scene."

Konsta was still at it. "In 2001, you tasted what you'd been dishing out for decades."

Susan's face went white. "The men who flew those missions

were honorable. They followed—"

"Orders, I know." Konsta's voice was flat. "Put this aside, and think about it. Really think about it. Your military isn't standing guard at home; it's flexing in everybody else's backyard."

Wang Lei covered a chuckle with a cough. As he saw it, the American was the rich, dotty uncle with a temper. Equipped with a blunderbuss and binoculars, he was dashing about, mindlessly blowing up things here, there, and everywhere. Racking up trillions of dollars on a credit card that his grandkids would be saddled with, the American was chasing phantoms through deserts and across jungles.

In contrast, China bombed no one and antagonized few. It didn't bleed itself dry on warfronts abroad but rather granted strategic loans to states that could not repay, like Sri Lanka.

As Wang Lei saw it, China's century of humiliation was drawing to a close; it was commanding the global stage, once again. In Australia, it owned everything from farms to factories, from an airport to a seaport, from wind farms to coal mines. Along with Africa, Australia was gradually being pulled into China's orbit, on its way to becoming a tributary state. Slowly through the generations, it would all work out. For Wang Lei, the *Zhōngguó Mèng* was no mere slogan; the ascension and rejuvenation of the mighty Chinese nation were inevitabilities.

"Americans," he observed aloud while meticulously buffing his nails, "the self-proclaimed, righteous global overlords, trampling over every humanitarian convention." Dressed in a smart dark suit with a white dress shirt casually open at the collar, Wang Lei exuded confidence. A gleaming red pack of expensive Chunghwa cigarettes jutted from his breast pocket.

Mr. Galecki looked over at the Chinese businessman in silence, his eyes hard and filled with dislike. "Spare us the sanctimony. More than ten thousand Chinese firms are operating in Africa," he said, the words sharp with distaste. "Your rapacious grip extends to every resource. West Africa's forests vanish into your shipping containers—Gambia, Ghana, Senegal, one by one."

"Quite so," Wang Lei agreed, giving his fingers a last inspection, "and let's not forget the forests of Indochina."

"'Quite so'?" Mr. Galecki repeated, his voice incredulous.

Wang Lei put down the nail file. "The word 'China,'" he explained, "is short for 'one-fifth of humanity intending to join the middle class.' You Westerners already enjoy your fine cabinets and dining tables. It's our turn now," he said, shrugging. "This translates to a lot of forests." Wang Lei was fortunate to have secured some of the rare, exquisite mukula wood from Zambia.

Listening to the ongoing exchange, Lee felt as if she were neck-deep in a murky swamp, their words pressing her ever lower. She could feel the blood pumping in her temples. None of the people seated nearby in the alcove paid her any heed.

"With you," Mr. Galecki was saying, "it's all about power and resource-grabbing. But mark my words, you'll never be as innovative as we are!"

Wang Lei grinned wolfishly. He pulled out a cigarette. "What difference does that make?" He lit it and waved it about. "Integrated-circuit manufacturing, pressurized-water reactors, genetically modified organisms, or high-end machine tools—what we don't get from you through trade, mergers, and acquisitions, we take from you in other ways."

He took a drag on his cigarette.

"We've hacked into your databases, pilfering your trade secrets, business protocols, and intellectual assets. We've coerced technology transfers in exchange for entry into the Chinese market. We've gained control of numerous startups in artificial intelligence, autonomous vehicles, augmented reality, robotics, and blockchain. We've meticulously reverse-engineered your innovations. We've deployed a vast workforce to trawl through your doctoral theses, government reports, and conference proceedings, channeling the extracted knowledge into our industries and research institutes. We have legions of people within your universities, national labs, innovation centers, incubators, and think tanks." Wang Lei blew a ring of smoke upward and smiled at Mr. Galecki. "You've become our innovation pasture, just as Africa is shaping up to be our resource larder."

And the Uyghurs your organ farm, Lee thought, the words rising unbidden, acid in her throat.

Mr. Galecki reddened. "However—"

"And now, look at you! You've lost much of your manufacturing capabilities. You depend on us for many of your medications and strategic minerals, from gallium to barite." Wang Lei burst out laughing.

Lee scrambled to her feet and, without looking back or acknowledging Susan's concerned call, walked away. She could bear it no more.

She was done with them, with all of them. Lee did not want to hear any more of al-Jabouri's plans for a global caliphate, the tally of atrocities of the Americans, or the resource takeover by the Chinese. They were all busy establishing brave new worlds.

At the far end of the hallway, she opened a door and shut it behind her.

CHAPTER 26

Undisclosed Location, Off-World, the Commission Building

"IRAQ SEIZED THE TINY OIL-SOAKED PEARL OF KUWAIT," Puddeck said. "This event ignited an international outpouring of support so stirring, it could moisten a veteran soldier's eye. From the UK to France, from Canada to Italy, a chorus arose, united by camaraderie and petroleum.

"With America at the helm, nearly a million troops piled in to liberate the Kuwaitis and their oil. Just the logistics of relocating all these personnel and equipment to various staging areas required sixteen thousand airborne sorties. Hell, the daily instructions alone could've filled an insurance claim binder. Everyone jostled for flight time, chomping at the bit to do their share to drive the Iraqis out." As he delivered this, Puddeck paced the hexagonal bamboo stage.

This was the first session focusing on Earth's violent conflicts. It'd started hours earlier in one of the larger meeting rooms. The hall was round, with a soft lime-green carpet. The walls and ceiling were decked out in hand-carved oak panels with a luster finish. Behind a tall desk, seven polished wood pedestals were in place. At that moment, four of these were occupied by commissioners, who were listening to the man in the violet robe, Puddeck, as he resumed his spot at the lectern.

"Fast-forward three years," he said, "when word reached the same governments that an extermination campaign was gearing up in Rwanda, the responses were glazed eyes and vacant stares. Experts estimated that less than ten thousand well-equipped, determined soldiers could prevent the genocide before the wheels started turning. Yet, no military could pencil in Rwanda on its jam-packed schedules."

He paused for a moment.

"When the systematic slaughter of the Tutsi population commenced in Rwanda, France advocated for a humanitarian mission. The United States suggested the UN council dispatch a symbolic delegation. Meanwhile, the United Kingdom urged everyone to steer clear of trigger words like 'forceful action.'

"The national piggy banks must've been scraped clean," Puddeck confided. "The Americans balked at the idea of even allocating funds to jam the radio station drumming up the call to murder. And when African troops stood poised and ready for a rescue operation, the United States failed to scrounge up the funding needed to provide airlift support."

"Has this reaction been typical?" one of the commissioners asked.

"Yes," Puddeck said. "The public back home—be it in Australia or in Colombia—has not given a rat's ass about extermination campaigns happening to 'other' people—not when two million Cambodians were slaughtered, not when six million Jews were exterminated, not when hundreds of thousands of Armenians, Greeks, and Assyrians were butchered. The decision-makers have been just as indifferent."

He continued, "The killing season in Rwanda went on month after month. It ended only when, in a dizzying five-day span, a staggering eight hundred and fifty thousand souls fled, crossing the border into Zaire."

With a grand sweep of his hand, Puddeck summoned a holographic video projection that materialized all around them, vividly capturing a ripple of the past. It showed them a long, silent march of a seemingly endless number of people. "This is when the international community leapt into action," Puddeck continued. "Thousands of aid workers were airlifted and rushed into the area. A nonstop stream of planes touched down in a nearby border town, hour after hour, bringing tent components, food, and medical supplies—arguably the biggest humanitarian deployment of the twentieth century. From Save the Children to Doctors Without Borders, over four hundred NGOs showed up. It was like a goddamn do-gooder convention."

The man in violet fell silent as the people in the room regarded the never-ending column of marchers. "It's certainly not every day that you see a mass parade of serial killers," he observed.

The Presiding Chair reared back. "What did you say?"

Puddeck motioned and the camera zoomed in close enough to make out the faces of the marching people in the column. "I did fail to mention that, didn't I?" He smacked his thigh. "Those are not the Tutsi fleeing the genocide. Those are the aggressors, the accomplices, the killers, the génocidaires: the Hutus."

A wave of scandalized murmurs swept through the chamber at his words. He had to raise his voice. "And mind you, we're talking here about people having a hearty breakfast, then, with a machete in hand and a song in their hearts, spending hours on end hunting and butchering Tutsi families. Then wake up the day after and do it all over again. Seven days a week; week in, week out; month in, month out. That is, until word reached them that a Tutsi-led army was advancing from the north, and the lot of them fled."

"Did the aid organizations not realize who they were provisioning and sheltering?"

"Your Grace, the humanitarians caught on soon enough," Puddeck said. "But what were they going to say to the people back home? 'We've used your donation money to stuff the bellies of murderers and their accomplices who are plotting to regroup and continue their extermination campaign'? Look, they'd been given the dough to feed hungry people with dark skin, and that's what they were doing. Why quibble over the details?" Puddeck asked.

"The Hutu leaders were only too happy to let the Western dumdums supply and house their people while they themselves got down to the serious work of smuggling weapons and rebuilding their forces to resume the genocide campaign," Puddeck said. "With the money they had carted off from Rwanda and the money they were skimming from the do-gooders, the Hutu leaders procured AK-47s, ammunition vests, mortars, and rocket launchers."

Puddeck threw his hands up in the air in a gesture of helplessness. "But in the end, it amounted to little; most of their killing days were behind them. Eventually, the Hutus were forced back into Rwanda, where many were to stand trial and be meted out punishment by the newly formed government."

He gave a short bow and took a seat.

The Chief Examiner strode to the hexagonal floor area and laid his notes on the lectern. "May it please the commission, I'll proceed with the presentation on the war in Iraq."

One of the commissioners nodded.

"After repeated warnings," Rafirre began, "the US-led military coalition launched a shock-and-awe campaign, bombing the Iraqis right out of Kuwait. However, it did not stop there.

"Coalition forces flew over Iraq and blew up water treatment plants, food-processing and sewage facilities, communication centers, roads, and bridges. Overnight, urban Iraq was driven back to preindustrial living conditions. For the next dozen years, the US-led coalition imposed economic sanctions upon Iraq on a scale possibly unprecedented in the modern history of Earth."

One of the commissioners waved her hand, signaling the Examiner to halt. "I'm struggling to follow the narrative here. They drove the Iraqis out of Kuwait. What was the rest all about?"

Aratta rose to his feet. "Your Graces, beneath the smokescreen of deceit and delusion, there were political objectives. And beneath those, there were motives. Politicians had their motives, as did the top brass. Volunteer soldiers had theirs. The defense industry and an assortment of other Beltway contractors had their own." He shrugged. "That's not uncommon with government initiatives and programs around here. Rather than trying to plaster on a semblance of coherence—or even cynicism—I suggest letting the events stand on their own."

"Your point is well taken, Lord Aratta," the Presiding Chair said and motioned for Rafirre to continue.

The Examiner nodded. "The massive bombing of the infrastructure, coupled with the sanctions, made it impossible for Iraq to recover," he said. "Almost every support system necessary to sustain human life was left in ruins.

"Unemployment soared; millions were thrust below the poverty line and were reduced to living on handouts from the state. With malnutrition widespread and water contaminated, Iraq's infant mortality spiked. In a country where serious childhood hunger had been virtually unknown, they were now dying of diarrhea, typhoid, and cholera. Hundreds of thousands of young ones died during those years.

"A sense of hopelessness and desolation had settled over the land. Families broke up, kids were pulled out of school to beg or engage in petty crime. A religious revival swept through the country, and the mosques took on prominent roles in society. There was also a rekindling of clan associations and deepening sectarianism.

"The crushing US-led sanctions finally ended after a grueling twelve-year stretch—when US-led coalition forces rained bombs on Iraq and their ground troops stormed the land, and shattered the Iraqi state.

"During the takeover, countless bullets were discharged into the environment. And in addition to the depleted uranium rounds fired years earlier, US-led forces now added more. These created toxic dust that filtered through the air, ground, and water, contributing to the explosion of cancers and birth defects that followed.

"After toppling the Iraqi leadership, the occupiers declared they would usher in a stable democratic country. Thereafter, the administrative members of the occupying powers retreated behind concrete walls and barbed wire to the air-conditioned palace complex in the heart of Baghdad.

"It did not take long for anarchy and lawlessness to descend on the land.

"Across the country, government buildings were looted and gutted. Everything that could be pried off the walls was: from doors to light fixtures, from air conditioners to piping. Ancient artifacts and cultural treasures were plundered. Bands of looters roamed residential areas, and fathers kept their girls indoors for fear of rape. Criminals acted with impunity and militias set up shop in the middle of the streets, terrorizing the local people in broad daylight. Malnutrition and disease rose sharply, and the number of child beggars increased. Uncollected garbage piled up, untreated sewage slithered about, and gasoline prices surged upward—along with the resentment and indignation of the public.

"In a country underlain by ethnic fault lines, there was a desperate need to rally the population around a positive, unifying element. The Iraqi military, whatever its sins, remained the only national institution with the manpower and reach to impose order. Alas, the occupying forces dissolved it. Moreover, they purged large swaths of the Ministry of Interior. These were the very people familiar with the detailed workings of the infrastructure, from the power grid and water resources to public transportation. Thus, in a one-two punch, the US-led administration not only undermined the foundations necessary for social and economic activity but also alienated and humiliated hundreds of thousands of Iraqis who could no longer support their families. Adding fuel to the fire, the occupying forces shut down unprofitable state-run industries, laying off still more people.

"Hence, the resistance was born, embarking on a campaign to drive off the occupiers. They began detonating bombs and firing barrages of mortars.

"The growing opposition to the occupation finally provided the American soldiers with something to do: house raids, collective punishment, detentions, and questioning.

"But things are never so bad that they can't get worse.

"The Iraqis held mass rallies, clamoring for a genuine democratic election. But that wouldn't do. Behind the high walls of the air-conditioned palace complex, the foreign powers decreed a new form of national government built explicitly on ethnic and religious quotas. They peddled the notion that sectarianism permeated everything in Iraq. And only those who claimed to speak for a specific ethnic or religious group were invited.

"The administrators brought ideologues to the table, not the moderate and thoughtful people who represented the broader interests of Iraq. Professional qualifications mattered little; group identity was paramount. The ministries rarely coordinated their actions, helmed as they were by political adversaries. Staff, often unqualified, were hired based on family ties, friendships, or party affiliations, leaving government agencies virtually incapacitated.

"Then came one final gift: The occupiers canceled all tariffs and import taxes. Overnight, the inflow of cheap foreign consumer products devastated the businesses of domestic producers and sellers."

The Examiner took a sip of water.

"Your Graces, almost none of the Americans who jetted in to restore public services and set Iraq on a prosperous trajectory spoke Arabic, understood the Iraqi culture or economy, were familiar with the local power plays—or really cared to. They reckoned that good intentions, coupled with wads of crisp hundred-dollar bills parceled out liberally, would pacify the natives and set the *Hajjis* on the right path: the American way of life, values, and economic system.

"The Americans would drive into town, round up people, and hand them a few thousand dollars to start a business. Break ground on a hospital, only to abandon it roofless. Provide wheat seeds to grow in the desert. Compile a Yellow Pages telephone book with several hundred listings. Encourage women to open cafés in streets bereft of running water or electricity.

"The Iraqis had no intention of spending their own coins on those bridges-to-nowhere and half-baked enterprises, and neither did the Americans involved. But it was borrowed money that saddled future US taxpayers with the bill, so no one really minded.

"Now, I don't want to give the impression that the Americans floundered in all they undertook in Iraq. They proved quite capable when it came to matters of significance," Rafirre said. "As a case in point, they commandeered a large area for themselves, where they proceeded to build a movie theater, a Turkish café, and an Olympic-sized swimming pool. They also set up air-conditioned dining halls, where troops and contractors could eat cheeseburgers, baked salmon, roast turkey, grilled pork chops, banana pudding, and cherry pie. The servants were imported from Sri Lanka and Bangladesh."

Rafirre continued, "Americans practically insisted on overpaying for everything, turning Iraq from one of the least corrupt to one of the most corrupt countries in the world. By then, many Iraqi professionals emigrated in search of a better life. The Americans ended up pushing piles of money across the table overwhelmingly to thugs, fawners, and tribal strongmen with narrow, vested interests.

"Streams of dollar bills were fed in. These were processed into models, mission statements, and contracts. On the other end of the assembly line, out came progress reports, photos, and ribbon-cutting ceremonies—to fuel career advancement up and down the foreign service totem pole. In contrast, essentials that the local population needed, like a functional electrical grid or trash collection services, were a big investment of time and resources for very little optics.

"By 2011, after eight years of US presence, over a trillion dollars had been rerouted, and millions of Iraqis had no access to education, electricity, and health care. The labor market was dismal to nonexistent. The population was terrorized by rampant criminal gangs involved in kidnapping, extortion, robbery, and rape. Millions were internally displaced. Electrical lines and oil production equipment were pilfered. The Shiite-dominated government turned into a murky kleptocracy bobbing on a sea of American dollars and bent on persecuting the Sunni minority. Numerous people were murdered each month. Identity politics took on a prominent role in people's lives, fracturing the country along sectarian lines. All things considered, the US forces deemed their rebuilding of Iraq complete and withdrew."

With that, the Presiding Chair struck his ceremonial hammer, announcing a recess.

WHEN THE SESSION RECONVENED, Aratta rose. "If it pleases the commission, I would like to close out my earlier analysis of the forces that have underlain many of the violent conflicts on Earth."

The Presiding Chair nodded.

Aratta said, "The modern international order treats it as axiomatic that population groups are to exist inside immutable state containers—even if a given state container happens not to align with kinship networks, sectarian realities, economic geography, or historical patterns of authority.

"Nigeria's blockade of Biafra—shored up by the international system—starved around a million people, mostly Igbo, who sought to secede. Among other things, this was the cost of 'territorial integrity, come what may.'

"The collapse of the state of Somalia could have seen a reversion to the ecology of clans governing through customary law and negotiated pacts. Instead, the insistence on one legitimate government in the entire territory, one sovereign interface to the world, turned power into a single, winner-take-all prize. This interface was the funnel through which billions in aid would flow; the chokepoint controlling ports and customs; the authority granting permits and awarding contracts. Compromise among various clans became irrational.

"In Congo, Kinshasa's sovereignty over the eastern territories exists largely on paper. On the ground, power is held by militias and warlords who control towns, mines, and trade routes.

"In any other century, they would already have evolved into a mosaic of durable polities that provide services and social stability. But the modern international order bars this. Militia groups may hold territory, but not legitimacy. They are locked out of law, trade, diplomacy, and development, and pushed into smuggling, extortion, and mineral rackets. Warlordism is not a transitional phase in Congo—it is the only political form the paradigm makes possible. The cost? Large-scale displacements, rape campaigns, child soldiers, and millions dead."

Aratta bowed. He was done.

For a few minutes, the commissioners conferred in low voices, discussing what Aratta had just shared with them. Finally, they motioned to Rafirre, who stepped up to the lectern.

"Your Graces," he began, "outraged by the punishing sanctions imposed by the Crusaders on the Iraqi population throughout the 1990s, offended by the Crusaders' military bases in the heart of the holy land of Saudi Arabia, and scandalized by the Crusaders' alleged plundering of the Gulf's riches, a small militant Islamic organization decided to act. In 2001, nineteen members of Al-Qaeda hijacked four planes and crashed them into two tall skyscrapers in New York and into a part of the Pentagon. In the process, they killed themselves and a few thousand Americans."

Rafirre signaled to Puddeck, who was to take over that portion of the discussion.

The man in violet said, "The American public had no idea what any of this was about. But with the help of their leaders and media, they reasoned out this much: from that day on, their lives would always be in danger—unless. Unless someone would care for them a whole awful lot."

"What happened next?" the Presiding Chair asked.

"Some people had to pay dearly for what occurred," Puddeck explained. "This was something of a predicament as the entire outfit involved with the attack on American soil numbered just a few hundred Kalashnikov-wielding Al-Qaeda militants. Even killing all of them wouldn't have been enough payback; more people had to be killed. Setting this aside, the generals and politicians wanted to make such a display of wrath that no one would ever again dare to inflict mass harm on their civilians or otherwise threaten the American way of life.

"More enemies had to be proclaimed and dealt with. Hence, the government of Afghanistan, offering a sanctuary for Al-Qaeda, found itself on the chopping block, its personnel to be hunted down like rabid dogs. Moreover, the United States set its crosshairs not only on all the group members associated with the attack but on every Jihadist group across the globe. In perpetuity. Admittedly, in those days, there might not have been many such terror groups, but that was not something US forces could not rectify over time.

"Within a few months of the invasion, the Taliban collapsed; its forces surrendered. There was nothing to fight, no one to kill." Puddeck frowned for a moment. "Consider the situation. Australia deployed its Special Air Service Regiment troops; Canada brought in its Joint Task Force 2; the Czech Republic dispatched its 601st Special Forces Group; Denmark flew in its Jaeger Corps; and the United States dominated the all-star field with its variety of special ops units such as the Army Rangers and Delta Force. Afghanistan became a giant operators' rally. They all came to kill bad guys and otherwise see their hard training put to use. But the Afghans were not playing."

Puddeck paced about and shook his head ruefully.

"The break came from an unexpected angle. The Americans

established a network of black sites in Thailand, Morocco, Poland, and Romania. There and elsewhere, they imprisoned thousands of ex-Taliban—ex-government employees and foot soldiers—and suspended them from the ceiling by their wrists, subjecting them to prolonged sleep deprivation and mock executions. What torture didn't extract in intel, it repaid in enemies.

"Soon enough, supply exceeded demand as various Afghan warlords who wished to settle old scores pointed fingers in exchange for wads of dollar bills from the clueless—or perhaps indifferent—Americans. Personal feuds and old enemies were recast as counterterrorism." Puddeck nodded to himself. "As the ancient proverb goes, 'The enemy of my Afghan-allied warlord is the enemy of the United States.' Past grudges, large bounties, and wild rumors were enough to get people arrested, tortured, or killed."

Puddeck's face bore a sober expression. "With the occupation came the inevitable, heartfelt yearning to transform Afghanistan into a modern, thriving democracy. Much like Iraq.

"Uncounted billions of US taxpayer dollars began to fall from the sky, and American contractors and NGOs rushed in to catch the rainfall. Then they set to work: building a school with no power, no plumbing, and no students. Delivering cargo planes with no spare parts. Planting soybeans in soil that couldn't grow them for people who didn't want them. Erecting a power plant that ran on diesel no one delivered. And as one official confided in us, the decision-makers back home were largely indifferent to how the money was used—so long as it was spent."

The commissioner nodded in acknowledgment, then motioned to Puddeck to resume his presentation.

"The contractors were making money hand over fist," Puddeck continued. "Well-placed Afghan officials got to build luxurious villas in Dubai. And the American politicians back home bolstered their credentials by being tough on terror and bringing democracy to the world. Granted, the Afghan population might not have been pleased with the US-propped government and acute malnutrition among small children, but let's get real: you can't make everyone happy."

One of the commissioners said, "We have here in our notes that in January 2006, Al-Qaeda offered a long-term truce and an effective end to Islamist militant activities. 'Both sides would be able to enjoy security and stability under this truce ... If you Americans are sincere in your desire for peace and security, so here it is—we have answered you.'"

"Perish the thought," Puddeck said with some heat. "Just like the War for Drugs, the War for Terror has been a success story that just keeps on giving. It doesn't matter if one cultivates a fruit tree or war," he said. "Either way, pruning is key to encouraging new growth. So you kill potential terrorists, terrorize others, who then go on to raise a fresh crop of terrorists, thereby perpetuating or expanding your counterterror campaign. Each drone strike clears a target and seeds the next generation. One cannot overstate the importance of building sustainability into the terror vision. Absent this, you risk grinding the terror-spawning, counterterror-sustaining, terror-reinforcing terror operation into the ground. At which point, defense stocks dip, and Americans get nervous."

"Put another way, thanks to the diligence of the United States Empire, Rebel Alliance bases have sprung up across the world: from Jemaah Islamiyah in Indonesia to ISIL in Syria; from Boko Haram in Nigeria to al-Shabaab in Somalia; from Ansar al-Sharia in Yemen to al-Mourabitoun in Mali. US forces have been operating across an arc of client and combat states—from Senegal and Gabon to Saudi Arabia and South Sudan. Assassin drones hunt those on the American kill list in Libya, Somalia, Yemen, Iraq, Syria, Afghanistan, and Pakistan. By our count, the American-led War for Terror has now touched nearly eighty countries—from the Philippines in the Pacific to Niger in the heart of Africa."

Puddeck gave a slow grin. "God bless America!" he proclaimed, and the session came to an end.

CHAPTER 27

Foothills of the Organ Mountains, New Mexico, Earth

Lee stood on the hillside in the shade of a small tree, her house within sight. Hagar and Aratta were standing next to her. She was leaving Earth.

"So this is goodbye," Lee said, a tremor in her voice.

"We'll visit," Hagar promised, her eyes wet. "This is a promise."

"It is," Aratta said, and he opened his arms to Lee. The two hugged fiercely and then kissed.

With her eyes also swimming with tears, Lee turned to Hagar, and the two women embraced for a long time, Hagar whispering something in her ear.

A moment later, Aratta and Hagar stood there smiling, regarding Lee. "Go on, kid, live it up," Aratta said, winking. Hagar waved, and the two disappeared in a rush of air.

Lee rested her hand on the gnarled bark of a juniper tree nearby. She then started toward her house. She could not bring herself to say goodbye to anyone else.

Owing to extraordinary circumstances, she might have impacted Earth and its people more than any human who ever lived. She had wanted to see the hearing to the end. But once the prospect of going to Qataria became real, her tolerance had quickly waned for the prevailing culture on Earth and its people. Now, as she approached the only home she had ever known for the last time, Lee realized there was an additional reason for her desire to leave this planet. She'd been instrumental in bringing outside attention upon this world and felt she no longer had the right to mingle with the Terraneans.

The house looked empty. A few hours earlier, two moving trucks had hauled away most of the belongings. She was donating the furniture to acquaintances. Aratta had already taken the stasis boxes and other sensitive items off-world, except for one small item.

Lee strolled through the familiar rooms she had walked so many times before.

Once more, she entered the concealed space in the basement. Its otherwise bare shelves held a single object: a recording device. Her parents had left it, with instructions to play it only if Lee ever departed Earth. At last, she would hear their message. Carrying it to the living room, she settled into the sole remaining chair and hit play.

"Lee'chelle," came a voice that sent a shock wave rushing down her spine. It was her father.

"Hi, sweetie," a soft feminine voice followed.

Lee took a shaky breath and pressed her fist against her mouth.

"Daughter." It was her father again. "If you're listening to this recording, it means we're dead. It also means you're about to depart Earth and go to our home planet, Qataria. You may be too young yet to comprehend what we are about to tell you."

In the wall mirror, Lee saw a reflection of a woman with streaks of gray in her hair. She looked away.

"Lee'chelle, on this planet, people may get in touch a few times with something within, something that comes from the root. It is an outlook on life. Blazing like a sun, this outlook is outside the spectrum of the existing cultures on Earth. It is an unarticulated sense of immense possibility."

For a few seconds, only a faint hissing sound came from the tiny speaker.

Her father said, "In Qataria, our homeworld, you will learn to dance with the unfathomed, with the irrepressible, and with the uncontrollable.

"Along with other young people, you will be coached to focus on the moment, to confront yourself and your deepest fears. You'll learn to have an all-out commitment of self, all-out intentionality toward a goal. You will learn to put principles before the expediency of the moment. You will cultivate a sense of inner balance. You will delight in the moment and come to have an awareness of the present."

"We could not be happier contemplating this prospect," her mom said.

For a moment, the only sound was the hiss of the recording.

Then the voice of her father came on one last time. "Seize the day, Lee'chelle."

"I love you, sweetheart," her mother said. There was a soft click as the recorded message came to an end.

For a few minutes, Lee sat on the wing chair in the otherwise empty house until the tears stopped flowing.

"I'm—" She rose from her seat, the recording device in her pocket. "I am ready."

And she was gone from Earth.

Then rematerialized hundreds of kilometers above Qataria.

The planet filled most of the sky, slowly rotating on its axis. Lee whooped in delight mixed with astonishment.

"Great view, huh?" came Big Carlo's voice.

She jolted. The three gods materialized by her side.

"Lee," Fat Frank began, "your parents gave their lives to this cause. Yours is about half over. We will return you to your home planet. However, in addition, we would like to grant you a boon in consideration of the critical role you've played in convening a hearing on Earth."

Lee was silent for a long time. "I did not choose to grow up and live on Earth," she said quietly. "Still, I don't regret it. My life truly mattered. Few can say that. If I'm to die now, I am at peace. And yet…"

She breathed audibly. "You said a boon." She glanced at the three. "Is this like one of those wishes in fairy tales?"

Fat Frank gave her a quick, reassuring smile.

She looked embarrassed, then the words tumbled out in a rush. "I would like to know the life I never had—but not as an aged woman past childbearing years, weighed down by the pain of the world I grew up in. I would like to be young again." She stopped speaking just as abruptly, cheeks turning red.

Frank asked, "You want to set back the odometer some—and then begin the aging process anew?"

Lee nodded.

Frank looked at Vito, at Carlo, and then back at her. "Yes, of course," he said. "The memories of your adult years will fade some. Your body will be youthful. The rest is up to you."

For a moment, the other two gods lowered their heads in farewell and then disappeared.

Lee'chelle and Fat Frank contemplated the giant orb beneath them as it slowly spun.

"So few lights!" Lee said.

The god wore a slight smile. "It figures. There are only around five million humans down here on Qataria, scattered about in small towns and hamlets."

Lee felt the excitement coursing through her. Something dormant within her was awakening.

"Well, *Mademoiselle*, where would you like to live?" The god gestured downward. "As you can see, the main settlement clusters are spread out. Some are in Sri Lanka, Madagascar, and along the California coast. Others occupy the Cook Islands, Morocco's coastline, the Central Valley of Costa Rica, and Namibia. You'll find clusters on New Zealand's North Island and in Colombia's Aburrá Valley. The largest concentrations are scattered through the tropical savannas and northern woodlands of Australia. These are the population clusters; solitary communities are scattered in many other regions."

"The grasslands of Africa and North America are totally dark," Lee observed. She wanted to stay up there with him a bit longer.

He nodded. "People here tend to keep away from the major grassland areas, where tigers, lions, and leopards reign supreme. Some of those lion varieties are bigger, and the prides are larger than what you're used to on Earth. Packs of dire wolves are no laughing matter, either."

When the eastern seaboard came into view, she pointed. "No Chicago or Jersey."

Frank shrugged. "Ever been there in the winter? Fucking miserable. Why would anyone want to shiver in cold winters or sweat buckets and be pestered by mosquitoes in the summer when you have an entire planet to choose from?"

Lee'chelle laughed. "Yes, figures." For a moment, she rubbed her nose. "So, I can settle down wherever I want?" She knew the answer, but it was nice to hear it.

He humored her. "Of course." A warm note of amusement entered his voice. "There are no countries or administrative controls down on this planet. Come with an open heart and a desire to contribute, and I'd venture to guess any community will likely welcome you."

"I wish to go home, Frank," she said, and he raised an eyebrow. "I mean, your godship," she amended, looking at him mischievously.

He gave a bark of a laugh and ruffled her hair. "So, you want to settle in Madagascar."

"Yes. It's where my parents were born and grew up. I think they would've liked that."

Fat Frank examined her face intently, reading her thoughts. "Very well … Going once, going twice …" He waited for a moment. "Done!" he exclaimed and clapped his hands.

The world disappeared in a rush, and she screamed in sudden pain.

CHAPTER 28

Undisclosed Location, Off-World, the Commission Building

"CHRISTIANITY HAS WITHSTOOD the test of time," Susan told a mildly indifferent Brandon. "It is not a fad, but the most revered religion on Earth. I am proud to have Jesus as my Lord and Savior."

Later, she repeated this to the Chief Examiner and his associates at the chambers of the Civilization Assessment Group.

Master Rafirre noted the golden cross around her neck. He wondered how it would have gone over if Jesus had died in recent times. Would she have adorned herself with a miniature replica of an electric chair?

"The New Testament is yesterday's news, boss," one of his aides said. "Things have happened on that front since it was composed. I got fresher stuff." He reviewed the information on his computer screen some more. "Here. A while ago, another prophet started a movement in Kenya—*the Lost Israelites.*"

"Oh?"

"Claims he's Jehovah, boss, and goes by Jehovah Almighty God Wanyonyi."

There was a prolonged silence as the assistant consulted the displayed data. "Says he came down to Earth after his son, Jesus, was rejected and that he wants to try to save humanity himself."

The Examiner smiled brightly. "This is good. We've got God visiting Earth here and now. I'd like to give you a fair hearing, you know."

But Susan was shaking her head violently. "This is not God; it's just some charlatan."

The Examiner's smile faded. "Charlatan, you say? Why? I mean, he says he's the father of Jesus. How can you speak ill of him?"

"Like heck he is the father of Jesus."

"You are a Christian! You're saying you don't believe in Jehovah Wanyonyi?"

"You think just because someone declares himself God, I would believe it?"

One of the assistants in the room smirked.

The Examiner settled back in his chair. "You haven't even been in His Presence. How can you dismiss his claim out of hand? Will you risk burning in Hell for this?"

Rafirre looked over his shoulder at his assistant. "What else have you got on him?"

"Jehovah Almighty God Wanyonyi says he's the one who begat Adam and Eve."

The Examiner was nodding encouragingly at Susan, who remained stone-faced.

"He also claims to have taken on all the sins and filth of the world."

"Well then." Rafirre spread his hands as if that settled it.

"There is more, boss. Says he'll wipe out all the heathens."

"Oh boy, that's not too good, is it?" the Examiner said. "Anyway, Wanyonyi does sound like the real deal to me."

Susan was gaping at him.

Rafirre took the printout handed to him and skimmed through it. He lifted his head. "Wanyonyi says he can treat all diseases, including AIDS." He extended the sheet of paper, offering it to her to see for herself.

She was livid. "Do you really believe that?"

"As much as I believe Jesus restored sight to the blind," he said, putting down the sheet of paper. Those religious types were all the same, Rafirre reflected, skeptical and level-headed when it came to all religious claims—except their own.

He sighed. "Anything suspicious about Wanyonyi?"

They were quiet as the aide studied his screen some more. Susan was flushed; the Examiner was unruffled. "Other people in that area claim he is a false prophet, boss. The government warns that he's dangerous."

"I told you he is a fraud!" Susan yelled.

"Come, come now." The Examiner leaned back and put his feet on the desk, enjoying the moment. "Jesus, your God, was also denounced as a false prophet and was executed as such. Be sensible now."

It took all she had to restore a semblance of calmness. "If it's all the same to you, why do you insist?"

Rafirre swung his legs down. "Dear lady, we have no firsthand account of what Jesus himself said. In fact, we have no firsthand account of anyone who met Jesus. The earliest writings that make up your New Testament were composed by people in far-off lands, and decades after he made his appearance. This is very soft evidence. Instead, we can investigate people who are living and have been miraculously healed. We can interview God himself."

Susan massaged her temples and eventually said, "Just trust me on this one. You'll do my people a great disservice if you use this man and his teachings as the cornerstone of your presentation about religions on Earth."

The Examiner regarded her, cocking his head to the side. Finally, he shrugged. What difference did it make? Let the Terraneans hand him the rope to hang themselves with.

⇒⇐

THE BRIEFING ON RELIGION TOOK PLACE IN THE GRAND HALL. Unlike the adjacent deliberation chambers, this one resembled an enclosed amphitheater and could hold an audience of one thousand people. It was the custom to open at least one session to the public. It often made for a tumultuous hearing, but the commissioners had soldiered through those sessions stoically. Invariably, the attendees came from the Reservation—from one or another of its hundreds of thousands of population groups.

A hearing, happening just once or twice a decade, always managed to pull in a crowd. True to form, the Grand Hall was packed.

Half a dozen seats were arranged in the hexagonal floor area in the center, reserved for a handful of Earthborn wishing to take a more active role in the session. Any of them who chose to sit there could be asked to testify, render an opinion, or be cross-examined. A bit away from them, the Chief Examiner stood with his hands resting on a burnished copper lectern. Against the wood-paneled wall, five of the commissioners sat, the Presiding Chair among them. Recognizing the significance of religion in the lives of many Terraneans, the commissioners sought insights into the religious doctrines and perspectives of Earth.

"The hearing is now in session," the master of ceremonies called out, and the Presiding Chair rapped the ceremonial hammer.

Rafirre bowed toward the bench. "With the commissioners' leave," the Examiner intoned. He turned back to face the large crowd and the few Earth people seated in front of him.

"Christianity postulates the existence of a divine entity that birthed the cosmos," he began. "They refer to this being as God. This entity is uncreated and everlasting. Furthermore, it is omnipotent, omnipresent, and omniscient. It is endowed with distinct will and personality and is said to govern the universe with profound love, supreme wisdom, and absolute justice.

"I said 'God,' but in fact, classical Christianity asserts that three discrete persons share one godhood and labor in perfect unity: God the Father, God the Son, and God the Holy Spirit.

"With relentless fervor, the Son proclaims the moral law of His Father," Master Rafirre continued, "and through their Spirit, they bind the believer to it. Paradise is promised for obedience, and eternal torment for defiance."

The Chief Examiner directed a query to the small group of seated Terraneans, "Would I be correct in assuming that devout Christians follow the Lord's commandments?"

"Absolutely," Susan said. "We endeavor to follow the Lord's Word, walk in righteousness, and lead godly lives to the best of our abilities."

Rafirre looked at Susan. "Would it be fair to suggest," he said, "that a cornerstone of evangelical Christianity is the belief that the Bible is self-authenticating, discernible to the rational reader, and the final authority?"

"Yes."

"The Lord decreed that a witch must not be allowed to live," Rafirre said. "I wish to commend you for having killed countless witches in centuries past." All around them, the gallery hummed with hushed comments and stifled laughter. The prosecutor simply nodded, seemingly deep in his own reflections. "Moreover, you have shown true commitment to your Lord by having consigned apostates and heretics to the purifying fire."

His smile turned to a scowl.

"You have grown lax in recent centuries, however, and sin has overflowed the land. The Lord commanded the extermination of mediums, yet they practice their eldritch arts unhindered. The Lord commanded the execution of blasphemers, yet they abound within your cities." He pursed his lips. "Dare I hope you have been carrying out death sentences for adulterers, as prescribed in the Good Book?" He shot Susan a sharp look.

Someone from the gallery yelled out, "Do God's will!" Hoots and laughter greeted this statement.

Susan sat silently and stone-faced.

The Examiner patiently waited for the commotion to quiet down. "I can see how your overpopulation crisis has come to be," he said, his tone laced with regret. "So many sinful souls, yet too few laborers in the vineyard of the Lord to carry out His holy work."

He sighed dramatically.

A chant started to swell among the crowd, "Kill! Kill! Kill!" Soon, more voices joined in. To the spectators, this session was nothing but theater. And the more outrageous the pronouncements, the louder the applause. The Examiner did not disappoint.

Raising his arms, Rafirre beckoned for silence, his face the picture of earnestness. "I'm afraid," he said, as the chant dwindled to muffled chuckles and murmurs, "to find out how many people willfully ignore God's holy commandment to put to death those offspring who treat their parents with contempt. Why do you question the God of Mercy?" he cried. "Why do you doubt the God of Love?"

The chant resumed. "Kill! Kill! kill!"

"Jesus never commanded this!" Susan cried out.

"Much as I am doing now, God the Son rebuked the doubters: 'Why do you, by your traditions, violate the direct commandments of God?' And He reminded them what God the Father said: 'Anyone who speaks evil of father or mother must be put to death.'"

"Kill! Kill! Kill!" The call echoed through the chamber, amplified by the jubilant foot-stamping of numerous spectators.

"It appears you accept God as your Lord," Rafirre said loudly. "It's just some of His commandments you have a problem with." He shook his head sadly.

"Those barbaric edicts were set by God for Iron Age people," Susan screamed over the tide of sneers and yells. Wrenched from her heart, it left her mouth without thought. "We've matured and evolved since!"

The Examiner held out both hands until silence returned to the Grand Hall.

"Did it not occur to you that if the almighty, all-knowing Father has not altered the Holy Book in modern times, it's because He expects you to follow the Bible as it stands?"

Rafirre addressed the members of the commission. "I posit that the standards of what's right and wrong are an articulation of

God's character. If His attributes do not change, then neither do His moral principles. What was wrong yesterday cannot become right today." The Examiner turned his attention back to Susan. "The very fact that Jesus had to die to satisfy cosmic justice means even the Lord cannot bend the fundamental, immutable order of the universe and waive any of the resultant laws. Yet, you presume to do so." He walked over to the seated woman. "What does it mean to regard the Bible as the final authority if you ignore some of its divine decrees?"

"By His precious blood, Jesus cleansed us of our sins," Susan said monotonously, a distant look in her eyes, as though she were reciting a litany. "Because of this, we are pardoned and forgiven. We're only human, imperfect, and incapable of always keeping the Lord's holy law." Mutters and jeers rose from the assembled crowd. A few of the commissioners regarded the Earth woman with unmasked disgust and incredulity.

"The Lord may forgive your failures," Rafirre countered, "but He does not absolve you from the obligation to do your utmost to comply with His laws. Be it bride-price or the prohibition of land sales. For it is said, 'Until heaven and earth pass away, not an iota, not a dot, will pass from the law.' It is also said, 'A person who keeps all the laws except one is as guilty as a person who has broken all of the Lord's laws.'" Rafirre crossed his arms. "And let's be honest here," he said in a reasonable tone of voice, "how hard is it to round up a few good people of faith and carry out the pre-scribed executions of men who commit the abomination of having sexual relations with other men?"

Much laughter and whistles greeted those words.

"You laid down your sword—and called your cowardice mercy."

One of the commissioners leaned in. "So that's the core of Christianity? A set of principles and statutes to abide by?"

"No, Your Grace. These are but the things contained in their holy book. Some are adhered to, some downplayed, some ignored."

"Let's get to the heart of this religion, then," the Presiding

Chair said.

Rafirre cleared his throat. "I'll put forward what could be regarded as a conservative evangelical view of Christianity. Keep in mind, each tenet I present has variants across the numerous denominations that abound.

"I've mentioned earlier that Christianity has three persons operating as one god. Well, this trio will bring the existing epoch to an end and institute a radically new one. This is what it all leads up to, so let me start with this.

"The beginning of the end will be heralded by wars, famines, and scarcity that will kill over one billion people. And then things will get really bad. But for the sake of expediency, I'll skip the graphic details.

"With the world in ruins and people in searing agony with no reprieve, everyone will be forced to their knees before God the Son as He makes His grand entry, accompanied by believers who will have risen from the dead in glorious, immortal bodies. God the Son will assume the role of a literal global ruler. He will reign in perfect righteousness and usher in peace and prosperity throughout.

"At the end of one thousand years of benevolent rule, a great battle will ensue. In its aftermath, everyone will be brought forth to stand for a final judgment, both those who will be alive during that epoch to come and those who have died in ages past. Those deemed sinners will be cast into the fires of Hell to suffer for all eternity. Those considered among the righteous will enter into the full enjoyment of life in the presence of God.

"While all sinners will experience an everlasting torment, there will be varying degrees of suffering. In determining the extent of horror to be meted out, every sin will be accounted for and tallied. Similarly, the righteous will also receive varying degrees of reward, as they are to take their place in the new Earth."

"A new Earth, you say?"

"Indeed," the Examiner said, "there will be a perfected

re-creation of the world. The new Earth will be a place of great beauty, abundance, and joy—with no death, pain, or sorrow."

The commissioner barked a laugh. "Is this their idea of a paradise?" she asked, her words tinged with annoyance. "How can you be truly alive if you do not comprehend your mortality? How can you be in ecstasy if you have no space for agony? How can you be really human if you cannot choose?" She regarded the seated Terraneans. "If life can be viewed as a web of interactions—such as these with the world at large, or with a spouse, or with a task, or with oneself—then paradise is a place where interactions are meaningful. Paradise is a place that empowers its inhabitants to brave interactions that engage them—interactions that are charged or fiery rather than casual or prosaic. What you portray as their loftiest vision is but a waiting room. A graveyard."

"Yes, Madam Commissioner."

"I take it that to gain admittance to their notion of paradise, one has to live in accord with the divine dicta," the Presiding Chair said.

"Your Graces, Christianity hinges on the idea that this is not truly possible, which brings us to the crux of this religion. Let me lay it bare for you to see.

"God the Father birthed the cosmos and every element in it—most notably life on Earth. Hence, He created the first female and male humans. Formed in His image, they were to be His crowning achievement. Their purpose for being was to glorify God."

There were titters in the gallery.

"However, things went terribly awry," the Examiner went on. "The first two humans, contrary to God's edict, ate a special fruit that gave them the ability to discern good and evil. In other words, it provided them with the capacity to develop a code of morality. Humanity could stand on its own two moral feet.

"The divine trio regarded this as a fundamental sin—an abomination that set a massive gulf between them and humans.

"This sin—this affliction—was passed down from one generation to the next. Every newborn is marked by a distorted conscience and a rebellious reasoning faculty. This renders humans incapable of aligning with the universal moral code in both deed and mindset."

There was a moment of stunned silence in the great hall.

"In my long years of service in this office," the Presiding Chair proclaimed, "this is surely the most abhorrent and depraved doctrine I've ever heard." He leaned forward and rested his arms on the bench. "The foundation of this doctrine is taking all that is evil and distilling it to its essence." He was glaring down at the small gathering of Earth people on the hexagonal stage area. "Using your own cultural references, this is not the religion of any god; this is a satanic religion authored *by the devil himself.*" He bellowed out the last sentence.

Deathly silence descended on the Grand Hall. Susan turned white. Konsta was whispering furiously to Wang Lei. Others sank down in their seats or vacantly stared at the walls. At that moment, the Terraneans wished they were anywhere but in that packed hall. The Examiner seemed as disconcerted as everyone else by this unprecedented outburst.

The Presiding Chair went on in a hushed tone, "Reasoning, conscience, and personal choice—these are the very things that define us as humans and make everything worthy in life possible. By definition, the capacity to choose right from wrong is the bedrock of morality. What perversion of mind could generate such an immoral creed is beyond my ability to fathom. The malevolence in its premise is so profound that it is almost beyond belief that it could have been conceived by human authors." For a long moment, his heavy gaze rested on the Earth people.

"Continue if you would," he said eventually.

Rafirre bowed. "Inherently, every person is destined to burn and be tortured in the afterlife for eternity," he said. "That is the penalty incurred by human nature—a mandatory sentence within the immutable system of justice governing the cosmos."

"But there is a way out of eternal damnation," one commissioner suggested, contempt thick in her voice.

The Examiner nodded. "There is a way out. Your Graces, at its core, Christianity is an afterlife salvation scheme. I'll explain how this works.

"Out of sheer love, God the Son took human form and lived a life of perfect obedience, so that His merits could be imputed to those who are counted as believers and transferred like assets on the cosmic scale of justice.

"In addition, He also took on himself the sufferings necessary to pay the penalty for their sins. And in the end, He sacrificed himself and died in their place. Or rather, He underwent a finite, temporary death-state for a couple of days. Thus, the guilt of the faithful was expunged, making people righteous and holy. From that point on, believers sin, confess, and move on—secure in the knowledge that the bill's already been paid."

One of the commissioners said, "I can only repeat what my esteemed colleague said: evil distilled. Destroying the fundamental tenet of self-accountability is but another dimension of it."

"It's not much of a scheme," another commissioner said. "There has to be more to it."

"There is," the Examiner said. And every eye was on him. Rafirre paused. Everything he'd presented was leading up to this point.

"Your Graces," he said, "to be saved from eternal burning at the Lake of Fire, a person must regard God the Son as their savior. Furthermore, one needs to experience repentance for their past sins, renounce them, and adopt a sincere commitment to lead a life in keeping with the precepts laid out by the Son and the Father." His voice cut through the rising mutters. "In other words, to receive salvation, a person must acknowledge their corruption, embrace the transaction, and sign over the deed to their own will. They must surrender all executive function to the deity."

The Examiner turned to face the Earthborn seated in front of him, those poor, deluded fools. "May the commission have mercy on your souls," he said to them.

CHAPTER 29

Aratta prevailed on two of the five commissioners who had attended the religion session to allocate a bit more of their time in the commissioners' private chambers.

"Christianity is widely recognized as a faith," Aratta was explaining, seated across from them. "And, for many, it is well on its way to being relegated to the dustbin of mythology. Conversely, when a set of beliefs possesses full potency, it is not acknowledged as such; it is simply treated as what's so, the truth," Aratta told the two. "The Terraneans are brimming over with those.

"Your Graces, I wish to bring up one such case in point. But for this, I need to first tell you a little story."

"Very well, Lord Aratta," replied one of the two commissioners.

"For at least a few centuries," Aratta opened, "smallpox has had a presence in Europe, leaving a trail of corpses and scars.

"In the late eighteenth century, a physician by the name of John Haygarth uncovered the chain of transmission of the virus: how it passes from one person to another, the proximity threshold, and the conditions conducive to its spread.

"Subsequently, he came up with a protocol, which he put to the test in 1778. Among other things, no one was to enter an afflicted house; no one who showed signs of infection would visit public places; no item suspected of being contaminated should leave the premises; and everything was to be carefully washed and scrubbed after the illness abated. Fourteen families adhered to his protocol and spread no disease. The smallpox they carried was contained.

"With the success of this test case, he put together a monograph in 1793 containing a detailed blueprint for rapidly eradicating smallpox from Great Britain. The plan entailed an extensive network of public health inspectors who were to enforce case isolation.

"His scheme was widely read and discussed, with some clergymen implementing his protocol and getting positive results. Other medical professionals joined their voices to his.

"In Germany, Dr. Bernhard Christoph Faust agreed with Haygarth that smallpox was not an unavoidable evil, but something that could—and must—be stamped out through determined action. He outlined a plan for isolation houses on the outskirts of each town. At the very first sign of infection, the patient was to be immediately relocated there. Faust was certain that strict quarantine and thorough disinfection of clothing and bedding would break the chain of contagion. He opined that if these measures were implemented, then within ten—at most twenty—years, smallpox would be a thing of the past in Europe.

"But then something else grabbed the imagination of the Western world with the promise of a perfect and everlasting cure."

"I gather this is where the plot thickens," stated one of the commissioners with a faint smile.

Aratta lowered his head in acknowledgment. "To tell you what unfolded, I first need to explain a few things.

"The universal belief was that whoever had once contracted smallpox never suffered a second attack," Aratta said. "In addition, it was found that there was a way one could contract the disease in a mild form. When you put those two things together, you arrive at the rationale for inoculation. Namely, the deliberate introduction of small amounts of infectious material from smallpox vesicles into the skin of healthy subjects. The intent was to induce a mild smallpox, which would result in immunity to the more severe, naturally-acquired disease.

"Occasionally, people died of inoculation, but many were willing to play the odds. The practice gained popularity in Great Britain around 1738 and really took off in 1765.

"But not all was well. It became evident that while the inoculated might stand less chance of experiencing the disease in a severe form, the practice had inadvertently been introducing the smallpox into towns and villages previously free from it. You see, those inoculated proved contagious, as they carried the virus with full potency. Mass inoculations may well have caused a net increase in death from smallpox in Great Britain.

"Contagion was a problem looking for a solution.

"Tales of people who avoided contracting smallpox through their acquisition of the non-contagious cow-pox were commonplace in farming communities. Several individuals deliberately inoculated themselves or a few others with the cow-pox. One of them was a physician by the name of Jenner. He inoculated a few people and then made some far-reaching claims. This got some attention. In 1799, Dr. Woodville and Dr. Pearson decided to put this age-old notion to the test.

"The two doctors inoculated a few hundred people with cow-pox, which—as it turned out—was partially contaminated with smallpox. Woodville and Pearson proceeded to ship out their microbial cocktail to other physicians, and the number of test cases rose to about two thousand.

"The big question was whether the new, cow-pox based inoculation would ward off smallpox.

"Rather than wait for natural exposure, the physicians recalled the subjects and exposed them to smallpox via inoculation—to test this claim.

"Alas, the smallpox inoculation that followed the cow-pox inoculation had an effect on the subjects. In fact, it produced for the most part the same conditions as it always did: while some reported just a local inflammation, others had a single pustule—pocks with pus in them—and others yet had eruptions of numerous pustules.

"Now we come to the peculiar part of the story. A surgeon at The Manchester Royal Infirmary who partook in the clinical trial, congratulated mankind on the success of the novel cow-pox inoculation. He wasn't the only one."

"Odd reaction, indeed. But at least the subjects did not succumb to the smallpox inoculation administered on the heels of the cow-pox one."

"Your Grace, as I noted earlier, the subjects rarely succumbed—that is, died—to smallpox inoculations, notably in the milder procedure used after 1765. The cow-pox inoculation they had administered beforehand did not affect different outcomes in the smallpox inoculation that followed. All that many of the physicians described were simply the signs one expects from smallpox exposure via inoculation.

"The study did not show that the cow-pox had any different effect. At any rate, given that some batches of the cow-pox were contaminated with the smallpox virus, the most charitable thing that can be said is that a haze of uncertainty surrounds this pivotal study.

"In July 1800, the *Testimonial in Favour of the New Inoculation* was proverbially nailed to the door of a church. Signed by a few dozen prominent physicians in London, it hailed the new inoculation and promised sure and everlasting protection from smallpox.

"*The Testimonial* had a great effect on the public mind; to the majority it proved irresistible.

"Its chief author challenged the world to produce a single person with experience of smallpox who wasn't a staunch convert. The coup was over; the new cow-pox inoculation, henceforth to be known as vaccination, reigned supreme from this point on. A new belief took hold of the Western world and beyond. It came to enjoy a peculiar protection from doubt; and in that respect, it did tend to provide a lifetime immunity.

"By 1802, the authorities were proclaiming that universal

vaccination would soon 'absolutely extinguish one of the most destructive disorders by which the human race has been visited.' Word of it spread fast around the world, and the vaccinations even faster. In the Indian city of Madras alone, a quarter million were vaccinated by 1807.

"It didn't take long for the first reports to emerge of smallpox fatalities among those previously vaccinated. But by then it was too late to stem the tide." Aratta got up. "I wish you to hear this firsthand, Your Grace. There are two gentlemen I wish you to meet."

The two inclined their heads, Aratta clapped, and they were elsewhere.

Musselburgh, Scotland, Summer 1809

THE THREE HAD ENTERED A REFLECTION that was old and heavily degraded; both the sky and the ground sported ominous black gaps.

The sun was close to setting as Aratta and the two commissioners found themselves in a broad, unpaved street facing a row of adjoining buildings that formed one continuous block. The building right in front of them held a sign proclaiming "Musselburgh Arms."

"This is as far back as I can take you, Your Graces. We're about eight or nine years away from ground zero—eight or nine years after the birth of vaccinism." Aratta motioned toward the doorway, and the three of them entered the inn, eyeing warily the rips in the fabric of the aging reflection.

Two seated men rose when they spotted them.

Aratta introduced them. "Gentlemen, this is Dr. Maclean, a medical doctor, and Mr. Brown, a local surgeon." The men all shook hands and took seats. Moments later, they ordered sage cheese and veal and shared a bottle of claret. Pleasantries were exchanged, then they turned to talk about the smallpox vaccine.

In reply to a question by Aratta, Mr. Brown said, "As it turned out, in an outbreak in Hampshire, dozens who had been vaccinated prior, contracted smallpox in the natural course of events and died. There was another outbreak in Chesterfield where nine vaccinated people contracted smallpox at a later date, and two died."

"As a matter of fact, there were earlier reports yet," noted Dr. Maclean. "Mr. Simmons, a farmer near Buntingford, was vaccinated in 1802. Three years later, he was infected with smallpox and died."

"How did the medical profession explain it?" inquired Aratta.

Mr. Brown sighed. "We started claiming there were genuine and spurious vaccines. You see, if the patient should die of inflammation of the puncture, we might conclude the material administered via the vaccine was not genuine. Others maintained that the good or ill success of the vaccine depended on the period in which it was given. New books, new instructions, have seemingly appeared every month. And the milder cases of smallpox were classified away as chicken pox, horsepock, or flea bites."

Dr. Maclean laughed. "Nothing but the most desperate and headstrong zeal can demand credit for such a tissue of absurdity." He took a sip of wine. "A few years back, England was swarming with vaccinators. All the fussy folk who had a taste for doing much good at little cost were playing the cow-pox lancet."

"They could not deny it was an experiment," said Mr. Brown, "of which the degree of security could only be ascertained by time." He gestured, somewhat resigned. "But we all insisted on the propriety of instantaneously subjecting the whole human race to a course of this experiment."

"You see," said Dr. Maclean, openly grinning now. "Mr. Brown here was an early convert."

"Guilty," the surgeon said, nodding. "Vaccination was introduced as a perfect antidote and security against smallpox without any exception or reserve. I accepted this, and as a result, I rejected and explained away many cases which were entitled to the most serious attention."

A waitress brought their food, and they all busied themselves for a few minutes.

Dr. Maclean blotted his lips with his napkin and chuckled. "Along with everyone else, Mr. Brown here has been afflicted by *cow mania*." He smiled sardonically. "To doubt its efficacy was among medical men to incur, if not the suspicion of insanity, at least the penalty of excommunication. The zeal with which the fanatics persecuted their opponents was scarcely ever exceeded by the *odium theologicum*. If they did not burn every unbeliever, they dexterously undermined his practice and ruined his reputation. Whoever had not taken the oaths of supremacy and allegiance to vaccination, or dared to question the infallibility of cow-pox, was treated as a traitor to the royal vaccinating state." He gave a slight bow, a slight smirk on his face.

The surgeon looked at him dubiously. "Well, yes," he said eventually. "Indeed, why do not the supporters of vaccination come out collectively and declare they are as much convinced as ever of its utility, its infallibility, in securing mankind against smallpox—now that seventy-five people who had been vaccinated died after contracting the disease at a later date?"

Aratta watched intently as a floating fragment of black void slowly drifted their way. The ripple they had entered was unsafe, close to a general collapse.

"Hear, hear!" said Dr. Maclean, banging his hand on the wooden table.

Without warning, the two commissioners found themselves back in the chambers of the commission.

"It was unsafe to stay in that ripple any longer," Aratta apologized to the slightly bewildered commissioners.

"WHAT happened next, Lord Aratta?" asked one of the commissioners, after they were seated again.

"In the subsequent decades, parents protested against the possible serious side effects," Aratta said. "They were paying too high a premium for the insurance, as one of them said. And in India and Ceylon, families who had vaccines forced on their children employed every means possible to rub out the vaccine, suck it out, or cauterize the area where it was administered.

"Widespread mortality from smallpox in vaccinated London generated outcries that the unvaccinated were the culprits. And in 1853, the government made smallpox vaccination compulsory. Reluctant mothers were made to come to the vaccination stations under threats of summons and fines. Schools were inspected in search of unvaccinated children. Consequently, by 1870, the population had the highest vaccination rates ever.

"Shortly afterward, a smallpox pandemic swept through, resulting in tens of thousands of deaths, many among the vaccinated. It was the deadliest smallpox pandemic in living memory."

For a moment, Aratta was silent.

"What happened next, Lord Aratta?"

"As the decades went by, more and more parents asked whether improved sanitation, good food, and quarantines were not, in fact, the best ways to deal with smallpox. Leicester was at the forefront of it. The vaccination rate of newborns in Leicester declined perceptibly, and by 1891, it dwindled close to zero. This was when another smallpox epidemic engulfed the United Kingdom.

"For many, this was the moment of truth when the city and the world were to find out whether the low rate of vaccination in Leicester was to be an epidemic 'powder keg,' as many predicted. There was a fear Leicester would be 'decimated.' The epidemic was to run like 'wildfire, unchecked.' They were 'in for it,' as one medical officer confided.

"The plague died out in 1894; the proverbial smoke cleared, and the results were in. Only 19 people per 10,000 living contracted the disease in Leicester. That compared to 63 per 10,000 in Dewsbury, 123 in Warrington, 192 in Sheffield, and on the far end of the spectrum—with no isolation and identification measures—was Gloucester, with 399 afflicted per 10,000 living.

"In fact, for Leicester, full-blown smallpox epidemics were a thing of the past. When a few were infected, the town was ready for it. With the report of a case, a phone call was made, and the smallpox van hastened to pick up the infected person and rush him to an isolated ward. All those connected to the contaminated house were placed for two weeks in a designated quarantine house. In the meantime, the house of the afflicted was fumigated, and the bedding was disinfected and subjected to a special hot air procedure.

"Following the lead of Leicester, cities quietly and gradually adopted—in addition to administering vaccines—case isolation and early notification measures. I cannot speak to the extent to which the vaccines contributed to the eventual eradication of smallpox. But I can say that much: The believers never questioned it. Not then. Not in the two centuries to follow. And canonized history records the vaccine as 'the world's most triumphant achievement in medicine and public health.' It eradicated smallpox."

CHAPTER 30

The Western End of Madagascar Island, off the Coast of Africa, Qataria

ALDABARA WALKED BRISKLY WITHIN the large wooden treadwheel. Through a series of pulleys and ropes, he gradually brought down the waxed canvas sheets into place, shielding the paper screen walls of his house from the oncoming storm. Minutes later, the first drops of rain started to fall, quickly escalating into a downpour. The sound of heavy rain mingled with the howls of strong winds, punctuated by the occasional deep rumble of thunder.

As was his habit during storms, the aging man sat cross-legged, eyes shut, letting the cacophony wash over him—until a loud thud jerked him upright.

Aldabara rose and hurried to the door. He flung it open, squinting into the downpour. There! Lightning flashed white, illuminating a naked woman sprawled just steps away on his porch. Raising an arm against the torrential rain, he blinked repeatedly, straining to see as night shrouded the still, prone figure in darkness. Unable to discern any details, Aldabara crawled to her, relying on touch to reach her shoulders.

The elderly man squatted behind the woman. His hands found purchase under her arms, and he hoisted her into the house, kicking the door shut behind him. He dragged the limp body across the floor mats toward the small room with a spare bed. All the while, the woman was muttering incoherently, seemingly delirious. Aldabara looked at her, then away—overwhelmed by a sudden dizziness.

Risking another glance, he registered nothing but boiling shadows and flashes of light. Aldabara screwed his eyes shut, gasping for breath, wiping away the rain and sweat that trickled down his face. He shuddered. There was something strange unfolding; it felt as if primal forces cloaked the woman in a black mist, thwarting his attempts to behold her.

For a moment, Aldabara remained rooted in his place. Shaking off his hesitation, he heaved the woman up again and managed to drag her the rest of the way. Keeping his eyes closed tight, he rolled her over on the mattress. For a long minute, the only sounds in the room were his labored breathing and her unintelligible mumbling.

Aldabara struggled to his feet, battling a bout of dizziness. He leaned on a nearby side table for support. Gathering himself, the elderly man left the room, returning moments later with a large towel in hand. He dried the mystery woman as best he could, then wrapped her in a sheet before sinking heavily against the wall. Little by little, he regained his breath, using the towel to blot his own rain-drenched face and arms.

What now?

He stole a glance at the occupied mattress and recoiled as a searing pain hit him between his temples. For the briefest moment, before the midnight fog shrouded her, he glimpsed her. Fair-skinned woman. Dark hair streaked gray. Eyes closed and lips writhing.

Aldabara gritted his teeth and peeked once more. For an instant, through the roiling cloud of darkness, he saw. The gray hair was gone; an adolescent lay there. He pressed his hands to his temples, squinting through the pain to take in the sight. A child. An older woman. A scream caught in his throat as the pain intensified, radiating from his skull. A young woman. A child. An adolescent. The agony reached an unbearable crescendo; darkness and flashes of light buffeted him as consciousness slipped away.

The elderly man regained his senses, awakening to the sound of pattering rain and urgent, unintelligible whispers. Opening his eyes, he surveyed the dim room. Outside, the storm was subsiding. His mysterious guest was still lying on the mattress nearby. From within the black cloud enveloping her, he could hear her thrashing about, mumbling incessantly. He strained to decipher her words, his eyes tightly shut.

He kept vigil at her side throughout the night until sleep finally claimed him in the quiet hours before dawn.

⇒⇐

ALDABARA AWOKE WITH A START, the sun already high in the clear blue sky. His eyes snapped open and immediately darted to the bed. It was vacant.

With a surge of adrenaline, he sprang to his feet and rushed out of the room. There she was! By the window, her back to him. She wore one of his oversized shirts, her long brunette hair still damp from a shower she must have taken.

She spun around at the sound of his footsteps. A young woman in her mid-to-late teens regarded him. There was a hint of astonishment in the intense, bottle-green eyes.

A moment of silence hung in the air between them.

"Is this home?" she asked in a small, unsteady voice.

"Home?" He approached her slowly until he was face to face with her. "Where is home?" he asked softly, gingerly.

"Madagascar Island, Qataria."

He gave a slight nod.

One hand flew to her mouth. Her eyes shone with elation and welled with tears. "Please," she whispered. "I need to go outside and see for myself."

"Of course." Swiftly, he strode over and flung the door wide open. She stepped onto the porch, squinting against the brightness.

Fields of tall, molten-gold grass thrashed about under the azure sky. The air was fresh, and a few hundred paces away, a group of towering baobab trees marked the horizon.

The young woman sank to her knees. She sobbed and gasped, overcome with emotion.

She got up, let out a jubilant whoop, and raced toward the majestic conical trees. Once there, she sprang up and skipped back, hollering all the while. Grinning widely, she bounded up the stairs, soon panting as she sat next to the elderly man on the porch swing.

He laughed. Her joy was contagious. "I am Aldabara," he said.

"Lee'chelle," the girl said between giggles. She could not stop herself; the giggles kept bubbling to the surface.

Finally, she calmed down somewhat. "How did I end up in your house?"

"It was last night, at the height of the storm." His voice was carefully neutral. "I found you unconscious, lying at my doorstep. I brought you inside." That was the least peculiar part of what had transpired. But he decided not to push things too fast.

She frowned, obviously puzzled.

He'd anticipated her reaction. "What *do* you remember?" he asked gently.

She brushed away loose strands of hair, her brows knitting as she grappled with her fragmented memories. "My parents... they died in an accident about two years ago." She hesitated, her certainty waning—was it three years? "It was not here. It was definitely not around here. It was..." She regarded the giant tortoises milling at the base of the short flight of stairs. "It was an entirely different place."

"Another place?" he asked.

The girl nodded gravely. "Another place." Another world, she suddenly recalled. *Earth!* The name popped into her head. But just as quickly as it surfaced, it seemed to slip through her grasp, like water flowing through her fingers.

"Oh," he said, not sure what to make of it.

They were quiet for a while.

"Don't spend all your money in Vegas, Kaminski," he said, breaking the silence.

"What?"

"It was one of the things you were mumbling about last night. You seemed delirious. Do you understand what the reference to Allah could mean?"

She grimaced.

"'We partner, *blan*. We make good money together,'" he quoted.

"I said that, too?"

He nodded.

"I confess, none of it made much sense to me," he admitted. "A bad dream?"

"Perhaps, yes." She lifted her hands to her face, tracing with wonder the familiar yet youthful contours—as she'd done multiple times since she awoke that morning. "I . . . I think I have a sense of what these phrases might mean," she said hesitantly. *Oh, God,* she thought. Had she just emerged from a colossal nightmare? Or were those memories of actual events and discussions? She would have to sort through it later. Much later, if she could help it.

Lee'chelle lowered her arms and gazed at him. "First things first," she said. "I don't recall arriving here or the storm you mentioned. I'm afraid I don't have any memory of last night at all. I'm certain, though, about one matter: I owe you my gratitude." She reached out and squeezed his hand. "Thank you, for whatever you've done."

He bowed his head. "You're welcome."

This was the first day of the rest of her life, and she planned not to squander or take for granted even a minute of it.

She beamed at him, then jumped to her feet. "Breakfast?"

CHAPTER 31

Undisclosed Location, Off-World, the Commission Building

"Your Graces, there is one thing I wish to show you."

The Presiding Chair nodded in affirmation. Aratta clapped his hands and transported the five commissioners in the deliberation chamber to a ripple from Earth's past.

Suddenly, they stood on a city rooftop, the wind carrying a faint scent of oil and dust. Below them, hundreds of people marched, their chants and cries floating up. Loudspeakers installed at every street corner blared strident rhetoric.

"We are in the city of Tianjin, in the fall of 1966," Aratta told the commissioners. He continued, "This was the year China descended, once again, into a ritualized frenzy of class enemies, public shaming, and struggle sessions." He fell silent, and they all surveyed the tumultuous scene below. "Those young people you see on the street truly believe in the cause, as young people are prone to do.

"It was an era of grievances, outrage, and hatred," Aratta said. "Those who were discriminated against or were mistreated by government officials sought to settle scores or gain a measure of control. Yet the most potent force driving the people was fear— fear of being denounced, of being cut off from resources, and of persecution; fear of unemployment, of a damaged reputation; fear of losing one's place in the social network. The only way to stay afloat was to out-denounce and out-proletarian others while getting as close as possible to the power hubs, which granted access to benefits and opportunities."

Aratta and the commissioners peered again at the street below. "Until a few weeks ago, the Red Guards were the in-group," Aratta explained, his eyes scanning the masses. "Some statements made in an influential publication changed things, and for the next month, it would be the Rebels who had their day under the red sun." Aratta observed the scene one last time. He clapped, and they were back at the real Earth. With one more jump, they were back in one of the deliberation chambers of the Commission Hall. Aratta and the five commissioners took seats, facing each other.

The commissioners absorbed Aratta's words in silence as he went on, "At least since the French Revolution, some territories on Earth have been convulsed at one point or another by movements purporting to bring about 'equitized' societies.

"Your Graces, this brings me to the culture of the West—still the foremost cultural influence in play. However, its essence is now tinged with a creed of victimhood and oppression, one rooted in group identities. This creed is soaked in grievances and accusations, intertwined with societal entitlements, racial preferences, and welfare benefits. This creed, Your Graces, fragments society into identity groups along racial, ethnic, and gender fault lines, and regards their interactions as a zero-sum struggle. This creed is a malignant cloud, corrupting and warping all it permeates."

Crossing his ankle over his raised knee, Aratta continued, "This doctrine views the dynamics of society as a power struggle among disparate groups within a vast spoils system of power and influence. It is the unholy union of three tenets: hereditary moral status; perpetual jockeying for power among groups bearing irreconcilable interests; and widening circles of condemnation and sanctity rankings among the different groups."

Grim humor flitted across Aratta's face. "It may sound like this identity train is on a journey without end through grievances and fatalism, or it may seem like it chugs its way to the never-never land of equivalent outcomes or equitable power-sharing among different identity groups. It's neither, really. Judging by the actions and history of socialist totalitarian movements, it is a power struggle for the 'deserving underdogs' to turn the tables on the alleged oppressors of the day and assume the coveted slot of exploiter and dominator, resulting in the dictatorship of the proletariat. That is, their variation of it.

"Your Graces, it's a power trip striving to become a power grab. The more alleged injustice there is, the more legitimacy the powers-that-be have in extending their authoritarian tentacles to redress it. Under the guise of civil rights, this doctrine has captured institutional power, subsequently normalizing its tenets and delegitimizing dissenting outlooks. After administrators and HR personnel fell in line, it was but a matter of time before almost everyone else would submit. And so it happened, from Hollywood celebrities to educators to corporate board members. Many who grew up in recent decades don't even have to pretend. They believe."

A cold gleam flickered in Aratta's eyes. "Contesting this orthodoxy is viewed as a symptom of having internalized one's oppression or of deep-seated misogyny or racism—hence, it could be dismissed out of hand. Challenging the faithful can never be valid; by definition, such criticism is construed as bullying or silencing. It's a bright new day. Language has been manipulated, terms mutated and weaponized, and reality and facts treated as malleable. In fact, the intent has been nothing short of creating a linguistic framework in which it is literally impossible to conceptualize heresies. In public discourse, the intent has been not merely to win the chess match but to set up a game board with rules and play pieces where no other outcome is possible."

"I see," said the Presiding Chair. "I find this information of some merit, Lord Aratta."

Aratta inclined his head. "This is but an example of what

I actually wanted to bring to your attention. Your Graces, at the core of this ideology stand the modern professional intellectuals."

Rising from his seat, Aratta paced about in the deliberation chamber.

"They are the architects—generating blueprints and permission structures—of nearly every calamity and failed policy on Earth in the last couple of centuries: from the utopian nightmare of the Khmer Rouge in Cambodia to the economic wreckage of Tanzania's Ujamaa; from the brutal French Revolution to the operatic tyranny of Mussolini's Italy; from pseudoscience used to justify slavery and eugenics in the United States to the extermination campaigns of Nazi Germany; from the delusional five-year plans of the Soviet Union to the War on Poverty; from militarized drug crusades and educational fads to outlandish foreign policies. This tragic pattern, repeating for centuries, has left indelible marks across societies on Earth.

"They're called 'intelligentsia,' 'the experts,' 'intellectuals,' or simply 'elites.' More aptly described as conceited wits—divorced from truth, devoid of wisdom.

"Draped in the mantle of credentials, bedecked with the regalia of Science, and cloaked with a sense of superiority and righteousness, they've assumed the role of shepherds, ushering the unwashed masses to brave new futures—whether they want them or not.

"They excel at rhetorical skirmishes, spinning convincing arguments from platitudes and hot air. They are armed with ad hominem attacks, fearmongering, and euphemisms. They provide themselves with self-referential legitimacy.

"The professional intellectuals are always confident, rarely correct, never accountable. Unlike people in most vocations, they never receive feedback from reality they need to heed. They may concoct the most outlandish precepts and can afford to dismiss the resulting catastrophes as unrelated—or simply pivot to a new idea, disowning the last. The bill is never theirs. It is paid by the people living under their broken visions.

"At its worst, this class of people ushers in devastation. At its best, it sows chronic dysfunction, subtly crippling society on Earth."

Aratta bowed and exited the chamber, leaving the commissioners deeply troubled by what they'd heard.

CHAPTER 32

Undisclosed Location, Off-World, the Commission Building

"It doesn't seem like they grow much of their food within the urban districts," the Presiding Chair said.

"No, Your Grace," Hagar said. "They have transformed vast swaths of nature for that purpose."

"I see," the Presiding Chair said. "If you would, High Mistress Hagar, please do continue with what you were saying earlier."

Hagar bowed her head. She was seated on a wooden stool near the front. Wearing ankle boots, low-rise tight jeans, and a black stretchy top, she drew unsettled glances from more than one Earthborn in the audience. All hundred or so Terraneans were in attendance.

She said, "On Earth, instead of grazing in grasslands, cycling nutrients, and providing vital services to the ecosystem, a large portion of that world's livestock is confined in giant enclosures. Feed is grown, harvested, processed, and delivered to them. A case in point is the United States, where tens of thousands of square miles of prairie have been plowed and primed for the cultivation of corn for livestock. In fact, the terrain they have commandeered for it is four times the land used for all your rice, vegetables, orchards, and legumes—combined."

"Is this as unhinged as it sounds?"

"I believe so, Your Grace," Hagar said.

Hagar swiveled on her stool to face the Earth people. "This is but one aspect of the environmental freak show you have wrought," she told them. "Had you rerouted all that livestock manure back to the croplands, you'd have closed the nutrient loop. But you don't. You pile it near the feedlots, creating nitrate wastelands in some areas and sterile soils elsewhere."

She continued, "In the same vein, everyone should also do their civic duty: urinate, defecate, and return the nutrients to the big happy circle of life.

"Hundreds of millions of tons of compost can be produced from human manure mixed with larger amounts of crop residues. However, most of the action is with the urine." She gestured at the group of people from Earth. "Irrigate the fields with your urine and return to the soil something like 30 million tons of nitrogen, 3 million tons of phosphorus, and over 10 million tons of potassium each year—nutrients you indirectly draw out of the fields annually for your consumption."

"How exactly do you fancy we'll pee on the fields?" demanded one of the Earthborn.

"Oh, please," Hagar said. "Use urine-diverting toilets and funnel the liquid to central processing facilities. Employ magnesium oxide or bittern to precipitate the pee into an odorless powder—and you end up with a slow-release phosphorus fertilizer. The leftovers, nitrogen and potassium, can be drip-irrigated."

The striking woman suggested that human excreta and urine could yield three million tons of phosphorus annually. The Terraneans were unsure of what to make of this amount, but one of them seemed decidedly unimpressed. "You do realize we spread nearly seven times that on croplands every year," he said.

Hagar shot the man a pointed look. "I do. That's like flooding an apartment to wash your feet. Recycled cattle manure and human waste, along with cover crops like white lupin and buckwheat, would have stabilized the system."

She turned to the commissioners. "The same thing's playing out with synthetic nitrogen fertilizer." She flicked her gaze toward the Terraneans. "Instead of planting legumes that fix nitrogen naturally, you drown the soil with factory-made nitrogen, far beyond what crops can absorb. Some of the excess bleeds into rivers, breeds toxic algal tides, and turns your coasts into dead zones. Some of it taints your aquifers, in the form of nitrates that can choke hemoglobin's ability to carry oxygen. Genius."

"Why do you till the land?" queried one of the commissioners.

"We till because it works!" the man in the front row snapped. "It buries the weeds and aerates the soil so crops can actually breathe. It's how you farm. It's how we've always farmed."

Hagar shook her head and sighed. "That rider's name was Tillage, and Hell followed it." She silently studied the Earth people. "You drag your disk rippers and disk harrows and disk chisels across the land—slicing, dicing, and churning. It's akin to running a termite mound through a giant tumbler—tunnels, conduits, termites, and all.

"Consequently, the fungal network is in disrepair, the life-harboring micro-cavities vanish, and the volume of nutrient exchanges nosedives. The soil's internal architecture collapses and eventually compacts into a dead mass as silt and clay choke what little porosity remains."

She went on, colder now. "Rain no longer enters. It runs off. You compensate with irrigation." She let this sink in. "You pump water from rivers and aquifers to irrigate. Overdraw them, and you start getting salt in some places. Then you stand there blinking as the land turns white and dies."

"You're saying tilling is the root cause?" a Terranean asked.

"One of them," she said. "Those who leave the field bare for months on end are also signing a death warrant for the fungi. The sun cooks the exposed earth, and the lack of living roots finishes the job. No plants, no fungal network. No plants also means no carbon injected into the soil during those months.

"Bereft of the fungal strands that bind soil, bare fields lose their ground to hard rain and harsher wind." She stared coldly at the Earth people. "Worldwide, tens of billions of tons of soil blow away each year."

The chair signaled her to halt, and the members conversed in hushed voices, conferring. At long last, he looked up. "Please move on."

"Yes, Your Grace," Hagar said. "Many Terraneans grow a single crop species in a given season." She pursed her lips. "Monoculture limits both nutrients and habitat, which causes insect biodiversity to crash. That opens the door for a few species to explode into pests. Which is a self-created problem in need of fixing—so they spray insecticides. Some of which kill the bees.

"By this point, the farm operators notice the plants don't look so hot or grow so well."

Titters and soft laughter rippled through the chamber.

"To fix it, they douse the soil with synthetic fertilizers loaded with macronutrients," Hagar said. "And the plants? They detect the buffet of free minerals and dial down the carbon spigot. Why waste precious energy feeding fungi and microbes when they can take nutrients straight, no symbiotic surcharge? But without that carbon fueling the soil life, things get grim down below.

"Hammering fields with nitrogen also juices the weeds; bare ground guarantees even more weed pressure. To the rescue come the glyphosate herbicides. Trouble is, glyphosate isn't just a weed killer. It's a mild metal magnet that binds essential nutrients. Starve the crops of those, and you're flirting with weaker immune systems and, in some cases, lower nutrient density at harvest."

"And undoubtedly they have devised fixes for all of those things," the Presiding Chair said dryly. "I believe the commission has heard enough."

"In that case, I am ready to proceed with my recommendation," Hagar said.

A few commissioners exclaimed softly. By pronouncing those

specific words, Hagar was telling them she had reached a conclusion. That much was expected. They just didn't expect her to do so before the hearing was over. By offering to state her conclusion, she was also signaling that her involvement in the hearing was coming to a close.

"Your Graces," she said. "I offer that this food-production system is the brainchild of buffoons and monkeys with wrenches. With its chemical spraying, it is demented. With the growth of grain expressly to feed cattle, it is deranged. With its crowding of animals into giant enclosures, it is monstrous."

Her eyes blazed with indignation. "Considering these thoroughly devastating practices and the underlying mindset, I feel I have no choice but to recommend that the commission approve the immediate relocation of the humans from Earth."

Cries of shock and outrage greeted her words as most of the Terraneans sprang to their feet. The notion of relocation had not been raised before, and its sudden introduction landed like a gut punch. The audience was in an uproar. The Presiding Chair released a weary sigh. The cat was out of the bag. In vain, the master of ceremonies banged his staff on the floor, attempting to restore order. The mood was turning ugly. Eventually three dozen armed security men filed in, marching down the aisles in lockstep.

"Terraneans!" the Presiding Chair bellowed. He waited until the angry voices fell silent and all eyes were on him. "Terraneans," he said in a softer voice, "these officers will escort you. You'll see for yourselves what fate awaits your people should our verdict be unfavorable." With a curt nod, he signaled the captain of the guards.

In short order, all the Earth people were ushered out of the chamber, muttering and grumbling. Minutes later, they found themselves crowded into three large freight elevators.

The elevator doors closed with a hiss. There was a jolt, and the slow, mile-long ascent to the surface began.

CHAPTER 33

Salt Flats of Lake Eyre, South Australia, the Netherworld of Earth

IT WAS THE NERVE CENTER OF THE NATURE Assessment Group. Millions of hidden sensors and cameras embedded across Earth streamed their data into the vast underground hub in real time. Projection platforms, computer terminals, and a bustling crowd of technicians filled the massive facility. The cavernous hall pulsed with moving projections—weather systems, migrating scars of deforestation, collapsing river basins—while technicians moved through it like attendants in a trauma ward.

"We are actively monitoring every square mile of the planet," the deputy director of the Nature Assessment Group told the seven commissioners and Aratta.

He continued, "Most of the ecosystems are at varying levels of degradation or have been entirely devastated. In just the last decade and a half, the combined wilderness area lost to human settlement, farming, and mining is roughly the size of Western Europe. The planetary ecosystem of this world has been undergoing death by a thousand cuts."

"I gather the destruction of the rainforests is ongoing," one of the commissioners said.

"Yes. In fact, you are watching it." The deputy director made a distinct gesture. And all maps and images displayed on the dome above them disappeared, replaced by an all-encompassing holographic projection with a top-down view of a forest. The video feed rapidly zoomed in on the island of New Guinea. "A fresh path, bulldozed through the heart of the rainforest in the last few months: a new segment of the Trans-Papua Highway. It will open the forest to fossil fuel extraction, mining, and timber harvest." He zoomed back out. "We observed a similar situation in the Congo Basin: more than eighty thousand kilometers of roads have been added, cutting through and crisscrossing the rainforest." He kept his voice steady. "By now, the apes and elephants have almost nowhere to hide."

"I thought I saw something," one of the commissioners said. "Please, take us back to Borneo."

The rainforest flickered and reshaped itself on the dome.

"There! What are those clouds of smoke rising from the lowlands?"

The holographic video feed was directed to the lower regions of the island. Now he realized what they were seeing. "Fire, Your Grace. Swaths of the lowland rainforests are being burned to clear the area for oil palm plantations." He zoomed in, and they could now see it clearly.

For a few moments, the commission members watched, aghast, as one of the most ancient rainforests in the world was put to the torch.

"Oil palm?" one commissioner asked.

"Yes. Along with utilizing this oil in an array of products, they use it to make biodiesel fuel." The deputy director grimaced. "In an effort to avert climate change, Terranean governments mandated vegetable oil as fuel feedstock."

He sighed. "The Terraneans got to work. A few months back, they moved in with earthmoving equipment and ripped out the rainforest. Over five million acres have gone under." A knot rose in his throat. "As you can see, they now torch the remains, releasing in the process massive amounts of carbon dioxide from the peatlands into the air—far more than would have been emitted by burning petroleum." His faint smile held a touch of sadness. "But tens of millions of Indonesians have become economically dependent on palm oil; some transnational corporations based out of Dubai and Singapore are making money hand over fist; and just as importantly, local district bosses sell land permits and rake in mounds of money to finance their reelection campaigns. So oil palm plantations are here to stay."

In dismay, they surveyed the charred stumps protruding from the blackened earth like tombstones of ash. In the distance, a green desert of oil palm trees stretched as far as the eye could see.

"Only a few tens of thousands of orangutans still roam the tropical forests of Southeast Asia, but business is business," the deputy explained. "Day after day, vast tracts of rainforest in Malaysia and Indonesia are bulldozed or torched for more oil palm plantations. It's no different in western Guinea, where we tracked the Terraneans clearing rainforest to access the bauxite. Just a few decades ago, there were over 150,000 Western chimpanzees. Now, more than two-thirds are gone."

The Presiding Chair's mouth was set in a hard line. "What of the oceans?"

The deputy's face was bleak.

"Just last year, tens of millions of sharks were killed. After the fins were removed, the remainder were thrown overboard. From Dall's porpoises to bottlenose dolphins, countless smaller whales and dolphins are also butchered."

"What is the status of whales on Earth?"

"People on Earth hunted down and slaughtered close to three million whales in the previous century, reducing some populations by as much as 99 percent. For about three decades, the Soviets were at the forefront of it."

"Why?"

"No real reason, Madam Commissioner," the deputy said. "They had to hit production goals—and the crews got substantial bonuses if they exceeded them. It was primarily a numbers game and a career move. The whales themselves were of little utility—the Soviets only removed the blubber and otherwise left the carcasses to rot. It was a contest of vanity, measured in carcasses: the Soviet state strove at all costs to outdo capitalist countries on any gross output matrix, whale hunting included. In addition, whale numbers were dwindling fast, and they were grimly racing to the finish line to have some sort of national hunting legacy to leave behind."

"The situation here on Earth is dire," one of the commissioners contended.

"Worse, actually," said a new voice. The director of the Nature Assessment Group approached the robed figures, walking briskly, her expression apologetic. "Please forgive my late arrival, Your Graces," she said, her voice steady. A few commissioners acknowledged her with nods.

"What do you mean by 'worse'?" asked the Presiding Chair.

"As I was walking in, I was linked and heard your earlier conversation. Your Graces, the so-called intact areas are, in fact, diminished ecosystems."

"Kindly expound," said one of the commissioners.

"The deputy talked of Siberia," the willowy director said. "Just a few millennia ago, that vast tundra was a bustling mammoth steppe, teeming with horses and reindeer, bison and mammoths, along with musk oxen, saiga antelopes, and woolly rhinos. At some point, they were largely wiped out, and the ecosystem unraveled. Subsequently, the meadows and grass gave way to moss, shrubs, and waterlogged soils. At present, it is mostly undisturbed, yet hollowed out.

"He mentioned the woodlands and savanna of northern Australia. Imported red foxes and feral cats have spread throughout, and wholesale decimation followed. This was merely the final pulse. The dispersal of humans across the continent tens of thousands of years earlier coincided with the demise of all the large herbivores, such as the large short-faced kangaroos, the giant wallabies, and the massive diprotodons.

"He spoke of the sagebrush steppe in North America's Great Basin, once a bustling region filled with horses and elephants, camels and helmeted muskoxen, along with a rich variety of grass species. Today, it's a ghost ecosystem, disturbed only by the wind, home to nothing but a handful of resilient brush species.

"In the Congo Basin, Africa, this saga is happening in real time," she said. "Its forest elephant, the ecosystem engineer, is being driven to functional extinction. In fact, just in the last decade, twenty-five thousand forest elephants were slaughtered in Minkébé National Park alone, a chilling testament to the relentless Terraneans' assault on Earth's ecosystems."

For a moment, no one talked.

"Doesn't a park area designate a wildlife territory as protected?" one of the commissioners asked.

The director found little merit in the question. In Madagascar, her team reported large-scale slash-and-burn forest decimation in Menabe Antimena Protected Area for agriculture, and similar decimation in the Tsaratanana Reserve for marijuana cultivation. In Laguna del Tigre National Park, Guatemala, the Terraneans have been clearing old-growth trees for industrial cattle farming and for airstrips serving cocaine traffickers. Beng Per Wildlife Sanctuary, Cambodia, has already lost more than half of its forest at the hands of business tycoons. And in the protected Marahoué National Park, Ivory Coast, they counted more than twenty thousand squatters busily cutting the native trees, replacing them with cocoa.

She said, "Your Grace, we have been tracking many elephant poachers coming over from the town of Djoum in neighboring Cameroon. They cross the Gabon border into the park unhindered." She didn't know what happened to the elephants there, but her team learned that in Myanmar, elephants were slaughtered for their hides, which were then processed into skin beads, jackets, and car interiors.

"Do they have a ban on ivory trade?" a commissioner asked.

"Indeed, Your Grace," the director said. "Naturally, after the ivory market went underground, the cost of ivory shot up."

"If anything, the situation with rhinos is even worse," her deputy interjected. "In Vietnam, the rumor that powdered rhino horn cures cancer has spiked its price to the point where it's worth more than gold by weight. As you can imagine, the Terraneans have consequently wiped out the Javan rhinos in Vietnam to the last."

"Cure for cancer, huh?" the Presiding Chair said darkly. "The horn consists of keratin. They could grind their own nails and get the same meaningless result."

For a moment, the director's mouth twisted in distaste. "This is not unlike what takes place in sub-Saharan Africa, where a brisk trade is conducted in body parts of gorillas and bonobos—sold as spiritual talismans, charms against sickness, fear, and misfortune, and as wards against evil spirits."

The director sighed. "Obviously, this extends beyond pangolins, elephants, and rhinos," she said. "To satisfy the demands of the Southeast Asian market, poachers strip forests bare—of porcupines, turtles, monkeys, parrots, otters, lemurs. Once home to tigers and leopards, these jungles now house nothing larger than a housecat."

She signaled to one of her team members, and a video of the Mar Piccolo lagoon sprang into view. "Southern Italy," the director said quietly. The camera panned across a shallow bay, seagrass swaying, seahorses drifting upright with their tails hooked around the blades. An operator maneuvered the cameras before locating a fleet of small fishing boats sailing under the cover of night, dragging nets through the meadow. When the nets were hauled in, the deck writhed briefly with tiny, contorted bodies, then stilled.

The director continued, "Tens of millions of seahorses are captured each year—killed, ground up, and then consumed by people in China who believe that ingesting them excites sexual desire." She drew her lips in a tight smile. "Evidently, the decimation of seahorse populations is a small price to pay for the promise of arousal." She folded her arms across her chest. "In the relentless pursuit of fleeting, self-indulgent vanities, Terraneans lay waste to Earth and the splendid tapestry of life it hosts, treating it as a pantry and a latrine."

She bowed.

The Presiding Chair returned the bow. "We thank you and your team for your work."

The director bowed once again and left, trailed by a few of her aides.

Aratta and the seven commissioners were making their way to the door when the Presiding Chair glanced toward the nearest wall and stopped. The others followed suit. "High Mistress Jilieth," he called out, approaching the woman seated on the floor, "I was unaware of your presence."

She looked up at him with her startling, yellow eyes. "I teleported here just in time to hear the end of what the director was saying."

"Anything you wish to add?" the Presiding Chair asked diplomatically, warily regarding the enigmatic, volatile woman.

She hugged her knees. "Not really." She bit her lower lip. "I was just thinking that the majority of large mammals had been driven to extinction thousands of years before High Mistress Hagar and Lord Aratta arrived on Earth." She regarded the commissioner with a measure of sadness. "Yet, if those two had brought me in just one hundred years earlier, my team could have salvaged a lot more." For an instant, her amber eyes smoldered with fire.

Aratta gave an ironic smile and shook his head slightly.

Jilieth added, seemingly to herself, "Why, the ancient forest of the Pacific Northwest was still intact back then, one of three forest remnants. Thousands of square miles of titanic coastal redwood trees." She looked away and said in a barely audible voice, "But then they came for them, too—with double-bit axes and two-man crosscut saws. In a forest possibly dating back to the dinosaur era, some of the largest and most majestic trees on Earth were made into log houses, cut into railroad ties, and pulped into newspapers."

"Take us there," one of the commissioners instructed a technician.

Once again, the room dimmed, and a holographic projection of the forest appeared.

"As you can see, High Mistress Jilieth, patches of coastal redwood rainforests have survived and are protected," said the Presiding Chair softly. "The fog, mosses, and ferns are still there. A few hundred years of growth, and a new generation of trees may take their places among the stately elders."

"A few intact pockets, somewhat under two hundred square miles in all. But yes," Jilieth whispered. "Maybe, yes."

Aratta pressed a hand against his ear for a moment, listening to some private communication. "Your Graces, the elevators carrying the Earthborn have just reached the surface," he said. "I'd better go." He bowed and then vanished.

CHAPTER 34

THE THREE LARGE FREIGHT elevators jerked to a stop, concluding their long upward journey to the surface. Their walls fell outward with loud clanks, raising puffs of parchment-yellow dust, leaving only their frames and roofs standing.

The hundred or so bewildered Terraneans stumbled out into the open, and the metal walls sprang back up. Moments later, the elevators plunged downward and—impossibly—a layer of earth materialized over them, leaving no trace that anything had stood there a short time prior.

Susan wove her way through the crowd, her eyes drinking in the staggering panorama. A seemingly endless expanse of grass and scattered trees stretched into impossible distances, arching upward until it merged with the sky above. Far away, at great intervals, spine-like ridges punctuated the horizon. The air was dense and warm, carrying a hint of an unfamiliar scent.

"You are inside a shell," a gruff, disembodied voice boomed, coming from all directions. The hundred people glanced wildly about but saw no one.

"It's a construct—vast beyond your ability to comprehend," the same disembodied voice blared. "A hollow sphere with a tiny dwarf sun at its core." At that, those who hadn't looked up finally did. Above them, a weak sun shone ivory-peach at the center of the colossal shell, tens of millions of miles away. "You could drop

Earth down here, and it would ricochet around like a ping-pong ball inside a steel drum the size of a building."

And suddenly he was there, standing on a boulder nearby, facing them. "We call this world the Reservation," he said. "The Res, for short. Though old-timers here have other names for it, too."

He jerked his thumb toward his massive chest. "I'm Vito the Barber. Along with Fat Frank and Big Carlo, I formed this construct."

Vito the Barber looked nothing like the man Lee had seen in the kitchen with the other two gods. He appeared here as a humanoid hulk, eight feet tall, with bronzed, pitted skin, and scarification on his gleaming head. With no visible neck, his giant head seemed to rest on two immense, broad shoulders. A shark tooth was strung on a chain across his bare chest. His eyes had purple irises and were deep-set.

Rafirre stood by his side.

He turned his massive head their way, finally deigning to study them. "This is you," he said, his voice tinged with the sound of gravel crunching under tank chains. "You spread throughout. You shit. You destroy." His purple eyes roved through the dazed-looking crowd. "The commissioners are investigating what you've been doing. You're to tell them why you are not going to screw up things further. They decide.

"You've been wondering what happens if they rule unfavorably. Well, you come here. If they tell me you go, you go. If they tell me you stay on Earth, you stay." He nodded toward Rafirre. "Along with his team of hundreds of compatriots, the Chief Examiner has been making the case for why you ought to be deported."

Vito paused, letting the weight of his words settle among the crowd. "Should you lot receive your marching orders, we've got legions at the ready, poised to spend the next few decades scrubbing away your mess." His words landed like heavy stones in silence. "I'm talking about the asphalt and concrete scarring the land, the cocktail of antibiotics and antidepressants fouling the rivers, the carbon dioxide you've belched from your vehicles into the air. There are dams to blow up, oil tankers to acid-dissolve, and strip-mined areas to rehabilitate."

He bowed his head to Aratta, who stood somewhere farther out, apart from the gathered group. "Lord Aratta'Gwa'Nar, High Mistress Hagar'Racina, and Puddeck have been monitoring that world of yours for several centuries. They have been providing expert testimony before moving on to their next assignment: monitoring another planet and alerting us if its people crap up."

For a moment, the Barber surveyed the far-off vista.

Then he was back, looking at them. "Should you be ousted and land here," he said, "there are a few things you need to understand.

"This is a regulated environment. The temperature's steady, and the weather is always the same. Land is everywhere, and its composition is relatively uniform. No lakes or seas, but we've got a very dense network of rapid creeks, bearing fresh water and keeping things sanitary.

"This world holds several hundred billion people from dozens of parallel planets, populating a number of sectors. Mostly, though, it's an impossibly vast, barren land with room for countless more people who don't give a rat's ass, who never balanced the checkbook, and who figured tomorrow would sort itself out."

A cynical grin split Vito's face. "When it comes to flora and fauna, you can bring down whatever you want, as much as you damn well like. Just the way you like it. You won't be able to hunt things to extinction here any more than you can wipe out gnats or flies by swatting them." He was smirking. "Everything here runs on spores."

He gestured expansively. "Our genetically engineered plants will stuff you full and grow back nearly as fast as you can hack them down." He raised a hand, ticking off on his fingers. "We've got rat-like critters that taste like chicken, and we have horse-like creatures that taste like goat's ass. Food isn't going to be an issue—unless you're hell-bent on hoarding it from others. I can appreciate the need to screw each other over to pass the time."

From his position atop the boulder, Vito scowled at the crowd of Terraneans. "Don't be really stupid in matters of sanitation, and you won't have to worry about diseases. Oh, yes. No mosquitoes here." He turned to the Examiner. "Ain't that right, Rafirre?"

"Sure thing, Vito." They fist-bumped. "You guys complained, so I wiped out those suckers. I did right by you," the Earth people could hear Vito say. And then he redirected his attention back to the aghast people in front of him.

"When you check out from Earth, you'll be lugging all your junk along—your trend-chasing outfits, Grandpa Billy's vinyl record collection, and Aunt Esther's jewelry and china. All these knickknacks will have to go, one way or another. However, we'll screen for contraband. Think sarin gas, anthrax spores, explosives, firearms—shit like that.

"I run a stone-, leather-, and fiber-based world here. This mainly comes down to granite, limestone and sandstone; fiber and lumber; animal hides; and various resins for sticking, flexing, and hardening.

"That being said, you'll be allowed to haul low-tech metal artifacts from Earth, from cookpots to hunting knives. Yet, before they dock, they'll get chemically treated. This means they'll keep their form and characteristics but, when they wear out, break, or grow dull, that'll be it. If you try to reforge them, they'll dissolve and reform as a glassy, hyper-brittle slug."

The large man fell silent.

"Is this some kind of test?" Susan called out eventually, red-faced.

"What about our rights?" Brandon demanded.

"How are we expected to build a civilization with Stone Age tools?" Wang Lei asked, waving his glasses about.

"You're not expected to," the Barber deigned to reply to that last question. "If you're relocated here, it means the time for expectations is over. We expect nothing from you and have made sure it's gonna stay this way. This world doesn't have the raw materials with which you could foul the nest.

"The Res is your journey's end. You'll live here, breed here, and drop dead here—over and over. No day, no night, just perpetual high noon. There's no next thing; there's just the Res." That last word seemed to reverberate oddly, hanging suspended in the air.

"You were brought to the surface a bit ahead of schedule. All the same, you were brought here so you can see and report back to your leaders." For a moment, his belly shook with silent laughter. "This was meant as a joke—the part about your 'leaders.'" He sobered up. "The rest was said in earnest, though. Take the information I've shared with you back to Earth. We want to light a fire under your asses so you realize the true stakes involved and put together the best defense case you can. However, unless you want to experience a breakdown of basic services throughout your world, I advise discretion. Some of your people should be made aware of what may befall your kind, but I wouldn't broadcast it on the evening news."

The giant man leapt down with a thud, raising a small cloud of dust. He glowered at them. "Listen well. If you apes get out of control down on Earth, we'll consider the hearing over and haul your sorry asses to the Res faster than you can imagine."

In one powerful leap, Vito was back on his rocky perch, gazing down at them. "This world has a number of ferocious predators," he said. "They'll get that old heart pumping. But primarily they are here to cull the morons and losers, making sure we won't have a human infestation on our hands in the next few millennia. The space may be vast beyond human comprehension, but it's not limitless. We average a group of humans—roughly a couple billion—every decade or so, and we need to keep the numbers somewhat in check.

"Given your lot's size, I'll grant you two full grid sections: fifty-seven and sixty-seven, which are adjoining. Each grid is about eighty million square kilometers. They'll be yours—if you can keep 'em. These grids are about a year's journey away from the nearest human cluster. But a year is all you got before hundreds of millions of marauders sweep through your territory." A semblance of a wintry smile creased his granite-like face. "Your arrival will be the most exciting thing since the last gang showed up a decade ago.

"Listen up, people! No need to sacrifice anything; help is not coming. Nonetheless, in case you guys are into worship and stuff, tell your kids … it's Vito *the Barber*." He was suddenly holding aloft a gigantic straight razor in one hand.

Rafirre pleaded, "I tried to explain, Vito. I told 'em it's not a sword, I swear."

Vito grimaced. "You people—does this look like a sword to you?" He gave it a slow half turn. "If your grandkids erect a statue to Vito the Barber, he'd better be holding a straight razor." The giant posed. "Something like this." After a moment or two, he made the razor disappear.

Some of the Earth people gaped open-mouthed. Others appeared slightly ill.

"For those of you who enjoyed the privileges of the first-class cabin back on Earth, the Res will be a setback," Vito said. "For your descendants, however, it'll just be reality. The accounts you bring with you of Earth will turn into stories in later generations. Over time, the stories will fade into myths."

Vito scrutinized them. "You're all in varying stages of shock. Normal. It'll pass," he said. "If I were to transport you back now, your sense of unreality would only intensify. You'll stay here for a few solid hours; it'll rub things in and take the edge off.

"No predators will bother you while you're here today. I'm taking the liberty of conjuring grub and providing shade." A few pavilions with food-laden tables materialized. "You can relieve yourself in the bushes; I'm not going to build you outhouses." He smirked. "You might as well get accustomed to doing it old school, *without* toilet paper." He smirked some more, then gave a short bow to Aratta and vanished.

For a long minute, the only sound was the rustle of leaves in a nearby thicket.

Some Terraneans slumped down where they stood; others broke out into small groups, and some wandered off by themselves, lost in their own gloomy thoughts or in a state of stupor.

There was a sense of finality—no appeals possible, no returns accepted. It was all in the hands of the seven-member commission and a yet-to-be-formed Earth delegation. The way of life they knew hung in the balance. For some, though, it seemed the scales had already tipped, and the grim prospect of exile was a fait accompli.

⊃⊂

SUSAN SETTLED DOWN AGAINST a boulder, resting her bones.

She looked up when she heard approaching footsteps. Aratta.

Susan waved him over. "Help me up," she said with a trace of bitterness. "I'm starting to feel my age." She paused. "Unlike you, in a few decades, I'll be pushing up daisies." She could feel her rage drowning out the panic and desperation that warred deep within her.

Aratta helped her to her feet, and she dusted herself off.

It took everything Susan had to restore calm.

Her eyes finally met his. "Penal colony, huh?"

"It'll provide you with unlimited food and land, no strings attached," he said to her. "Those are the givens. The rest is up to you." *Once you survive the initial wave of raids, that is.*

Susan took a deep, shaky breath. "How do you plan to do this?" she asked.

"We'll deploy one million gateways throughout Earth that lead to decontamination and screening centers, and from there, to the Reservation."

She was quiet for a while. "Do you really believe people will willingly go to this prison planet of yours? They'll fight, Aratta—to the bitter end if they must."

"In Cambodia, the Khmer Rouge forced everyone to abandon the cities and relocate to the countryside. And millions did, Susan—old, infirm, and all—when commanded by gun-toting teenagers with megaphones. I don't see why people would fight any harder to avoid crossing over into a new world." He tossed a pebble into the air, catching it as it fell. "It might not be as cataclysmic as you think."

Susan laughed. "So that's the great plan for evacuating humanity?"

Aratta shrugged. "It works."

"There must be more to it than that."

His gaze traversed the impossible stretches of land that dissolved into a haze hundreds of miles away. Finally, he returned his attention to her. "Should an expulsion order be issued, an engineered microbe will be released worldwide, spreading via spores, winds, and ocean currents. A metal-eating microbe." Susan stiffened visibly at this. "It will self-terminate after seven days. By that time, weapons, telephone lines, cars, and power generators will all look like Swiss cheese. Your entire civilization will collapse on its collective metallic ear, and it'll be all over." His voice lost its lightness. "People will have just enough time to leave the cities before the girders topple over their heads. Hunger, coupled with shock, is a potent motivator." As he spoke, Susan's face gradually turned pale.

"So what was all the talk about allowing us to bring some metal artifacts here?" Her voice lost its strength.

"We'll announce the relocation two days prior to activating the metal-eating microbe; this is the carrot. Many will scramble to grab whatever they can and rush to the gateways ahead of the stick coming down."

She turned away. "Why are you telling me all this? I could warn people. We could find ways to protect our weapons and other essentials made from metal."

"You'd be surprised what this microbe can dig through to get to the metals. Regardless, giving people hope is worse than useless; you'll be killing them."

"Some might prefer to die," she said, her voice barely audible.

"And they'll be given the option; anyone who successfully evades the evacuation will die as a matter of certainty."

She stared at him in disbelief.

Aratta said, "During World War I, a safety valve was set in place."

"World War I," Susan repeated, trying to latch onto a thought.

"An engineered virus was released worldwide, and a few years later, the genetic code of every Earth inhabitant was imperceptibly altered. This genetic modification is hereditary and is innocuous on its own." He gestured almost apologetically. "If you are made to go, we'll introduce *another* engineered virus, which exploits the genetic vulnerability we introduced among the Earth's inhabitants. Within three weeks, all of you should have made it through the portals. However, by week four, any Terranean still on Earth will be dead. No one would die unless they choose to. But let's be clear: The prime objective is the restoration of Earth's ecosystem. Your well-being is of secondary concern."

Bile rose hot in her throat. "Once we enter the gateways, will this virus be neutralized?"

"Essentially, yes. It'll go dormant the moment people relocate to—What did you call it?—the prison planet. For the microbe to be active, it requires a specific concentration of argon present in Earth's atmosphere. A different concentration of argon, which happens to occur here, will keep it inert."

He wasn't telling her everything. Over the past two years, they had tracked all weapons of mass destruction. In the event of deportation, a specialized force would neutralize them. This would be the first thing the commissioners would authorize, even before word of the ruling went public. They were concerned about the destructive power of these weapons, and what the Terraneans might do to the remaining pockets of the natural world—if they resolved to depart Earth with a spiteful parting gift. "But you're right, Susan; I shouldn't be telling you all of this." He met her gaze and held it. In a modified, strange voice, he said, "You *will* forget all the things I've just told you."

"I will forget what you've just told me," she repeated mechanically, eyes glazed.

"Attagirl," he said in his usual, softer voice. Her eyes focused again, eyeing him curiously.

Aratta brushed some dirt from her sleeve. "For what it's worth," he said, "remember this: When you are the cancer cells, relocation beats chemotherapy."

He moved to leave but then stopped and turned. "Your civilization has never worked," he said, his tone flat. He hesitated as if about to say more. "Over eight billion people," he eventually said, then shook his head in dismay and walked off.

⇒⇐

"I WAS BORN HERE," RAFIRRE SAID as he sat down beside Josh on the stone ledge. "In fact, my people have been here for centuries. Some groups have been here for a lot longer."

He waited, but Josh just kept staring at some far-off point, seemingly in a daze. The distant buzz of insects, the dry wind—none of it reached him.

Rafirre leaned back, resting on his elbows. "The weather is warm and constant. The land is for the taking. And you never have to file an insurance claim or worry about HR. It's not as bad as some make it to be."

Josh finally stirred, scuffing the dirt with his shoe. "What was that talk about us being a one-year journey away?"

Rafirre didn't answer right away. Then:

"So here's the thing. Food's nourishing—but sometimes people hunger for real meat, if you catch my drift." He shot Josh a look. "That's why raids are the main pastime here. Word's out—and hundreds of millions will saddle up when you arrive.

Marauders . . . they'll sweep through your territory."

Josh looked up, his voice wooden. "Marauders, you say? Who are they?"

"Actually, that would be my people," Rafirre said with a little ironic smile. "Our brightest minds trained their whole lives to be on the Assessment Group. And after decades of intensive study, we spent the last few years in the field, researching and building up a case. Given that, the Barber let our people have the 'first cut,' as it's called.

"But for you, does it really matter who the raiding horde is?" He winked and jabbed Josh. "Other raiders might sweep through later, but the real action is always in the first cut. One day, your people will get their turn. You'll catch on."

He scooted closer, eyes glinting.

"They're coming for your stuff—the good stuff you bring over from Earth: silk, compound bows, girls, hiking boots." He looked pointedly at Josh. "So don't go 'identifying' as a woman." He burst into a braying laugh.

"The captive men will have a raw deal, too," Rafirre admitted, sobering. "They'll be castrated and made to guard settlements from encroaching grissloirds and panarenians. Then, when they're too worn out to be useful, they'll be fattened up and served."

Lounging back, Rafirre closed his eyes, soaking in the sun, the only sun he'd known before his Earth jaunt. His legs swung idly. "In the Res, normalcy will return," he said, pensive. "Meaning: you'll breathe again. Back on Earth, compliance departments, legal review, and HR have been keeping your collective balls in a vise."

He eyed Josh. "Your men need it. Earth's made them soft. Bodies fed on sugar and chemicals. Fearful of pain and conflict. Glued to glowing screens, jacking it to pixelated pussy, and arguing like bitches online. The Res scrapes the softness off a man like rust off steel."

Rafirre noted Josh's startled look. "I watched you long enough down there to learn how you lie to yourselves," he told him, and for a moment his dark eyes glinted.

He fell silent.

Some time passed, and he noticed a young Earth woman seated a stone's throw away, leaning against the trunk of a tree. She wore a tight crop top, tighter jeans, and boots. She noticed his gaze and gave him the finger.

"Look at her," he murmured. "Pretty little thing." He chuckled darkly as he regarded her anew. "Washing machine does the scrubbing. Push-up bra keeps the tits looking perky past expiration. Courts make sure she never has to say sorry. Pregnancy undo button. Government plays daddy—pays some of the bills, sends men with guns. Unplug her, and she won't stay modern long. Same as you, same as all of you."

Josh felt his skin crawl. He raised his head long enough to look at the young woman across the rocky expanse.

Rafirre stretched. "Boss bitch—until the grid's gone and her belly's full of baby. Then she's crying in the dark, ready to trade whatever she's got to latch onto the first resourceful man who gives a damn."

"What do—"

Rafirre plowed on. "No wonder your offspring numbers are circling the drain. Your males drift alone like stunned cattle. Your homes are fractured. Your young numb themselves on pills and chase likes and dopamine on glowing pixels—don't build anything, don't belong to anything, aren't even sure what sex they are."

Josh just shook his head numbly.

"You think I'm exaggerating? Even in the Siege of Leningrad—when people survived on rats and wallpaper paste—their women still pushed out more babies than in some of your softer countries now."

Rafirre leaned in, his voice lowering. "Here, you'll sweat. You'll bleed. This place will slap you people back to reality and get you off the Self-Extinction Express." He leaned back. "You want to survive? You come together in clans. You protect your mate and your offspring. Everything else is noise."

Josh's voice sounded hollow, detached. "Hold on," he said. "I'm Josh Pruitt, online sales manager for mainframe cooling systems." He fumbled for a business card, holding it up with trembling fingers. "See? It's all there. I have a critical meeting in Frankfurt next month. Management booked me a hotel. I can't skip it. I can't."

Rafirre laughed, jabbing Josh's shoulder. "You've got cold feet, but don't worry about it. Like the rest of us, you have a respectable, long tradition; you're just out of practice, is all." Rafirre jabbed him in the shoulder again. "Just find your people and stick close."

Josh shook his head, trying to clear it. "Got some misunderstanding here. You don't understand; I work for a big corporation. I have an important meeting a month from now."

Rafirre narrowed his eyes. "Hey, stay here with me. I'm giving you some good, valuable information about the raids. Forget about Frankfurt. What good are Frankfurt and cooling equipment going to do for you now?"

Josh was shaking his head, repeating some unintelligible phrases over and over.

Rafirre jumped off the ledge. "Anyway, remember the tips I gave you." He squeezed the other man's shoulder and strode off, leaving Josh to stare intently at the trails of dirt he was stirring up with the tips of his shoes.

CHAPTER 35

IN THE CONCLUDING DAYS OF TESTIMONY, THE CIVILIZATION Assessment Group focused on the power dynamics of world governments, saving the influential United States for last. Basile led the presentation. He was a tall, balding man with an air of calm and perceptive eyes.

As Aratta stepped into the chamber, Basile was drawing his comments to a close.

"The F-35 Lightning II, a fifth-generation fighter jet, offers a case in point," Basile was saying. "A financial black hole, this jet program has been mired in technical failures and cost overruns. More than one decision-maker has wondered about the wisdom of financing it. Yet, they continue to pour taxpayers' money down the program's gullet. It's about the employment opportunities and economic benefits that this aircraft program provides. And as its supply chain and manufacturing facilities are spread across nearly every state, everyone has skin in the game. No member of Congress wants to explain to their constituents and donors how the member's own actions contributed to the loss of their livelihoods or to the undermining of their financial interests because this venture doesn't make sense. It doesn't need to make sense; it just needs to generate taxpayer-funded jobs.

"Your Graces, a small donor class and outside groups contribute an outsized share for all congressional seats. Their donations afford them significant influence and cement enduring relationships. Consequently, no political will exists to hold them accountable or object to infusing them with taxpayers' money during times of dire need. Put bluntly, inside the Beltway, it may be political suicide to go against the interests or bidding of Wall Street, Big Pharma, Big Oil, agribusiness, and the defense contractors." The commissioners, now well acquainted with the details of these entities, nodded in understanding. "And quite a few senior officials are former executives or board members of major corporations and are likely to have business ties to them.

"It is a playground of members of the ruling class, of billionaire ideologues, and of oligarchs. They inject the arteries of power with dark money through charities and foundations, nudging voting patterns and sponsoring candidates who will carry their water. The elected officials in Washington are routinely beholden. The policies they enact are oftentimes contrary to the interests of the American public."

A man in white-and-silver livery went around and refilled the carafes with water.

Basile gave an appreciative nod, taking a sip from his glass. "In addition to whatever else it may be, the Hill essentially operates as a giant call center. Representatives spend much of their time cold-calling potential donors, seeking contributions. Realistically speaking, who has the impetus to take on crumbling bridges, aging water pipes, and deteriorating roads? These things neither contribute to re-election war chests nor do they help post-congressional career prospects."

"Please elaborate on that last point."

"Yes, Your Grace. Senior government officials who prove themselves may be offered positions and graduate to become lobbyists or executives, with far better pay. Hence, their attentiveness to the pleas of those who may one day sign their paychecks." He waved his hand. "That's how we see career trajectories like the Director of the National Reconnaissance Office joining Lockheed Martin's board, the CDC's Director becoming president of Merck's vaccine division, the former Speaker of the House getting on the payroll at Squire Patton Boggs, and the FDA Commissioner transitioning to the board at Pfizer."

"Could you delve deeper into the topic of special interest groups you mentioned this morning?"

"Of course, Presiding Chair," Basile said. He thought for a moment. "They can best be described as inward-looking and narrowly defined. For instance, the gun lobby persistently derails any legislation aimed at stringent gun control, while the trial lawyer lobby exists primarily to safeguard the unrestricted prerogative of suing. Special interest groups have no mandate to negotiate a compromise or collaborate for the greater good.

"Your Graces, the political arena is crowded with interest groups, each jostling for a spot at the teat. Interestingly, some of them represent foreign interests. Whatever entitlements a given organization has secured for its constituency, it will fight tooth and nail to protect them, indifferent to the wider societal costs. A case in point is the corn ethanol lobby. It has secured a mandate that compels refiners to blend—or finance the blending of—billions of gallons of fuel distilled from Midwestern corn each year, whether or not it makes sense. Because the first presidential contest is held in a state steeped in corn, no serious candidate dares to question the arrangement. The broader costs be damned; woe to those who suggest unwinding the subsidy. The special interest groups circle overhead like harpies, ready to swoop down with talons extended at any whiff of reform. Congressmen prudently confine themselves to the safe haven of Status Quo Island."

With a bow, Basile indicated his readiness to conclude his remarks about the US Congress. "In an environment where genuine governance and the advancement of the common good are sidelined, political posturing, symbolic gestures, and pretenses become the mainstay of the legislators' actions. They churn out bills that won't see the light of day. They fire off tough questions in subcommittees, showing their folks back home they're in the fight. They record their speeches in a near-empty House Chamber to make supporters feel listened to. They grandstand on hot issues, often butting heads with those on the other side of the aisle.

"To sum up, aside from fundraising and theatrical posturing, the predominant use of congressional time is bestowing subsidies, tax relief, and immunity from regulatory interference to benefactors and those with influence—and not much else."

He bowed one last time. After one year of research and five hours of testimony, his work was done. He nodded to Aratta and Puddeck as the two men made their way to the lectern.

⇒⇐

"YOUR GRACES," ARATTA BEGAN, "MASTER BASILE HAS predominantly explored the democratic exterior. But if we delve beneath the hood, we find the United States government largely consists of an unaccountable, permanent, and unelected bureaucracy. Real power is not harbored in the corridors of the Capitol but within a multitude of sprawling agencies. Their tendrils extend into almost every facet of American life.

"Actual authority is wielded by managerial bureaucrats and technocrats and regulators and administrators and activist legal authorities. To these individuals, elected politicians, who are part of an ever-shifting cast, are little more than transient irritants, while the citizens, ostensibly the sovereigns, are deemed short-sighted subjects requiring the state's firm guiding hand. The United States is increasingly becoming an administrative totalitarian state, its presence ever more pronounced in its inhabitants' lives.

"And when I speak of an administrative state, I mean it in the full sense. The managerial bureaucratic caste has assumed preeminence in all large organizations—both private and public, both for-profit and nonprofit.

"Your Graces, strictly speaking, the US government is the hundreds of agencies to which I've just alluded. More broadly, however, it's an interwoven web of power hubs that sets the United States' policies and priorities—a web whose nodes include giant corporations, financial institutions, nonprofits, media, academia, government agencies, and advocacy groups. When the leading social media companies ejected a democratically elected, sitting president from their platforms—the modern public square—it laid bare where true power resides in America."

Puddeck, standing alongside Aratta, interjected, "That last was but a manifestation of the war to eradicate disinformation from the public sphere."

One of the commissioners raised an eyebrow. "Speak more of this."

"The aim of this war is to safeguard the American citizen's right to be exposed to the Truth, and nothing but the Truth," the man in purple explained.

"Your Graces," Aratta said, "this campaign seeks to establish a narrative monopoly and manufacture consent as a way to assert power and control. It discreetly filters what individuals view online, effectively sculpting public opinion and discourse, creating a uniform narrative for public consumption."

A murmur of interest rippled among the commissioners.

Puddeck said, "Disinformation commissars are embedded in major media outlets, governmental agencies, academic institutions, and non-governmental organizations. Working in tandem with fact checkers, conspiracy theory detectors, and claim debunkers, they act as gatekeepers of discourse—determining which utterances are safe, responsible, and inclusive. From Germany to the United Kingdom, many Western countries have instituted laws against wrongspeech, at times served with early morning police raids."

There was silence for a moment.

"Your Graces, as this campaign solidifies its grip," Aratta said, "it blurs the once-sacrosanct boundaries between the public and private spheres. It acts as a muzzle on those who threaten the establishment, those who undermine Truth and Science, those who obstruct social justice. This consortium 'de-amplifies' problematic mass movements, neutralizes 'threat actors,' protects the individual's 'cognitive infrastructure,' and combats information pollution by applying 'friction' and 'intervention.' In essence," Aratta said, "it is another step toward the fascistic vision of 'Everything in the State, nothing outside the State, nothing against the State.'"

Some of the commissioners nodded thoughtfully.

"Allow me to delve deeper into some of the implications of living within the institutional leviathan."

Aratta was quiet for a moment. He finally said, "The complexity of life requires human judgment: a continual consideration of things that come one's way, set against ever-changing circumstances.

"From the marketplace of ideas to the commercial sphere, society draws its vitality from the freedom to exercise one's judgment and to own one's daily choices, doing what one deems prudent and sensible. It is the possibility of a choice that provides people with a sense of personal fulfillment, challenges them, and keeps them engaged.

"Your Graces, laws ought to form outer bounds within which freedom of judgment and action can flourish. Alas, the cobwebs of regulations, statutes, and insurance stipulations pervade every facet of industry and human interaction. There are rules on everything and for everything—taking the place of discretion and judgment. Their sweep is one the Soviet central-planners of old could have only dreamed of.

"This expansive framework of directives gets between people and plain old common sense. It discourages individuals from leveraging personal insights acquired over the years, pushes aside firsthand judgment, and disengages one's moral compass.

"Exact, unmalleable statutes and insurance stipulations do not permit case-specific adaptations and are ill-equipped to navigate situational nuances. The body of regulations is often too detailed, on one side, and decoupled from common social norms, on the other. It's impossible to internalize and truly make it one's own.

"Constraining the exercise of sound judgment saps people of their stamina. Their spirit of initiative fades. They no longer feel one can effect change—or one should bother and try to.

"Within professional settings, personal discretion takes a backseat; codified directives guide behavior. Decisions are measured against potential liability and legal risks. As the saying goes, the limits of freedom are defined by what one can be sued for. A barrage of insurance stipulations, governmental regulations, human resources guidelines, and company procedures forms a formidable maze of deterrents and red flags.

"From a heritage of 'damn the torpedoes' to a present mired in code compliance and rigid protocols, Americans have traded their once vibrant, can-do culture for a risk-averse society of drone bees performing tasks by the numbers.

"During World War Two, American manufacturers retooled their factories and new, giant plants were built throughout the country. Millions of Americans rolled up their sleeves and nearly one hundred thousand aircraft were constructed in one year— machines that flew, fought, and worked. There was no time for a three-year feasibility study, and the oversight had a heartbeat. Today, the heartbeat is gone, and the stack of paperwork is thicker. Much thicker.

"Take cancer clinical trials," Aratta said. "Getting from concept to activation requires navigating hundreds of prescribed tasks—a recursive loop of IRBs, institutional contract offices, and privacy mandates that add bureaucratic layers with marginal safety value."

Aratta flashed a grim smile. "How things have changed from the days Oliver Evans built a high-pressure steam engine, mounted it on a hull, and with a single nod from the Board of Health drove that amphibious monster down a road in Philadelphia and into the Schuylkill River. One permit. One giant leap for the annals of history.

"Your Graces, risk-averse culture coupled with all-pervasive regulations throttles bold innovations and technological advancements. It's doubtful whether insulin, general anesthesia, or even flight could have emerged in today's regulatory climate.

"In practice, even if they wished to, government officials of today cannot lay out a transcontinental ultra-high voltage electrical grid; the regulatory morass renders plans of any magnitude nearly unfeasible. After all, even the elevation of the deck of the existing Bayonne Bridge in New Jersey, to allow taller ships to pass through, necessitated years of approval processes: thousands of pages of environmental assessments and thousands of pages of documents related to various regulations and permits.

"There are no longer public servants who can attack a problem or resolve an issue armed with acumen. In their stead, there are legions of worker drones who dutifully execute some of the millions of regulations that legions of lawmakers churn out. No one knows what they all say. Typically, older statutes just slowly submerge beneath the weight of newer ones.

"This brings us to the way things are: regulations, impervious to context and nuance, that shape and solidify every facet of life.

"This is the era of the institution on Earth. Your Graces, a culture that once supported human initiative and sound judgment has been supplanted by clockwork mechanics of regulatory cogwheels, liability insurance gearwheels, corporate locks, and the absence of thoughtful human intervention."

CHAPTER 36

The Western End of Madagascar Island, off the Coast of Africa, Qataria

THE MORNING BREEZE TOUSLED Lee'chelle's hair, rousing her from sleep. As her eyes flickered open, a curious rodent was already darting away. She sniffed at the impertinence and stretched, arching her back against the straw mat.

Sunlight spilled through the sliding paper screens as she opened them. Brightness everywhere. She squinted at far-off, pearl-white clouds sailing across a sky of light blue and savored the feel of the wind on her bare skin. It was going to be another gorgeous early summer day.

She didn't need to check the main house to know Aldabara, her adoptive father, had already left. He always left at the break of dawn. Lee'chelle, on the other hand, preferred to start late and work into the night. On some days, she didn't reach the business district until noon.

Since arriving a couple of weeks ago, she'd taken a few airship rides to the village hub, floating in mesh cocoons hoisted by winches. But on a day like today, when the sun's heat wasn't oppressive, she preferred to walk. The brick road, a stone's throw from home, lay hidden beneath waves of tall, golden savanna grass. She waded in and soon was swallowed by the flaxen sea.

Half an hour later, Lee'chelle walked into downtown. A warm

wind swept the streets, and a honeyed scent drifted from nearby balsam poplars. As had become her habit in recent days, she popped into a few shops, learning what was new, helping unload heavy cargo, and chatting with some people.

As always, she stopped by Terno's bakery.

As she entered, Lee'chelle was greeted by the smell of baking bread and the scent of fresh cheese. From a supporting pillar hung wooden boards stacked with mozzarella, whey still dripping. A reed basket of glossy black olives rested on a low stone ledge.

Terno must have been at the oven, baking. Pity. Lee'chelle wanted to say hi. She pulled out a buffalo mozzarella ball, wrapped it in wax paper, and tucked a loaf of sourdough under her arm. The crust was golden-brown, blistered in places. As she left, she smiled to herself. She could get used to the moneyless economy on Qataria.

For the past two weeks, this had become a ritual. After picking vine tomatoes from a nearby vegetable garden, Lee'chelle would head to her workplace. There, she would tear into the warm bread, slather it with pesto, and relish each chunk that she paired with soft white cheese and deep-red tomatoes.

The overall shape of her adoptive dad's work studio resembled a see-through dovecote. As she came in, stray sun rays reflected off the iron of the old proof press. Manuals and type specimen books were scattered about. In the center of the shop stood two tall swivel chairs and three bronze desks.

She went over to her adoptive father's office and kissed him on the head. Aldabara looked up and returned her kiss. "Had breakfast?" he asked.

"Brought it with me."

"Darr will be here soon. I'd like you to sit in on the meeting. In fact, I would like you to take the lead."

She was surprised and excited. "Really?"

He nodded. "You've worked diligently and produced pleasing work since you got here. You've earned it, Lee'chelle."

She gave him a mock salute, excused herself, and went over to the small low table overlooking the quiet street below. She ate, occasionally gazing with serenity at the tall canopies of the majestic baobab trees outside. After finishing her breakfast, she cleaned up. Then, she closed her eyes and meditated.

"Lee'chelle," Aldabara said softly. At the sound of his voice, she opened her eyes and turned.

A man stood at the doorway with a faint smile on his face. Aldabara walked over, clapped the man on the shoulder, and led him in. "Darr, may I introduce my adopted daughter, Lee'chelle? Lee'chelle, this is Darr O'haera."

She stood up.

Darr came over and kissed her hand. "*Viorette* Lee'chelle," he said formally. "It's an honor." He straightened and for a moment frankly regarded the pretty young woman with dark hair, animated face, and bright green eyes.

He only knew what was widely known. She had appeared a few weeks earlier in the dead of night, at the heart of the storm. Aldabara had found her naked, wet, unconscious at his doorstep. It was said that her parents had died in an accident two years ago in a distant place. Undertaking a long solo journey, she had found her way to Madagascar. Beyond these scant details, nothing more seemed known, save perhaps by Aldabara himself.

She gave a deep bow. "The pleasure is all mine." The young woman wore a cornsilk-white summer dress with a fitted waist. Her flared skirt swayed gently as she led him to one of the studio spaces. The three took their seats on bamboo legless chairs around a low table stacked with technical drawings and specimen books.

For many years, the community had been aware of Darr's efforts to put his vision into writing. Aldabara had wanted to do the honors for a long while. Now, the opportunity had finally presented itself. They were going to typeset his book.

Father and daughter faced the author who sat across from them. Darr was eyeing one of the type specimen books. Lee'chelle noted it was opened to Cerlio. "Beautiful," the man said. She glanced at the giant letters and saw what he meant.

Aldabara smiled at her encouragingly, and she dug up some specimen sheets and spread them in front of Darr. "Every typeface has an effective size range," she said, then leaned over his shoulder, pointing at some of the typed sentences. "Post Medival blossoms only at the very small sizes. Madrounnea can only look attractive at large sizes. And few, like Fatt Face, need to tower over one hundred points to acquire their full flavor."

Darr studied the folio sheets and eventually looked up. Lee'chelle was smiling faintly at him.

Aldabara elaborated, "The typesetting community continuously works to broaden the effective size range of the fonts we use."

"How do you mean?"

Aldabara said, "The shapes of the letters ought to be modified at various sizes. A master image designed for optimal appearance at standard text size can result in letters appearing clogged at smaller sizes, such as in footnotes." The older man leafed through some of the folio sheets and then handed a number of them to Darr. "There's a need for a separate set of master letters designed specifically for use at small sizes—with thinner stems, extended letterforms, and an increased white space within the characters."

Lee'chelle smiled brightly. "This goes beyond adjusting for readability. Take the Stones font. At smaller sizes, it has piquancy. However, magnify the master design, and the characters start to lose their zest. By adding these almost-undetectable quirks and irregularities to the outlines of the letters, Stones can maintain its sharp look and feel at large sizes."

"Fascinating," Darr said.

Aldabara turned to Lee'chelle. "Why don't you show him what you've been working on during the past week?"

"Yes, Father," she said. For a moment, they shared a private smile. It still sounded odd to be calling each other "father" and "daughter." Lee'chelle went to the next room and, a moment later,

came back with a stack of sheets. "This is a Gille Sans font." She
crouched by Darr. "In this typeface, the letters 'r,' 't,' 'f,' and 'y' do
not play well with others. And so I've been creating variant letters. Or look at this. See the question mark symbol? It's useful.
Yet, there is also a need for a question mark variant that suggests
exclamation, wonder, or urgency. In fact, there is a need to create
a whole set of softer punctuation marks, for those times in which
the Gille Sans is used in works of fiction." She gazed at the author.
"Darr, hundreds of supporting letters are called for in any given
typeface."

"And so you work on Gille Sans."

Lee'chelle laughed. "One among many, and a novice at that, but
yes, I was told refining a typeface is a process that spans decades."

She regarded Darr. The things she had mentioned were but
the tip of the iceberg; she did not think he grasped the possible
extent of it. The young woman thumbed through a book sitting
nearby, then pointed. "Look at this sentence. What word grabs
your attention? Don't reflect on it; just tell me what's the first word
you noted."

"'Water.'"

"Is it written using the same character set as the rest of
the words?"

He studied the page. "Yes."

"Actually, it isn't. In this word, I used variant letters with a hint
of quiet intensity. Hence, it caught your eye—as I meant it to."

"But the letters of this word look identical to all the other letters in this font!" Darr cried.

Lee'chelle winked, then burst out laughing.

They chatted a bit longer with Darr and, at some point, saw
him to the door. Lee'chelle bowed. Aldabara shook hands, and
the author left.

"I'm happy, Father," Lee'chelle said.

"So am I," he said and gave her a tender smile. "Tell me, do you
still ponder about your time before your arrival here?"

"Yes," she said. "At least, now and then." Her eyes flickered with deep emotions. "I remember most of the seventeen years of my life." Or was it sixteen? Unsure, she went back and forth on that one. "I did a lot and traveled far. To an astonishing degree, it seems. Yet those memories are fading away, and I've begun to wonder in the last few days if it was just a nightmare I had, you know? Some aspects of it appear so … disconnected from reality. Maybe even implausible."

"What does it feel like?" he asked, concern in his voice.

She smiled ruefully. "It felt like wading neck-deep in sludge, but you know how it is in a dream: everything feels perfectly natural when you're in it."

Aldabara studied her from under his bushy, gray eyebrows. Finally, he patted her on the shoulder, climbed to his feet, and returned to what he was doing.

After a moment of meditation, Lee'chelle opened her eyes and walked over to her large work desk.

It was time to get started.

She pulled out the tools she typically used: a pencil, a point ruler, a razor blade, a highlighter, a translucent triangle, and a 15x magnifying glass.

Lee'chelle pondered a line of copy she'd begun working on the day before. The general look of the sky ride announcement had already been set by the designer. What Lee'chelle had to do was to … hone the text.

For several minutes, she examined the arrayed letters. They had to come together as words. During the setting of type, one could not regard the characters as standalone components. A word had to be considered as a unit—an agreeable interplay of black lines and white spaces. One of the startling implications of this was the need to create uneven letter spacing.

A chain is only as strong as its weakest link, a principle Lee'chelle applied as she ferreted out the least manageable character combinations in the heading. So far, she had spotted two areas of darkness, which would force the other parts of the word to adjust accordingly. But then she couldn't really do that, as she had a letter that trapped a lot of white space and dictated an overall lighter appearance. Interesting…

She played with the letters on the screen as long as it was productive, then made some notes and pushed the steam keyboard aside. In the evening, she planned to have another go at it. She needed to give her subconscious some time.

There was a knock. A messenger boy stood at the doorway. Lee'chelle walked over and thanked him, pleased. She had just received the text and some samples for the upcoming community fire dance. She was to design some of the related announcements.

EVENING WAS FALLING OVER THE GRASSLAND, its red glow heating the sky.

As Lee'chelle closed her eyes, some of the stories in Darr's story collection came back to her.

Which typeface to choose?

She reckoned typesetting was either the highest form of art, or the lowest. But it surely was one of those. It was the art of invisibility. The typeface was the medium to carry the flavor, the weight of the text. If the font was too sterile and severe, it could not contain the quality of the story. If the font was overly ornate, it would draw attention to itself.

This was the truth, albeit oversimplified. Clumsiness, grace, and vigor clung to a typeface through associations and the context of an era.

Lee'chelle read one of Darr's stories again, and then another. She dropped the manuscript and opened the first of five ring binders. She thumbed through the thick volume, jotting down names of typefaces to try out.

Itaian Old Style's main merit was that there was nothing bad to say about it. Yet, the font held no exceptional attributes that could have reflected the spirit of the story. Goldenn Type was in a way the best candidate, but the font suffered from a real drawback: it was inherently dark and bore harsh overtones. Post Medival conveyed the appropriate storytelling quality: bookish and jovial. But—and that was a big "but"—at text size, the flares and jaggies of the letters were too pronounced, making it appear cutesy and decorative. And then there was Dela Rubia, a trifle eccentric, but she thought that it just might be the typeface she would end up going with.

To finalize her decision, she printed some pages from Darr's manuscript.

A whole range of black hues existed, each designed to impart a different mood or provide a better match for a particular paper. These subtle variations were essentially black ink with green, red, blue, or white additives—producing pleasing black colors with all but imperceptible undertones of one hue or another.

Lee'chelle instructed Agni how to ink up the rollers of the proofing press. The little apprentice weighed the black and magenta inks he had scraped from the jars, keeping a close watch over the black-to-magenta ratio. Aldabara had told Lee'chelle that none of the children who had occasionally walked resolutely into their shop stayed longer than a few days—at most. It just wasn't the kind of craft kids connected with; it had too much of the subtle and the understated.

In short order, Agni printed a number of samples for Lee'chelle to contemplate. This was what she had pictured. With an almost imperceptible red tint, the severity of the font went away, and the characters became lively and organic.

Lee'chelle had made her decision. The book would be typeset in Dela Rubia.

She continued working long after Aldabara and Agni left.

Down below, on the street, a pair of children were wheeling a loaded cart fastened with glowing paper lanterns, loudly inquiring if any of the people toiling late needed dinner brought up to them.

Lee'chelle was grateful. She waved at the two. And moments later, she was eating a warm sandwich wrap, frowning in concentration and frustration at the growing pile of text samples on her desk. She had covered all the bases, and it still wasn't working.

Darr's manuscript was now set in Dela Rubia. The size of the letters was 11 points; the line spacing was 13.25 points; the line width was 305 points. So far so good.

Dela Rubia was a very organic typeface. It looked somewhat off-putting with the left margin straight and stiff. This issue was taken care of; she had created very gentle slopes and jaggies on the left margin, giving the body of text subtle, natural edges—on both sides.

She had optimized the letter size, linewidth, line spacing, and line endings. Yet something was still off. Any time she closed her eyes, she could see the rightness. And when she opened them, she saw the reality. There was a gap between the two.

It was apparent that this lovely typeface still had some kinks in need of adjustment. The lowercase "s" of Dela Rubia appeared caved in. Capital letters, notably the "T" and "H," were too wide. The question mark was too dreamy, while the other punctuation marks were too harsh for their own good.

More hours passed as she spent her time stretching all the letters infinitesimally, after which she considered the result in the galley proof. Yes, things *did* look better. Alas, the sense of wrongness lingered. Something was still eluding her.

Lee'chelle logged onto the typesetter network and accessed the file on Dela Rubia. Only half a page had been written about that font. She read through it quickly. Evidently, someone had started working on this typeface earlier, but the project was aborted. The typesetter had pointed out the overly wide caps. "There is something else. I will have to re-visit it," he had noted. No help there. She added her entry and attached the character variants she had created.

Lee'chelle turned back to the large work table.

She studied the groups of letters she'd marked earlier. The problematic letter combinations varied each time. An "e" was a problem in one group, but not in another... Then, it was the "h" causing trouble, but only on one occasion. Then she saw it. It was in the combinations. Whenever letters like "e" and "a" stood next to airy ones, such as "h" and "u," there was a spike—a sudden jolt of color on the page. She could see it now. She could see it.

CHAPTER 37

The Reservation, Deep Underground, the Commission Building

"What's the antidote to market saturation?" Ms. Hill asked rhetorically. "You grow the market, of course. You sell illness. Plain heartburn becomes 'acid reflux disease.' People take prescriptions instead of baking soda."

It was the last round of presentations and testimonies by the Civilization Assessment Group. Aratta, Puddeck, and the Chief Examiner, Rafirre, were in attendance. And so was the second Earth person who wanted to stay for the remainder of the hearing.

Unlike the other Terranean, Ms. Hill had significant ties waiting for her back on Earth. But she also had a bone to pick—or at least some bitter, firsthand experience she wished to testify to. It had something to do with her long years as a pharmaceutical sales representative. Back home, she was a whistleblower. Predictably, her podcasts and interviews changed nothing. But then those people whooshed from the sky, or from wherever. She reasoned that if anything or anyone could undermine the stronghold of Big Pharma, they were it. Ms. Hill had a personal score to settle and wanted to stick it to the drug companies.

"Pharma invests in what brings the most profit, not in what may do the most good," Ms. Hill was saying. "In developing countries, the demand for better, cheaper drugs for treating malaria and schistosomiasis may exist, but the money does not. It's far more sensible to focus on less serious ailments that afflict the middle class. I'm just being honest. The best maladies to invest in are common ones requiring lifelong treatment. So you can appreciate why children are recognized as the most lucrative market niche. The earlier the diagnosis, the longer the revenue tail."

"Give us a concrete example," Rafirre prompted. Through Hill's testimony, he was exposing Earth's greed: its ugly, profit-hungry core.

"Sure. Antipsychotics prescribed in childhood often turn into long-term dependencies, since they don't cure the underlying condition but merely suppress the symptoms," she said. "They're difficult to discontinue, which guarantees a steady revenue stream. And because they disrupt neurotransmitter systems, they frequently require additional drugs to manage the side effects."

She paused. "As it turned out, stimulants and antidepressants can trigger manic symptoms in kids. Within a decade, a new diagnosis exploded into existence. Now you treat the mania—sometimes with a stabilizer, sometimes straight to an antipsychotic. Either way, the side effects demand their own drugs. One pill bought us entry; the complications bought us the whole system." A cold light came into her eyes. "This is the point where pharma's propaganda arm revs up."

"Propaganda arm?" Rafirre asked.

"Yes," Ms. Hill said. "They roll out disease-awareness campaigns to inflate new disorders. Celebrities suddenly discover they've 'suffered in silence.' Funded 'patient groups' appear overnight, demanding access to treatment. Fear-based ads fan the flames of disease paranoia. And by the time the drug arrives, the disorder already feels familiar—approved by repetition."

"What of clinical trials?"

"Pharmaceutical companies spin clinical trials, massage the data, and obtain the results they need," Ms. Hill told them. "You design for success: compare the new drug to a placebo, not the current gold standard—that sets the bar at zero. You manipulate time, keeping follow-up windows too short for neurological damage to surface. You run ten trials, publish the three that succeed, and bury the seven that fail. And if a competitor can't be avoided? You overdose it so your drug looks clean by comparison."

"A while ago, the government commissioned a large, long-term clinical trial for the treatment of high blood pressure. As it turned out, diuretics were as effective as the newer drugs in lowering blood pressure and, more to the point, better at preventing heart failure. Alas, the diuretics carried no patent, so they were cheap. As you can imagine, no company had a financial interest in promoting them. Not surprisingly, the far more expensive, yet no more effective, patented drugs got pushed and overwhelmingly prescribed."

"What about government watchdogs?"

"Watchdogs? Government advisory boards are *crawling* with industry insiders."

"All the same, with all the billions Big Pharma has been paying out over the years in court-imposed fines, hasn't that served as a deterrent to their shenanigans?"

"No," Ms. Hill said. "For vaccines, they operate under a special liability shield—most injury claims are diverted into a government compensation program instead of the courts. As for their other products, honestly, those penalties are little more than rounding errors."

"What if a news outlet is about to run a story unfavorable to a new drug?" Rafirre asked.

"This rarely happens, as pharma advertisements keep the lights on."

"What about innovations?"

Ms. Hill grimaced. "Innovation is a crapshoot; Big Pharma usually goes with what it considers the safe bets. When the patent monopoly for a lucrative drug is about to lapse, the company can tweak the product in question ever so slightly, and suddenly there's a freshly patented version that can lock out generics for years to come."

She added, "When the disease is rare and the affected population is too small to attract competition, the firm owning the related drug gains a license to print money. The worst price spikes come from drugs owned by hedge funds, private equity, and financial arbitrage firms."

Ms. Hill helped herself to some water.

"Each year," she said, "tens of thousands of well-compensated sales reps give out billions of dollars' worth of free samples. I say 'free,' but the cost of these—along with the entire immense marketing budget—is really paid for by the end-consumer in the form of jacked-up drug prices and fat insurance premiums. What pharma discovered is that once physicians and patients get into the habit of using the medication, they'll want more of it after the samples run out.

"Speaking of physicians, the majority of states require doctors to receive continuing medical education, with most earning their necessary credits by attending numerous meetings and lectures. But here's the kicker: A large share of dinner programs, symposiums, and medical conventions is underwritten by pharma. And as they pick up much of the tab and host posh parties during the night, they get to set the agenda and hold the microphone during the day."

Ms. Hill paused and sipped her water. "Pharma also employs influencers, physicians who champion certain products and essentially shape the prescribing habits of other physicians. Benefiting from academic freedom and industry support, these key opinion leaders present industry trials at medical conferences and educational sessions. Often, their views—amplified by the industry—conflict with the actual evidence, thereby perpetuating an industry-serving narrative."

"What about doctors?"

"What about them?"

"Are they in on all of this?"

She shrugged. "They went into medicine to help people. But when you owe more than a house and the only jobs are corporate, you put on the polo shirt and do what the company protocols say."

The Presiding Chair nodded in understanding. "I thank you for your testimony, Ms. Hill," he said. "Ready for a closing statement?"

Ms. Hill nodded and took a moment to collect her thoughts. "Your Honors," she finally said, "pharma permeates and dominates the entire ecosystem. It has co-opted every aspect of medical education, medical research, and medical practice. It steers the media, pulls the strings of legislators, and has quietly captured the health agencies. It's not a coincidence that Medicare is prohibited from negotiating down prescription drug prices." She shook her head in amused wonder. "Follow the money. Just follow the money."

She nodded toward the commissioners, and some nodded back.

Ms. Hill exited the hexagonal, bamboo-floored area.

"Thank you, Ms. Hill," Aratta said as he took to the stage along with Puddeck. "Your testimony was most fitting, as it does capture many facets of the existing economic system."

He was going to give testimony on the economic setup on Earth.

As Aratta saw it, this was one of the most important testimonies—one that would delve into the primary engine of their world.

CHAPTER 38

ARATTA TOOK HIS PLACE AT THE LECTERN AS the chamber stilled.

"Esteemed Chair, respected commissioners," he began. "A good economic system meets four conditions. One, it facilitates human flourishing through its end products and services. Two, it operates within the regenerative limits of the physical world. Three, it lets the wild remain wild—as an end in itself. Four, it makes economic participation itself an endeavor of worth—pursuits that awaken a sense of ownership and pride, foster meaningful human interactions, or spur self-actualization and originality. As I speak, I ask that you keep these criteria before you."

He drew lightly on the pipe and then exhaled, letting the silence settle around his words.

"First, let us dispense with the banal.

"For a time, an administrative command system governed the daily lives of hundreds of millions of people on Earth. It sought to replace the judgment of countless individuals—each an expert in their own circumstances—with the edicts of a small cadre of central planners who controlled raw materials, set quotas, fixed prices, and dictated production.

"Such a system could not accommodate the spontaneous order, emergent properties, and adaptive dynamics of a complex marketplace. Decisions made in distant hubs lacked the feedback mechanisms to respond to the ever-shifting needs and desires of people living their lives."

He paused again, tasting the stem as if to punctuate the obvious.

"Not surprisingly, the administrative command systems proved to be bleak affairs. Innovation withered; local initiative died; apathy, cynicism, and self-serving agendas took prominence. Life under them ranged from the drab and stifling to the outright calamitous."

Some of the commissioners nodded in acknowledgment.

"By contrast, decentralized, money-driven markets are good at accommodating the complexity of the modern economy. They adapt. They signal. They respond. Like the enchanted pasta pot in their tale of Strega Nona, they helped raise living standards across much of the world: food became abundant and storable, running water and flush toilets became common, and electric light pushed back the night so that work and study could continue after sunset. They don't just incentivize marketable innovation; they compound it—iteration under competition, adoption by imitation, scale by default. But as in Strega Nona, the pasta kept pouring out, overflowing the pot and flooding the streets, smothering everything in its path."

A murmur ran through the benches.

"I'd like to start by introducing the grand precursor—centuries old, but the pattern for everything to come." The pipe tapped softly against the lectern as Aratta gestured toward Puddeck.

The man in violet inclined his head. "It was a grand vision," Puddeck began. "It reshaped continents, galvanized many, and generations gave their lives for its fulfillment. The goal was nothing short of adding sugar to the marmalade and tea of the European moneyed class.

"Everyone was on board, except the people who did the work. Hence, the refrain of the Portuguese in the Brazilian rainforests, 'Whoever wants to profit from his blacks must make them work well—and beat them even better.' And beat them they did. With whips and hot irons, they drove the chronically hungry great masses of people, day and night, to feed the canes into rollers— thus crushing the stalks and extracting the liquid. And from there, to the boiling houses, where roaring furnaces and bubbling cauldrons threw off intense waves of heat and clouds of steam.

Generation after generation, millions of Africans were transported into this system and processed through its gates: lumps of coal for an insatiable engine. A crowbar and an ax were kept by the rollers so that, if a body was caught, its arms could be chopped off before the rest followed—thus preventing damage to the sugar-making machinery.

"They fed black flesh into one end; white crystals came out from the other—to sweeten the day of the many, and to rot the teeth of the few, those truly fortunate to wallow in the pure extract."

For a moment no one said anything.

Aratta broke the silence. "To keep the boiling houses fed, they chopped the coastal rainforests to stumps. The cane, planted and replanted without rest, leached the soil dry of nutrients. Where forest loam had been, there remained only baked clay and rills of mud."

Puddeck shook his head, bemused. "It is astonishing, truly, what Terraneans can accomplish when they set their mind to it."

"What about honey?" asked one of the commissioners, bewildered.

"Honey?" repeated Puddeck with uncertainty.

"Your Graces," Aratta said, grateful for the question. "Before sugar became big sugar, there was honey: the most common sweetener in Europe, and costing no more than butter, which was cheap and abundant.

"The Europeans developed tiered beehives that let colonies grow naturally. They added extensions to harvest honey without killing the bees. They managed to winter the hives successfully. In short, they had the tools and know-how to scale honey production as needed."

"Incredible," murmured one of the commissioners. He eyed Aratta and Puddeck skeptically. "Why, then, go through with that horrendous sugar-production process, tyrannize people, and indirectly kill countless?"

Aratta took a long draw from the pipe, then blew out a stream of silvery vapor. "This brings us to the crux of the matter, Your Graces. During the 18th century, honey was not more expensive than sugar. In fact, honey as a source of sweetener was superior in most ways. However, two things eclipsed the rest. One, the consumption of sugar had an aura of status. Two, it would have been hard to become a honey tycoon. Beekeeping was too … diffused, democratized. Across Europe, people of little means could have constructed and set up beehives and sold honey."

He let his hands rest on either side of the lectern now.

"In contrast, the money that gushed out of the sugar refineries was highly concentrated, allowing a few to amass power and prestige. And with a blend of enterprise, ruthlessness, and luck, some did clamber atop the sugar heap. They commissioned sprawling manor houses. They paraded in suffocating European fashions through the tropical heat. They gorged nightly on suckling pigs, turkey hens, and joints of mutton, drowning it all in claret and rum. They were the undisputed avatars of success.

"This economic system has borne no relation to community, self-actualization, ecological integrity, or the common good.

"Subsequent centuries sanded down the worst excesses, but the fundamentals remained: manufacture demand, concentrate rewards, externalize the harms. And label the result 'prosperity.' You will find this DNA embedded in large-scale modern enterprises.

"Consider the family farms, which were the lifeblood of rural America." Aratta took a sip of water. "A number of decades ago, the ground started to fall out from under them as diversified, family-run enterprises were driven out by colossal, mechanized operations.

"The takeover has sapped not only the economic base from America's rural communities but also their vitality. Across much of rural America, the investment that still comes knocking is for landfills, fracking fields, and prison complexes. From dignity, ownership, and livelihood, the landscape has in part become one of low-paying, exploitative jobs, which many native locals want no part of. Your Graces, industrial and factory farming is a pyramid of gloom and woe with a glittering apex of capital. One of these controlling agribusiness dynasties commands a net worth in the tens of billions."

"Please elaborate, Lord Aratta. If the locals, as you stated, want no part of it. Where does the labor come from then?"

"Migrants from poor territories have taken their place, Your Grace. Incidentally, whether in a clothing factory in Gazipur, Bangladesh; a poultry processing plant in Arkansas; a tomato plantation in Puglia, Italy; or a dormitory factory complex in China's Pearl River Delta—one encounters this dynamic throughout."

"Do the large-scale operations offer increased efficiency, driving down production costs?" one of the commissioners asked. "Is that it?"

"In hogs, most of the cost advantages are captured by scaling up to a few thousand animals. Beyond that, the per-unit costs barely budge, even as the environmental burden and infrastructure demands spike."

It was time to lay bare the heart of the matter, Aratta thought.

"Your Graces, money is not merely a token of exchange. It is a force, with a gravity well all of its own. Over time, it reshapes incentives, perception, and even desire itself.

"It is said that financial incentive is the engine of human endeavor. There is truth in it—just as there is truth in pervasive grading in schools. Yet, grading displaces the love of learning with the pursuit of approval. It conditions people to optimize for the metric. It penalizes risk, ambiguity, and failure—the very conditions from which discovery arises.

"Work, when meaningful, is inherently fulfilling. The firefighter does not require a commission on each life saved. The physician in a public emergency ward is not less diligent than one in a private clinic. Despite saturation in the ideology of competition and reward, the impulse to contribute, share, and matter persists. Millions, without pay, built the largest encyclopedia in their history. It was not profit that coordinated this feat, but shared purpose.

"Quality is a perishable item," Aratta said from atop the podium. "It can be sensed via the ripples of water at a lagoon, but it cannot be put in a watertight container and taken home. The moment one tries to capitalize on it, quality slips away. Sometimes, the better choice is to leave it be—transient, out of reach, unnamed. But under their economic order, there is an impetus to do something—anything. Brand it. Package it. Scale it. Earth people keep commodifying profound, charged experiences and then sell themselves on a diminished life. In the main, they sell, but they don't enrich."

Aratta exhaled a stream of cinnamon vapor. "The goal is to make money," he said.

"One doesn't make money by producing a valuable commodity. One makes money by producing a commodity more valuable than the competitor's. On Earth, businesses aim to get ahead of the pack; they don't aim to elevate humanity. It's a race for favorable attention, not an expedition to heighten the quality of life.

"The 'customer' aspect of one's persona is a reaction to what's out there, which in turn is a response to this customer persona—ad infinitum. A hall filled with mirrors, bearing endless reflections of nothing worth looking at.

"In line with that, ratings-driven talk shows and formula-proven movies have been devised; inane products bearing alluring veneers have been formulated. Terraneans invest their time formulating sixty-nine competitive kinds of toilet paper to wipe the consumer's personalized arse."

Frowns and thoughtful glances were exchanged around the bench.

Aratta continued, "Until recent times, children met the world on its own terms—mud, arguments, scraped knees—the full agony and ecstasy of being a fully dimensional child. Now they're often parked in front of glowing screens or shuttled to one orchestrated experience or another. Their childhood has been leased out, leaving them entertained and lonely.

"When monetary incentives are introduced," he said, "they do not merely reward behavior. Consider: attempting to reduce late pickups, a daycare center introduced late fees. Subsequently, the rate of late pickup nearly doubled. The fees were treated as just part of doing business—extinguishing any sense of social responsibility to show up on time. In another instance, financial compensation reduced willingness to host nuclear waste—by dissolving what was felt to be one's civic duty.

"An increased dependency on paid-for products and services reduces the need to cooperate, to have mutually supporting interactions. What was broadly satisfying, meaningful, and collaborative got transformed into 'every family for itself'—the nuclear family as a cocoon.

"Commercialization corrodes the bonds that hold communities together. It erodes generosity of spirit, and it thickens the alienation."

He took his time with the pipe.

Finally, he said, "To maximize moneymaking, a ravenous consumer culture was contrived, peddled, and pushed on people. Advertising clamors for their attention when they fill gas tanks, turn on the television, listen to the radio, answer the phone, open the mailbox, flip through magazines, check emails, browse the internet. It lines the highways on billboards, waits at bus stops, hides in product placements and celebrity interviews. Invitations, pleas, suggestions to consume and acquire intrude when the Terraneans are still in their cradles and follow them all the way to the twilight days at the senior home.

"Under the annual rainfall of thousands of commercials per square person, the moneymaking paradigm generates needs and problems and desires where none existed before. Products and services fill up every nook and warp every cranny of the social ecosystem."

Silence.

"The goal is to make money," Aratta said. "What if hustling people pays better than earning their respect? What if it is more profitable to build things just sturdy enough to survive the warranty—thus ensuring repeat sales? What if it is more lucrative to pour the budget into media blitzes than into honest field-testing? What if the biggest margins lie in bloating simple tools with needless features so new tiers or models can be justified? What if it is better business to turn buyers into tenants—unable to repair what they bought or forbidden to own it outright? What if the easiest profit comes from engineering addiction, amplifying insecurity, or exploiting the need to belong? What if the easier sell is not the better good?"

Aratta looked down for a moment.

"From fortified compounds in Myanmar, Cambodia, Laos, and elsewhere, coerced workers operate computers, messaging apps, and fake investment platforms, flooding the wider world with scripted courtships, counterfeit exchanges, fraudulent offers, and manufactured emergencies. Their handlers train them to prey on loneliness, cultivate romance, amplify fear, and stoke greed—then harvest those impulses into deposits, fees, transfers, and vanished savings. The effluent of these operations seeps into society, corroding ambient trust and making suspicion the common weather.

"Entire sectors produce no nourishment, shelter, or durable goods," Aratta said. "They exist to intermediate mistrust, speculate on valuation, arbitrate opacity, and extract tolls from complexity. In excess, such functions become parasitic overhead. Deceit gives rise to verification industries. Manipulation produces compliance regimes. Mistrust becomes a standing market opportunity. Vast energy is diverted not toward creation, but toward guarding, hedging, litigating, insuring, and outmaneuvering.

"The economic system on Earth resembles a Rube Goldberg

contraption—an elaborate arrangement of superfluous parts that expends enormous effort to accomplish what a simpler system could achieve directly. It buries humanity beneath layers of friction and mutually assured distrust."

Aratta spread his hands.

"Your Graces, stripped down to its essence, their dominant economic system is piles of money striving to get bigger. Just that. All the rest is but means to that end, humans and natural resources alike. And those piles of money commission the services of the shrewdest and brightest to impregnate the broader culture with the essence of the moneymaking dynamics.

"A marketplace absorbed in devising winning formulas and appeasing the stock market in the short term doesn't hold time or inspiration to conceive spaceships that will send the human race into the galaxy—literally and metaphorically. The allegiance of the marketplace is to romance the consumer's money. When push comes to shove, this allegiance overrides any aspiration to advance the quality of human life.

"Your Graces, they could have been cultivating a paradise on Earth. Instead, they make money."

He bowed.

"Thank you, Lord Aratta," said the Presiding Chair. He rapped the hammer, signaling the end of testimony for the day.

CHAPTER 39

The Western Part of Madagascar Island, off the Coast of Africa, Qataria

BRIGHID AWOKE. HER GREEN eyes opened to slits, and she peered at the inert ocean of sand dunes under a clear night sky.

The hot breath of the summer night swept across her body, and she stirred. Her long legs uncrossed and stretched over the sand—fluid muscles moving underneath smooth skin.

She grinned, teeth flashing briefly in the moonlight, and eyed the two girls who lay on the sand next to her. "Is the Skirmish about to start?"

The girl to her right, Chryseis, opened her eyes, glanced up, and gauged the position of the stars. She kicked sand at Brighid. "Does the term 'patience' exist in your dictionary, sand-queen? Or did you replace it with 'let's wake Chryseis up for no reason'?" From the other side, Lee'chelle propped herself up, grinning.

Brighid rolled away with a groan of disappointment. Then she burst out laughing. "Over here," she hollered, standing up. Her voice carried through the hills and dunes, addressing the invisible male opponents far in the distance. "Hello, everybody! We're here, ready to unleash a reign of terror—" With shrieks of protest and laughter, Lee'chelle and Chryseis pulled her down. "I introduce—" Brighid gasped, her words intermittently muffled as she pulled at the hand covering her mouth. "I introduce Lee'chelle—to

the world—the hottest—girl in the known—universe!" More outcries and laughter. "Lee'chelle is ready to—"

Her call was cut off as Lee'chelle leaped on her. The two fell in
a heap. Grappling and kicking, they tumbled down the massive
dune, a cloud of sand rising in their wake.

They rolled down and down, gasping and laughing, until they
came to a halt at the base of the dune.

"Your kicks flattened my butt," groaned Brighid. "Now none
of the boys will want to wrestle me in a dune melee." She touched
her raw backside, wincing.

"Hey," Chryseis shouted from the top of the dune. "She's right.
We've got to help her."

"Uh-oh," Brighid said, struggling away.

"Yeah," Lee'chelle said thoughtfully, shaking the sand from her
long hair. "Yep, we need to pump some air into her butt; it'll inflate
her buns—restoring them in no time."

With a squeal, Brighid sprang away from Lee'chelle, rapidly
somersaulting backward across a flat, rocky expanse nestled
among the dunes, toward the conveniently placed pile of their
belongings at the edge of the area. The red staff practically leaped
into her hands.

She spun around and advanced on Lee'chelle, her staff twirling and blurring. Lips working silently. Green eyes blazing—the
eyes of a tiger.

Lee'chelle cried out in excitement. From afar, she heard
Chryseis's battle cry as she raced down the dune. But then Brighid
was upon her, and Lee'chelle was in the midst of the whirlwind,
dancing with the padded staff, dodging its swings.

Suddenly, a low-flying desert bird swooped down, crossing
Brighid's path. Startled by the unexpected feathered visitor, she
lost her footing and dropped like a stone. Seeing this, Lee'chelle,
who was already off balance from their mock fight, stumbled over
her fallen companion. Meanwhile, Chryseis, already halfway down
the dune, couldn't stop her momentum and landed squarely on

her friends. The result was a tangled mess of limbs and laughter that carried across the desert.

The sounds of their merriment subsided. The three disengaged and remained sprawled on the ground, listening to their own labored breathing.

A steady beat of drums broke their reverie, stirring something old and primal within them.

Just as suddenly as the drumbeat had started, it stopped.

Silence descended upon the land, the silence before a storm. "Has the Moonshadow Skirmish just begun?" Lee'chelle asked her two friends in a hushed voice.

"No," Chryseis said. "For the next two hours, we will be alone. From this moment, no words will be spoken."

They joined in a three-way embrace. Then, they withdrew and stood apart, bowing silently.

Each walked her own way.

⇒⇐

One Mile West

Hush and darkness.

A faint warm breeze passed through the thicket of giant bamboo.

The leaves in the upper reaches fluttered.

Quiescence returned. Gradually, time came to a stop.

Far below, the undergrowth of the thicket was rife with bioluminescent fungi. A blue-and-white glow bathed the pond, the light passing through the surface of the clear water, rendering the shallow bottom visible: a patchwork of large, pink-and-white slabs of quartz, streaked with black obsidian.

Silence.

A single leaf dropped, twirling and fluttering down until it touched the water, sending out ripples. And a giant tortoise that had been grazing at the water's edge raised its head.

Silence.

A burst of warm desert wind swept through the bamboo thicket. The small lake stirred, wavelets rushing in all directions. Next, a school of fish suddenly spurted above the water and, in a flash, disappeared beneath the rippling, shimmering surface.

A breathing tube vanished underwater, and a head bobbed up. Lee'chelle opened her eyes and filled her lungs with balmy air.

The young woman rose, then marched toward the distant, rocky bank. The water became shallower with each stride. Her full breasts emerged, their nipples dark against her fair skin. Moments later, her broad hips broke through. Her powerful thighs rose and fell, stirring up foam and waves.

On the edge of the water, a pygmy hippo opened its jaw, and Lee'chelle let out a ferocious hissing sound, arms over her head, fingers curved. The pygmy hippo turned and made its way elsewhere, disappearing shortly afterward amid the thick vegetation.

Lee'chelle reached the shore, then followed a narrow stone path that wound through towering bamboo. Her bag was on the boulder where she had left it. She climbed to the top, turned to face the lake, and sat down. Out of the corner of her eye, she noted a pair of elephant birds picking through the foliage, seeking fruited trees to browse on. Each massive flightless bird must have been ten feet tall. They ignored her, and Lee'chelle tracked them with her eyes until they disappeared.

Her bag at her feet, she rummaged through it.

She put on pale yellow pants and a matching tie top. She brought her long hair over one shoulder, then brushed it unhurriedly, eyes staring at nothing. Finally, she tossed the brush into her open bag. Lee'chelle lowered herself—legs crossed, head held high, buttocks flat against the rock. She took a deep breath and slowly exhaled.

Everything felt . . . right.

She had good friends and a father once again. She lived in a world that made sense to her. She could pursue her passions untrammeled by a broader, deadening culture and a corrupting economic climate.

Lee'chelle Lainraad was finally home.

CHAPTER 40

The Reservation, Deep Underground, the Commission Building

IT WAS LATE AFTERNOON when Aratta started the last segment of his presentation on Earth's economic system.

"I understand that earlier today," he said, "Puddeck highlighted how government intervention in the economy magnifies the existing flaws of their economic system to produce grotesque dynamics and outcomes. This involvement creates incentives that breed corruption, stagnation, and waste. This is undeniably true. With your permission, I will continue with my presentation.

"Yesterday, you were told of the Great Depression, when many Terraneans went hungry. One might expect that, under such conditions, the production of food and basic necessities would increase. Instead, it collapsed. Millions stood idle though they wished to work, and bread lines lengthened though fields still yielded crops. This alone reveals a critical defect: Their economy does not organize itself around human need; it organizes itself around the circulation of money.

"At the closing of that era, during the 1940 Annual Clinical Congress of the American College of Surgeons, it was suggested that smoking might cause lung cancer. By the mid-fifties, rigorous studies had made the link between smoking and lung cancer impossible to ignore. By the mid-fifties, a multitude of physicians and public health experts acknowledged the hazards of smoking. By the mid-fifties, only the most obtuse, uninformed, or nicotine-dependent could ignore the link between smoking and lung cancer.

"Now, under an economic setup oriented toward human well-being, such findings would have led to the demise of the cigarette industry. But that's not the economic setup they've been operating under. An emergency meeting was convened by major tobacco company executives who, in their singular pursuit to maximize the sales of cigarettes, established an institute with scientific trappings designed to generate a fog of confusion, which ended up being an accessory to the premature death of millions of people in the decades to follow.

"Once the employees—from the CEOs to the assembly line workers—realized that, one would expect a massive wave of resignations. However, virtually no one walked away. Not in the nicotine industry. Nor for that matter, in the glyphosate-herbicide industry, generations later. And society did not expect them to. Earth people have come to accept that, when it comes to it, their economic system is decoupled from morality and from any overarching goal of enhancing societal welfare."

His fingers drummed once on the wood, then stilled.

"Your Graces, in the city of Hyderabad, pharmaceutical plants dump in the nearby Musi River effluent containing a chemical stew of antidepressants, contraceptives, steroids, antihypertensives, and antibiotics. Downstream, the river turns into a breeding ground for resistant bacteria and a delivery system for hormones and toxins. Women miscarry. Children are born wrong. And others come into the world already at war with infections no ordinary medicine can touch.

"Now, instead of inflicting misery and ecological woes, they could have done the obvious. Pharma could have allocated a fraction of what they annually spend on advertising to plasma arc facilities: systems hot enough to break complex toxins down to basic chemistry. The inorganic fraction—and the captured residues from scrubbing—is melted into a vitrified, inert slag suitable for construction aggregate. The remaining off-gas is cleaned and discharged as mostly water vapor and carbon dioxide. Instead, companies have reckoned that fines, lawsuits, and bribes are more cost effective than remediation."

Aratta rubbed his thumb along the edge of the lectern, tracing the worn grain.

He said, "This logic extends through global manufacturing. When price becomes the final arbiter, efficiency is achieved not only through ingenuity, but through wage compression, unsafe conditions, and evasion of labor law. Model factories are built for inspection. Real production occurs elsewhere. Retailers suspect. Legal teams protect. Plausible deniability suffices."

He set his glass of water down with quiet deliberation.

"When it's said that the bottom line is what matters to a publicly traded company, what's really meant is the shareholders' bottom line. In fact, the board of directors has a fiduciary responsibility toward the shareholders.

"In turn, the shareholders are typically mere speculators, trying to outwit and second-guess one another. Most of them have no interest per se in the corporation, the quality of its products, or its long-term vision—just in having the stock price go up, for any damn reason. Children coughing due to black lungs is a pity, but the price of a stock is a serious matter. If it stays flat over a prolonged period, shareholders sell it off without any compunction and move on to more promising prospects. This is nothing more than a giant speculative dreamscape of stocks, futures contracts, options, and other derivatives circulating endlessly. Trillions upon trillions of dollars course through the electronic nodes and arteries of the financial world, detached from anything productive, in search of ways to multiply themselves."

Aratta took his place at the lectern when the session was resumed. "In a finite physical system, the sensible thing to do is to make products with the lowest ecological footprint possible, which also means maximizing durability and longevity. But this is not how their economy is set up.

"A T-shirt might start as a bale of cotton in Mississippi. It is then hauled thousands of miles over the Pacific to be spun into yarn in Indonesia. Then, that yarn gets shipped back thousands of miles, this time to Colombia, for more processing. Finally, it comes back to the United States, right where it started. This makes no ecological sense. However, within the existing economic system, only production costs and perceived scarcity of raw materials compute and matter."

He chose his next sentence with visible care.

"The capacity of humans for avarice and for conjuring wants may be boundless, but the physical system underwriting these is not. The bedrock of their economy is Earth. It is finite. It has fixed land and water, specific rates of regeneration, a quantifiable energy budget from its sun, and certain ecological tolerance levels.

"Their economic system, however, is built upon perpetual expansion. It is a shark, which must swim ceaselessly to force water over its gills. The moment it rests, it suffocates. Growth is not merely desired—it is required. The process of sucking the natural world dry can neither be halted nor seriously slowed down. It's an onward march to the bitter end, to the last twang of the ax and the fall of the last tree.

"This has set human activities on a collision course with the planetary ecosystem. This is where the dominant system reveals the full scope of its pathology and harm.

"As long as money is made by utilizing natural resources, and as long as they have entities whose purpose of existence is to amass money, there will be a fundamental conflict of interests.

"The defects inherent in their economic setup make it impossible to reverse environmental course. Their economic system has a foundational structural flaw and cannot be used to effect any needed transformative measures.

"They need another economic engine, one whose express purpose is the well-being of humanity and the broader natural world. Nothing short of that will put a stop to the withering of the living environment and the biosphere."

He bowed his head.

"I regret to say, I don't believe they are capable of doing away with the current scheme and engendering a new, viable one."

CHAPTER 41

Later that day, Aratta testified for the last time.

"I will conclude with something that encapsulates much of what has been discussed throughout this hearing," he said, voice steady. "I refer to a global miasma born of mass delusions and anxiety, bolstered by groupthink and an illusory sense of control over biological dynamics, propelled by corruption and thirst for power, and marked by an apparent inability to grasp the multifaceted nature of the situation. As a result, millions needlessly died, tens of millions needlessly suffered, and thousands of millions needlessly paid a toll. This episode stands as the definitive testament to the follies of the existing human society on Earth in recent times.

"The Chinese modified a coronavirus. At some point, we think it escaped the lab and started to do what viruses do: first, seeding itself in the city of Wuhan, next, ripping across the population centers of the world."

"What were the health effects on individuals?" the Presiding Chair asked.

"This became clear fairly quickly, Your Grace. The virus hit hard the very old and those already battling health issues. However, with a certain regimen of supplements and repurposed drugs in the first seventy-two hours, its impact on these demographics was no more severe than that of the common flu, perhaps less. For the broader population, especially the young, the effects of the microbe were negligible irrespective of treatment or lack thereof."

"Understood. Proceed, please."

"World governments waged a war on the virus, mobilizing citizens and funneling trillions of dollars into a quixotic quest to vanquish it. Daily death tallies—in some regions swollen with unrelated fatalities—fanned the flames of anxiety. Under the cloak of necessity and cracking the whips of fear, public health authorities assumed far-reaching powers.

"Countries hit pause on non-essential operations, decreeing indefinite social distancing to slow the spread of the virus. No one questioned the rationale. And even granting the premise, the toll that lockdowns would impose on society was always going to be severe—and a fraction of the economic fallout of such measures could have funded makeshift treatment centers for a hospital overload that never came. No one in power ran a cost-benefit analysis; no one in power balanced these virus containment measures with broader medical, economic, or social needs.

"Rather than offering the vulnerable the option to self-isolate and shop during designated hours, technocrats and bureaucrats forced everyone else to do so—countless people who were not at risk or were asymptomatic and thus unlikely to spread the virus. Not that the transmission rate of the virus was meaningfully affected by the ensuing crude, erratic lockdowns and social distancing. Everything else, however, was."

Aratta lit his pipe.

He said, "From shuttered churches and canceled weddings and funerals to barred nursing home visitations and the closure of schools, gyms, and restaurants—the once-vibrant tapestry of society leached away. An array of afflictions set in across the land: disconnection and chronic anxiety, job loss and addiction, educational deficiencies and erosion of social bonds. Predictably, self-harm, apprehension, and depression spiked among kids in the first-class cabin during the era of lockdown, while down in the steerage cabin, with parents jobless and schools closed, some children were thrust into the seedy underworld of sexual exploitation, forced into marriages, or compelled to beg. During the lockdown era, the poor got poorer, the affluent got richer, and the billionaire class exploded with wealth.

"The populace was also compelled to fix masks to their faces—a mandate that was surprisingly effective in demoralizing and breeding conformity. It served as a successful coping mechanism for some and provided a talisman for many."

Aratta continued, "Within a month or two of the outbreak, a number of front-line doctors in various regions of the world had formulated a wide array of highly effective, inexpensive protocols, combining topical antiviral measures, repurposed host-directed antiviral and immunomodulatory drugs, anti-inflammatory therapies, nutritional supplementation, and—where clinically warranted—corticosteroids and anticoagulants. Treated early with these protocols, the death count collapsed—in many clinics, to zero. This turning point was announced during a press conference by a group of independent physicians standing outside the United States Supreme Court building. The declaration swiftly exceeded seventeen million views.

"This was not to be.

"The video was taken down by the main social media platforms for 'sharing false information about cures and treatments for COVID-19.' Physicians disseminating effective early treatments were declared beyond the pale and forced into clandestine networks. Pharmacists refused to fill prescriptions when they suspected the medications were intended to treat the illness. Hospitals fought court orders compelling them to administer these treatments. Insurance providers severed ties with clinics that continued to use these drugs. Intimidation, censorship, and professional reprisals were leveled against physicians by medical boards.

"The ordained standard of care required the infected people to isolate at home and take no active measures—until they developed severe breathing difficulties. This was the point they were consigned to hospital wards, administered an anemic dose of dexamethasone and the costly, ineffective remdesivir—a drug associated with significant renal injury. Sometimes hospitals also resorted, notably early on, to mechanical ventilators, which were a cumbersome, expensive way to kill many of the afflicted elderly.

"Compromised government technocrats and healthcare corporate administrators decreed this standardized, one-size-fits-all—or rather, one-size-fits-none—medical treatment, foisting it on frontline doctors and, by extension, on the population at large. That was unprecedented.

"Doctors followed orders; their judgment was set aside. The refrain was familiar to history: 'I only did what I was told.'"

He tapped the pipe against the lectern.

"A year into the pandemic, Spain recorded 69,000 virus-related deaths, while Uganda, comparably populated, reported just 350. Both countries had their first reported cases in the same month. Belgium mourned 65,000 deaths; Burundi, only 3. In crowded Rio de Janeiro, close to 19,000 people died. Meanwhile, in crowded Lagos, with more than twice as many people, only about 200.

These vast disparities in mortality might have been partly due to the routine use of antimalarial drugs, pointing toward inexpensive, widely available treatments. Such a possibility imperiled the vast revenues expected from a patented pharmaceutical poised for release."

"Explain."

"Your Graces, the liability-free Emergency Use Authorization for the novel treatment hinged on the absence of adequate, approved, and available alternatives for treating the disease. Furthermore, you must understand that the health agencies have served chiefly as the enforcement and marketing arm of the pharmaceutical companies when it comes to injections, which the new product was set out to be," Aratta said. "At stake were hundreds of billions of dollars in potential revenues from the novel treatment itself and additional potential long-term revenues from its possible adverse effects.

"The experimental injectable product was launched with much fanfare—every news outlet and government spokesperson chanting that the shot was 'safe and effective,' assuring that those injected 'do not carry the virus and don't get sick,' warning that those who don't get jabbed would face 'a winter of severe illness and death' while also 'putting grandmas in harm's way.' Furthermore, they touted that the injection 'halts transmission' of the virus. As it turned out, it did not."

A murmur passed through the benches.

"What is the significance of that?" the Presiding Chair asked.

"It's a civil and individual rights matter," Aratta said. "Pressuring citizens to take the shot to prevent transmission to others may be one thing. Requiring them to take it merely to supposedly lessen their own symptoms if they were to later contract the virus is an entirely different matter."

"Ah, yes. I see your point."

"Informed consent was thrown out the window. Leveraging fear, threats, bribes, and stigma, governments and their affiliates were relentless. Everyone was pressured to be injected—regardless of an individual's history of adverse reactions, natural immunity from previous contraction of the virus, or minimal risk due to youth and good health. Or as the chairman of the World Economic Forum warned, shaking his fist, 'Nobody will be safe if not everybody is vaccinated.'"

Aratta went on with his account, "In the following months, countless related adverse-event reports from the shots began to pour in, the more serious of which were hospitalizations, permanent disability, and death. The genetic instructions compelled the body to mass-produce the viral protein, triggering a wide range of physiological disruptions. These ranged from Bell's palsy to second-trimester miscarriages to heart inflammation to flare-ups of aggressive cancers. This fact was widely suppressed. UK government data showed a marked increase in all-cause mortality among the injected. This fact did not make the front pages. There was a significant rise in reported severe, life-threatening illnesses and injuries among US military personnel on the heels of the introduction of these genetic-instruction shots. This fact was explained away as data glitches. Scores of injected athletes collapsed from cardiac arrest while playing their sport on live TV. This fact was explained away."

Aratta's gaze swept the commissioners. "Authorities have quashed dissent in response to criticism of their pandemic policies—namely, the ordained troika of masking, confining, and jabbing. This crackdown has extended to digital platforms, where authorities have exercised stringent control, indirectly censoring social media posts and breaking up online groups, obstructing COVID-related reports, and shutting down non-compliant outlets. In South Africa, Ukraine, and India—government agents physically assaulted journalists or bloggers for reporting on COVID. In Poland, Australia, and Bangladesh—government agents detained and prosecuted people expressing opposition to authorities' pandemic policies. In Mexico, Hungary, and the Philippines— government agents outright prevented related reporting. In Canada, Ukraine, and Sri Lanka—government agents broke up large protests.

"And the population?" Aratta asked rhetorically. "The majority was in the grip of mass delusions and acute anxiety: a safety-first, safety-only pandemonium. They put pressure on decision-makers to act, or if not that, then to at least appear to act. People were hoarding guns and toilet paper and disinfecting their mail. People were ratting out their neighbors for noncompliance. And some healthcare physicians stated that the 'unvaccinated' deserved to die. The stink of fear permeated everything. They traded their liberty for the mirage of safety—and paid the toll in flesh, livelihoods, and a social trust that will take a long while to mend."

Aratta regarded the seven members of the commission, and he

nodded once. "I am ready to proceed with my recommendation, Your Graces."

"Please proceed," said the Presiding Chair.

"In light of all presented here," Aratta said, "I recommend that humanity be removed from Earth."

His judgment delivered, Aratta fell silent.

He bowed, and the commissioners bowed back.

Thus the surveyors concluded their final session, and the fate of a world stood before the commission.

Rafirre and his two-hundred-member team were to return home, above ground, and await the verdict. His people, having bided their time for a century, could wait another week or two.

CHAPTER 42

The Reservation, Deep Underground, the Commission Building

AGAINST A WALL COVERED IN DRAPERY OF intricate design, the chief commissioner slid into a chair with a high back and drew about him his dark forest-green ceremonial robe.

With the main segment of the hearing concluded, he was to give a short address, to be broadcast to the people of Earth.

He folded his arms over his lap.

"Social reality is not everything," he began. "However, it is the nearest thing to being so.

"Social reality is the set of channels through which you flow and articulate a personal identity. Social reality is the set of options from which you choose what you wear, the career you pursue, and the opinions you hold. Its soil nourishes some things, while those incompatible wither and die. Its web dictates which notions and ideas entwine within the cultural matrix, becoming integral, and which, lacking connection, are left alone, bound to waste away.

"For all practical purposes, you are a creature of the social reality around you. Yes, each life is as unique as a snowflake, but all are fabricated from the same elemental stuff, imbued with an underlying common essence, and bear the same basic flavor.

"And in the case of Earth, I am afraid the flavor is not vanilla.

"It all comes down to the way you, the people of Earth, have predominantly chosen to interact.

"To interact wholeheartedly, meaningfully, and earnestly entails the agony and ecstasy of being violently alive. It is a choice fraught with risks and requires an incredibly high personal investment. On the other hand, a low-quality interaction requires little of you, as it involves predictability, passivity, reassurance.

"Reality continually asks you to choose the depth and authenticity of your expression. And the quality of the resulting interactions defines the quality of your life, your world.

"The choices people of your world have made throughout your collective history are as numerous as grains of sand.

"Different people on different occasions have made choices of differing quality. Yet, a trend has existed—a trend that solidified through the millennia into a cultural roadway paved with the countless trillions of choices people have made. These choices were largely characterized by fear, by evasion, by apathy, by silence, by avoidance, by blindness, or by mental capitulation.

"Millennia have come to pass. A culture shaped by apprehension, marked by low-quality interactions, has given birth to specific social and economic structures and endorsed philosophies that rationalize and reinforce such behaviors.

"A social reality has coalesced.

"This is your past. This is your present.

"Tomorrow, you will come and tell us what you intend the future to be—and why it would be other than an extension of the past. Tomorrow, a delegation of your people will present their case, and we will listen to your arguments."

The Presiding Chair rose to his feet.

"It is in your hands now," he said.

CHAPTER 43

Somewhere on the Reservation

THOUSANDS OF PEOPLE FILED IN AND TOOK SEATS ON the stone benches that ringed the large, covered amphitheater carved into the face of a hill. These were the chieftains and their deputies, representing most of the clans of the Nation. It was an extraordinary gathering, the like of which had not been seen in many years. But then again, it was the eve of an extraordinary occasion, the one they had been preparing and discussing for generations. This was to be the year the Nation would rise as a mighty empire.

All eyes were on Rafirre, who, along with two dozen of his most loyal men, made his way to the open flat space at the base of the amphitheater.

The last session of the surveyor groups had come to an end a few days earlier. Their work was complete. Rafirre and his two-hundred-member team had returned home, above ground, and were awaiting the verdict. His people, having bided their time for a century, would wait another week or two.

Master Rafirre spread his arms wide, and murmurs throughout the amphitheater died down. "Brothers," he hollered, his amplified voice booming, "here is something that happened on Earth a couple of decades ago. Something that holds the key to our nation's ascension to power. Something we ought to study and emulate."

He motioned, and a hologram materialized all around them. This technology was a gift—by way of a temporary loan—from the Commission Building.

The holographic video transported the thousands of viewers to another place and time, a ripple from the Earth's past, where it was dawn. They could see far down below numerous families wading through a thicket of reeds in an immense marsh that extended to the horizon. The mass of people split into progressively smaller groups and dispersed into the vast wetland.

As the holographic projection of the wetland subtly narrowed its focus to home in on a particular section, the amphitheater was filled with the sounds of houseflies buzzing and the metallic hum of dragonflies. From somewhere in the distance, the spectators in the arena could hear the shrill hoots and howls of macaque monkeys and observe one group of people after another crouching in the mud and camouflaging themselves until they were hidden from view.

"Like actors taking their places before the curtain rises," came Rafirre's voice. "Those who survived came back to the marsh every dawn in the hope of seeing another day."

The crowd watched, riveted.

Rafirre gestured, and the video blurred as it rushed through two hours, then slowed down to a normal playback speed. A few minutes passed, and then they heard it: the sound of people singing in the distance. "Watch," Rafirre said in a soft voice as he adjusted the viewing angle. The sounds of singing came closer. Then they came into view: numerous people wearing hats and carrying machetes on their shoulders. "Here come those who slaughter," Rafirre said.

When they reached the edges of the swamp, some of the incoming people blew whistles and shouted, and all of them waded into the deep, oily-black mire.

"They're hollering, 'Here we are! We are here!' 'We come to prepare Tutsi meat!' and 'We must exterminate you all!'" Rafirre narrated. He panned out, and within a few minutes, they could see people hacking others apart. Cries and screams of pain pierced the tranquility of the wetland.

"Who are they killing?" someone yelled from the risers.

Rafirre smiled nastily. "Their next-door neighbors. Could be their kids' school teacher or the vendor with the cart down the street."

Titters and whispers broke out among the seated chieftains and their lieutenants.

Rafirre skipped forward a few hours.

It was now midday, the sky boiling with buzzards and crows. He zoomed in on a certain point on the ground. He spotted a family that was made to stand up. "Watch this. First, they'll slaughter the father. Then the mother. The children will go last—so they get to watch the parents die."

He dexterously navigated the invisible eye to zoom in on one of the killers. He paused the video. A giant face, contorted in hatred, filled the night sky of the amphitheater.

"Daily mass-killing operations had been playing out across the land. On a productive day, the Hutus might uncover and hack to death thousands of people. Day after day, month after month. During the long season of killing, no one wanted to marry or watch a soccer match. Everything appeared inane and insignificant except the kill."

The audience was mesmerized. They had never seen anything of the kind: a methodical extermination campaign.

"What you're seeing is the mop-up operations. The first weeks were far more prolific. They butchered in churches and in other public buildings where people sought refuge."

He skipped forward again, to when the sun was low on the horizon, casting long shadows. It was silent in the swamp but for the occasional curse or grunt as the killers slogged through the quagmire and pushed through the foliage. Finally, a whistle was heard, notifying the Hutus that the workday was coming to an end. In twos and threes, they struggled out. The large group of men then walked toward the town, conversing in low voices.

"Kill together, loot alone," came Rafirre's voice. "Many would now head out to round up cows whose owners they'd killed, pry out windows, and haul off corrugated metal siding. This aside, evening was a time for a nice warm supper and a refreshing beer."

The holographic video came to an end, and with it, the sounds from that faraway world.

The torches were relit until they all blazed brightly in the arena and on the risers above.

"Brothers," Rafirre called out, "what we have here is a how-to manual to take people who have lived side by side, fan old flames, and turn them genocidal toward one another. What we have here is a working blueprint to devise and put into operation a large, unified extermination machine. This is our ticket to gain dominion over the entire sector!"

A roar of applause and stomping of feet filled the amphitheater.

"The details will be discussed at a later date," Rafirre said, "but let me give you an overview. A few core elements—tried, tested, and scalable.

"First, you need provocation," Rafirre said, pacing about. "You can't just give the order. You seed the rage. The architects of the genocide alleged that the Tutsis were plotting total war—no Hutus left alive.

"A few schoolchildren were said to have been attacked. That part was staged, of course. But it served the purpose. Emotional leverage. It doesn't have to be true—it just has to be believable enough to move men to act.

"Framing is critical," Rafirre said flatly. "You don't ask citizens to commit murder. You call it self-defense. You redefine the enemy as accomplices, not civilians. The act itself? It's not slaughter—it's work. Tools, not weapons. Machetes become agricultural implements. The killing becomes a communal labor obligation.

"Every morning, the units assembled outside a church or on the soccer field with machetes, axes, or clubs. From there, they would split into smaller teams and head out to work. Each crew had at least one or two individuals responsible for organizing the day, setting the tone, and motivating the team.

"Soldiers and police personnel led the first wave of the genocide. But then it scaled; everyone lent a hand. Councilmen signed up for kill teams. Butchers supplied the blades. Teachers pointed out who hadn't shown up to class. The shopkeepers paid and provided transportation. Local businessmen supplied food and drinks to those staffing the checkpoints. And everyone went about flushing out the surviving Tutsis.

"And just as importantly, the organizational hierarchy was agile and responsive; those most committed to the cause floated to the top." Rafirre nodded grimly to himself. Neighborhood-level intelligence networks. Localized logistical coordination. Broadcast command-and-control via radio. Kill quotas. Kill lists. Checkpoints. Supply chains for food, fuel, and blades—it was the most well-executed decentralized extermination model he'd encountered. Earth was a blessing, and in more than one way.

Rafirre surveyed the assembled delegates. "The time is now at hand," he shouted. "The extermination of our enemies will secure our supremacy in this sector. The long wait is almost at an end.

"In the meantime, I've brought something that will make the interval a bit more agreeable and the genocide we are preparing a bit more real." He beckoned and dozens of his people sprang into motion.

They wheeled large wooden crates into the arena. Whispers and murmurs of anticipation swept through the amphitheater. By the time Rafirre's team was done, approximately fifty crates were arrayed about. Rafirre strode to one of the sizable chests and slashed the plastic straps securing it with a knife. "Before the extermination campaign got underway down on Earth," he hollered, "the Hutu leadership secured about half a million machetes." He pried open the lid and pulled it aside, revealing thousands of gleaming metal blades underneath.

A roar went up.

"Here it is, brothers!" he shouted. "The first shipment of machetes from Earth." Rafirre grabbed one by the handle and lifted it high to the roar of the crowd. "There are enough blades here for all of you who have gathered here tonight. And this is but a taste of what's to come."

This brought down the house. Rafirre amplified his voice further to be heard over the din. "What's more, we'll recruit some of those Hutu field leaders once they come through the portal. Men with experience. Men who delivered results!"

He waited for the shouting, cheers, and stomping to subside.

"Some of you have been asking me if the Terraneans are really coming." The crowd fell silent. "You know how it works. The commission is evaluating whether the Terraneans are going to be good stewards for their planet. Our team presented the evidence we have gathered and researched these past few years. The Earth delegation will make its case. The commissioners will reach a verdict.

"But let me share with you *my* conclusions. Let me tell you something about the Terraneans.

"One of the large animals that still exists in their world is the rhino. Yet, they are decimating it. You may ask yourself why. Is it for food? No. Is it for self-defense? No. Is it to prove one's prowess in battle? No." Rafirre stopped pacing, his gray eyes bright with silent laughter and glee. "They're killing it for the horn, ingesting its powdered form to make their hangovers milder."

General laughter and hoots rippled through the arena. They loved to hear that. The Terraneans were seedy and foul! That meant that the Terraneans would be deported, ergo, they were coming!

Rafirre raised his arms until the amphitheater was quiet again. "I have been to places where they breed and confine thousands of lions in pens so rich tourists can gun them down like poultry and their skeletons can later be suspended in large barrels containing alcohol to produce a special bone wine. To all of this, I have but one thing to say—"

Rafirre paused.

"They are one of us!" he bellowed, fist clenched and raised high.

Thousands of people sprang to their feet. "One of us! One of us! One of us!" the people chanted over and over and over, joyful about the prospect—the apparent certainty—of the Terraneans' arrival at the Reservation.

"Our forefathers set in motion a plan a century ago," Rafirre said, with an arm raised, pointing outward. "In partnership with Lord Aratta, they did their part to delay this hearing for as long as possible. And that made all the difference. Had the hearing been conducted a few generations earlier, why, the bounty would have been so much paltrier. Their technology would have been so much less rewarding to loot."

Murmurs of agreement swelled in the amphitheater. Of course, they all knew this; they'd grown up hearing it. A century-long scheme had been hatched and, over time, matured. They were the generation to harvest its fruits and make the Nation the greatest and most powerful in the sector.

"Yes!" Rafirre was hollering. "It is as you've suspected and wished for. The fattest bounty ever is soon to arrive—for us to plunder!"

The stomp of thousands of feet was felt a mile away.

Master Rafirre raised his arms until silence was restored.

"Hear me now," he yelled and let the words linger.

"Among the Terraneans, you'll find hundreds of millions of garden-fresh women for the taking—to be made into second and third wives. Unspoiled, prime stock: from alabaster and peaches-and-cream skinned girls to those with deep amber and rich-coffee hues. Some are built for labor. Some are better suited for display. Those last ones will need breaking in, but they've got spunk," he said to general laughter. "Myself, I plan to snatch three."

His smile lingered for a beat.

"Brothers! The Terraneans are coming. And in their trunks and rucksacks, they will haul with them the riches of their world, the fruits of thousands of years of culture and technology.

"They will bring light, breathable shoes; steel knives for hunting and scissors to trim hair; feather-light collapsible tents; and engineered compound bows. They will carry with them potent mind-altering drugs to sniff and snort. They will lug works of art.

"Speak to your women and daughters of lustrous silk, of the softest vicuña wool, and of engineered fabrics in which one sweats but little. Speak to them of platinum-embossed Noritake porcelain, white as bone and thin as a petal. Of Dior perfumes. Prada suitcases. Cartier jewels. And top it off with Dom Pérignon White Gold Jeroboam—an alcoholic beverage the color of pearl with light, tiny bubbles, coming in bottles sheathed in white gold."

Rafirre paced about. He was laughing exultantly, swept away in the roar of applause and the yells from thousands of throats.

"I'm sorry," an amplified voice cut in. "Is this a bad time?"

The roars and laughter abruptly stopped.

And suddenly Hagar was there on the circular stone arena at the base of the amphitheater, her hands jammed in the pockets of a knee-length wool coat. Seconds later, Aratta materialized, a multi-barreled minigun strapped to one shoulder.

Rafirre sought to recover. "High Mistress Hagar, Lord Aratta," he said in a mild tone and bowed. "It's a . . . surprise."

"Hell, yeah," Hagar said. "Sorry to crash your make-believe party, boys. Just thought you would want to be the first to hear the news." She turned around and looked at her companion.

"It is as Master Rafirre said," Aratta said. His voice filled the night air. "About one hundred years ago, I teamed up with some of your people. I had my own reasons to see the hearing delayed. You had yours. If I have any regrets about the choice I made, it is for me, and me alone, to bear."

The mood in the vast amphitheater was on a razor's edge.

Aratta continued, "Your people were aware of the whereabouts of Hagar's stasis box. They feared that if I took out Hagar from the timefold, she would convene a hearing sooner rather than later.

Long story short, your people relocated the stasis box and faked her death. As I've recently discovered, they were also behind the bombing of the building in Warsaw that had originally stored it. Those two things are entirely unacceptable.

"Your collective greed indirectly brought Earth to the brink of ecological disaster—to a far greater extent than I would have allowed. But by then, as you already know, I was unable to open a gateway on my own."

"For years, you've worked hard to mount an effective presentation," Hagar announced, "and you've earned the machetes—these ones here and the millions more you've ordered."

Rafirre grew horror-stricken as it dawned on him what was coming next. "Nooo," he mouthed, a flicker of panic in his eyes.

"Yes," Hagar said quietly. She then shouted, "Vito the Barber caught wind of your little double-cross. As a result, he decreed that the Earth people—if it's decided they are to be deported—will not be brought into sections 57 and 67, after all."

A wave of murmurs rustled through the amphitheater.

"They're being reassigned to sections 81 and 91—"

Everyone rose to their feet, and bellows of rage all but drowned her voice.

"—which are, of course, on the other end of the populated region of the Res, hundreds of thousands of kilometers away from here," Hagar said. "So other nations will get first pick of the Terraneans. No compound bows. No silk. No prime stock. Not for you boys."

Heedless of the minigun that Aratta held, hundreds of chieftains, then thousands, came barreling down the risers, their faces red with fury, roaring.

Hagar gave them a mock salute, then she and Aratta vanished— just as the mob burst into the stone clearing they had occupied a moment earlier.

CHAPTER 44

Salt Flats of Lake Eyre, South Australia, the Netherworld on Earth

HAGAR STOOD ATOP THE PLATFORM next to the seven commissioners, who conversed in hushed tones. On the ground below them, the master of ceremonies waited attentively, his ceremonial staff in hand. Farther out, an honor guard formed two rigid lines, their dark forest-green capes stirring in the breeze that swept across the vast expanse of the salt flats.

Suddenly, Hagar exclaimed, "Here they come." Her voice was tinged with anticipation.

Indeed, about two football fields away, a swirling, circular portal materialized in the distance. The commissioners stopped their conversations and strained to make out details through the haze.

The first vehicle emerged. Overcome with emotion, Hagar felt a knot rising in her throat. It was too far for her to make out the identity of the driver, but she knew it was Aratta. He led the procession in an old pickup truck, one arm draped over the side window as he drove slowly onward.

Aratta's vehicle veered aside, coming to a gradual stop. Within moments, he had materialized beside Hagar, a comforting presence. Their brief embrace was a shared moment of understanding, before they refocused their attention toward the distant portal.

A pair of motorcycles burst forth, their yellow and blue lights flashing, splitting the haze. They were soon followed by a score more, their lights also flashing as they moved forward in a precise V formation.

"The Earth delegation is arriving," hollered the stoic master of ceremonies from the base of the platform. He swung his ceremonial staff sideways, striking the giant suspended gong.

A black Cadillac limousine emerged from the portal, followed by another, then another, and another, until over a dozen gleaming identical vehicles drove in a procession, lights on. Each limousine sported a flag—a detailed representation of Earth, imprinted in pale yellow against a rich, cobalt-blue backdrop. Hagar cast a curious glance at the unfamiliar flag. It must have been something created recently. Very recently.

The motorcade made its way toward the waiting dignitaries and halted with measured precision a few paces from the honor guard. A command rang out from the guard commander, and hundreds of sabers went up in salute and flashed in the sun as limousine doors swung open. Men and women, mirroring the cultural mosaic of Earth, stepped out of the limousines and walked toward the stage, their faces alight with congenial smiles. Another yelled command, and the swords thrust high up and over, forming an honorary saber arch under which the first Earth delegates marched between the two rows of ceremonial guardsmen.

The seven commissioners stepped down from the platform to greet them.

CHAPTER 45

1968, on the Outskirts of Hangzhou, China

THEY FOUND PUDDECK SITTING on a ledge with an almost empty bottle of dark rice wine and another, drained, beside it. He was muttering to himself and singing drunkenly.

Hagar and Aratta helped their squat companion to his feet. Puddeck put his arms up, one arm around each of them, and they helped him walk.

"I'll miss it, Aratta," Puddeck said, looking blearily at Aratta and then at Hagar. "My beloved China," he crooned, half-shuffling, half-walking between his two comrades.

He broke into song.

Chairman Mao loves the people,
Chairman Mao, he is our guide.
To build a new China,
He leads us forever forward.

Hagar caressed Puddeck's bald head. "He always gets sentimental when we're about to depart a world," she reminded Aratta. "You know how much the Cultural Revolution meant to him."

She kissed a morose Puddeck. "There will be other worlds with civilizations like this, hon."

"Who is like Chairman Mao?" he mumbled.
He broke into another song.

The east is red, the sun is rising.
China has brought forth a Mao Zedong.
He works for the people's happiness,
He is the people's great saving star.

They came to a stop on a hilltop.
"Look!" Aratta said. A red sun rose in the east, heralding a new morning, and Puddeck, encouraged, gave a faint smile.
The wind stirred their garments.
"Ready, Aratta?" Hagar asked.
"Always, dearest," he said.
The three smiled at each other and vanished from Earth.

If you found this book worthy, please take a moment to leave a review. Your feedback helps other readers discover the book. You can rate or review it at any major retailer or on Goodreads.